Linc's big hand covered her cheek and he placed thumb in the center of her bottom lip.

"I want you, too," Tate admitted. "It's inconvenient and crazy and there are a thousand reasons why it's a bad idea—"

But she didn't have the strength or the willpower to walk away. This one time, she couldn't resist temptation. But, because she had to, she could protect herself. So she did what she always did—she laid out the rules of engagement. That way, there couldn't be any misunderstandings.

"This is a very temporary arrangement, Linc. We're just two adults who are wickedly attracted to each other." This couldn't be anything more and he needed to know that. "This is temporary. So, no expectations, okay?"

"Understood," Linc said.

The fist clenching her heart relaxed. She could do this, and she would be fine. She had to be—anything else wasn't an option.

"So, to spell it out, I look after the kids and you... well, you do what you do. Do we have a deal?"

Linc smiled. "Yes, we have a deal."

* * *

The CEO's Nanny Affair
is part of Mills & Boon Desire's
No. 1 bestselling series,
Billionaires and Babies: Powerful men...
wrapped around their babies' little fingers.

THE CEO'S NANNY AFFAIR

BY
JOSS WOOD

MILLS BOON

First Published in Great Britain 2017
By Mills & Boon, an imprint of HarperCollins*Publishers*
1 London Bridge Street, London, SE1 9GF

© 2017 Joss Wood

ISBN: 978-0-263-92830-3

51-0817

Our policy is to use papers that are natural, renewable and recyclable products and made from wood grown in sustainable forests. The logging and manufacturing processes conform to the legal environmental regulations of the country of origin.

Printed and bound in Spain
by CPI, Barcelona

Joss Wood loves books and traveling—especially to the wild places of southern Africa. She has the domestic skills of a potted plant and drinks far too much coffee.

Joss has written for Mills & Boon KISS, Mills & Boon Presents and, most recently, the Mills & Boon Desire line. After a career in business, she now writes full-time. Joss is a member of the Romance Writers of America and Romance Writers of South Africa.

One

Tate Harper had eaten deep-fried crickets in Thailand and snacked on guinea pig in Peru. She'd been lost in a jungle in Costa Rica and danced the night away in a run-down cantina in a Rio favela. She'd been propositioned by both rich and poor men in every corner of the world. As the host of a travel program exploring different food cultures, she'd faced some unusual situations in her life.

But nothing gave her the heavyhearted feeling that a meeting with Kari did.

Tate pushed her fist into her sternum and gripped the handle of the door to the diner. It was a wintry Wednesday afternoon in early January, and she'd touched down at JFK just after six that morning. After already having spent the morning with the executive producers of the travel channel she worked for, discussing her options for hosting a new travel series, she was mentally and physically exhausted.

She simply didn't have the energy to deal with her older-in-years-but-still-a-child cousin.

Adopted sister. Whatever the hell Kari was.

Not for the first, or hundredth time, Tate wished that she and Kari were closer, that they were each other's best friends, but, despite she and Kari sharing the same house since she was eight, they'd never really clicked.

That old familiar wave of resentment twisted Tate's stomach into knots. She looked down the snow-dusted road and thought about walking away. She was tempted; her life was so much easier without Kari in it. She shook her head. She wasn't tough enough to ignore Kari's request to meet, and, while she knew she was risking being disappointed for the umpteenth time, a part of her still hoped that they could establish an emotional connection, be a family. Resigned, she pulled open the door to the diner and stepped into its warmth. She shrugged out of her coat, pulled the floppy burgundy felt hat from her head and looked around the diner for Kari. Because their mothers were identical twins, they looked more alike than most sisters did. They shared the same wavy light brown/dark blond hair and long, lean build, but the last time Tate had seen Kari, she'd dyed her hair platinum and was the proud owner of a new, bigger pair of boobs she'd conned someone — probably a boyfriend—into paying for. They also had the same generous mouths and high cheekbones, but Kari had the twins' bright blue eyes while Tate inherited her grandfather's cognac-colored eyes and straight nose.

Not seeing Kari, she caught the attention of a waitress rushing past. "Sorry, excuse me? I'm looking for someone who looks a lot like me. Her text said she was here, waiting for me, but I don't see her."

The waitress nodded. "Yeah, she's sitting at that empty

booth. I think she went to the bathroom. Take a seat, she shouldn't be long."

Tate thanked her and walked toward the empty booth, her attention caught by a beautiful biracial baby fast asleep in a stroller parked between the booth and the table next to her, where a couple sat. The baby, Tate decided, had hit the genetic jackpot by inheriting the best of her stunning African American dad's and Nordic mom's genes.

Sitting down, she nodded at the offer of coffee. Hell, yes, she wanted coffee. She wanted to wrap her freezing hands around a warm mug and gaze out the window, happy to be out of the bitter wind and snow-tinged rain. It had been years since she'd been in the city in the middle of winter, and she'd forgotten how miserable it could get.

Next to her, chairs scraped, and Tate turned to watch as the gorgeous man and his blonde partner stood up, gathering their coats and shopping bags. From their intimate smiles and heated looks, Tate realized that they shared a deep connection. Electricity buzzed between them, and she wrinkled her nose as jealously pricked her soul.

She'd never had a man look at her like she was the reason the earth spun on its axis, the pull of the moon on the tides, the strength of the sun.

You've got to be in the game to play it, Harper, Tate quickly reminded herself. *But you chose independence, freedom and to live on your isolated island.* The consequence of that choice was emotional safety.

And, sadly, the sex life of a nun.

But that didn't mean that she couldn't admire a masculine butt in well-fitting jeans. Because he had an A-grade ass, it took Tate a while to realize that they were leaving. Her eyes dropped to the baby still asleep in the stroller, and she shot to her feet. "Hey, wait!"

The couple turned around and they both raised their eyebrows.

Tate gestured to the stroller. "Your *baby*. You're leaving without her."

They responded with frowns and matching is-she-crazy expressions. "That's not our baby. The lady who was sitting there came in with that baby," Sexy Guy told her.

Wait! What?

Tate caught the eye of the waitress as ice flooded her veins. "Who came in with this baby?"

Tate was subjected to another she's-a-nut look. "The woman you asked about, the one who looks like you, she came in with this cutie."

Oh, God, oh, God, oh, God. Tate fought for air and managed to compose herself long enough to ask the waitress if she'd, please, check the bathroom to see whether Kari was in a stall. Tate's eyes bounced between the sleeping baby and the small hallway leading to the restrooms, and when the waitress reappeared, biting her lip and shaking her head, Tate started to tremble.

Déjà vu, she thought. She knew, without a fraction of doubt, that Kari had slipped out the door when her back was turned. *God, Kari, don't... Please don't abandon another of your children. Breeze back through that door, toss me a weak explanation, and we'll pretend this never happened. Just don't walk away; please don't confirm my worst beliefs about you.*

Tate turned around to look at the door to the diner and waited for it to open, waited for the world to stop tilting. When a minute passed and then two, she sighed and turned around again. Feeling moisture on her cheeks, she wiped away her tears and blinked furiously. She wouldn't cry, she wouldn't fall apart. Taking a deep, calming breath, Tate sent another anxious look to the door, hoping for a miracle.

After ten minutes passed with zero miracles occurring, her shock receded, and air rushed into her lungs, clearing the fog from her brain. *Think, dammit. Think.* Legally, this child was her niece, and she was responsible for her. As much as she wished she could run away, her mother had already bolted from the diner, and leaving her alone wasn't an option.

Kari was in the wind… So, what now? Looking down, she saw a diaper bag in the storage area under the stroller, and Tate pulled the heavy sack onto her lap. Resting her arms on the diaper bag, and trying to keep the panic at bay, Tate stared down at the sleeping child.

Angelic, she thought wistfully, because that was the only word that made sense. Her skin was the color of lightly burnt sugar, wispy espresso curls covered her head and her rounded cheeks were pure perfection. The little girl had the wide Harper mouth and pointed chin.

Tate unzipped the diaper bag and peered inside. Seeing a brown envelope flat against the side, Tate pulled it out, her heart hammering. She opened it with shaking fingers, yanked out the papers and slowly flipped through them. There wasn't much besides inoculation certificates and medical cards and a birth certificate stating that the baby was Ellie Harper, the mother, Kari Harper, and father unknown.

God, Kari. How could you not know who the father was? Or did she know and just decided not to inform the state? The last piece of paper was a letter scrawled in Kari's handwriting.

Tate,
I know what you are thinking and I don't blame you. This looks bad; it *is* bad. I need you to take Ellie.

Something has come up and I can't keep her. You'll figure out what to do with her.

If you're freaking out—and you probably are—call Linc Ballantyne, your nephew's dad. His number is below. Ellie is Shaw's half sister and he'll help you out.

I know that you won't believe this but I do love her.

K.

Her eyes still glued to the letter, Tate shoved her hand into her bag and pulled out her smartphone. Feeling like she had a sumo wrestler sitting on her chest, she entered the phone number and held her breath as she stared down at the small screen.

What was she doing? Linc Ballantyne's connection to Ellie was tenuous at best—he was Kari's ex-fiancé and, yes, the father of the now-four-year-old son she'd abandoned. Linc had lived Tate's current reality four years ago, and maybe he could help her make sense of Kari's crazy. It wasn't in her nature to ask for help, but desperate times trumped pride.

Tate lifted the phone and held it to her ear and listened to it ringing. She was transferred from one efficient Ballantyne employee to another before a deep male voice muttered a harsh greeting in her ear. As Linc Ballantyne's sexy voice rumbled through her, Ellie opened her eyes, and Tate was struck by the burst of bright, cobalt blue.

Kari's eyes…

"This is Tate Harper, Kari's sister, and I have a massive problem. Can we meet?"

Some days, running a multibillion-dollar company gave Linc Ballantyne a splitting headache. Hell, make that most days lately. Needing an aspirin, Linc walked into the middle office separating his and his brother Beck's office, and, ignoring Amy's concerned expression, he pulled out a bottle of aspirin from the top drawer of her desk. He tossed two into his mouth and dry swallowed, very used to the bitter taste.

Amy, the executive assistant he and Beck shared, tucked her phone between her neck and ear and reached across her desk to throw Linc an unopened water bottle. He caught it, cracked the lid and looked through the glass walls to see his still-slim, still-pretty mother walking down the hallway and, as he always did, said a quick, silent thank-you to whatever force that had driven her into the arms of Connor Ballantyne.

Well, not his arms—as far as he knew Connor and his mom were never romantically involved—but into his house, at least. Moving into the brownstone known as The Den and meeting the kids who would become his siblings was the best day of his life; losing Connor, the worst.

Linc hurried across the office to open the door to her and bent down to kiss Jo's cheek.

"Hi."

"Hello, darling," Jo replied. Her eyes were gray, like his, but hers were the color of gentle rain while his were a darker, edgier granite. "I'm sorry to drop in on you without warning."

"That's never a problem," Linc assured her.

Jo greeted Amy with a kiss and a hug, and gestured to his office. "Have you a minute for me, Linc?"

"Always."

In his office Jo sat down as he perched on the edge of his desk and folded his arms across his chest, feeling the burn in his biceps. He'd pushed himself last night, storming through his late-night workout, hoping that the exercise would ensure a good night's sleep. It had helped somewhat; he'd slept for a solid four hours only to be woken up by Shaw having a nightmare. It had taken an hour to get his son to settle again, and by then he was wide-awake.

"Gary has asked me to move in with him."

Linc jerked his attention back to his mother, trying to contain his shock. "You want to leave The Den? But why so soon?"

Jo rolled her eyes. "We have been in a relationship for more than six months, Linc, so stop acting like I met him two weeks ago! You like him, you told me so."

That was before he was encouraging you to move out, Linc silently groused. Every time Jo mentioned Gary, her eyes glowed and her cheeks warmed. If he believed in love and all that crap, he'd say his mom was head over heels in love with the ex-banker. Since he didn't, he looked past all that and saw two intellectually and socially compatible people who simply enjoyed each other's company. Truth be told, he still didn't like the fact that Jo was choosing Gary over Shaw, the grandson she'd been helping Linc raise since he was six weeks old.

"I think that we'll marry eventually, but I—" Jo continued, rubbing her forehead with the tips of her fingers. "I've lived in The Den for twenty-five years and I love it, but now I want my own home, Linc. I want a place that's all mine, and we want to travel." His mom lifted worried eyes to his. "You know I love Shaw and I was happy to help you when he was a baby because, frankly, you needed the assistance. I still want to help out but—"

"But you don't want to do it every day," Linc said and Jo nodded.

Linc cursed. *Bad time to defect, Mom!* He had a massive company to run and grow. They were rebranding the business, he was considering investing in a diamond mine in

Botswana, they had a strike looming at a mine in Colombia, they were opening new stores in Abu Dhabi and Barcelona, refurbishing stores in Hong Kong, LA and Tokyo.

His business life was ridiculously busy and consistently stressful, and he was only able to do what he did because he didn't have to worry about Shaw. His home life ran like clockwork: he took Shaw to pre-K, Jo picked him up and spent the afternoon and early evening with him, feeding and bathing him if he was running late. It worked so damn well because he trusted his mom implicitly, and he never worried about his son's emotional and physical welfare. She was irreplaceable.

"I've been looking after kids for so long." Jo shrugged, lifting delicate shoulders. "I'm nearly sixty, Linc. I want to have some fun, take a break, travel. Have a glass of wine at lunchtime if I feel like it. I'm tired, Linc. Can you understand that?"

Linc stood up and walked to the window, conscious of his accelerated heartbeat and his constricted throat. He hated change, especially in his personal life, and now she'd thrown him for a total loop. Keep calm and think it through. As a father of a mischievous four-year-old and as the CEO of a Fortune 500 company, keeping his head while everyone else was losing theirs was how he navigated his life.

He'd had a lot of practice at being the calm port everyone ran to in a storm. When he was eleven, Jo had secured the position to be Connor Ballantyne's housekeeper and to help him look after his orphaned nephews and niece. His mom told Linc to keep out of the Ballantynes' ways, but Connor, with his huge heart and lack of snobbery, insisted that if they were going to live in The Den, then they had to *live* in The Den. They all ate and played together, and Linc attended the same expensive school as Jaeger and Beck. He read in the library, slid down the banister and peppered the magnificent chandelier in the foyer with spitballs.

To his utter surprise and delight, Connor embraced Linc's presence at The Den, and he never once felt like a third wheel. Maybe that was because Jaeger, Beck and Sage latched onto him, and though he'd been a kid himself, a little less than a year older than Jaeger, he somehow became the person they'd gravitated to. For more than a quarter of a century, he'd been the glue holding the Ballantynes together, and while Beck helped him run Ballantyne International and all four of them held equal shares in the company, he was—despite the fact that he was not a Ballantyne by blood—the leader of the pack.

Linc didn't mind. When he formally adopted the four of them when Linc turned sixteen, Connor made it clear that Linc was the oldest child, that he expected him to look after his siblings, to look after the company, to do him proud.

He had no intention of disappointing the only father he'd ever really known. But Shaw's welfare was his first priority, always. How could he place his son's care in the hands of a stranger? How was he supposed to run this company, nurture and grow it, if he was worried about whether his son was receiving the same attention at home?

Linc opened his mouth to throw himself at her mercy and ask for a time extension but then immediately snapped it shut. As much as he hated change, he couldn't put his needs above Jo's. Especially since she'd dedicated the past thirty-five years putting him first.

Crap. Having integrity sucked.

He turned and forced himself to smile. "So, what do you suggest I do?"

Linc saw the shock and relief in her eyes, ashamed

to realize that she'd expected him to argue. "You need a live-in nanny."

Ack. A stranger in his house, looking after his kid. Shoot him now.

"I'll contact the most reputable agencies and select a few for you to interview," Jo said before lifting her eyebrows. "Or do you want to do this yourself?"

Linc shuddered. "No, thanks. I'd rather shower with acid."

His mom cocked her head. "You know what you need, don't you? More than a nanny?"

Sex? A decent night's sleep? A skiing vacation with lots of sex and lots of sleep?

"You need a wife," Jo empathetically stated.

Linc shot her a glare. He so *didn't.* Once upon a time he'd nearly acquired one of those and lost her two weeks before they were supposed to say "I do." For the past four years he'd managed perfectly well without a wife. But he'd had Jo's help... Dammit.

"I've heard all the reasons why you're not interested, Linc. Women are fickle, untrustworthy, they just want your money or the Ballantyne name. Et cetera...et cetera."

"Mom." Linc closed his eyes, looking through the glass wall in Amy's direction. He had a full day ahead, multibillion-dollar decisions to make, and he did not need to talk about his crappy love life. Amy, as she often did, suddenly lifted her head and met his eyes.

"Help me," he mouthed.

"Amy's not going to bail you out," Jo said, not bothering to turn around to look at his assistant. "Besides, she and I agree that you need someone in your life."

"Like I need a needle in my eye," Linc muttered, mouthing "You're fired" at Amy. His assistant just grinned and turned back to her monitor.

"You need someone to challenge you, to make you laugh, to make you think. Someone interesting and independent and smart," his mom insisted.

Why were they even discussing this? Thanks to his ex-fiancée, Kari, he was now determined not to risk his heart, and especially not his son's, on another woman. They were fine on their own. They had to be because there wasn't a woman alive who was worth taking a chance on. He'd learned that lesson well. "Mom, I have work to do. I don't have time to dissect my love life or my relationship with my crazy ex."

Jo stood up and pushed a finger into his chest. "You need to start dating again."

Linc shuddered. Hell to the no. Time to move on. And he could only do that if he deflected the conversation onto one of his siblings. "Talking about relationships, Cady is in Beck's office, right now."

Jo's eyes immediately brightened with curiosity. "Cady? Is she back?"

Linc put a hand on her shoulder and gently directed her to the door. "Amy will explain it to you. I need to get back to work."

Jo glared at him as he reached around her to open the door. "You just don't want to discuss your love life anymore."

"I don't have a love life," Linc corrected, bending down to kiss her cheek. "And I like it that way."

Jo tossed another hot look his way before addressing Amy. "He needs to date."

"I know," Amy answered without missing a beat, her fingers dancing over her keyboard. "I'm working on it."

"You're working on nothing," Linc retorted, "because I freakin' fired you!"

Amy rolled her eyes at Jo, who smiled.

"You're delusional, Linc. We all know that Connor left me in charge. Hold that thought," Amy told him, before answering a call. She listened for a minute before lifting suddenly serious eyes to meet Linc's.

"It's Tate Harper and she needs to speak to you. It's private and, in her words, it's pretty damn urgent."

Linc glanced at his Rolex and glared at the imposing front door of The Den, his brownstone just off Park Avenue that had been in the Ballantyne family more than a century. In the four years since Kari bolted—taking two of his credit cards and her flawless yellow diamond engagement ring with her—he'd had precisely zero contact with the Harper family. He knew that Kari had been adopted by her aunt and had a cousin she'd been raised with, but she had hardly spoken about them.

They certainly hadn't been invited to their wedding, and, at the time, Linc had thought that there was bad blood between them. Now he knew that Kari hadn't bothered with wedding invitations because she'd never intended to marry him. He would've saved himself a bundle in both time and money if the damned woman had let him in on that little secret.

He once thought that she wanted what he did; a home, a family, a traditional family life together, but Kari had run from the life he'd offered her. Most shocking of all, she'd also relinquished all parental rights to Shaw. When she did that he assumed that all connections to Kari and her family were permanently severed, so he couldn't understand why Tate needed to see him.

And why he'd ever agreed to meet with her was equally confounding. But he'd heard something in her voice, a note of panic and deep, deep sorrow. Maybe something had happened to Kari, and, if so, he needed to know what. She was still Shaw's mother, after all.

Linc heard the light rap on the door and sucked in a breath.

The first thought he had when he opened his front door to Tate Harper and raked his eyes over her was that he wanted her. Under him, on top of him, up against the nearest wall…anyway he could have her, he'd take her. That thought was immediately followed by, *Oh, crap, not again.*

Kari had been a stunning woman, but her beauty, as he knew—and paid for—had taken work. But the woman standing behind the stroller was effortlessly gorgeous. Her hair was a riot of blond and brown, eyes the color of his favorite whiskey under arched eyebrows and her skin, makeup-free, was flawless. This Harper's beauty was all natural and, dammit, so much more potent. Linc, his hand on the doorknob, took a moment to draw in some much-needed air.

He scanned her face again, unable to stop drinking in her dazzling beauty. The rational part of his brain wanted him to tell Tate Harper that he had nothing to say to her, no help to offer and that he and Shaw did not need the aggravation dealing with a Harper almost always caused.

The rest of him, led by his very neglected libido—he was a super busy single dad who rarely had time to chase tail—wanted to start stripping off her clothes to unveil what he assumed was a very delectable body.

"Tate? Come on in."

She pushed the stroller into the hall, holding the bar with a white-knuckle grip. Linc, wincing at the realization that he was allowing a whole bunch of trouble to walk through his front door, was about to rescind his invitation for her to step into his home and his life. Then he made the mistake of looking into her eyes and gauged her terror, her complete and utter dismay, and her-what-the-hell-did-I-do-to-deserve-this expression.

She'd jumped into the ring with Kari and had the crap kicked out of her, Linc realized. And, for some reason, she thought he could help her clean up the mess. And, because his first instinct was to protect, to make things right, he wanted to wipe the fear from Tate's eyes.

God, he was such a flippin' asshat.

Annoyed with himself, Linc turned his attention to the occupant in the stroller... Ten or eleven months old, he guessed, clean and well fed. And cute, man, she was cute. He loved kids, and this adorable little one, with those bright blue eyes looking up at him, was born charming. He recognized those lapis lazuli eyes; they were Kari's eyes and this was Kari's kid.

But if this was Kari's kid, then why was Tate on his doorstep with her?

Her hands tightened around the bar of the stroller, no color left in her face. She read the question in his eyes and slowly nodded, devastation glimmering in her eyes as she confirmed his worst suspicions. "She was there, at the place we had arranged to meet. She must have seen me arrive and slipped out when I linked Ellie to her."

Linc placed his hands on his hips and tipped his head back to look at the ceiling. He swore quietly, before returning his gaze back to Tate, who was rocking on her heels. "So, what do you want from me?"

Because I know what I want from you and that's to unbutton that blouse, slide it off your sexy shoulders and feel your silky skin beneath my hands, your made-for-sin mouth fusing with mine. I want to know the shape of your breasts, dig my fingers into the skin of your ass...

Sex? That's where his head went after her shocking statement. What the hell?

For God's sake, Ballantyne, get a freakin' grip! Why, after all the crap Kari had put him through, did he have the hots for her sister?

Linc rubbed the back of his neck. "I need coffee. Would you like a cup?"

"Only if you don't poison it. Or spit in it."

Linc felt his lips twitch and fought a smile. So, she had a bit of a mouth on her. Back in the world he normally lived in, *the one that made sense*, Linc didn't mind sassy women. There was nothing more annoying than someone who agreed with everything he said, so desperate to please. He'd dated quite of few of them.

He didn't like this woman, he reminded himself sternly; he didn't have any intention of liking her, ever. They were going to have coffee, a conversation, and, hopefully, in ten minutes he'd be back at his desk and life would return to normal.

He looked down into the stroller again. "What's her name?"

"In her letter, Kari calls her Ellie."

"Pretty name," Linc said, undoing the harness that kept Ellie in the stroller. He picked her up and placed her on his hip, his arm around her little butt. God, it felt weird, but almost right, to have a baby in his arms again. He'd always wanted a big family, tons of kids. But, since babies usually came with a mother and that species came with complications and drama, he was resigned to being a one-child dad. And that child was pretty damn cool...

"Follow me." Linc led Tate through the second floor of the brownstone and hit the stairs leading to the garden level. Stepping into the large open-plan room, he walked into his, and Shaw's, favorite area of the brownstone—

the living room that flowed out from the kitchen and informal eating area. It held long, comfortable couches, a large-screen TV, books and Shaw's toys. Massive French doors led to the enclosed garden with pots of herbs and garden furniture. The rest of The Den held priceless art and rare antiques, but this room was functional, lived-in and cozy.

Linc, still holding the baby, headed to the coffee machine and hit the button to power up the appliance. It was nearly 4:00 p.m., was it too early for something strong and alcoholic? After making coffee, Linc walked back into the sitting area and placed their mugs onto the coffee table.

Tate looked as white as a sheet, shell-shocked and more than a little panicked. She needed to calm the hell down.

"Take your coat off, sit down and breathe," Linc instructed her, relieved when Tate nodded her agreement. In real life, she wouldn't be so quick to acquiesce, Linc mused. It might have been her snarky comment earlier about him spitting in her coffee, but he just knew that Tate wasn't a pushover. It added a layer of intrigue to the sexy.

He watched as she removed her coat, revealing more of that almost perfect body and her glorious blondish-brown hair. "I've lost my hat."

"I think you have bigger things to worry about than a hat," Linc stated, leaning forward to pick up his coffee cup.

Questions that had nothing to do with his ex and her baby jumped into his mind. Would her eyes deepen or lighten with passion? Was she a moaner or a screamer? Would she be…

Linc closed his eyes and forcefully shook his head, reminding himself to start using his brain.

He needed to hear her story so that he could hustle her out of the door and get back to his predictable, safe, sensible world. She was pure temptation, and being attracted to his crazy ex's sister was a complication he most definitely did not need.

"So, start at the beginning and tell me how Kari managed to sucker you into looking after her child."

Two

Tate sank back into the cushions of the super comfortable couch, wishing she could just close her eyes. When she woke up, this would all be a horrible dream, and she'd have a vacation to start, a career to obsess over.

She wouldn't have a baby to think about or to care for, and she certainly would not be in Linc Ballantyne's fabulous mansion on the Upper East Side, looking at Manhattan's hottest and most elusive bachelor.

The photographs of him online and in print publications didn't do this man justice. They simply told the world that he was incredibly good-looking. And by *good-looking*, she meant *fantastically hot*. It was toasty warm inside his house, but she was still shivering, partly from shock but mostly from a punch of "throw me to the floor and take me now."

Under Linc's button-down shirt and tie was a wide chest and, she was sure, a hard, ridged stomach. His shoulders

were broad, his legs long and muscular and his short, thick
dark hair was just this side of messy. And those eyes, God,
his eyes. They were a deep and mysterious gray, a color
somewhere between summer thunderclouds and pewter.
Short, thick black lashes, a slightly crooked nose and dark,
rakish eyebrows added character to his too-sexy face.

But the photographs didn't capture the power sizzling
under his skin, the intelligence radiating from those eyes,
the don't-BS-me vibe emanating from him. They certainly
didn't capture the sheer and unrelenting masculinity of
the man.

The man she was fiercely, *ridiculously* attracted to. Of
course she was, Tate sighed, because she was a Harper
woman and Harper women never made life easy for themselves.

Her eyes moved from his face to the baby tucked into
the crook of his elbow, and she swallowed hard. She remembered his earlier question about what she wanted from
him, and, not for the first time since stepping into the
brownstone, she wondered what she was doing here. She
wasn't the type to fall apart in a crisis, who needed a man
to sort her life out and she'd learned, at a very early age,
not to depend on anyone else to help her muddle through
life. People, she'd found, and especially those who were
supposed to love her, were generally unreliable.

Ellie was her responsibility, not Linc's. So, really, there
was no point in extending this very uncomfortable visit.
And the zing of sexual awareness dancing along her skin,
making her heart bounce around her chest, added a level
of awkward to their encounter.

Tate got to her feet, walked over to him and reached for
Ellie, pulling the little girl into her arms. Eleven months
old and abandoned, Tate thought. How could Kari do this?
Again?

"I'm sorry, Linc, we shouldn't have come here." Tate heard her words running together and tried to slow down. "We'll get out of your hair now."

Linc leaned forward and placed his muscular forearms on his thighs, his eyes penetrating. "Take a breath, Tate. Sit down, drink your coffee and let's talk this through."

"I should let you go back to work."

"My day is already shot," he admitted. "Tell me what happened."

Tate gave him a quick rundown of her day, and when she was finished, Linc asked, "Where's the note she left you?"

Too tired to argue, she told him where to find it and sat down with Ellie propped on her lap. Tate took her little hand in hers and thought that Ellie was amazingly docile for a child that had been dumped with a stranger.

"So, though this note is short on details it seems to imply that you now get to call the shots with regard to Ellie," Linc said.

"*Imply* being the *operative* word," Tate bitterly replied. "And what am I supposed to do with her? Look after her? Place her in foster care? Give her up for adoption?"

"I don't think you have the legal right to do the last two," Linc said, and she saw the anger burning in his eyes. "But why couldn't she just do any of this herself? Why involve you?"

"I don't know. I didn't even know about Ellie until I got to the diner. I haven't seen Kari for two years." Tate rubbed her thumb gently over the back of Ellie's hand. "And that meeting was tense."

"Why?"

She started to tell him that they'd had a huge fight because Kari abandoned her son. Tate had been so incensed at her cousin's blasé attitude toward Shaw that she'd stopped communicating with her. Tate noticed Linc's hard eyes and knew that he wouldn't appreciate, and didn't need, her defending his son. Linc Ballantyne was obviously very capable at fighting his own battles.

"Family stuff." Tate eventually pushed the short explanation out.

Linc linked his hands together and leaned back, placing his ankle on his knee and tapping the sheaf of papers balanced on his thigh. "So, what are you going to do?"

Tate forced herself to think. "Right now, I suppose I need to find us a place to stay—"

"Whoa! You're homeless, too?"

Tate glared at him and held up her hand in an indignant gesture. "Hold on, hotshot, don't jump to conclusions. I'm a travel presenter, out of the country for most of the year, so I live out of hotel rooms. Once a year, I get a long vacation, and I came back to New York to meet with my producers. I was planning to find a hotel for a night or two, until I decided where I wanted to spend my vacation. I might have to rethink leaving New York now, since I have Ellie with me."

"Do you have enough cash? She needs diapers and clothes and…stuff."

Stuff. Tate wrinkled her nose. How unhelpful.

She did have enough money. Her living and travel expenses were paid for by the production company, so her hefty salary went straight into her savings account. Kari was a flake, but she wasn't. "Yes."

"You don't seem like you have much experience with babies."

"Or any," Tate replied self deprecatingly. "I'll buy a book," she added.

"God." Linc muttered, shaking his head. "Do you know how to change a diaper at least?"

"I'm sure I can figure it out," Tate huffed.

Linc rubbed the back of his strong neck, above the patch of tanned skin between the collar of his shirt and his hair. It was the dead of winter—why was he tan? And why did she feel the insane urge to taste his skin?

"Are you going to call Child Services and place her into foster care?"

It took Tate a moment to pull her attention back to the conversation... Ellie and what to do with her. *Focus, Harper.*

Tate looked at Linc and saw the wariness in his eyes and realized that this was a test, that this moment would make him form an opinion of her that wouldn't be easy to change. Wariness and distrust would slide into contempt.

Strangely, she felt the need not to disappoint him, since she felt like Harper women had disappointed him enough already.

This wasn't about him, she chastised herself. It was about Ellie and what was best for her, so Tate tried to imagine how she would feel watching a Child Services officer walking away with Ellie, and she shook her head. "No, I can't do that."

Tate saw, but ignored, the flash of relief that crossed Linc's face.

"I'm on vacation, and I can look after Ellie as well as any foster mother could, once I figure out the basics." She sighed. "I think I need to consult a lawyer and find out whether I can, temporarily, keep her."

He nodded but remained silent.

"Just so you know, I intend to track Kari down and make her face the consequences of her actions. I want her to make the decision to give Ellie up for adoption, not me," Tate added.

"That can be arranged." Linc held her eyes, and in that

instant she saw the edgy businessman, the man who made hard, complicated decisions on six continents.

"What do you mean?"

"My best friend owns a security company, but he started out as a private investigator. He tracked down Kari the last time she skipped town. I'm sure he could do it again." Linc's words were as hard as diamonds and twice as cold. Oh, her sister had obviously done a number on this man's head. *Dammit, Kari.*

"I'll think about hiring a PI. But right now I just need to get us settled for the night and meet with a lawyer."

"I'll get Amy, my assistant, to find someone who specializes in family law," Linc said, leaning sideways to pull his ultrathin phone out of his pants pocket.

Tate started to protest but snapped her mouth closed when he issued terse instructions into the phone. God, he sure didn't waste time and was clearly a take-charge type of guy. Would he be like that in bed? Of course he would be; he'd be all "do this" or "do that," and any woman alive would jump to be under his command. Including her. Tate knew, instinctively, that the pleasure he'd give her would be worth any amount of bossiness…

Someone slap me, please, Tate thought. Right…well, Linc wasn't going to take charge of her…in or out of the bedroom.

Tate waited for him to finish his conversation, intending to tell him exactly that. Okay, she might be in his house, having run to him as Kari suggested, but it wasn't his job to fix this.

"No, I am not going to tell you why," Linc spoke into his phone, exasperated. "Jeez, Amy, you don't need to know everything about everybody. Concentrate on your wedding arrangements or, better yet, do some work."

Linc snapped the phone closed and tapped it against

his thigh. "I share an assistant with my brother Beck and, unfortunately, she is scary efficient, which leaves her far too much time to meddle in our lives."

Tate nodded, thinking that his crooked smile was charming, the grudging affection she heard in his voice endearing. She should go, she really should. But it was so nice in this warm house, and looking at Linc wasn't a hardship. Tate yawned, fighting the urge to close her eyes. Jet lag and having her life flipped on its head was not a great combination.

Tate fought her tiredness, decided that it was time to leave and was about to stand when she heard the sound of feet on the wooden stairs, the piping voice of a little boy and the measured tones of an older woman. Shaw was home, she thought. Both excited and nervous to meet her nephew, Tate shot Linc an anxious look.

"He knows who Kari is," he told her as he stood and stretched. "I'll explain about Ellie when I think the time is right."

Fair enough, Tate thought.

Tate heard the loud, excited "Dad!" and turned around to see a little boy fling himself at Linc's legs. Tate couldn't help noticing, and appreciating, the way Linc's biceps bulged as he scooped his son up and into his arms, easily holding the three-foot dynamo.

"Dad! You're home! What are you doing here? We made clay dinosaurs at school. Billy made Jamie cry. I fell down and scraped my knee. But I didn't cry or anything."

"I am home, buddy. I needed to meet someone here. I'd love to see the dinosaur you made… Where is it? Who is Billy and why did he make Jamie cry? I'm glad your knee is okay," Linc calmly replied, sending a quick smile to the dark-haired, older woman who walked into the room. "Hey, Mom."

Tate's gaze danced over Shaw's features; he had Kari's blond hair, the same spray of freckles she remembered her sporting in her childhood and Kari's spectacular eyes. Give him twenty years and he would be fighting off girls with a stick.

Shaw must've felt her eyes on him because his head whipped around, and his mouth dropped open with surprise. He wiggled out of his father's arms and belted across the room to stand next to her. "I'm Shaw. Who are you?"

Keep it simple, she thought, seeing Linc's concerned frown. "My name is Tate. And this—" she lifted the little girl's fist "—is Ellie."

Shaw placed his hands on his hips and cocked his head. "Okay. Did you come for a playdate with Dad?"

Tate held back her laugh. Oh, God, she wished that this situation was that simple. "I needed to chat with your dad." She stood up and held out her free hand to Linc's mother. "Hi, I'm Tate Harper, Kari's sister."

Linc frowned. "I thought she was your cousin."

"Legally, we're sisters. My mom adopted her when we were kids," she explained.

Tate expected Jo to give her a very frosty reception, so she was very surprised when the older woman ignored her hand to lean in for a quick hug.

"You're the travel presenter. I love your program! And who is this?" Jo looked at Ellie and shot Tate a sympathetic gaze, and her mouth tightened. "Don't bother answering, I see the resemblance between her and Shaw. She's done it again?"

Tate forced herself to meet Jo's eyes, and saw a mixture of sympathy and anger. Sympathy for her, anger toward her ex-almost-daughter-in-law.

To her dismay, her eyes started to burn with tears. "I flew in from South America this morning. I had a meeting with my bosses. A few hours later and I'm suddenly responsible for a baby!" She waved her free hand in front of her face in an attempt to regain her composure. "Sorry! I'm not a crier but I'm so mad."

"You need a cookie," Shaw said, looking up at her, his expression concerned.

Tate let out a tiny laugh. "I probably do."

"I'll have one with you," the little boy stated, his tone confident. "Then you can feel twice as better."

Linc shook his head, and the amusement in his gray eyes made her heart stutter. "Nice try, mister. You can have an apple, and if you want a cookie, you can have it for an after-dinner treat. That's the rule." Linc placed both his hands on Shaw's shoulders. "In the meantime, you can take your schoolbag upstairs and say hello to Spike."

Shaw nodded and bounded away.

Tate lifted her eyebrows. "Who is Spike?"

"His bearded dragon," Jo replied, shuddering. "Ugly little thing."

Jo reached out and took Ellie from Tate's arms. Ellie touched Jo's cheek with her little hand, and Jo pretended to bite it. The older woman then turned her megawatt smile onto Tate. "Now, what are we going to do about you two?"

Tate darted a look at Linc and shook her head. "No, really, this isn't your problem. I'll make a plan, figure something out. I'll buy that baby book and muddle along. We'll be fine."

"I think you should stay here tonight," Jo said, her tone suggesting that she not argue. "Judging by your career, I doubt you have any experience with babies—"

"Try *none*," Tate interjected.

"—and I can, at the very least, help you through your first night with her."

Oh, God, she'd love that. Tate knew she could figure

it out, eventually, but being shown how to do the basics would make her life a hundred times easier. Then Tate saw Linc's forbidding expression, and her heart sank. He didn't want her in his house or in his life, and she couldn't blame him. The last time a Harper female dropped into his life, she caused absolute havoc and a great deal of hurt. "That's extremely kind of you but—"

"Where are your bags?" Jo demanded.

"Um, still at my company's office," Tate replied, suddenly realizing that if she wanted a change of clothes and to brush her teeth, she'd have to collect the suitcases she'd left in the care of Go!'s security. And she'd have to lug said luggage and a baby to whatever hotel she could find on short notice.

Damn.

Tate straightened her shoulders and injected steel into her spine. She'd faced down bigger challenges than this in cities a lot less sophisticated than New York. She wasn't powerless and she wasn't broke; she'd just have to get organized. "Thank you but no. I'll be fine." She forced herself to meet Linc's stormy gray eyes. "I'm so sorry to have called you. I suppose I panicked."

As Tate went to take Ellie, Jo turned her shoulder away and shook her head. "You're not going anywhere, young lady. You are my grandson's aunt, and I insist that you spend the night. It's not as though we don't have the room."

"Mom—"

Tate heard the warning in Linc's voice even if Jo didn't.

Jo narrowed her eyes at her son. "Linc, arrange for the Ballantyne driver to collect Tate's luggage and have it delivered here. One of those many interns you have hanging around at work can purchase some baby supplies. I'll make a list, and it can be delivered with the luggage."

Linc pulled his hands out of his pockets and lifted his

hands in resignation. He looked at Tate and shrugged. "My mother has made up her mind."

But you're not happy about it, Tate thought. She looked at Jo, thinking that she'd try another argument, but Jo's expression was resolute.

"Just for tonight," she capitulated. "Thank you and I do appreciate your hospitality."

Jo walked toward the kitchen, taking Ellie with her. When she was out of earshot, Tate gathered her courage to look at Linc. "I promise you, I won't abuse your hospitality."

Linc nodded, his face granite hard. "I won't let you. Trust me, I have no intention of being played for a sucker again. So, fair warning, whatever you think you can get out of me, it's not going to happen. One night, Tate. That's it. Tomorrow, you're gone."

Tate wanted to explain that she wasn't like her sister, but quickly realized that Linc wasn't interested in her explanations and, worse, didn't care. She was the dust on the bottom of his shoes, and the sooner he could shake her off, the happier he'd be. "Tomorrow, I'm gone," Tate agreed.

"See that you are. My mother got her way this time. She won't again." Linc lifted his wrist to look at his expensive watch. "I've got to get back to the office. I'll arrange to have your luggage collected if you give me the address. Amy's working on finding that lawyer, and I will ensure that whatever my mother wants purchased gets delivered."

"Thank you. I do appreciate your help," Tate said, her back still straight and her eyes still clashing with his.

Linc surprised her when he stepped up to her and gripped her chin in his large hand. An inch apart, she could feel the heat of his hard body, smell his sweet breath. She could see the faint scar in the corner of his mouth, count each individual bristle of his sexy stubble. Her pulse raced. She wanted that mouth on hers...wanted to wind her arms around his neck, to push her aching breasts into his wide chest.

She wanted to know what he tasted like, how he kissed.

"I fell for the machinations of one pretty Harper woman before. I won't do it again." Linc's gaze darted to her mouth and back up to her eyes again. She saw desire smoldering under his layers of anger and frustration. "So don't get any ideas, Tate."

"One night, Linc." It was all she could think of to say, the only words she could force through her lips. "I promise."

Derision flashed across Linc's face as he dropped his hand and stepped back. "Sorry, but Harper promises mean less than nothing to me."

Fair enough, Tate thought as he strode away. If her fiancé had bailed on her and her child two weeks before their much-anticipated society wedding, she, too, would still be furious and not inclined to play nice with his relatives.

And she most definitely wouldn't have been as calm as Linc had remained with her. Tate placed her hands on her hips and stared at her feet.

She'd been granted a reprieve, and she'd use that time wisely to rest and pick Jo's brain on the basics of childcare. Tomorrow she'd move on.

Between now and then the one thing she would not do was fantasize about Linc Ballantyne. Yes, he was insanely hot, but if she were to have a type, he wasn't it. Within ten minutes she'd pegged him as a traditional guy, someone absolutely committed to his son and his family, to his stable, conventional life.

He was everything she was not. And that was perfectly fine with her, because in the morning she would be moving on.

After all, moving on was what she did best.

Three

In the space of an afternoon, Tate had fallen in love.

She absolutely adored her niece, was partly in love with Jo, was pretty much there with Shaw and utterly entranced with the brownstone the three of them called their home. It was after midnight, and Tate, barefoot and dressed in a pair of yoga pants and a T-shirt, padded down the imposing wooden staircase, her hand sliding down the banister. How many hands had repeated the same action since the house was built in the late 1800s? How many guests had snuck down these stairs to head for the kitchen for a late-night glass of milk or a glass of wine to aid sleep?

Clutching a baby monitor, Tate stepped off the last tread and turned into the enormous room on the ground floor. Jo had taken her on a tour of the five-story home earlier in the day, and every room was a delight. The huge entrance hall opened up to reception rooms and formal living rooms, a library and a smaller sunroom.

The second floor was Linc's domain, comprising a master bedroom, a home office/library and Shaw's bedroom and playroom.

She was on the third floor, in the middle bedroom, which was linked by an interleading door to Shaw's old nursery.

Jo occupied the top floor but this ground-level floor was already Tate's favorite. As a food lover, she was delighted by the state-of-the-art kitchen. She loved the way the kitchen flowed into an informal dining area and then into a relaxed living space filled with books and toys and... mess. Magazines and coloring books and handheld computer games. The mess reassured her that a family lived here.

Oh, she did love the house but... What was it about it that made her feel out of place? It wasn't the luxury; she didn't care about the expensive furnishings and the exclusive address. It was the permanence of The Den, Tate realized, that made her feel twitchy. Like Ballantyne's store on Fifth Avenue, their flagship store, it was an institution. It screamed tradition, solidity...everything she, the ultimate rolling stone, was not.

She was a product of her tumultuous past, Tate decided as resentment twisted her stomach into knots. Her life had been perfect before Kari and her mom, Lauren, Tate's mother's twin, came to live with them for what was supposed to be a month or so, until the single mom found a job and her bearings. A month had turned into six, and her dad had moved out, threatening divorce unless their lives returned to a normal, Kari-and-Lauren-free existence.

Her mom, Lane, chose her twin. Tate had lost her dad, her home and her mother, who seemed to prefer Kari to her, all in less than a year. They all had lost the financial security her father had brought to the table. Then when she was eight and Kari eleven, her aunt had been diagnosed with breast cancer and quickly passed away, leaving the three of them to muddle along, moving from one rental to another. Lane had managed to scrape enough money together to cover the legal fees for her to formally adopt Kari and to petition the courts to change Tate's surname to Harper, with no objection from her father.

All her life Tate had felt like the third wheel and a stranger in her own house. Her teenage years with Kari had been pure hell. Kari had an uncontrollable temper, a sense of entitlement and was a master manipulator.

Tate had coped by dreaming of running away to places like Patagonia and Santorini, Istanbul and Ethiopia. Anywhere, she decided, was better than sharing a small house with a selfish, irresponsible drama queen and her enabler. When she left home to travel the world, she'd realized her teenage instincts were correct and that she was much happier having an ocean and a couple of continents between her and her mother and Kari. She liked being alone and free, not having to answer to anyone but herself. It wasn't that she didn't like people, she did, but her mom and Kari were emotional leeches. At a young age she'd learned to create little pockets of solitude around herself and tried to spend as much time there as possible.

When you didn't rely on anybody for anything—companionship, love, company—they had no power to hurt you.

It was funny how two melded-together families, hers and Linc's, could be so different. When Kari and Linc had become engaged, Tate made it her mission to study the family her sister was marrying into, and she'd been impressed by what she'd learned from press reports and interviews with various members of the famous family.

Their story was a modern-day fairy tale. Jaeger, Beck

and Sage Ballantyne were orphaned young and placed into the care of their uncle, Connor Ballantyne. Linc was the housekeeper's son, but Connor adopted all four children as his, and they were now one of the most powerful and influential families in Manhattan, known for their fierce love and loyalty to each other and the family name. If you messed with one Ballantyne, it was said, you messed with three more.

Their commitment to each other was absolute.

The Ballantynes functioned as a cohesive unit, whereas her family was a train wreck, and her only commitment was to her job and to avoiding Kari. That entailed staying on the move, never allowing herself to put down roots. Without roots and connections she couldn't disappoint people and, more important, open herself up to being disappointed.

Using the light from the hallway, Tate headed for the stainless steel fridge and pulled out a bottle of milk. After opening cupboards she found a glass and sat at the informal table to drink her milk. She'd love a cookie, but she felt that rummaging about in the Ballantyne cupboards was an abuse of their hospitality.

Despite feeling like she was camping in the middle of enemy territory, Tate had enjoyed her evening with Shaw and Jo. It was a relief not to have Linc there, glaring at her as she ate; thank God for whatever it was that kept him at work past dinner and bedtime. Though, possibly, working late was just an excuse to avoid her. Truth or lie, Tate silently thanked him—the evening had been far more relaxed with Jo and Shaw than if she'd had to make awkward small talk with the deliciously sexy Linc.

She'd never understood why Kari walked out on the man. Kari craved status, and Tate had expected her to grab onto Linc like the lifeline that he was. After all, he had been—still was—New York's biggest catch. Seriously smart and successful, devastatingly handsome, filthy rich. And judging by the way that Shaw's eyes lit up when he spoke about his dad, he was an excellent father.

Linc was the type of guy women dreamed about. A full-time, fully involved father. Someone stable, committed, responsible.

Tate had never believed in fairy tales, in handsome princes and happy endings. But she did believe in the power of lust… It was simple attraction to Linc that made her heart thump, her blood heat and her panties a little uncomfortable. Images of them together, on his huge bed upstairs, bombarded her. She could easily envision herself naked on his sheets, his big body covering hers, his long, muscled legs tangled with hers. Chest to chest, breaths and mouths and hands mingling… Had he loved Kari like that in that same bed?

The thought barreled in from nowhere and Tate groaned. God, she now needed brain bleach to wipe out that thought. They might have made Shaw in that very bed!

Tate scrubbed her face as her heart constricted. She scowled at the unfamiliar sensation. Thoughts of Kari and Linc together made her feel totally off-kilter. Why? Tate didn't like the only, and obvious, explanation. She was jealous; jealous of Kari, envious that she'd had that sexy mouth on hers, his broad hands stroking Kari's skin and not her own. Tate shuddered at the thought of Linc and Kari, naked, doing what naked people did.

You are not allowed to lust after Kari's ex, Tate told herself sternly. It was against the sister code, the cousin code, against the laws of nature.

Besides, Linc was the last guy on earth she should be attracted to. Like his house, he had an air of tradition, permanence, solidity. Kari had informed her—during their awful fight—that she and Linc agreed that she would be a stay-at-home mom, that they would have a traditional marriage, with Linc as the breadwinner. But that was too conventional for her sister, so she'd run.

Like Kari, Tate was a drifter. But unlike her sister, she was determined to keep her distance from people—men!— and she guarded her independence, like a mommy bear guarded her cubs.

She and Linc were noon and midnight, cliffs and sea, trains and planes…

And really, she had bigger problems to deal with than this inconvenient desire to see Linc naked. *Get a* grip *for goodness' sake!* Lusting after Linc was a stupid waste of energy, and, besides, she knew that he would rather kiss Shaw's bearded dragon than kiss her.

She was under no illusion that when Linc looked at her, he saw Kari, and, on the surface, they were alike. But if Linc took the time to get to know her, which he wouldn't, he'd quickly see that they couldn't be more different. She might not have the trappings of wealth, but she had a very healthy bank account, thanks to saving most of her salary for the past seven years. She worked hard, and she was committed to her career and her independence, but those came at a price. On occasion, she was desperately lonely, and sometimes she craved company, someone else to talk to besides her production crew. Sure, she wasn't interested in a relationship, but she sometimes hungered for a connection, a pair of strong arms around her, a masculine chest to lay her head on, a deep voice whispering dirty things in her ear as hot hands explored her body.

She could handle sex, a fling, even a temporary affair— provided there was an end in sight—but her lifestyle, and career, made that difficult. Most of the men she met were backpackers and travelers, and she understood that, for them, hooking up while traveling was a major part of the "experience." Apart from the icky diseases factor, she really didn't want to be another in their long line of sexual conquests. And sleeping with her coworkers was out… As a result, she'd been celibate for more years than she'd care to count.

Linc, damn him, made her remember exactly how long it had been. Why did he have to be such a sexy, sexy guy? He made her remember what being uncomfortably horny felt like. That had to be why she felt like she wanted to jump out of her own skin whenever he was around.

"Can't sleep?"

Tate screeched and hurtled up from her chair, knocking over her glass of milk. She tried to grab the glass, but it rolled away from her, off the table and smashed on the tiles below. Tate swore and, as she put her foot down, she felt a shard of glass pierce her heel. She groaned and dropped her butt onto the chair, hoisting her heel up onto her knee to look at her wound.

Tate blinked when the kitchen filled with light and turned her head to look at Linc, who was walking toward her. She started to apologize for breaking the glass, but her words, and the moisture in her mouth, disappeared when she saw that he was dressed in nothing more than athletic shorts and shoes. Earlier, dressed in his suit, he'd looked urbane and sophisticated, but this Linc—perspiration glinting on his bare skin, bulging muscles, a defined six-pack and muscled thighs—was pure masculine power.

"Sorry, I didn't mean to scare you." Linc said, walking over to her and bending his head to look at her heel. He winced at the shard of glass in her heel. "Can you pull it out?"

Tate quickly removed the sliver and dropped her heel.

"Careful," Linc warned. "There's glass everywhere."

"Sorry," Tate said. "I'll replace the glass."

Linc frowned. "It's a glass, Tate, not a Picasso. Relax. And sit down. I'll clean up."

"But—"

"I'm wearing shoes. You are not," Linc said and turned to walk into the expansive utility room behind the kitchen, returning with a broom and dustpan. Within minutes he'd swept up the glass, mopped up the milk and was chugging down a bottle of water he'd pulled from the fridge.

"Do you normally work out at midnight?" Tate asked, trying to break the heavy silence between them.

Linc lifted a big, broad shoulder, and Tate wondered how it would feel to run her hand through his light sprinkling of chest hair. "I work out daily. Sometimes I have crazy days, and that means that my workout happens at crazy hours." Linc lowered his water bottle and nodded at the baby monitor on the table in front of her. "Did she go down easily?"

Tate shook her head. "Not really. I had to rock her to sleep." She made herself meet his hard eyes. "She's probably missing Kari."

Linc bent down and rested his forearms on the granite island of the kitchen, his expression broody. "So, have you decided what you're going to do?"

"About Ellie?" Tate clarified and waited for his nod before continuing. "I'm still thinking it through. My plan is still to get legal advice and go from there."

"Are you going to talk to my PI?" Linc leaned his butt against the kitchen counter and crossed his ankles. His hands gripped the granite countertop behind him, and his muscles bulged and tightened. Raised veins—a fine indication that he was super fit, in case she didn't catch a clue from his zero-fat, all-muscle body—snaked over his forearms and biceps.

Concentrate, Harper!

Tate squirmed under his hard, penetrating stare, sensing that he was frustrated by her lack of decisiveness. He wanted answers, an immediate plan of action. It was the CEO way, she decided.

But this wasn't his company; it was her and Ellie's lives. She'd take all the time she needed to make a decision she felt comfortable with. Besides, he would be free of them in the morning, so what did he care?

But he'd been kind enough to let her stay here tonight, so she thought she might, maybe, owe him a brief explanation.

"I'm conflicted and feeling a lot overwhelmed, Linc. I need time to process what's happened," Tate admitted, she jumped up from her seat at the table and walked toward him.

So much for a brief explanation, she thought, as words rolled off her tongue. "I know I can't look after a baby, and I don't want the responsibility of making decisions for Ellie. I have two months before I go back on the road and can't take a baby with me! Ellie is her daughter, not mine. I mean, God, she's cute and sweet and pretty damn easygoing but I'm not mommy material!"

How could she be? Lane, Kari, even her aunt Lauren, had been—were—shockingly bad mothers, and there was no reason to think she'd be any different.

Having a baby was the ultimate commitment, so keeping Ellie was out of the question. Besides, conventional wisdom stated that the child was always better off with their mother so restoring Ellie to Kari was her ultimate goal.

"Along with your killer body and gorgeous hair, that seems to be a trait you share with your sister," Linc said, his voice flat.

His words were an acid-tipped arrow straight to her heart. She wanted to lash back, to tell him that she wasn't anything like Kari, that she wasn't irresponsible and selfish and so very screwed up. But the suspicion in his eyes told her that, no matter what she said, he wouldn't believe her.

But she had to try. For some crazy reason she didn't want him to judge her by her family name. She was better than he thought. "I'm not my sister, Linc."

Linc didn't acknowledge her words. He just held her indignant look, and she watched as his eyes turned from granite to a smoke gray. Oh, God, she recognized that hot, masculine look of appreciation, and it had nothing to do with liking her mind or her personality and everything to do with liking the way she filled out a T-shirt.

He was as attracted to her as she was to him. Oh, Lord, what was she supposed to do with that thought, how was she supposed to process it?

The smart reaction would be to walk away, to turn her back on him and hightail it out of the kitchen and up the stairs. Tate wanted to be smart, she really did. But more than that, she wanted to taste him, to press her breasts into his bare chest, to feel that hard, sweaty skin under her hands. She wanted to inhale him, devour him, climb inside him...

An unintelligible curse erupted from Linc's mouth, and his hand shot out to grab her wrist. With a hard yank, he pulled her into him, and her hips slammed against his erection—ooh, nice—and he ducked his head to cover her mouth with his.

He didn't bother to sip or suckle, he didn't tease or taunt; Linc just slid his tongue into her mouth to tangle with hers, challenging her to give as good as she got. Tate responded by twisting her tongue around his, answering his silent dare.

Something hot and hard arced between them. Tate felt heat zinging through her as Linc's big hand slipped between the fabric of her shirt to cup her, his hand easily covering her small breast. His thumb swiped her nipple, and she made a guttural sound in the back of her throat, rising on her toes to align her mound with his erection, wanting more heat, more hardness.

Her hands, by their own volition, skated up his rib cage, across his chest, flirted with the ridges of his stomach. Linc responded by placing his arm under her butt and lifting her off her toes. It made sense for her thighs to grip his waist, to hook her ankles behind his back, to rub her long-neglected core against his hot-and-hard-as-hell length. She wanted this man. She wanted him in the worst possible way.

She wanted no fabric between them, she wanted them slick and hot…battling to breathe and crazy with need. Because feeling Linc inside her, touching all those neglected, lonely places, was what she needed, craved. Tate thought about asking him whether he had a condom as she pushed her hands down the back of his shorts to thrust her fingers into the hard muscle of his butt. A wave of desperation rose within her. They had to rid themselves of the barriers of clothing, mostly hers, that kept him from sliding inside her, stretching her and filling her.

Words, she needed them, but she couldn't bring herself to stop kissing him long enough to get her point across. Tate swirled her tongue around his, pulling on his bottom lip, but, unlike earlier, he didn't respond. Tate frowned. Taking stock, it occurred to her that his hands had stopped exploring her body, that she was sliding down his big frame, that her toes and then her feet were touching on the cold floor. Shaking her head, she tried to work out why he'd stomped on the brakes.

Had she done something he didn't like? Did he think that she was a wild woman? A slut? Oh, God, did he think he was kissing Kari and suddenly realized that it was her?

Tate shoved her hands into her hair and looked up him, dreading the expression of cool disdain she knew she'd see.

Linc, however, looked calm and in control and not at all like he'd just tried to inhale her. Where did all that passion go? What had he done with all that hot, unbridled desire? Tate looked down and saw that he was no longer rock hard… *That's an amazing amount of control, Ballantyne.*

It pissed her off.

Tate opened her mouth to utter a very snarky comment, but he spoke first. "Ellie is crying."

Tate blinked, trying to make sense of his words. *Who? What? Where?*

"The baby is crying, Tate. You need to go to her."

Through the monitor on the dining table Tate heard Ellie's soft wail, heard the desolation in her muffled cry, and she snapped back to the here and now. Oh, God, the poor thing sounded like her heart was breaking. How long had she been crying? Minutes? An hour? Longer? How long had she and Linc kissed? She couldn't tell, she'd lost all sense of time, and of reality.

Oh, my God… She almost lost her freaking mind. She'd been a heartbeat away from asking her sister's ex to do her on the kitchen counter!

What must he think?

And more important, what must Ellie think? Did she think that Tate had abandoned her just like her mother? Not wanting to make the little girl wait another minute, Tate whirled away from Linc and sprinted for the stairs.

Yes, she was desperate to get to Ellie, but honesty made her admit that she was equally desperate to get away from Linc. She had absolutely no control of herself around him, and she thanked God for Ellie's interruption. And for his keen ears because she hadn't heard a damn thing.

She'd been deaf, dumb, blind with lust for him…

It was a very good thing, Tate thought as she sprinted up the stairs, that she was leaving tomorrow.

Four

Linc, after a night short on sleep and long on aggravation, hustled Shaw through his morning routine, trying not to think about the fact that he'd been so close to taking his ex's sister on the kitchen counter the night before. He'd been desperate to know if she was as hot and honeyed as he expected, and his hands had been in her pants, about to push the fabric over her hips, when he'd heard Ellie crying. Would he have stopped if she'd slept through?

Possibly. Maybe. Not a chance in hell.

In his bedroom, Linc muttered a curse as he pulled on his shoes. What the hell happened last night? Yeah, he was horny; it had been a while since he'd last got lucky, but, crap, he never lost control like that. Even as a teenager and at his craziest with Kari, he'd never felt so desperate for a woman, so utterly and incomprehensibly caught up in pleasure.

And the fact that he felt this way about his ex's sister

just pissed him off. Bloody Harper women. They had a way of turning his life upside down and inside out. But, he was compelled to admit, he hadn't, not once, thought of Kari when he'd been kissing Tate. Thank God, because this situation was weird enough without getting them confused.

And thank God again that Tate was leaving today because he didn't know if he could spend another night tossing and turning and talking himself out of the urge to go to her room and finish what they'd started.

The sooner Tate left, the better. The world could then stop trying to spin off its axis.

She was the exact opposite of the woman he thought that he and Shaw might someday want. On those odd times when he wished that his life had turned out differently, he fantasized about a sexy, funny stay-at-home mother and lover, someone who adored Shaw. Someone who'd put him and his son at the center of her world, someone he'd trust to stay with him, surfing the waves of life with him and never swimming away.

If he ever got to that place where he felt he could trust again, risk again, Linc knew that he'd want someone who believed in traditions, in order, someone who could fit into his life and who looked the part. He wanted a woman who was easy, and he wanted calm, a lake and not a storm-swept sea.

Tate was exactly what he didn't want or need. She'd create waves and whirlpools, the turbulence he tried to avoid at all costs in his personal life. The woman didn't have a conventional bone in her body; her clothes were bohemian, and, according to Kari, they'd had an unstable upbringing. Tate was a modern-day nomad, a free spirit, innately unconventional.

But, God, the way she kissed; it was a goddamn miracle they hadn't set the brownstone and most of the block on fire.

Linc walked into his closet, yanked a tie from his collection and draped it around his neck, fuming over the fact that he couldn't think about Tate and her mouth and knot his tie into his customary perfect Windsor.

He didn't have enough blood in his brain to do both at the same time.

"Dad, hurry up, Granny Jo is making pancakes," Shaw shouted from the doorway to his room.

Linc frowned. "She's up?"

Shaw nodded. "And she's wearing lipstick. Hurry!"

Linc followed Shaw downstairs, wondering what was going on. Jo was not a morning person, and he and Shaw rarely saw her before breakfast. He did the morning shift, Jo took the afternoons and, if he was slammed, the evening shift. Then Linc remembered that she wanted him to hire a nanny...

Crap.

Linc felt his stomach clench and wondered how he was going to solve that problem. He understood her need to spend more time with Gary, and it wasn't an unreasonable request. His mother was entitled to a life that didn't include the responsibility of looking after his son.

But how was he supposed to trust a stranger with his heart and soul? If something happened to Shaw, he'd crumble. He trusted his mom, his siblings, but anyone else? Hell, no. Nobody would ever love Shaw or look after him like he did, but Jo came damn close.

Well, thankfully, he didn't need to figure it out immediately. Better off thinking about it when he didn't have a came-close-to-having-sex-but-didn't hangover, a headache from too much frustration and not enough sleep.

Linc noticed Tate's bags in the hallway, ready to be

loaded in a taxi, and his heart bounced off his rib cage. He tasted panic in the back of his throat and briefly considered whether he was losing his mind. He definitely wanted her to leave; she couldn't stay. Tate was cut from the same cloth as Kari, and the fabric was damaged, stained, torn. He needed another Harper woman in his life like he needed a hole drilled into his head.

But, God, she looked good, Linc thought, as he stopped in the doorway to his kitchen. She looked, and Linc spat out a silent swear. *Right*. Tate sat at the kitchen table, bouncing Ellie on her knee as she listened to Shaw telling her about his favorite teacher at school.

"She sounds really nice." Tate ran a hand over Shaw's head, totally engrossed in what he had to say. Tate leaned forward, her beautiful eyes sparkling with amusement. "And do you have a girlfriend?"

"Yuck." Shaw looked horrified.

Tate laughed, and Linc felt as if she'd punched him in the throat. Her laugh was similar to Kari's, but not. It was full-bodied and genuine and long on amusement and short on insincerity. Ellie, hearing her laugh, waved her hands around and laughed, too.

God, this was what he'd wanted. Laughing kids, a gorgeous partner, Connor's house filled with joy. He'd wanted this…with someone.

But having it with a Harper woman was utterly out of the question.

"Linc, you're here. Excellent," Jo said, noticing him hovering in the doorway. He kept his eyes on Tate's face, and the laughter in her eyes faded along with the color of her skin. Then a blush appeared on her high cheekbones and mortification flashed in her eyes. So she was regretting last night's madness, too.

He still wanted to kiss the hell out of her, suck her nipples, slide his hand between her... *Ballantyne! Pull yourself together!*

Linc headed for the coffee machine and, keeping his back to the room, yanked a cup from the cupboard and punched a button, mentally begging the machine to hurry up. He needed caffeine. Or a brain transplant. Either would do.

Shoving his hand through his hair, he frowned at his mother. "Is there a reason that you are up and making us pancakes?" he asked, ignoring his mother's narrowed eyes at his surliness.

"Yes!" Jo retorted, sounding far too chipper for someone who was not a morning person.

Something about his mother's cat-eating-canary expression made the hair on Linc's neck rise. He lifted a hand and scowled at her. "No." He nailed her with a hard look. "Whatever it is, just no."

Jo pointed her spatula at the table. "Sit down. And maybe you can remember your manners and say good morning to our guest."

How old was he? Ten? Linc shot Tate a look and saw the twitch on her lips suggesting amusement. "Good morning, Tate." He ran his hand over Ellie's soft curls. God, she was cute. "Morning, honey."

Ellie leaned away from Tate and smiled at him, revealing two little teeth. She lifted her chubby arms, so he picked her up and settled her on his hip where she immediately grabbed his tie and wrapped it around her fingers.

"You don't have to hold her," Tate said, sounding subdued.

"I like kids," Linc told her. It was the truth; he did like kids. Babies didn't scare him; he'd raised Shaw from the time he'd been born, and he never once regretted having him in his life. Shaw was the best thing that had ever happened to him. What the hell was Kari's problem pulling this crap twice? Whether Tate decided to track her down or not, he was going to find his ex and force her to take responsibility for her kid.

She'd refused to be part of Shaw's life, and he no longer wanted her to be, but, God, she wasn't giving up this baby without, at the very least, a reality check from him. He owed Shaw's half sister that.

Linc turned to see Jo, holding a platter of pancakes, staring at him. The corners of her mouth kicked up, and she nodded as she approached the table. "You're going to track her down, aren't you?"

Not bothering to issue a denial—his mom wouldn't believe him if he did—he just took his seat at the table and tucked Ellie into the crook of his arm.

"I think that's the right thing to do," Jo said, placing the platter on the table between them. Linc forked up a couple of pancakes to put on Shaw's plate before pushing the platter in Tate's direction.

"You're going to find Kari?" Tate demanded, her eyes flashing a hard-to-miss warning.

"I'm not going to let her get away with this again. It's b…" Linc looked at Shaw and swallowed the swear. "It's not acceptable, Tate."

"I never said it was," she protested. "It's just that I have a problem with you pursuing this. It's my problem." Tate's hot gaze threatened to singe his skin. "I will handle it."

"My PI already tracked her down once. He will again," Linc stated, using his best don't-argue-with-me voice.

"I'll use your PI, but I'll pay for him and I'll deal with him," Tate insisted, adamant. Linc heard the bite in her voice and sighed when he realized that her lifted nose and snotty expression turned him on. Yep, the party was starting to happen in his pants again…

"He's expensive."

"My problem, my money," Tate leaned forward, and he was distracted by her gaping shirt and the fantastic flash of rose-lace-covered breasts and a cleavage he wanted to ravish with his tongue. Ah, damn, he thought as his blood pumped into his penis. Smooth, fragrant skin, her breathy encouragement in his ear, those small hands on his—

"Linc will pay Reame, the PI. And you will pay him back by staying here and acting as Shaw's nanny for the next two months."

Wait! What? Had he really heard what he thought he heard?

"Mom! What the hell?" he demanded, dropping his fork and yanking his eyes off Tate's fabulous cleavage. Ellie let out a squeal at his raised voice, and he gently patted her thigh to reassure her, and she quickly settled again.

"I'm leaving today, Ms. Taylor," Tate said, panic coating her words.

"Call me Jo, darling." Taking her seat next to Linc, she sent Tate a serene smile, but he immediately recognized the determination in her eyes.

"And, no, you're not. You need a place to stay, and you need to spend some time with Shaw. I need to spend some time with my man... We're thinking about flying to the Bahamas for a week. Linc needs someone to look after Shaw." Jo picked up a pancake from the platter, placed it on her plate and, not appearing to have a care in the world, cut a piece off and lifted it to her mouth. She winked at Shaw, who tried to wink back. "It's the perfect solution for everyone."

"No, it's not. That's not going to work for me," Linc stated, in his coldest voice, the one he never recalled using on his mother before.

"It won't work for me, either." Tate said, her voice shaking.

"Well, it works for *me*," Jo replied, still as cheerful as a sunbeam. She looked at Linc, and he immediately noticed the build-a-bridge-and-get-over-it look that was a feature of his teenage years.

"Linc, with your trust issues and your protective streak, it'll take you months to make the decision to hire a nanny and another six to choose one. I choose Tate. She's related to Shaw, she's lovely—"

He knew exactly how lovely she was, but that had no bearing on this conversation. "She knows nothing about kids! She's unconventional and a free spirit and jet-setter!"

Tate glared at him, looking like she wanted to argue, but at the last moment she nodded, surprising him by agreeing. "All true."

Jo looked from Tate and then at him. "What nonsense! Yesterday afternoon, I called her boss, the executive producer, Keith someone, and asked for a reference on Tate."

Tate looked aghast. "You did what?"

Linc groaned. "God, Mom."

"According to her boss, Tate is punctual and easy to work with. As smart as a whip. She writes and coproduces her show and helps out with the logistics. But, best of all, she's utterly reliable."

His mother, Linc thought darkly, could be damn annoying.

"Oh, God," Tate muttered, putting her head in her hands. After a moment she dropped her hands and narrowed her eyes at Linc. "She's your mother, talk to her."

He'd try. "Mom, you can't ambush us like this."

"Just did," Jo replied, and Linc heard the familiar sound of a text message coming into a phone. Jo pulled her cell out of the back pocket of her designer jeans and swiped her finger across the screen. When she looked up again, her eyes glinted with amusement.

"Gary's booked our flights, and we're leaving for the Caribbean at noon. Yay!" Jo stood up and shoved her phone back into her pocket. She grinned at Linc. "Unless you can find another nanny by noon or play hooky from work, Tate's your only option to look after Shaw. And, Tate, stop being stubborn. You need a place to stay, and Linc, while he can be incredibly annoying and bullheaded on occasion, does know what he's doing when it comes to babies. Stay here, spend some time with Shaw, enjoy the house."

Jo dropped a kiss on Shaw's head, then Linc's, then Ellie's before wrapping her arms around Tate's shoulders and hugging her tight.

Linc had to strain his ears to hear her softly spoken words. "This is a good house, Tate. It can heal you if you let it."

Tate watched Jo walk away and rubbed her suddenly throbbing forehead. What had just happened? She dropped her hand and looked at Linc, whose eyes held the fury of a hundred hurricanes.

"Bloody Jo," he muttered, and the words were barely out of his mouth before they heard the rumble of deep voices in the doorway. Tate turned around and blinked when a petite, stunning woman with long black hair stepped into the room, followed by two tall, well-built, immaculately dressed men. Damn, the Ballantyne men were a sexy bunch.

The room filled with noise as Shaw jumped up to greet his aunt and uncles, flinging himself against hard legs before being boosted up and over rugged shoulders. Linc rolled his eyes and after ribs had been tickled and hair ruffled, he told Shaw to sit down and finish his breakfast.

When Shaw resumed his place at the table, Linc glared at his siblings.

"Yeah, you three are exactly what I need right now," he said, sarcasm coating every word.

Tate felt a flutter of nerves and bit her bottom lip, bracing herself for their hostility.

"Pancakes! Sweet." The tallest of the three Ballantyne brothers slid onto the chair opposite Tate and grabbed a plate. He flashed a grin as he forked a pile of pancakes onto his plate. "Tate, right?" he asked her. "The bride of Satan's sister?"

There was humor in his voice, and while his eyes remained wary, he didn't seem to direct any hostility toward *her*. "I'm Tate and you're… Beck?"

Beck waved his fork at his older brother, who took a seat at the end of the table. "Yep. And that's Jaeger and our sister, Sage."

Jaeger nodded a greeting as he pulled out a chair, clasping the ball of Linc's shoulder before he sat down. "You're looking a bit rough, dude."

"You have no freaking idea," Linc muttered, glaring at Tate. She returned his blistering look, silently telling him not to blame this situation on her. This was his meddling mother's idea, not hers!

"Tate?"

She turned her attention to Sage, who stood next to her chair. The young woman held out her hand, which Tate shook. "Hi, there. We understand that Kari has run off again?"

"Yep." Tate flicked an uncertain glance at Linc, who was pouring juice for Shaw. "I take it that your brother filled you in on my situation?"

"We don't keep secrets in this family," Jaeger said, his voice growly. Tate looked at him, and she saw the warning in his eyes, on his face. Mess with my family and I'll take you apart. Tate knew that this wasn't the time to cower, so she held Jaeger's eyes, and eventually, maybe, she saw a flicker of respect cross his face. A faint smile touched his lips, and then he turned to Linc. "So, what's the plan of action? And leave some pancakes for me, Beck!"

"The plan of action was for Tate to leave this morning. She was going to see a lawyer, I'm going to talk to Reame about tracking down Kari—"

"Reame's going to be pissed at doing that again," Sage commented before asking Tate if she could pick up Ellie. When Tate nodded, Sage took the little girl from Linc's lap. Ellie's hand immediately curled into Sage's long black hair, fascinated.

Linc quietly instructed Shaw to run upstairs to brush his teeth. When his son left the room, he turned his still-annoyed eyes back to his siblings. "Jo has thrown a monkey wrench into those plans."

Tate looked down at the table, shocked to see that the massive pile of pancakes had all but disappeared. Obviously Jo had advance warning that Linc's siblings were coming over; either that or she'd invited them. Tate suspected that they were very aware of Jo's plans and, worse, approved of them. "What's she done now?" Sage asked, rocking from side to side, her cheek on Ellie's head.

"Left me high and dry." Linc placed his forearms on the table and closed his eyes. "She's taking off to the Bahamas with Gary at noon, leaving me without anyone to watch Shaw. And I have a crazy afternoon."

"She didn't provide you with an alternate solution?" Beck asked, draining the rest of Shaw's orange juice, his smile hidden by the rim of the glass. Oh, hell, yeah, his siblings knew about Jo's plan. Tate leaned back in her chair and folded her arms, trying to make sense of Jo's machi-

nations, but all she could think about was the Ballantynes'
reactions to her. She'd expected them to hate her, to trans-
fer their animosity about Kari to her. But they seemed to
want her to stay with Linc, live in this house and act as
Shaw's nanny?

Why? What was their agenda?

Jo could offer her the moon to stay, but Tate knew that,
while Jo had conned Linc into letting her stay for a night,
he wouldn't be steamrollered a second time. No, this would
be Linc's decision…

And hers, obviously. So, what did she want to do? Stay
here or go? It would be easy to stay, Tate admitted. On a
practical level, if she remained at The Den, there was a
fully equipped nursery full of baby equipment for her to
use, and she could save the expense of buying equipment
she'd only need for a month of two, because, really, how
long would it take an experienced PI to track Kari down?

Practicalities aside, she did want to spend some time
with Shaw; he was Kari's son, and she adored the blond
dynamo. She wanted to make up for all the birthdays and
Christmases she'd missed with him, maybe do some fun
activities with the little guy. And maybe if he came to care
for her as much as she cared for him, Linc would let her
spend some time with him when she returned to the Untied States during shooting breaks.

But if she stayed in this house, she would be living
with Linc, and the chances of finding herself naked with
him were stratospherically high. The guy just had to step
into the room, and the urge to jump him was strong. Tate
closed her eyes, remembering the feel of his lips on hers,
his broad, hard hands on her bare skin. She just had to
look at him to turn into a raging inferno. Why Linc? Why
now? And why, dear God, did he have to be Kari's ex?
Why was she even attracted to him? She'd never been a

fan of the Mr. Traditional type of guy, the type who expected his woman to run the household and take care of the kids, ending the day by cooking a gourmet dinner. She was *not* that woman.

"Linc, concentrate!" Beck snapped.

Tate jerked her attention back to the present and saw that Linc was staring at her mouth, his fists resting on his thighs, clenching and unclenching.

"Big Brother is rattled," Beck said, amused.

"What was Jo's suggestion, Linc?" Sage asked, her eyes darting from Linc's face to Tate's and back again.

When Linc spoke, his voice sounded weary. "Well, she suggested that Tate take over as Shaw's nanny until I find someone else, someone suitable."

Sage tipped her head to the side. "Why isn't Tate suitable?"

Linc glared up at his sister. "I don't know her."

"You won't know anyone an agency sends, either," Beck pointed out, standing up to head for the coffee machine. He pulled cups from the cupboard, took milk from the fridge.

"Yeah, but they would've done background checks, have references from other parents," Linc said, glaring at her. "Tate arrived on my doorstep yesterday!"

"Some would call that fate," Sage suggested.

"Fate, my ass," Linc growled.

"You do know that I am sitting here, listening to you talk about me?" Tate interjected, feeling her temper start to bubble.

"You need a nanny, Linc," Beck told him, ignoring Tate's protest. "Unless you plan to take some time off."

"I am not leaving my son with a stranger," Linc said, his jaw rock hard.

The new nanny would be a stranger, too, but that pertinent fact seemed to have escaped Linc's steel-trap mind.

Tate's hand gripped her coffee cup, reminding herself that throwing the object would accomplish nothing. Unless the cup hit his head and knocked some sense into him.

"No, what you are really saying is that you won't leave Shaw with a Harper," Tate said, pushing herself to her feet.

Their eyes clashed and Linc nodded. "Yeah, I won't leave him with Kari's sister. Just like I wouldn't leave him with your mother.

"Not that she's ever asked to see him," Linc added, his voice bitter. To Linc, who obviously valued family so highly, her mother's lack of interest had to be a knife to his heart. Tate wanted to tell him that her mother was dead, she wanted to put him in his place, but those words died when she opened her mouth to retaliate.

"Stop comparing me to Kari." It took all her effort to keep her voice calm. "I'm not my sister."

"If it walks like a duck…" Linc said, his words deliberately careless.

Tate heard Jaeger's groan. "Dammit, Linc. Stop being an asshat."

Linc threw up his hands, his handsome face dark with suppressed anger. "It's not like I'm making assumptions here, Tate. Kari spoke about you. You never went to college, wanting to travel instead. You missed countless family events because you had something better to do. You can't wrap your head around commitment, and you'd rather have your freedom than stay in one place. You make a habit of quitting jobs and ending relationships on a whim. Knowing all this, how can I trust that you won't ditch my kid if you have something better to do?" Linc linked his hands behind his head as his chest rose and fell in agitation. "He's my life. I'd never forgive myself if something happened to him on your watch!"

This was why she'd kept her distance from her family,

why she'd worked so very hard to create another identity. All her life comparisons had been drawn between her and Kari. Linc was just another in a long, long line of people who'd assumed she was just like Kari and condemned her for it.

She sighed. She'd lived most of her life feeling trapped between two worlds—her family's perceptions of who she was and who they thought she should be.

Now, far away from the life she'd left behind, she felt free, like she could finally be who she really was. People either liked her, or didn't, for who she was without reference to Kari. She made it a point to not worry about what people thought about her, to try to live her life on her own terms according to her own truth.

But, unfortunately, Linc's assumptions about her hurt, and feeling hurt annoyed her. She'd known him for a few hours; his opinion shouldn't matter to her.

But, dammit, it did.

Tate, feeling as if she was fighting a riptide, took Ellie from Sage's arms and dropped a kiss on her silken head. Determined not to let Linc, or his siblings, see how upset she was, she tossed her head and gritted out, "You got all your information about me from Kari, yet here I stand, holding her child, the second one she's dumped. I think there's something wrong with that picture."

Tate walked toward the stairs, feeling the acid burn of tears in the back of her throat. At the door, she made herself turn, to look at Linc once more, probably for the last time. "I'll call for a cab, and I'll be gone in an hour. Good luck in your search for a perfect nanny."

Five

As Ellie played at her feet with plastic toys, Tate looked out her bedroom window to the tree-lined street below. Tate watched as Beck swung Shaw up onto his shoulders, the little boy laughing with delight. Sage was walking alongside Beck, and Jaeger stopped to close the wrought iron gate behind him. They were taking Shaw to his pre-K, Tate surmised. The Ballantyne siblings were a close-knit unit, something she and Kari had never managed to be.

She was, once again, alone. Tate looked down at Ellie's dark head and smiled. Well, she wasn't completely alone; for the next few weeks or so she had this precious little girl for company. Tate bit her lip, wondering if she'd ever see Shaw again. She wanted to be part of his life, but whether Linc would allow that was a tenuous possibility at best. However, there was one thing she *did* know beyond a shadow of a doubt. When she restored Ellie to Kari she'd be a constant and consistent presence throughout Ellie's life, whether Kari wanted her to be or not.

Well, as constant and consistent as her travels and job allowed. Shaw and Ellie were her nephew and niece, the only family, apart from Kari, she had. She wanted a better, healthier relationship with them than she had with her sister and her mother.

The Ballantyne crew turned the corner, and Tate realized that it was a bit of a shock to realize how envious she was of them, of the deep love they shared. A part of her wanted to know what unconditional love felt like—how it felt to be supported, to have a backstop, a soft place to fall. Tate shoved her hands into her hair, frustrated with herself. These thoughts were dangerous and counterproductive. Besides, love's favorite sport was to push her heart through a grinder.

"I handled that badly."

Linc's words danced over her skin, and her stomach quivered. As angry and hurt as she was, he still made her feel like she'd been plugged into a source of pure energy. Unable to face him, Tate sat down on the seat built into the window and watched the road below.

"I'm sorry. I was rude and dismissive and judgmental," Linc stated.

Tate lifted her hand to rub the back of her neck and closed her eyes, wishing that he'd just go away. It would be so much easier if she could just wait for the cab in peace, if she could slip out of the door and avoid this confrontation. She realized that she'd hardly spent any time with him, but she was already so sick of him looking at her and seeing Kari.

Hell, he'd probably thought that he was kissing Kari. It was highly possible that his attraction to her had nothing to do with who she was and everything to do with him taking a walk down memory lane.

Out of the corner of her eye Tate watched as he walked

past Ellie to sit beside her on the bench, lifting his ankle up onto his knee. "God, I'm exhausted."

Tate felt his broad, warm hand on the back of her neck and turned her head to look at him. She wanted to pull away from his touch but his fingers pressing into the knots in her neck felt amazing. *Not going anywhere, not going to pull away*, her body told her stubborn brain.

"You must be exhausted, too." Linc dug his fingers into the tight cords of her neck, and it took every ounce of determination she had not to moan from sheer pleasure. "Did you sleep last night?"

"Not much, no."

"Me, either," Linc admitted. "Let's talk, Tate. And this time, let's try not to kiss or yell at each other."

They could try, but she didn't know if they'd succeed. Because she still wanted that mouth on hers. If he tried to kiss her she didn't think she could resist him. Embarrassingly, her brain had lost all control over her body…

"Okay."

Linc dropped his hand and pulled his thigh up on the bench so that he could look at her. "I *am* sorry for earlier. As Jaeger pointed out after you left, I acted like an ass because I don't like change."

"And you don't know me so you don't feel comfortable leaving Shaw with me. It's okay, I get it. It's a big, bad world—I've seen most of it—and I'm thankful that you are a protective dad."

"I appreciate that. It's been just Shaw and me since Kari left."

"Shaw and you and Jo," Tate corrected.

Linc rolled his eyes. "At this moment she's on my hit list, so I'm not talking about her. She did tell me, *yesterday*, that I should start looking for a new nanny, that she wanted to be a grandmother, not Shaw's caregiver. I never thought that she'd pull this, though. *Blackmailer.*"

Tate heard the love under his frustration, but his anger was gone. Not sure what to say, she looked down at Ellie, who was babbling to a doll she'd found in the box of toys. "I've called a cab. It should be here soon. We'll get out of your hair."

"I think you should stay."

Tate's jerked, completely astonished. "You want me to stay?" She frowned. "To look after Shaw?"

Linc shrugged. "Maybe." He held up his hand when she opened her mouth to protest. "Just listen, okay? I need a nanny and you need a place to stay. As you said, I don't know you, and when it comes to Shaw, I'm very slow to trust. Your sister—"

"Messed with your head," Tate finished his sentence for him. She shrugged. "I get it, she's been messing with mine all my life. What else did she say about me?"

Tate saw his hesitation and waited for him to speak. "Nothing much more than what I already mentioned. She didn't speak much about you except to say that you were jealous of her."

Tate rolled her eyes. "As if." She looked him in the eye, desperate to get her point across. "I am not my sister. I didn't go to college, but, over the years, I managed to study part-time to get a degree in world history. I did miss many family events, but I also wasn't invited to many. I like being free to do my own thing. That's why having Ellie to look after is a shock. Kari was flat out lying when she said that I quit jobs and end relationships on a whim—I've had the same job for the past six years, and I haven't had a significant relationship to quit, on a whim or not."

Tate just stopped herself from telling him that keeping

her distance and remaining independent were essential to her. *Too much information, Harper.*

"Oh, and my mom didn't contact you because Kari told her that you threatened to have her arrested if any of her family tried to reach out. She convinced my mom that you had the power and money to do that."

Linc gripped the bridge of his nose and shook his head. "God, she's a piece of work. I did offer to let Kari have visitation rights with Shaw, but she wasn't interested. But if your mom wanted to meet Shaw, I'd make that happen. Supervised, but it could happen."

Tate's heart bumped against her rib cage at his generosity. "Thank you, but she died a couple of years ago."

Linc squeezed her knee. "I'm sorry, Tate. I wish I'd known…" His voice trailed off. "Anyway, I was wrong to judge you by your sister's actions but she…" Linc rubbed the back of his head, looking uncomfortable. "She ripped the rug out from under me."

"You really loved her," she stated, the familiar mixture of regret, guilt and sadness rolling around in her belly.

"I loved what thought I was getting," Linc gruffly admitted.

"Which was?"

"A complete family, my family within a family. She told me that she wanted to be a mom, a wife, my partner. I thought she would be the person I could come home to, normality after a crazy day."

Tate raised her eyebrows. "You associated Kari with *normality*?"

Linc grimaced. "Very briefly. Anyway," he said, moving the conversation off Kari and the past, "getting back to what we were discussing, you moving in…" He took a deep breath. "Stay for a week, and I'll work from home. I'll help you with Ellie, and you can spend some time with

Shaw. If, at the end of the week, I feel comfortable hand-
ing Shaw over to you to look after, I'll go back to work and
we'll do a trade. I'll feed and house you and pay for the
PI, if you look after Shaw until I find a full-time nanny."

Tate considered his offer, quickly running through her
options. It was a fair offer, she acknowledged, except for...
"I want to see Shaw in the future, I don't want to walk
away and never see him again."

Linc's expression softened. "I can make that happen."

Tate nodded her thanks. "Feed and house Ellie and me,
and I'll pay for the PI myself."

"He's expensive, Tate," Linc protested.

"I have money, Linc, and nothing is more important to
me than restoring Ellie to Kari," she replied, her tone firm.

"Okay, deal. But what if you find Kari, and she refuses
to take Ellie back?"

Her heart lurched. God, she couldn't think about that.
Not now. "She will. I'll make her."

"I hope you're right," Linc said. "But, because we are
talking about Kari, maybe you should have a plan B."

Tate heard the insistent horn of a taxi and looked out
of the window, seeing the yellow cab outside. She took a
deep breath and nodded. "Okay, deal. One week and we'll
reevaluate."

Linc placed a hand on her shoulder as he stood up,
squeezing gently. "Thanks, Tate. I'll go down and tell the
taxi he's not needed, and I'll bring your bags back up."

She pulled her knees up to her chest, thinking that
she shouldn't ask the question burning her brain. But she
couldn't stop the words. She had to know. "Linc...?"

He placed his hand on the doorjamb and turned.
"Yeah?"

"When you kissed me last night. Were you thinking
about Kari?"

Linc released a sound that sounded like a half snort, a half laugh. "No, that was all you, Tate Harper." His dark gray eyes dropped from her face to her chest, and back up to her face again. Then his gaze lingered on her mouth, and his eyes heated as his hands curled into fists. Tate thought that he might be trying to stop himself from reaching for her.

Or was that wishful thinking?

"It was all you," Linc repeated his words, his voice sounding like sandpaper. "*Only* you."

Linc disappeared, and Tate heard him heading down the stairs. "Damn, Ellie."

At the sound of her name, Ellie looked up and gifted her with a gummy grin.

"How the hell am I going to resist him?"

The child, not understanding the question, threw her doll at Tate's legs.

He was living with another Harper woman, Linc grumbled to himself a couple of days later, running down the stairs from his home office to open the front door.

God help him. Kari had been, generally, a pain in his ass, but Tate, well, she was trouble on a whole new level. Because no matter how hard he tried, he couldn't get her off his mind.

And he didn't like it. Not one bit.

Linc looked at his watch and thought that he'd known her for less than three days and every minute they were together he fought the urge to take her to bed. Her perfume was in his nose, the memory of her smooth skin was on his hands, and the image of those warm cognac brown eyes, foggy with passion, were burned into his retinas. He was *so* screwed, metaphorically speaking. Sad as that was.

Stop thinking about sleeping with her, Ballantyne. Think about business and the fact that you are less than useless working from home, mostly because you are so easily distracted by a pair of long, sexy legs and that that tumble of long, wavy hair you want to sink your hands into.

He bit back an oath. Work was piling up, and he couldn't leave Beck to carry the load for much longer. It wasn't fair and it wasn't right. Jo was having a ball with Gary, and Linc knew that he'd lost her as his full-time caregiver; he had to find someone to look after Shaw on a permanent basis.

Tate seemed to be doing okay, he reluctantly admitted. She and Shaw seemed to click, helped by the fact that Tate was able to spend hours with him in the afternoons, building forts and racing cars, Ellie close at hand. After sampling his runny scrambled eggs on day one at Frustration Central, she kicked him out of the kitchen, cheerfully stating that she'd cook. She quickly and with the minimum of fuss, whipped up meals that both Shaw and Ellie could eat and then tossed together a more adult meal the two of them could share while exchanging polite conversation and pretending that they weren't imagining each other naked. So far he'd eaten a Thai curry and a pork-and-beans dish from the deep South. If she wasn't a Harper, and he didn't want her in his bed, he'd probably employ her on the spot as his housekeeper/nanny.

Lusting after the nanny, such a cliché. And if that thought wasn't enough to dampen his raging libido, then he should remember that she was the last person that he should be interested in. She was a nomad, she'd only be around until she reunited Ellie with Kari, and then she'd shoot off to parts unknown.

She was also his ex's sister, and he'd been burned by one Harper blonde before. Did he really want to risk repeating *that* crappy experience?

If it meant getting her naked then…maybe. But probably not.

God, he was arguing with himself, a new low.

Linc opened the ornate wooden door and glared at Reame Jepsen, his oldest, closest friend and owner of the best investigative company in the city. His green eyes sparkling with amusement, Reame lifted his eyebrows and gave him a knowing look.

"What's up, dude? You look pissed," Reame drawled, walking into the hallway, taking a moment to look at the stained glass windows on either side of the door. "God, I love this house. Always have."

Reame was his one friend who knew him from BC—Before Connor. They'd both lived in the same run-down apartment building in Queens, but, somehow, their friendship survived his move to Manhattan when Jo landed the job of Connor's housekeeper, his subsequent adoption by one of the wealthiest men in the country and his very privileged lifestyle.

Reame had no idea how much Linc admired him; he'd grown up poor, joined the military, served with distinction in the Special Forces and established one of the most respected security and investigative companies in the city.

Reame said that he couldn't have done it without Connor's, and then Linc's, business, but Linc disagreed. His buddy never gave up and never gave in. He would be exactly where he was, with or without Ballantyne business.

"You're wearing your pissed-off-with-women expression," Reame stated, after they exchanged a one-armed, super brief hug.

"Thanks for coming over," Linc told him as they walked deeper into the house, heading for the downstairs family room. Reame shrugged off his thanks, and Linc knew that, like his brothers, Reame would move mountains for him if he needed him to.

"So, who's the woman?" Reame asked, not allowing Linc to change the subject.

Knowing that his friend wouldn't let the subject die, Linc pushed frustrated fingers through his hair. "Kari's sister."

Reame's eyes narrowed with suspicion. "Satan's bride's sister is here? Why?"

"Long story, we'll go into it," Linc said, rubbing the back of his neck. "She's actually going to be your client… I'm just doing the introduction."

Reame shook his head. "Nope. Not happening. I'm not interested."

"Hear her out, Reame. She's not like Kari." Linc hesitated. "At least I don't think she is."

Reame groaned, looking appalled. His fist rocketed into Linc's shoulder. "Are you freaking nuts? What is it with you and these Harper girls?"

"God knows," Linc replied, rubbing his shoulder. "Just listen to her, please?"

"Okay." Reame folded his arms over his chest. "But if I don't like her or what she has to say, or think she's trying to scam you, I'm not taking her case."

"Fair enough," Linc said as they moved farther into the house. They half jogged down the stairs leading to the kitchen and great room. Linc's eyes scanned the room and saw Tate standing by the doors to the garden, looking at the barren winter garden. Her head resting on Ellie's, her hand was patting the little girl's back in a rhythmic, soothing motion. She kept saying that she wasn't mommy material, but for someone who had been thrust into the role a few days earlier, she was doing fine.

And she looked stunning. Unlike the women he dated

who looked effortlessly chic and glamorous, Tate looked relaxed. She wore tall laced-up combat boots and gray over-the-thigh socks, and there was a gap of a few inches between her socks and flowy skirt. Her rust-colored sweater showed off one creamy shoulder, and her long wavy hair tumbled down her back.

Linc looked at Reame, saw his hell-yeah, appreciative look and jammed him in the side with his elbow. His pal nodded slowly before tossing Linc an amused look. "So… wow," he said, sotto voce.

"Tell me about it," Linc muttered. He called Tate's name and watched as she turned around and gave him a quick, hesitant smile. Her gaze moved on to Reame, and her eyes widened, a common reaction. Reame had a Turkish mother and a Danish father, and the combination of olive skin and light green eyes and big, muscular body, resulted in appreciative looks and flirty smiles. Reame's power over women had never bothered Linc before, but seeing Tate's reaction to his friend pissed him off.

Big-time.

"Tate, Reame Jepsen, the PI I told you about. Reame, Tate Harper. Potential client."

He made a big deal of emphasizing the word *client*. Reame had a cast-iron rule about not sleeping with, dating or having a friendship with his clients. Not that he'd allow Reame to make a move on Tate; he'd rip his old friend's face off first.

God, jealous much, Ballantyne?

Tate moved toward them and held out her hand for Reame to shake. As Tate got closer, Linc saw the tears in the baby's blue eyes, the track marks on her chubby cheeks. Ellie, noticing him, leaned forward, waving her arms at him, silently asking him to take her. Linc obliged and cuddled her close, holding her head to his chest. "What's the matter, honey?" he crooned.

Linc raised his eyebrow at Tate who shrugged. "I have no idea," she replied, frustrated. "She's clean, has had a bottle and she ate her lunch."

"This is a new house, new people, and she's probably feeling a little scared," Linc said.

To his surprise, Tate's eyes filled with tears. "I think so, too." She hauled in a deep breath. "That's why I was rocking her."

"It's all you can do." Linc nodded. "As much as she wants, when she wants it."

Tate sucked in a breath, nodded once and sent him a grateful look. She was holding up well, Linc thought, impressed. Most of the women he knew, with the exception of Jo and Sage—and Jaeger's fiancée, Piper—would be whining about how having to look after a baby interfered with yoga or Pilates or a pedicure.

But Tate just sucked it up and did what she needed to do. He admired her for that.

"Let's have coffee," Linc suggested, suddenly uncomfortable. It was one thing to lust after Tate, but he was playing with fire if he started liking her, too.

"I'll get on that," Tate offered, "since you have your hands full."

"Let's talk while you do that," Reame suggested, walking to the counter and pulling out a stool. "I don't have that much time, and it sounds like you have a story to tell."

Tate nodded. "I understand that you located Kari four years ago after she disappeared?"

"Yeah."

"I need you to find her again," Tate insisted, and Linc heard the bitterness in her voice. She sent Reame a determined look. "Find her so that I can take Ellie back to her, so that I can talk some damn sense into her. Find her so that I can tell her that she cannot dump her children whenever she feels like it!"

Tate closed her eyes as if she were suddenly realizing that she was shouting. She pulled in a long breath, and her chest lifted and fell. When she opened her eyes again, her anger, her frustration and her embarrassment were visible. She sent Reame an imploring look. "Please, just find her. For Ellie. She needs her mom."

Reame looked from Tate to Linc and back to Tate again. He nodded once and held out his hand for Tate to shake. Her small hand disappeared into his, and Reame covered the back of his hand with his other, his face serious. "I'll find her, Tate. I promise."

He would, Linc thought, feeling relieved. His buddy never made promises he couldn't keep. Linc's eyes met his, and Reame gave him a sharp nod, as if to reinforce his promise to Tate. Then Reame's expression changed, and amusement jumped back into his green eyes and lifted the corners of his mouth.

Tate turned her back to them, busy with the coffee machine, and Linc raised his eyebrows at Reame. "What?" he mouthed.

Reame gave him a thumbs-up before lifting his index finger and pulling it across his throat. Linc quickly interpreted his gestures. Tate was okay, and he was in so much trouble.

Which was nothing he hadn't already realized.

When Linc returned to the kitchen after seeing Reame out, Tate sent him a weary smile. She was exhausted; partly because she felt drained from talking about Kari and the little she knew of her life but mostly because she'd spent the previous night thinking about Linc and their volcano-hot kiss.

"I need to collect Shaw soon," Linc told her. "His pre-K isn't far from here. Do you want to walk with me? It's supposed to snow soon, so we'd better hustle."

Tate looked out of the window to the gray, freezing day. "Have you heard of a cab? A car?"

Linc smiled. "I need fresh air or else I get twitchy. Come on, don't be a girl."

"I *am* a girl," Tate told him, and his gaze darkened. Yeah, when he looked at her with male appreciation in his eyes, she felt intensely feminine and super sexy.

Dropping her eyes, Tate looked from Linc to Ellie, sitting on the carpet at her feet, and back again. "How far is far? Will Ellie be okay in the cold?"

"I'll find Shaw's old snowsuit and I'll carry her. She'll be fine."

Tate nodded and stood up, feeling Linc's hot gaze on her legs. She raised her eyes and caught his smile, the molten desire in his expression. "As much as I appreciate what you're wearing, I strongly suggest that you put on a few more layers or else you will freeze," he told her, his voice bone-dry.

Tate felt her cheeks warm. "I usually follow the sun. I don't have that many winter clothes."

"You look good," Linc murmured, his voice husky.

Tate shoved an agitated hand into her hair, wishing that he'd stop looking at her mouth. Even better, she wished he'd do something *with* her mouth, like kiss it stupid. Their eyes clashed and held, and Tate swallowed, wishing his big, strong arms were around her, that she could taste his breath, count each bristle on his chin. She wanted him to rip her clothes off her, to undo the buttons of his shirt and push the fabric aside so she could touch his chest, explore the hard ridges of his stomach.

"When you look at me like that, it takes every inch of willpower to stop myself from doing exactly what you are asking for."

Tate touched her top lip with the tip of her tongue. "What am I asking? Bearing in mind that I didn't say a word."

"You don't need to speak. Your eyes say it all. You want to see me naked. And more."

Tate didn't bother to play games by denying his very accurate observation. She just met his direct gaze and nodded. "You want to see me naked, too."

"And do more," Linc rasped, jamming his hands into the pockets of his pants and rocking on his heels. "A lot more."

Tate groaned and had to stop herself from flinging herself against his chest and doing what biology was urging them to do. "This is insane!" she muttered. "Do we not have enough to deal with without this crazy thing zinging between us?"

"Seems not."

"We shouldn't be attracted to each other!" Tate cried.

"Yet, we are."

Tate nodded. "But we don't have to act on it."

"We did the other night," Linc pointed out.

"Only because we both thought that I'd be moving on in the morning! I would never have let that go so far if I thought I was staying."

"Honey, you didn't even hear Ellie crying. I did."

Tate glared at him. "I would have. At some point." She pulled in a long breath and raked her hair back from her face. "Linc, it was a momentary madness. It won't happen again."

Linc sent her a hot, frustrated look. "Want to test that theory? I think that once we start, we won't be able to stop, not again."

Dammit, how was she supposed to resist him? Tate

didn't know, but her gut told her that she should. Instinctively, she knew that, while sleeping with Linc would be a delightful way to pass the time, the consequences of their actions would be huge. What those consequences were, she couldn't quite discern, but her instinct was telling her that they would be dire.

Feminine intuition aside, falling into a fling with a hot guy should be the last item on her agenda. She had to look after a little girl who was pining for her mom; she had to find her sister and reconnect mother and daughter. She had a career to return to, places to visit, people to meet.

Living with Linc, *sleeping* with Linc, would make this situation too intimate, too much like the fairy tales she'd never believed in. He was like this house, stable, solid and rooted. He was Manhattan royalty, successfully established and easily juggling his roles as a brilliant businessman and an excellent single father.

Whereas she was a transient, someone who could pack light but who carried far too much emotional baggage. She ran from relationships, from commitment, from anything and anyone demanding that she dip below the surface.

Her attraction to Linc scared her, but the fact that she liked his mind as much as she liked his body terrified her even more.

It's imperative you keep your distance, Harper.

Tate bent down and picked Ellie up. "Let's walk, Linc. Maybe if we get to know each other better, we'll realize that we don't, actually, like each other, and this crazy attraction between us will disappear."

"Here's hoping," Linc said, pushing his hands in the pockets of his pants. "But I think we're kidding ourselves if we think this is going away."

Six

Dressed in layers, Tate pulled the front door closed and headed outside, wincing as the bitterly cold air burned the back of her throat. She fought the urge to run back into the warm house behind her.

Too much sunshine has made you soft, Harper. Suck it up.

Tate drew level with Linc, concerned that Ellie wasn't warm enough. She touched her fingers to the baby's cheek, and Ellie sent her a gummy smile, obviously cozy in the snowsuit that Linc had found in the top of Shaw's cupboard. Ellie seemed very happy in Linc's arms, so Tate shoved her bare hands into the pockets of her parka and her chin into the scarf she'd wound around her neck.

Tate felt Linc's hand on her arm, pulling her left, and she shot him a glance. "Puddle," he explained and she smiled her thanks. Linc stopped and, with his free hand, pulled his knit hat off his head and thrust it at her. "Your lips are turning blue. Put this on."

"Are you sure?"

"You're turning into a Popsicle," Linc muttered as she positioned the hat over her hair, still warm from his head. "Do you want to go back?"

She didn't. The temperature was dropping rapidly, and she couldn't remember the last time she felt this cold, but with a little exercise she'd quickly feel warmer. She wanted to walk with Linc, breathe in the snow-tinged air and clear her head.

"I'll be fine, thanks." Tate pulled her hands out of her pockets and wiggled her fingers. "But I do need to buy some gloves."

He grabbed her hand and, winding her fingers through his, tugged it into the pocket of his leather-and-sheepskin jacket. Warmth from his hand flowed into hers, and she sighed as they walked shoulder to shoulder down the sidewalk. "Better?"

"Better," Tate replied. "How's she doing?"

"Fast asleep."

Ellie, her curls covered by the hood of her snowsuit, rested her cheek against Linc's black cashmere scarf, and her deep eyelashes were smudges against her caramel skin. She looked like a doll, Tate thought, lifting her free hand to gently rub the back of her knuckle across Ellie's cheek. "She's so beautiful, Linc."

He nodded, dropping his head to look into Ellie's face. "She really is," he said, his voice tender. Tate wondered if any of his employees or business associates knew that the strong, powerful CEO of Ballantyne International could be brought to his knees by a sleeping baby. "It's cold, Tate. We need to walk."

Her hand still in his, Tate felt grateful when he shortened his long stride to accommodate her shorter legs. Feeling a lot warmer and almost content, Tate rested her head against Linc's shoulder and tasted snow in the air.

What would Kari think if she knew that she was walking hand in hand with her ex-lover, the father of her son? Would she care? Would she think it one big joke? Or would she be jealous as hell? Tate recalled that Kari had never liked to share. When she'd moved in with them after her mother's death, Tate's room became hers, Tate's clothes and toys became hers. Kari, and what she wanted and desired, came first.

No, her sister would definitely not like the idea of Tate cozying up to Linc.

Well, tough. It was her idea for Tate to go to Linc, her decision to abandon her daughter, just like she'd abandoned her son. Kari could shove her jealousy and her what's-mine-is-mine-and-what's-yours-is-mine attitude straight up her—

"Whoa, I can practically see steam coming out of your ears," Linc said. "And you're squeezing the hell out of my fingers."

Tate winced and sent him an apologetic look. "Sorry. Thinking about my sister sends my blood pressure skyrocketing."

"I can relate," Linc stated bitterly.

She gave his fingers a gentle squeeze. "I really am sorry for what she did to you and Shaw, Linc. I was out of the country, but I was furious with her. Nothing I said could change her mind. I tried to talk some sense into her, I promise."

Linc nodded his head, a fine mist on his dark hair. "I appreciate that. I can forgive her for leaving me, God knows that I'm not perfect, but leaving Shaw? Bailing on our son is what I can't forgive. I can't abide people who don't, or won't, shoulder their responsibilities."

Tate heard a note in his voice that suggested Kari wasn't the first person in his life who'd disappointed him. "Who else bailed on you?"

Surprise followed by annoyance flashed across Linc's handsome face. *Bingo*, Tate thought. "You don't have to answer the question if you don't want to. I was just being nosy."

"It was a long time ago, Tate. BC."

"BC?"

"Before Connor."

"That was a long time ago," Tate commented. "It had to have been a hard knock because I can tell it still hurts."

Tate fell quiet, not wanting to push him where he didn't want to go. Not that she could push Linc Ballantyne. She didn't have that much power over him.

Or any at all."My dad walked out on my mom and me when I was five," Linc said, staring straight ahead. His voice deepened when he was upset, Tate realized. Or when he was feeling emotional. "We'd been Christmas shopping. We bought him a pair of golfing gloves." He choked out a small laugh. "Funny the things you remember."

"You came home from Christmas shopping…" Tate prompted, wanting him to finish the story.

"And he was gone. He cleared out their joint bank account and his clothes and vanished. Never to be heard from again."

Tate grimaced. "Your mom couldn't track him down?"

"Tracking someone down takes money and, pre-Connor, there wasn't that much floating around."

He had so much, yet he still remembered how it felt to be poor, Tate thought, amazed. Needing to thank him for opening up, she decided to repay him by doing a little of the same. "I can, sort of, relate. My parents divorced, and my dad faded from my life, and he seemed to forget about me when his new wife got pregnant. After my half brother's birth, I ceased to exist."

Linc pulled his hand from hers to run it through his hair. "One hundred and one ways to screw up your kids."

"You seem to be doing a great job with Shaw," Tate murmured, blowing air into her hands. Linc noticed and pulled her hand back into his pocket.

"Thanks to Connor and Jo."

His tone suggested that he was done with this conversation, so Tate decided to switch gears. "Getting back to Kari, she's always been…" Tate hesitated.

"Selfish? Narcissistic? Self-involved?"

"All of the above," Tate admitted. "I was eight when she came to live with us—"

"Because her mom died?" Linc interjected. He shrugged, and Ellie moved up and down his chest. "Kari didn't talk about her past and would never discuss the future. It was one of the many things that drove me nuts."

She and Kari were alike in that way. Tate rarely opened up about her childhood and torturous teenage years, and as for the future? She didn't make plans beyond the next year or two. That was a Harper trait.

But Linc deserved an explanation. He needed to know who Kari really was, what drove her and why she acted like she did. One day he would have to explain to Shaw why his mom left him, and she never wanted Shaw or Linc to think that they were at fault.

Tate explained how Kari ended up with them and about her aunt's death. "My mom and her twin were exceptionally close, and when she passed away my mom turned all her energy onto Kari, nursing her through her mom's death."

"And where were you in all this?" Linc asked gruffly. Tate jerked her head back, surprised that he'd asked. She'd told this story a few times and most people immediately and, rightfully so, empathized with Kari losing her parent at such a young age.

But Tate also lost her mother at the same time; she'd moved from being Tate's mom to Kari's.

"Lost," Tate quietly admitted. "Kari lost Lauren and I lost Lane. Everything changed that autumn."

Linc's fingers tightened against hers, and in that small gesture she felt comfort and sympathy. It gave her the courage and strength she needed to continue. "My mom created a monster in Kari, something she would never admit. I had to toe the line, but Kari, because she'd lost her mom, was given a free pass. At eleven she was a brat, by thirteen she was uncontrollable and at sixteen, she dropped out of school and moved in with her twenty-four-year-old boyfriend."

"I never knew any of that. I thought she went to college, studied art." He shrugged, his eyes bleak. "I met her at an art gallery."

Tate stopped to look up at Linc, and she felt the frown between her eyes. "Do me a favor? Whatever Kari told you, take it with a very small pinch of salt."

"Did she travel to Europe? Spend some time modeling in Paris? Did she work in Hong Kong in the marketing department of an upmarket clothing company?"

Tate didn't answer. Of course she hadn't, and Linc knew it. Instead of answering, Tate shoved her hands back into the pockets of her parka and shrugged. "In her defense, she probably believed in every lie she told you. For a while, until her attention was caught by something or someone more interesting than you—and by *interesting* I mean *edgier, dangerous, illegal*—she bought into her own lies."

"Yeah, what do they call people like that?" Linc muttered as he snapped his fingers, pretending to think. "Oh, yeah…sociopaths."

"I just want you to know that it wasn't anything you did or said. Or what you didn't do or say," Tate explained. "Kari isn't the type to stick around."

Linc's steel-gray gaze pinned her to the spot. "Are *you* the type that sticks?"

Tate bit her lip and looked down the wet street. Was she the type to stick? No, thanks to her tumultuous past, she'd shut down and retreated into her own world. She was intensely wary of commitment, of risking her heart. And, like her mom and sister, she wasn't good with routine, with traditions, with rules and regulations. That was why she'd chosen a career that gave her plenty of flexibility and a lot of different experiences.

"I don't stick." Tate lifted her chin and looked into Linc's eyes. "That's why I can't take care of Ellie, why I can't take full responsibility for her. It's not who I am, not what I want to do. I need to be free."

A sad smile touched the corners of Linc's mouth. After a minute of tense silence, he lifted his hand to rub his thumb over her bottom lip.

"At least you're honest, Tate." Linc looked across the road to a brightly painted purple door, and Tate followed his eyes. To the side of the door she saw the discreet sign stating that this building was home to ChildTime.

Even Tate, who had little to no knowledge of kids and schools, had heard of the most expensive and exclusive pre-K in the city. Of course Shaw would attend this pre-K; she kept forgetting that his father was a Ballantyne, one of the most influential and respected businessmen in the city.

She was also finding it difficult to remember that he probably would, in a week or so, be her boss. She would be, officially, his nanny. They had a deal.

And, really, sleeping with her boss—in any capacity—would be so very tacky. Of course, her long neglected libido and her common sense didn't give even half a hoot.

Tate, one hand on Ellie's stroller and the other holding Shaw's hand, heard her phone ringing in her pocket and knew that the call would be from Linc. *Again.*

It would be his fourth call in ninety minutes, and Tate debated answering. But, genetically unable to ignore a ringing phone, she sighed with resignation and pulled her phone out of her pocket.

She rolled her eyes at the name on display. Yep, Mr. Paranoid was checking up on her. Over the last week or so, they'd found some sort of routine. Linc took Shaw to school, and then he went to the office, leaving midafternoon to collect Shaw from pre-K. At The Den, they shared a cup of coffee, and then Linc went into his home office to work while Tate took charge of the kids.

They both spent a lot of time thinking about what making love would feel like. Well, Tate knew she did. Far more than was healthy.

But today was different as Linc had called around lunchtime to ask whether she could collect Shaw from school, stating that he couldn't get away from his desk. He then called her forty-five minutes later to remind her to collect Shaw, and then Amy, his assistant, called her to check that she was on her way. The man had serious trust issues, Tate thought. Then again, he *had* lived with Kari, so she couldn't blame him.

Tate looked at her still-ringing phone. There was no doubt that Linc wanted to know that she had Shaw.

Knowing that the call was about to drop, Tate finally answered. Linc's voice, deep and sexy, but holding a trace of anxiety, flowed into her ear. "I didn't think you were going to answer."

Tate rolled her eyes. "Hi, Linc."

"I'm just checking to see if the school released Shaw to you without any problems. They are sticky about who picks up the kids and when."

Tate decided to have some fun with him. "Oh, God... Is that the time? Was I supposed to collect him? Is it really half past three?"

There was a long beat of silence. Linc was probably deciding whether she was messing with him or not, or he was making plans to put a hit out on her so Tate handed her phone to Shaw. "Say hi to your dad."

"Hi, Dad!" Shaw said into the phone, always happy to talk to Linc.

Linc spoke, and Tate's eyes hit the back of her skull when she heard Shaw's answer. "Yes, Tate was waiting for me when I came out. No, I didn't have to wait for her. Oh, and Dad? I need a lot of cupcakes for tomorrow. Like, *hundreds*."

Tate heard Linc's loud groan and bent her fingers at Shaw, gesturing him to hand the phone over. Lifting the phone to her ear, she pushed the stroller with one hand and headed for home. "You sound like you are about to have a coronary, Ballantyne. I have your kid and we're heading home."

"Did you hear what he said about cupcakes?" Linc demanded, and Tate could imagine him running his hands through his hair.

Okay, this wasn't a big deal. "There are about a million bakeries in Manhattan. Send one of your minions to buy however many you need. Easy peasy."

"Nothing about ChildTime is that easy." Linc growled. "Hold on a sec. I'll see if they sent an email about this."

Tate pushed the stroller and idly listened to Shaw talking animatedly to Ellie as she waited for Linc to come back on the line. When he did, there was tension in his voice. "Yep, I found it. It was something I thought Jo would handle, so I ignored it. And, as per usual, they've complicated the process. They would prefer the twenty-four cupcakes to be homemade, preferably with the child being involved in the process."

"So buying the cupcakes is out."

"Yep, the school actively promotes families spending time together. Crap, I need this like I need a hole in the head. I have this damned photo shoot tonight, and the family is coming over for supper, and I now have to make cupcakes! Shoot me already."

"Twenty-four?" Tate demanded. "How many kids are they feeding?"

"They are asking for extra so that they can donate them to shelters for abused women and kids."

That's a nice gesture, Tate thought, slightly mollified. "What photo shoot?" she asked, recalling his previous comment.

"Our PR expert has the four of us in a series of print advertisements, all of us dressed the same and holding a piece of jewelry or a gemstone we have an emotional connection to," Linc explained. "The idea is to get people to the website to read up on our stones and the story behind them, hoping that they will see something they like on the site and part with their cash to have it."

Tate remembered seeing the ads featuring Jaeger. She'd done exactly what he'd mentioned—she'd read up on how he'd proposed to Piper with the Kashmir sapphire featured in his ad. "It's such a great idea. Is the campaign working?"

"Yeah, we've had good responses to Jaeger's and Beck's ads," Linc replied.

Shaw tugged on her sleeve, and she looked down to see his worried expression. He was four, and he wanted to take cupcakes to school. Tate sent him a reassuring smile.

"Hold on a sec, Linc, while I talk to Shaw." She turned to Shaw and asked, "What if I make the cupcakes and you and Dad decorate them? Would that work?"

Shaw nodded enthusiastically. "Can we make animal cupcakes? Or space monsters?"

Oh, dear Lord. What had she got herself into? Animals? Space monsters...? Well, with the aid of the internet, hopefully she'd figure something out.

"Is that okay with you, Linc?" Tate spoke into the phone again.

"I know you can cook, but can you bake?" Linc asked in her ear, his tone doubtful.

Tate pulled a face. She was a travel and food journalist and a fairly good chef, so whipping up a batch of cupcakes wouldn't strain her culinary repertoire.

"Can you? And more important, do you want to try and fit making twenty-plus cupcakes into your very busy afternoon and evening?" Tate pertly replied.

Linc's sigh was heavy. "No, I can't and, no, I don't."

Tate smiled. "Then your part-time, fill-in nanny will make them."

"My part-time, fill-in nanny is about to get a huge raise."

"I'm sure we can work out a repayment plan that would be a lot of fun," Tate replied, lowering her voice seductively. God, what was she *doing*? She heard Linc's swift intake of breath and knew that she was playing with fire. Tate slapped her hand against her forehead and groaned. She had to resist him, and she should not be making flirty comments!

"What, exactly, did you have in mind?" Linc asked, his voice low and husky and vibrating over her skin.

Tate closed her eyes, mortified. "Ignore me, I should not have said that."

"Why is your face red?" Shaw demanded. "Are you sick?"

Tate heard Linc's wicked laugh in her ear. "Are you blushing, Tate? What, exactly, are you thinking about?"

"I am not about to tell you that!" Tate admitted, lifting her hand to her burning cheeks.

"Spoilsport. But it's okay because my imagination is vivid enough for both of us. I'm just glad I'm alone and sitting behind a desk." Linc admitted.

Tate blushed again at the visual that popped into her head and wished that she were with him, touching him, running her hands over the hard-ridged muscles of his stomach and into the back of his pants to push her finger tips into the hard muscle of his butt.

"We can't do this, Linc. We really can't complicate our lives by having—" Tate glanced at Shaw "—doing that!"

"I know that. I've tried everything to talk myself out of taking you to bed, but I want you, Tate. I'm wrong for you, and you're wrong for me, but hell…I keep thinking of the patterns I want to draw on your skin, how I want to go about discovering every perfect inch of you. Then I want to make love to you until you forget your own name."

Oh, God, her panties just caught fire. Tate felt the throb of desire start in her womb and spread through her body, causing sparks to ignite under her skin.

"You're diabolical," she wailed. "This isn't a good idea, Linc. You know it's not!"

"Screw good ideas," Linc muttered.

Thinking that she'd plow the stroller into a light pole if they continued with this conversation, Tate tucked her phone between her neck and jaw, gripped the handle of the stroller with one hand and tightened her grip on Shaw's hand. She had children to get home, cupcakes to make; she wouldn't manage either if she kept fantasizing about the naughty things she wanted Linc Ballantyne to do to her.

They couldn't. They shouldn't.

They *wouldn't*.

"Do you have the ingredients for the cupcakes?" she asked him, thinking that they really needed to get to safer ground.

"Changing the subject, Tate?"

"Absolutely. Let's be smart and keep things simple, Linc."

Tate clearly heard his frustrated sigh, and when he didn't respond she chose to believe that he agreed with her. "So, about those ingredients?"

"I have no damn idea what is in the pantry," Linc eventually replied. "I'll get Amy to send an intern shopping for whatever you might need."

"Flour, eggs, icing sugar, food coloring," Tate rattled off. "Don't go overboard. And do your interns do any real work or are they just there to make your life easier?"

"Both," Linc said. "I'll try and be home as soon as I can. If I'm not home by five, can you let Cady and the photographer into the house?"

"Yep. And I'll even send you a text message to tell you that we are home safe, just so that you have one less thing to worry about," Tate told him.

"Thanks, Tate," Linc said. "I know that you think I'm overreacting and being paranoid but he's—"

"Your life. The reason the sun rises every morning," Tate said softly. God, she'd never been that to anyone, not even to her mom. For Lane, her first, most important connection was to her twin, then to Kari, who was all she had left of Lauren. And then, miles behind, was Tate.

What would that feel like, to be the object of Linc's fierce devotion? His love? Pretty damn awesome, Tate decided. Fully fantastic.

"Tate?"

"Hmm...?"

"You and me? We can try to keep resisting each other, but I suspect it's going to happen and when it does, we're going to blow the damned roof off."

Seven

By five that afternoon, Tate felt like she'd run the New York Marathon, fought off an alien invasion and gone ten rounds with a heavyweight boxer. Twenty-four cupcakes were cooling on the rack, Shaw had a sugar high from licking the sides of the mixing bowl, and Ellie needed her diaper changed. After today, she'd gained a newfound respect for stay-at-home moms and child minders. This job was *not* for the faint of heart.

Tate settled Shaw in front of the TV to watch his favorite show, then crossed the room and picked Ellie up from her playpen. The little girl's hand bounced off her lips, and Tate kissed her fingers. Ellie's laugh, deep and husky, just like Kari's, rumbled across her skin, and Tate cuddled her close, burying her nose in her silky curls. God, she was pure magic, utterly sweet and ridiculously good.

Looking toward the kitchen, she winced. Shaw had insisted on helping her bake, and the kitchen looked like it was ground zero in the flour wars. She still had to pack the dishwasher and sweep the floor, and then they had to decorate the cupcakes.

Tate cast a dark glance at the three massive bags of supplies sitting on the dining table. If Linc's intern had merely sent over some icing sugar and food coloring, they could just top the cupcakes with icing and a sweet. But, no, despite Tate's earlier request, the Ballantyne intern had gone way overboard. There were cutters and stencils, edible flowers and iced animals. Decorating the cupcakes was not going to be a simple affair.

Ellie wiggled in her arms and gave a little wail to remind Tate that she was both dirty and hungry. Tate dropped a kiss on her grumpy lips and, after telling Shaw to leave the cupcakes alone, walked up the steps to the first floor. As she turned the corner, she heard the front door open, and people spilled into the hallway, led by Jaeger Ballantyne, who was carrying a little boy not that much older than Ellie.

"Hey, Tate," Jaeger said, standing back to hold open the front door. "Rough day?" he asked, his expression amused.

Before she could answer, a slim woman walked up to her and leaned forward to drop a quick kiss on her cheek. "I'm Piper. I've been looking forward to meeting you." Piper put her hand on the little boy's thigh. "This is Ty, our son."

"Hi," Tate said warmly, as more people drifted into the hall, including Beck, Sage and a harassed, petite brunette holding a clipboard.

She exchanged greetings with Linc's siblings and watched as Beck grabbed the brunette's arm.

"Cady, meet Tate. She's…" Beck sent Tate a puzzled look. "What are you?"

"A friend of the family. Also Linc's part-time nanny,"

Tate replied, holding her hand out for Cady to shake. Not wanting to go into her convoluted history with Linc, she nodded to a harassed-looking man dressed in solid black. Behind him, two young women looked equally stressed.

The photographer and his assistants, Tate figured.

"You look like you have your hands full," she said, addressing Cady.

Her back to the photographer, Cady rolled her eyes. "You have no idea." She glanced at her watch and frowned. "We've all had a long day, and Jose is on a tight schedule. I presume Linc is upstairs, dressing?"

Tate pulled a face. "Uh…that would be a no. He's not home yet."

Tate's statement was met with a series of groans, the loudest of which was from Cady. "Seriously?" Beck asked, placing his hands on his trim waist.

"Seriously," Tate replied.

Cady released a strangled moan and scowled at Beck, who threw up his hands. "What? I am not my brother's keeper."

Cady drilled a finger into his flat stomach. "Find him. I have Jose here for the next two hours, and I need to nail this down."

Piper, carrying two grocery bags, lifted them into the air. "And Jay and I will get supper going."

Tate winced. "Uh, sorry. The kitchen is in a bit of a mess. I've been making cupcakes for Shaw to take to school tomorrow. I'll just change Ellie, and then I'll clean up. Can you give me five minutes?"

Sage stepped up to her and took a very willing Ellie from her arms. "I'll change Miss Gorgeous here, if that's okay with you?"

"She's a bit of a mess," Tate warned her.

"I lived with Linc and Shaw and Jo for years. I've

changed many diapers. We'll be fine," Sage assured her and headed up the magnificent staircase, crooning to Ellie as she did so.

Right, okay, the kitchen. Tate was about to follow Piper and Jaeger downstairs when the front door banged open, and Linc stepped through the entrance. His eyes immediately clashed with hers, and Tate felt her skin tingle as his stormy eyes roamed over her face, down her long-sleeved T-shirt. His gaze heated, and Tate was quite sure that her panties were about to catch fire.

"Hi."

"Hi back." Tate forced the words up her throat and wished she had the right to step into his arms, to lift her face to be kissed, to feel his big hands in her hair, changing the angle so that he could kiss her with hot abandon.

"You look—"

Stunning? Gorgeous? Sexy? Doable? She'd take any of the adjectives.

"—like you were dunked in a vat of flour."

Tate glanced down at her shirt and saw the streaks of flour and the blobs of batter in her hair.

Oh, shoot! Okay, not her best foot forward. "Cupcakes."

Linc briefly closed his eyes. "Dammit, I forgot. How much is there still to do?"

"A lot."

Cady, looking impatient, stepped between them and glanced at her watch. "Linc, we've got serious time constraints, and you're already fifteen minutes late. I need you changed and in the downstairs library in five minutes."

Linc dropped his laptop bag onto the hall table. "Dressed in jeans and a white button-down shirt?"

"Yes…casual, hip, no shoes," Cady quickly replied and, hearing the photographer shouting for her, she rushed down the hallway. Tate was about to turn away to head back downstairs to clean up the kitchen when Linc grabbed her wrist and tugged her to the stairs.

"Linc, Piper is cooking, and the kitchen looks like the world ended in there," Tate protested, yet her feet followed his hurried pace up the stairs.

"They can handle it," Linc replied. "Where's Shaw?"

"Downstairs, watching TV."

"Ellie?"

"Sage is changing her."

"So, you can spare me ten minutes?" he asked, as they hit the landing to the second floor.

"I suppose."

Linc led her down the hallway and reached past her to open the door to his bedroom, his hand on her back urging her inside. Tate's quick glance of the room registered brown and creams, a masculine space, but then Linc's arms were around her and his mouth was on hers, hot, deep, dark and breath-stealing sexy.

Oh, Lord, he could kiss, Tate thought dreamily. His mouth was assured and clever, his tongue silky, his breath sweet. Strong, muscular arms held her flush against his tall, hard frame, and Tate was grateful for his support because she was quite certain that every joint in her body was on the point of liquefying. Linc left one hand on her bottom, and the fingers of his other hand speared into her hair, gripping her head and, just like she'd imagined earlier, tilted it to allow his tongue deeper access into her mouth.

She could kiss Linc for years, eons, the rest of her life, Tate mused. When his big hand found her breast and his thumb drifted across her puckered nipple, she whimpered, groaned and whimpered again. Tate's hand caressed his back, his rib cage before both her hands came to rest on his lean hips, her stretched-out thumbs very close to his hard erection.

She wanted to unbuckle his belt, pull down the zipper, slide her hands into his underwear—

Linc pulled back to rest his forehead against hers. "I've thought about doing that, and more, all day. I've been less than useless."

"I burned the first batch of cupcakes because I was fantasizing about you," Tate admitted, her voice husky.

Linc's eyes gleamed with pleasure. "What was I doing?"

"This, pretty much," Tate whispered.

"This is pretty tame compared to what I've been imagining." Linc's big hand covered most of her cheek, and he placed his thumb in the center of her bottom lip. "I want you, Tate. Badly."

"I know. I want you, too," Tate confessed. "It's inconvenient and crazy, and there are a thousand reasons why it's a bad idea—"

"But you're going to let me take you to bed?"

She didn't have the strength or the willpower to walk away. This one time, she couldn't resist temptation. But, because she had to protect herself, she laid out the rules of engagement. That way, there couldn't be any misunderstandings.

"This is a very short-term arrangement, Linc. We're just two adults who are wickedly attracted to each other and who want nothing more than some no-strings-attached fun." She could do sex, she could do a fling. This couldn't be anything more, and he needed to know that. "This is temporary and an emotion-free zone. So, no expectations, okay?"

"Understood," Linc said. "Relax, Tate, I'm not asking for anything more. I'm not expecting anything from you but to share your body with me. No offense, but if I was looking for someone to settle down with, and I'm not, you're not what I'm looking for."

Dammit, why did she feel like he'd jabbed an ice pick

into her heart? Stupid girl! "Because I am the least stable, traditional, least likely to stay at home, woman you know?"

Linc shrugged. "But you're, by far, the sexiest woman I've ever met, and I want you more than my next breath."

The fist clenching her heart relaxed, and Tate sent him a hesitant smile. She could do this; she'd separate sex from emotion and she would be fine. She had to be; anything else wasn't an option.

"And, last request, outside this room, we act normal," Tate insisted.

Linc smiled teasingly. "What's normal?"

She was trying to be serious, but Tate's mouth curved upward. "Fair point. But, to spell it out, I look after the kids and you…well, you do what you do."

"Doing you is high on my list," Linc growled.

Tate punched his shoulder, but her fist held all the impact of a puff of air. "Be serious. Do we have a deal?"

Linc grinned. "And I thought that I was a pushy negotiator." He laughed at her glare and held up his hands. "Peace. And, yes, we have a deal."

Linc replaced his hands on her hips and dropped his head to nuzzle his lips against her temple.

"Shall we seal it with another kiss?" Tate asked, surprised at her brazen words.

Linc looked tempted and then regretful. With a groan he stepped back and moved his hands from her waist to her hands. "Tate, if we go there again, we're going to get naked, very fast. And if I'm not downstairs soon, Cady will send Beck up to light a fire under me."

"We have such crap timing," Tate said, her tone mournful.

Linc laughed. "We really do." He glanced at his watch and sighed. "Our ten minutes are nearly up. Jeans and white shirt. What type of jeans? Which white shirt?"

Tate pulled her hands from his and walked into his spacious closet, sighing at the racks of suits, dress shirts on hangers in a myriad of colors and what seemed like a hundred ties.

"You have more clothes than I do," she stated, looking at his pile of jeans.

"Since you live out of a suitcase, most people do," Linc said, walking past her to flip through his selection of white shirts. His shoulder brushed hers, and he hauled in a breath and closed his eyes. "You smell divine, like chocolates and perfume. And vanilla."

"Chocolate and vanilla cupcakes," Tate replied, picking up a pair of designer jeans from a pile and discarding them. When she saw a pair of jeans with a rip in the knee and a very pale blue from too many wash cycles, she held them up. "These."

"I meant to throw those away," Linc said, looking doubtful. "They are seriously old. I wear them to—jeez, I never wear them anymore."

"They are perfect," Tate reassured him. "There is nothing sexier than a guy in a pair of ripped, well-worn, well-fitting jeans and a good shirt."

"If you say so." Linc pulled his tie from his neck, undid some shirt buttons and pulled his dress shirt out of the waistband of his suit pants. Gripping the back of his shirt by its collar, he yanked it over his head and dropped it to the floor. Tate stood, openmouthed, taking in his broad chest softly dusted with hair, his mouthwateringly sexy six-pack and the bulging muscles in his arms.

She placed her hand on her stomach and softly whimpered. "Holy cupcakes with sprinkles on them."

Linc's head shot up, and his hand, about to unzip his pants, stilled. "Problem?"

Tate shook her head and met his eyes, allowing him to

see the raw desire she knew was blazing there. "It's just you, I..." She waved her hand as if to fan herself. "So damn hot. I could jump you right now."

Linc scrubbed his hands over his face and swore. "I'm holding on by a thread here, Harper, and you're not helping."

"You're the one stripping!" Tate huffed.

Linc dropped a hard, quick, open-mouth kiss on her mouth. "God, you are so sexy, and I love the way you look at me."

Smiling coquettishly, she dragged her index finger down the middle of his chest and over the ridges his six-pack. "Very pretty, Ballantyne. I'm happy to taste as well as touch."

"*Shut up*, Harper. You're playing with fire," Linc muttered, unzipping his pants and pushing them down his hips. Tate dropped her gaze, and she saw the proof of his desire for her straining against the soft fabric of his underwear. Tate licked her lips and took a step toward him. Determined to have his mouth on hers, her hands on all that tanned, masculine, sexy skin.

Linc's hands on her shoulders stopped her in her tracks. "As much as I want your hands on me, I can't. Not now. So, do me a favor, please, honey?"

Honey? Lord, she'd never been called that, never heard the words from a deep-voiced guy with lust and need and appreciation in his eyes.

Anything. She'd do *anything* for him, but, man, she hoped the favor involved getting naked and up close and very, very personal. Tate cocked her head and begged her racing heart to slow down. "What?"

"Later tonight, I promise you I am going to make you scream, over and over again, from unrelenting pleasure."

Oh...gulp.

"But for now? Please, walk your seriously fantastic ass

out of my bedroom and down the stairs. I need you to go so that things—" Linc gestured to his groin "—can settle down."

This was nuts, Tate thought. She'd never had such an intense, crazy, take-me-now-and-damn-the-consequences reaction to any man before. Why Linc? Why now? Why with the one man who was the embodiment of everything she'd never wanted? And why did she suspect that walking away from Linc—and she *would* because that was what she did—might end up breaking her heart?

She needed to back away, that was the clever thing to do. Get some distance, some air, try to settle down. Tate nodded. Yes, walking away was the sensible choice. And she would. In a minute.

But before she did, she reached for a white dress shirt she'd seen earlier. It was plain white with black buttons, designer, expensive but interesting. She pulled it off the hanger and handed it to Linc. "Wear this, roll up the sleeves to the middle of your forearms. Don't wear that watch. Wear the one you had on the other day."

"The one with the black leather strap?" Linc asked. "It's vintage."

"It's seriously sexy. As are you." Tate dropped a quick kiss on his bare, big biceps. "And, Linc?"

"Yeah?"

"Remember to smile," she told him softly. "Your smile… It's dynamite."

Heat flared in Linc's smoky gray eyes. "I'll be down in…" He looked down at his erection and he groaned. "Give me five minutes. Then again, it's been a while…I might need ten."

It took all Linc's fortitude and willpower to sit through that interminable photo shoot, to take directions from Jose, the anal photographer. But a millennium later—okay, maybe ninety minutes later—Jose declared himself satisfied and Linc, wearing Connor's massive alexandrite ring on his middle finger, was finally released from hell, previously known as Connor's magnificent and lushly decorated library.

Needing a minute, Linc ducked into the bathroom, turned around and leaned his back against the door. He turned Connor's ring on his middle finger, fascinated, as always, by its colors. When he'd stood by the windows of the library, the stone, in the natural light pouring in from the windows, had looked like a fine emerald, but now, under artificial light, it was the raspberry red of a fine Burmese ruby.

Connor had still been alive when he'd asked Kari to marry him, and thank God that he had been. Had he not, Linc might've been stupid enough to give Connor's ring to Kari on their engagement. She would've pawned it as she had her very expensive, stunning five-carat yellow diamond solitaire he'd handed over with his proposal. He could live with losing the diamond, but if he'd lost Connor's ring, he'd never forgive himself.

He still wanted to give it to his wife one day, if he ever found the one woman on whom he could take a chance. Linc pulled the ring off his finger and stared down at it as he imagined sliding the ring onto a feminine finger, looking tenderly into the eyes of the woman of his dreams. But instead of the blue or green eyes he normally conjured up, honey-brown eyes flashed on his mental big screen. Sparkling, warm, expressive eyes, a mobile mouth, tumbling, crazy blondish-brown hair.

Tate.

Linc shoved his ring back onto his finger and stood up

to grip the edge of the tiny basin. He glared at his reflection in the mirror above the wall and told himself to get a clue.

Tate would never wear his ring because Tate was not marriage material. Tate was a free spirit, someone who associated marriage and commitment with all the freedoms of jail.

Yes, they were wildly attracted to each other, and as soon as he could get rid of his family, as soon as the kids were asleep, he intended to discover every nook and cranny of that glorious body. He'd taste her, feed on her, but what he *wouldn't* do was get attached to her.

That way madness lay. Harper women didn't like restrictions or commitment. He'd learned his lesson with Kari and he'd learned it well. This time he'd be better prepared. This was about sex, pure and simple. Later tonight, he and Tate would light the match, set their attraction on fire and, like other chemical reactions, they would burn hard and fast, rocketing their way to a quick end.

Because they were on the same page and reading the same damn book, they'd be able to walk away from each other with only a couple of scorch marks and the wish that their spark could've burned longer and harder but understanding that intense reactions never lasted.

This was chemistry, nothing else. They hardly knew each other, were complete opposites and lived totally different lives. Chemistry was all they had…

Chemistry was all they *could* have, Linc reminded himself when a pang of longing coursed through his system. She was bold and mouthy and intense and complicated, for God's sake. She wasn't the quiet, stable, calm person he wanted.

She wasn't bland or boring, either, his inner devil told him, and Linc closed his eyes, frustrated at his turmoil. He hadn't felt this overwrought in years, not since…

Not since the other Harper woman dropped into his life and flipped it upside down.

Linc opened his eyes and ground his back teeth together. He would not allow Tate to upend his calm, controlled, orderly world. They'd have sex—there was no way he could deny himself that—but that was where their relationship started and ended.

In bed.

God, he couldn't wait to get that party started. Did the kids really need a bath? Shaw could, this once, miss out on his nightly story. There were a million places to eat in the city, his siblings could find food somewhere else…

He wanted, this one time, to put his needs and wishes first.

Eight

Linc jogged down the steps and stopped in the doorway to the kitchen and great room, taking in the chaos. A lasagna bubbled in the oven. Cady and Piper sat on the big leather couch closest to the kitchen, and Sage was in the chair opposite them, Ellie on her lap, holding her bottle and fighting sleep. Ty, Jaeger and Piper's son, sat in the high chair next to the granite-topped counter, and Shaw was perched on the counter itself, a piping bag of shocking green icing in his hand, biting his lip as he squeezed the contents onto a cupcake.

His burly brothers were standing on either side of Tate. Beck was using a small roller on what might or might not be bright yellow dough, and Jaeger was pressing a cookie cutter into garish purple icing.

These were going to be the brightest and messiest cupcakes in the history of pre-K bake days, Linc decided as he walked into the room.

Tate was the first to notice his arrival, and their eyes clashed and held as he walked across the great room. Judging by her glazed eyes and half-open mouth, she was reliving their X-rated, happened-in-the-closet kiss. He dragged his eyes off her before he embarrassed himself, and greeted Cady and Piper, bending down to drop a kiss on Sage's head. Because he could and she was cute, he kissed Ellie's head, as well. He walked over to the kitchen area and ran his hand over Shaw's bright head, taking a moment to connect with his son.

Shaw's eyes, that intense blue he shared with Kari, met his. "This is the best fun *ever*, Dad. We're making spacemen cupcakes."

Beck lifted his head and mock frowned at Shaw. "Spacemen? I thought we were making dinosaurs!"

"And I thought we were making monsters," Jaeger chimed in, joining the teasing.

"Spacemen," Shaw told them, his tone suggesting that they were both village idiots. He gestured to the badly decorated, messy batch of finished cupcakes, beaming with pride. Linc had never seen anything that looked less like spacemen in his life.

"They are so cool," Shaw said, his eyes sparkling with excitement.

"They really are, buddy," Linc lied, straight-faced. "How many do you still have to do?"

Shaw held up a half-decorated cupcake in his hand and looked a little disgusted. "Just this one. Tate says that she has to make some that girls will eat, so she's going to do the rest later." Shaw sent Tate a hard look. "No pink and no fairies."

"But I can do flowers, right?" Tate asked, her mouth twitching.

"Just a few," Shaw reluctantly agreed.

Linc walked over to the huge fridge and pulled out three beers, opened two and placed them in front of his brothers. Unable to resist touching Tate, Linc allowed his fingers to slide up and under her shirt to find the band of soft skin just above the waistband of her leggings. "Wine, Tate?"

Linc noticed that Tate sucked in her breath as his fingers trailed over her skin. Oh, God, this waiting was killing both of them. Good to know that he wasn't alone in this madness.

"I'm good…thanks," Tate said as if she were battling to find her words.

Linc checked on the levels in the wineglasses across the room before twisting the cap off his beer bottle and taking a long sip. He was thirsty, hungry and tired but, mostly, he was horny. He'd ditch the beer and the food in a heartbeat if he could kiss that sexy spot where Tate's neck met her jawline…

"Have you made any progress finding out who is buying up Ballantyne stock?" Jaeger asked him, leaning his butt against the counter.

Linc, pulling his mind from the bedroom, shook his head. "No, not yet. But I will."

"As a family we own controlling shares, and as long as we stick together, we are safe from a hostile takeover, so I don't seen the point of anyone buying up big blocks of stock. Combined, we own sixty percent of the company, but this company, Lach-Ty, now owns five percent. Worrying," Beck stated, picking up his beer.

Worrying about Ballantyne International was his job, as was protecting his family. But he'd done a crap job so far in regard to finding out who was behind the purchases of the shares. He had a company name, Lach-Ty, but little else. He loathed operating in the dark and decided to ask Reame to look into the situation. His pal had the skills, or employed people with the skills, to dig up the information he needed.

Linc placed a hand on his brother's shoulder. "I'll get to the bottom of it, Beck. It'll be okay, I promise."

"As long as we stand together," Beck replied, his tone giving away his concern.

"We always do. We always will," Jaeger told him, and Linc flashed him a grateful smile.

Jaeger nodded briefly. He glanced at the oven and bellowed, "Who is hungry?"

"Me!" Shaw shouted, waving the icing bag around. Linc saw splatters of radioactive green land on Tate's chin and chest. Reacting quickly, he reached across the counter and grabbed the bag from Shaw. "Easy, Shaw." He grinned at the streak of green in Tate's hair, the spots on her cheek. "Tate now looks like a spaceman."

Instead of rushing off to the bathroom in a panic to clean up, in order to look perfect, Tate dragged her finger across her chin and popped the icing she gathered into her mouth. Her gaze met Linc's, and his knees buckled at the lust and laughter in her eyes.

"At least I taste good." she murmured.

That he could vouch for...

"Well," Jaeger drawled, his eyes bouncing between them, "I have a feeling that dinner is going to be quick, and that big bro is going to be kicking us out of here as soon as we are done eating."

Linc didn't drop his eyes from Tate's.

"Damn straight," he muttered as Tate blushed. "Feel free to leave now. You can even take the lasagna with you."

Tate, feeling sticky and a little headachy from tension and anticipation, piped a pale yellow swirl onto a vanilla cupcake and reached for a premade bumblebee, carefully placing the little bee at an angle. Nine cupcakes down, three to go. Looking around the relatively clean kitchen, she couldn't help but smile. She'd been surprised, and grateful, when the Ballantyne brothers had cleaned up the mess they, and Shaw, had made in their effort to create their spacemen cupcakes. The dishwasher was loaded, the counters wiped down, the ingredients put away. Sage had even stayed to help her mix up four colored bowls of icing and had even offered to help decorate the next batch of cupcakes.

But Tate knew that Sage still had hours of work ahead of her, so she'd gently refused her help. Besides, she wanted to be alone with Linc. Well, as alone as they could get with two kids in the house. She just needed to get these last few cakes decorated, and she could take a shower and rid herself of her grimy jeans and sticky T-shirt. And then, God willing and children cooperating, Linc would blow her mind...

And, hopefully other parts of her body, as well.

Tate's head snapped up when she heard Linc's footsteps and sucked in her breath as he walked across the room to her. He stopped just behind her, slid his strong arms around her waist and laid his chin on her shoulder. "How many more to go?"

Tate tipped her head back to rest it against his collarbone, inhaling his masculine cologne and the underlying scent that was all Linc. "Three. It'll go quick, if I'm not distracted."

Linc nuzzled her temple before standing up straight. He dropped his arms and moved to stand next to her, his hip pushing into the counter. "What can I do to hurry this process along? I mean...to help?"

Tate lifted her eyebrows, trying not to laugh. "Are you any better at icing than your brothers and son?"

Linc smiled. "Not really." He gestured to her pretty cupcakes, a complete contrast to the other messy ones. "Yours look fantastic. Are you going to fix the spacemen?"

Tate shook her head. "I'm not going to do a thing."

"They aren't exactly of ChildTime standards," Linc said, and Tate heard the doubt in his voice.

"Screw the standard," Tate cheerfully told him. "Shaw made them, he loves them, that's all that matters. Besides, they are bright and sugary. The kids will inhale them."

Linc pushed his fingers into his short hair. "You're right. What Shaw thinks is all that's important." He walked over to the cupboard, pulled down two tumblers and a bottle of really expensive whiskey. Linc placed a half-full glass close to her, and she murmured her thanks.

"How was the photo shoot?" Tate asked, trying to think of something to talk about to keep both their minds off the smoking hot sex they were about to have.

She also needed a distraction from the realization that she'd loved everything about this evening, had so relished feeling like an integral part of a family, like she was needed and important. Normally, she would've avoided anything that smacked of Harriet Homemaker and run at the first hint of domesticity, but she'd thoroughly enjoyed herself. She even—dare she think it?—wanted more.

You're losing your mind, Harper. You're just overexcited because you're about to get laid, and your brain is working overtime.

Get a grip.

"Long," Linc replied, boosting himself up to sit on the counter next to her work space. God, how was she supposed to concentrate on her swirls when his long, muscled thigh was a few inches from her hand, when she could see his tanned flesh through the rips in his jeans?

Tate noticed the unusual ring on his middle finger. "Jaeger had Kashmir sapphires. Beck, red beryl. Sage, red diamonds, but I don't recognize your stone."

"Alexandrite." Linc pulled the ring off his finger and held it between his thumb and forefinger. He turned it, and in the red depths Tate caught a flash of green, then yellow, maybe a hint of orange. It was stunningly beautiful.

"Emerald by day, ruby by night," Linc explained. "It changes color depending on the light source."

"I've never seen you with it before." Tate picked up the bag of yellow icing and pulled a bare cupcake toward her.

"Despite my job, I'm not a jewelry-wearing type of guy. This was Connor's ring. I was with him, the day he discovered this stone," Linc explained, his voice low.

Beneath the lust hovering between them, she heard nostalgia and longing in his voice as he shared an incredible memory. Yes, of course she wanted to explore his fabulous body, but she didn't mind taking a stroll through his amazing mind. "Tell me more."

"It was about six months after we moved in here, and I was recovering from chicken pox. I was better, but the doctor insisted that I stay home, and I was bored out of my mind. I couldn't believe it when Connor invited me to attend an estate sale with him, somewhere upstate. He bid and won this box of what was mostly costume jewelry. But amongst the junk was a stunning ruby pendant and this ring. Connor was beside himself, alexandrite was his favorite stone, and the ring slid onto his finger as if it were made for him. He never took it off until the day he died."

"And you inherited it."

Linc's big shoulders rose and fell. "He was my dad, the only dad I knew. Or wanted. He never married, but, with my mom's help, he raised four kids and made us feel loved every damn day."

"And he and your mom?"

Linc smiled. "They were best friends, and she was devastated when he died, but nothing, as far as I knew, sparked between them."

"And she had no problem with him adopting you?"

Linc shrugged. "I think she did in the beginning. But they worked it out. He wanted me as much as he wanted the others, and I was his son, with or without her permission. Connor convinced her that him becoming my dad didn't stop her from being my mom."

Tate placed her hand on his knee and squeezed. "You must miss him."

"So damn much. He was my North Star, my magnetic pole. Funny, so smart, so full of life. He was, in so many ways, the glue that held us together. He was our charismatic, fearless leader."

"And now you've taken over that role," Tate observed, thinking how much responsibility Linc carried on his big, broad shoulders.

"Yeah, I suppose," Linc replied, his voice scratchy with emotion.

"And are you okay with doing that?"

"Connor would expect it, and that's reason enough. Though, admittedly, there are days when I'd like to run away." Linc lifted his glass to his lips, and Tate noticed the slight tremble in his fingers. "While this family mostly, runs on discussion and democracy, the buck has to stop with someone, and that someone is me."

"Your siblings would probably disagree with that. And, to be honest, they look like they are very capable of running their own lives."

"They are," Linc admitted. "And they do, but they all know that I'm standing behind them, ready to catch them if they fall. As for the company, I'll protect the Ballantyne wealth and assets with my last breath."

He would, Tate realized. His son, his family and their loved ones, were at the center of everything Linc did. He existed to protect his family and the company his father had loved and created. But where did that leave his wants and desires? He was so busy giving that he rarely took, probably didn't think that he had the right to be loved and protected and cherished himself.

I could, if I was braver, less independent and not terrified of staying in one place, I could love him. I could give him what he needed.

But, realistically, all she could give him was sex. Hot, intense, hopefully mind-blowing sex. Sex that he wouldn't forget.

Tate reached for a pink rose, plunked it on top of the last swirl of icing and ignored the last bare cupcake. She tossed the piping bag on the counter and pushed her hair off her forehead with the back of her wrist.

She was done. She wanted a shower and this man. Now.

Tate looked at Linc. "Shaw asleep?"

He nodded.

Tate gestured to the baby monitor. "So is Ellie."

Linc, not moving a muscle, just looked at her, his eyes blazing. Oh, God, was she going to have to spell it out for him? Maybe she could write *Let's Strip* on the counter with pale pink icing. Tate held her breath as Linc dropped to his feet to stand so close to her that her breasts brushed his chest. He picked up a strand of her hair and twirled it between his fingers. She sighed when she saw the green icing from her hair now smeared on his fingers. "You're a mess, Harper."

She agreed. "I know. I'll go shower and—"

"You're a hot, sexy mess," Linc murmured, ignoring her interruption. "You smell of sugar and chocolate and some perfume that drives me insane. You aren't wearing a shred of makeup, yet your face looks like it should be on the cover of a fashion magazine."

Linc placed his hand on her cheek, and his thumb drifted across her cheekbone. Tate gripped his strong wrist as his sexy words flowed over her, into her, heating her blood and drying up the moisture in her mouth.

Linc's thumb moved to her mouth. "I can't wait to touch you, taste you, to see you naked. I know that my fantasies will not match the reality."

Tate placed her hands on his chest and sucked in a deep breath. "All I need is a quick shower," she begged.

Linc bent his knees and in one fluid, easy movement, scooped her into his arms. Tate wrapped her arm around his neck, as she absorbed the heat from his hard, lean body. "You can shower later, sweetheart, preferably with me. I've waited too long for you. I'm not waiting any longer."

"But—"

Linc ignored her protest and strode over to the couch, holding her close to him before allowing her feet to drift to the floor. "I need you, Tate. Now."

Since she sensed that Linc rarely, if ever, used *need* and *you* in the same sentence, she just linked her arms around his neck and stood on her tiptoes to brush her mouth across his. She couldn't give him what he needed, deserved, on a long-term basis, but she could give him what he needed tonight. *That* she could do.

"I'm here, Linc. Take me."

Linc, smart man that he was, didn't need any further encouragement, and he quickly pulled her shirt up and over her head. Dropping the sticky garment to the floor, Tate watched his face as he looked down at her chest, his hands moving to cup her breasts in his big, masculine hands.

"So pretty, Tate."

To Tate's surprise, Linc lifted his hands from her breasts

to tunnel his fingers into her heavy mass of hair, and he angled her face to receive his no-holds-barred kiss. Tongues tangoed as he devoured her mouth, learning her taste, her essence, silently telling her that he wanted more.

That he wanted all that she had.

Exhilarated by his passion and his low, guttural murmurs of appreciation, Tate undid the buttons of his shirt and pushed it open so that she could explore the hot skin of his wide chest, to discover the hard muscles underneath.

So sexy, she thought, pure masculine strength. Tate's fingers traced the ridges of his stomach and moved on to the long muscles on either side of his hips and couldn't resist the urge to dance her fingers across the powerful erection that tented his jeans.

Oh, yeah. He felt amazing, and, judging by Linc's sudden gasp, he liked what she was doing as much as she did. And she liked it a *lot*. Teasing him, Tate traced his long length with the tip of her finger.

"Tate."

He muttered her name against her mouth, but she heard the desire and the demand in his voice. Linc's hands skated down her back to find her bra strap which he snapped open with a minimum of fuss. The cups of her lace bra fell away, and Linc pulled the fabric off her bare breasts, revealing her hard, pink nipples to his gaze.

"Yeah, so damn pretty," Linc breathed as his hands moved to the waistband of her leggings, pushing the fabric down her hips to reveal her tiny panties to his hot, hungry gaze.

His hands gripped and released her hips as he looked down at her, past her flat stomach, over the neat landing strip showing through the transparent fabric to her long legs.

"You are sheer perfection."

She wasn't, but she appreciated the words.

"You're not too bad yourself, Ballantyne," Tate whispered, dropping a wet, open-mouth kiss on his bare chest as she attempted to undo his belt buckle.

Linc slid his hand between her legs and cupped her, his thumb immediately finding and brushing her sensitive spot through the fabric of her thong, causing her to moan into his chest. If she didn't get her hands on him soon…

"Help me, Linc. I need to feel you," Tate told him, looking up as she laid her flat palm on him, wishing that she had a spell to magically make clothes evaporate.

Linc's hand pressed hers against his erection, and she heard his ragged breathing, his low curses.

"We need to slow this down. If we don't, I'm going to toss you onto that couch and take you, right here, right now."

And that would be a problem? "Since that's exactly what I want—hot, fast, furious—I'm wondering why you are waiting."

Linc reached behind him and pulled out a strip of three condoms from the back pocket of his jeans. He ripped off a packet with his teeth and allowed the rest to fall to the floor. He dropped the packet into her hand with a wicked, tempting smile. "You said that you want to get your hands on me," he teased.

"If you helped me with your pants, I would," Tate retorted, opening the foil packet.

Linc lifted an amused eyebrow. "Feeling flustered, sweetheart?"

Tate looked him in the eye. "Aren't you? We have all this raging heat, and I can't wait to stand in the ring of fire and burn with you."

Linc undid his belt and, using just one hand, flipped open the buttons to his jeans. He pushed his jeans and underwear down his hips, and Tate caught her breath when she saw his big erection standing straight and proud.

She flashed him a grin. "Wow. Talking about pretty…"

Linc groaned when her small hand encircled him, and nipped her jaw with his teeth. "*Pretty?* Try another, more manly adjective please?" he teased, laughter in his voice.

"Impressive? Masculine? Bold?" Tate rubbed her thumb lightly over the head of his shaft.

"Those will work," Linc growled, pushing her thong over her hips. When they were completely naked, he sat down on the couch and pulled Tate onto him, so that her knees straddled his thighs.

As his hands moved between her legs she curled her hand around his long and thick erection. She didn't want to wait. She wanted to be pushed, possessed, filled, taken to the limit. She wanted to feel as if she like belonged here, with him, just for this brief slice of time.

As Linc tested her readiness by sliding his finger into her, Tate pulled out the condom and swiftly rolled it over him, sucking in her breath as he hardened even more.

"Tate, I don't think I can wait any longer. I need to be inside you," Linc said, his voice rough with need. "I know it's our first time, and I should be taking it slow but…dammit, I don't think I can." Not giving her time to reply, Linc hooked his big hands under her thighs and lifted her up, spreading her legs so that the head of his shaft probed her wet, feminine core. Linc's hands on her hips gently guided her down as he thrust into her with one long, confident stroke. Tate felt herself liquefying, her entire focus on how Linc felt inside her. Her vision tunneled and there was just the two of them in the world, and making love was all that was important, all that could matter. Linc's hands on her skin, his mouth under hers, him filling those long neglected spaces was all she could focus on.

Linc held her breasts in his hands, his fingers caressing her ultrasensitive nipples, and his tongue in her mouth mimicked the thrust of his hips, the sure strokes as he lifted her closer to the sun.

"Come for me, honey, let me feel you," Linc coaxed, his forehead against hers.

Tate was beyond speech, so she replied by grinding down on him as lightning danced along her skin.

Linc moved his head so that he could speak directly in her ear. "You feel so good. So sexy. Take me, Tate, take all of me. Yeah, like that."

Her mind and body full of him, Tate reached for her release, and she shouted as another bolt of lightning skittered through her and splintered her body into a million pieces. Somewhere, from a place far away, she heard Linc's demands in her ear, his words not making sense. But his body did, and she understood the silent demand that she reach for more. She wanted to tell him that she couldn't, that it was all too much, but then he touched a place deep inside her and she exploded again, harder and faster than before.

A century might've passed, or maybe it was only a minute or two, before she came back to herself, her cheek against his chest, his arms holding her tight.

"We did it," Linc murmured, his hand brushing her hair off her cheek.

"We most certainly did," Tate agreed, her mouth curving into a satisfied smile.

"The sex was fantastic, I agree, but I was referring to the fact that we managed to make love without one of the kids waking up."

Oh, right. She'd forgotten about the kids upstairs. But until one of them yelled, she wasn't moving a muscle. "Yay."

"Want to see if we can do it again while the going is

good?" She heard Linc's smile in his words, felt the curve of his lips against her bare shoulder.

Tate nodded. Nobody could ever accuse her of not being up for the challenge.

"Slow and sexy this time?" Tate asked.

Linc's wonderful mouth curved upward. "Sexy every time, sweetheart."

Nine

Tate, always slow to wake up, pulled a strand of hair out of her mouth and groaned into her pillow. Fighting the urge to slide back into sleep, she yawned, frowning when she realized the pillowcase was a deep chocolate color and not the snowy white fabric she normally woke up to.

Linc. Sex. All night long. They'd started on the couch and ended in his bedroom. Twice, three times, four if you counted the heavy petting they'd shared in the shower. They'd been insatiable, turning to each other time and again, consumed by the need to give and receive pleasure.

He was the best lover she'd ever had… Admittedly, she hadn't had that many men in her bed, but she was convinced that if she had, he'd still be the best. Tender, demanding and confident and, surprisingly, uninhibited, Linc seemed to shed his calm, reserved, everything-can-be-worked-out attitude with his clothes and morphed into a dirty-talking, demanding, unrestrained lover.

Tate had no complaints. Nope, she couldn't think of one. Well, maybe a little one: she was in his bed and he wasn't touching her. That, she decided, could be easily remedied. Tate rolled over, and instead of encountering Linc's hot, hard, naked warmth, her hand landed on a small body wearing flannel pajamas covered in helicopters. Tate immediately glanced down at her chest and sighed her relief when she realized that she was wearing one of Linc's T-shirts.

Thoroughly confused, she lifted her head to look over Shaw's sprawled-out body and saw Ellie lying on Linc's T-shirt-covered chest, her face tucked into his neck and his hand covering her small back. His eyelashes were spikes against his cheeks, and heavy stubble covered his jawline.

Tate noticed the baby monitor on the bedside table next to him and tried to make sense of the time between falling asleep naked and now. She'd acquired a shirt, Linc had pulled on some clothes, and the huge bed they'd made love in had been invaded by two little people.

They looked like a family, Tate thought, panic creeping up her throat. This was what she'd had as a kid, two parents, lazy Saturday morning sleep-ins.

"Welcome to life with kids," Linc drawled, his growly voice dancing over her skin.

Tate pushed her elbow into the bed and rested her head in her hand. She looked across Shaw to Linc, who had yet to open his eyes. "When did they wake up?"

Linc cracked open one eye and lifted his wrist to look at his high-tech watch. "Shaw wandered in at about five, Miss Ellie was bellowing at six."

Tate winced. "I didn't hear a thing. You should've roused me."

Linc rolled his head and his smoky eyes met hers. Heat curled through her at the appreciation in his gaze. "I tried. You didn't even stir when I poured you into my shirt."

"That might be because we only got to sleep a few hours ago." She gestured to Ellie. "But thanks. I owe you."

"You do," Linc replied, his smile lazy. "If we were alone, I'd show you how you could repay me."

Tate blushed, thinking of how well he'd loved her. She opened her mouth to make a witty retort, but her brain had nothing. Zip. Not because Linc was six feet something of pure, primal male but because she'd rolled back in time. Remembering the little girl she'd been, climbing into her parents' bed at the crack of dawn, waking up in her dad's arms, her face tucked into his neck, hearing his whiskey-rough voice telling her to go back to sleep.

She'd had a few years of happiness and security, but that had been ripped away when Kari and Lauren dropped into their house and lives. Nothing lasted forever, and as sweet and wholesome as this little scenario was, her past reminded her that it wasn't hers to keep. Sex was one thing, but playing happy family with Linc and these gorgeous children was not something she could indulge in. She might come to like it and, worse, come to yearn for it. She'd lost one family unit; she wasn't going to set herself up to lose another.

Tate was about to sit up when Ellie's eyes slowly opened and focused on her face. She yawned and lifted her little hand in Tate's direction, her extraordinary blue eyes full of love. Smiling, she crawled off Linc's chest, over the still-sleeping Shaw and into Tate's arms. Ah, dammit, Tate thought as Ellie's chubby arms wound around her neck and the little girl burrowed closer, her nose under Tate's jaw, her hands tangled in her long hair.

This was trust at its purest form, Tate thought, holding Ellie tight and closing her eyes, feeling the wash of love breaking over her, holding all the pent-up power of the sea. Oh, God, she couldn't fall in love with Ellie, couldn't start thinking of being her family, her primary caregiver, of making a family with her.

How was she supposed to look after a little girl with the type of career she had? Babies and border posts were not a happy combination at the best of times, and taking Ellie with her would be utterly impractical.

Keeping Ellie with her would mean sacrificing her career—a career that earned her a lot of money and that she loved. With Ellie in her arms, Tate stood up and walked over to the window of Linc's bedroom, pushing aside the heavy drapes to look down at the icy road below. She released a heavy sigh. If she even dared to imagine giving up her freedom and her independence to raise Ellie, how would she support them? She had a healthy bank account and she could probably buy an apartment—not in Manhattan obviously—and ensure that they had a roof over their heads. But she'd still have to feed them, clothe them, pay the utilities, and to do that she'd need a job. A job, in this context, meant staying in one place, and Tate shuddered. She hadn't had a fixed abode in years, and she didn't think she could do it.

A bigger worry was that Ellie was starting to attach to her, as she'd just shown by leaving Linc's arms to crawl to her. Would she psychologically damage her niece when she gave her back to her mom? How would being a human equivalent of pass-the-parcel affect Ellie long-term? Would she have trust issues? Tate wouldn't blame her if she did.

Tate felt Linc's hands on her waist and sighed when his big body pressed up against hers, her back to his chest, his chin resting on the top of his head. "Is this all feeling a bit too real?" he asked, his deep voice gentle.

Tate nodded, a ball constricting her throat. "I don't think I can do this, Linc."

She had to pull back, she had to find that place of inner

solitude that served her so well. She had to retreat to her mental island where emotions couldn't affect her.

"Do what, Tate? Us?"

"No, that I can do because I know it's just sex." Not understanding the reason for Linc's sudden tension, she ignored it.

"I'm not sure I can be what Ellie needs," Tate said, her voice cracking. "She's starting to trust me, starting to rely on me, but in a couple of days, or in a few weeks, I'm going to hand her back to Kari—"

"If you find her."

"Reame will find her," Tate stated. He had to; she couldn't imagine having to make the final and crucial decisions about Ellie's future. That was Kari's job, dammit. "I'm worried that I will end up hurting her by loving her, by bonding with her knowing that that bond will be severed soon."

Linc rubbed his chin over her hair, and Tate felt the reassuring squeeze on her hips. "Tate, trust is a learned skill. When we teach children to love and to trust by being loving and trustworthy, they learn that they can expect that from other adults."

Tate snorted her disbelief. "Can't see Kari teaching Ellie those life lessons."

"Me, neither." Linc released her to stand beside her, leaning his shoulder into the wall, his face solemn. "I accept that you are worried about Ellie's well-being, but I suspect that you are also worried about your emotions, your state of mind."

Tate rubbed Ellie's back with her hand, realizing that the little girl had fallen back to sleep. She tipped her head to the side, not sure if she wanted to hear what Linc was about to say.

"You don't like the emotions and you're worried for

yourself, worried that you are becoming too attached to her. You're worried that you will be hurt when she moves on."

Oh, damn, she really was. She didn't want to miss Ellie, or Shaw, didn't want to miss Linc. She *so* didn't want to miss Linc. And she would. She'd spent so little time with him, but this house, this stupidly big mansion had become a place she loved, and the people who lived inside it, and who were associated with it, people she had come to truly like. Leaving The Den would hurt like hell.

"The thing is, getting too attached is exactly what Ellie needs from you even though it might break your heart one day. Because showing her love and affection is the right thing to do. She's the innocent party here, Tate. She didn't choose a damn thing, so if you withhold love and affection, you'd be punishing her for something she didn't create." Linc lifted his hand to clasp the back of her neck, dropping his head to rest his forehead on hers. "The only thing you can do is to make it as easy on her as possible. Even if that might make life harder for yourself."

"This isn't me, Linc!" Tate cried. "I don't want this responsibility. I want to be free and independent and only want to be responsible for myself."

"That's the easy route, sweetheart," Linc said, his voice low and rough. "Having no ties, no commitments, no responsibility is an easy—possibly lonely—way to live. You only have to think about yourself, all the time. It's a way to protect yourself from life and from all the crap it throws at you. And it's a really good way to avoid getting hurt."

He was right, of course he was. His words felt like hailstones smacking her soul, but he was speaking the truth, and she appreciated his honesty.

"Why the traveling, Tate? Why do you keep running from place to place?" Linc gestured for her to sit down on the large wing chair next to the bed, and Tate lowered herself and Ellie to the chair, grateful to get off her wobbly legs. She stared out of the window, watching cold raindrops slide down the windows.

Linc sat down on the edge of the bed, his knee nudging hers, his forearms on his thighs, his expression intense. "Talk to me, Tate. God knows you need to talk to someone."

Ellie, disturbed by her aunt's movements, sat up, rubbed her eyes and spat out her pacifier. She pushed Tate's hands off her, crawled off her lap and dropped her feet to the floor, one hand holding the chair and the other holding Linc's leg for balance. She wobbled before plopping down onto her butt. Smiling, she started to crawl away. Tate reached for her, but Linc's hand on her bare knee stopped her. "She's fine, Tate, let her crawl. Talk to me."

Tate knew that if she told Linc that she didn't want to talk about her past, he would respect her wishes, but she wanted him to know the forces that shaped her into the person she was. Keeping it simple and brief, she reminded him about her childhood, her parent's divorce, her mother's preference for her niece and why she and her sister didn't speak for years.

"Thanks for defending me—us." Linc said.

"My fight with Kari, about her leaving you and Shaw the way you did, caused an additional strain between my mother and me. We didn't speak much after that. Then she died and our relationship could never be repaired."

"I'm sorry, honey."

Tate crossed her legs and turned, resting her head against the back of the chair. "I'm sorry that two more Harper women have turned your life upside down again."

Linc's eyes gleamed with amusement. "That's okay… last night was worth any aggravation."

She needed to say it, needed to express another apology. "I'm especially sorry that Kari's actions caused you to shy away from love and relationships, Linc. You've given her too much power. Not all women are like that. You should try again. You're a good guy, and you deserve to be happy."

Linc kept his eyes pinned to hers, and she saw the flash of annoyance in those granite depths. "Pot calling the kettle black, Tate? Her actions have dictated the course of your life, too. You're the one who has run from commitments and people and stability because your family pushed you aside. Are you brave enough to change that?"

"No, I don't think so."

Linc released a long, slow breath before standing up. "Yeah. Me, neither." He ran his hands over his head, his shirt inching up his stomach to reveal the dark trail wandering down from his six-pack abs. "I'm going downstairs to make coffee. Want me to take Ellie with me so that you can grab a shower?"

Discussion over, Tate thought with relief. She nodded her thanks and watched as Linc scooped up Ellie and held her like a football, Ellie laughing in delight.

He looked down at her and then back at Tate, his gaze suddenly serious. "The trick is to enjoy them, Tate, for as long as you have them."

He was talking about Ellie but also about them, about the night they shared. He was right—she should just live each moment and deal with whatever life threw at her when she could see it barreling her way.

No promises and no guarantees. Especially from him. *Got it, Ballantyne.*

A week passed and it was another cold Saturday afternoon, and Tate had The Den to herself. Linc had taken Shaw to a birthday party and wasn't expected to be back until the early evening. Ellie had fallen asleep in the middle of Tate's bed after lunch, so after transferring her to the crib, Tate went downstairs, feeling a little at a loss. She hadn't spent much time on her own for more than three weeks, so how was she going to fill the next couple of hours?

She supposed she could work out. Linc had told her to make use of his gym in the basement, but the last thing she felt like doing was spending her alone time sweating. She could watch some TV, but that didn't appeal. A movie? Tate wrinkled her nose...

What she really wanted to do was to climb into bed with Linc and spend a lazy afternoon enjoying that delicious, masculine body. At the bottom of the stairs, Tate halted, her hand on the newel post. God, she was seriously addicted to Linc, her mind constantly occupied with thoughts of him, in bed and out.

Tate plopped her butt onto the bottom stair and placed her chin her hands, her elbows on her knees. She wasn't acting anything like the nanny she was supposed to be.

Oh, she collected Shaw from school, entertained him in the afternoons allowing Linc to put in a solid day at work. When he came home she didn't, like a good nanny, walk up the stairs and retreat to her own quarters. Nope, instead she ran straight into his arms. Sometimes, depending on what the kids were doing, they hustled up the stairs, taking a few minutes to rocket each other to a body-blasting orgasm, something to take the edge off until they fell into bed later.

She missed work, of course she did, but not as much as she had expected to. For someone who liked being alone, who felt itchy when she was pinned to a spot for too long, she was remarkably content. And that scared the pants off her. And when she imagined going back to work, to returning to her life of airports and customs control, impersonal hotels and tourist traps, to living life on her own, her heart rebelled. She couldn't imagine giving up her job, relinquishing her independence and her freedom—she loved what she did far too much—but the notion of giving up Linc and the kids threw her into a tailspin. She didn't want to live a life without them in it. And deep down in her heart she knew why.

She'd kind of, sort of, fallen a little bit in love with The Den, with the Upper East Side, with being Ellie's mommy and Shaw's nanny.

It was also very possible that she was in love with her sister's ex.

Oh, crap!

Tate dropped her head between her bent knees and sucked in a choppy breath. *Say it isn't so!*

No, no, no, Tate.

No! You weren't supposed to fall in love with him, you idiot. This was about sex, about a mutual fling; it wasn't supposed to get this intense this quickly.

Tate cursed herself, thinking that she'd definitely forgotten to pay her brain bill.

She couldn't be in love, she *wouldn't* be, Tate decided. She'd just been temporarily seduced by this lovely house and two cute kids and a man who made her catch her breath every time he walked into the room. She was just reliving the last time she'd been part of a family, and she was projecting that happiness onto the here and now.

Reality check, Harper. Reame was going to call, someday soon, and tell her that he'd found Kari, and then she'd return Ellie to her mom's not-so-loving arms. Man, that would bite. Then, because she had nothing to keep her in the city—she and Linc were as temporary as a social media trend—she'd move out of The Den, and maybe they'd see each other now and again until her vacation was over. She'd receive her next assignment, start working on a new series and she'd be sent God knew where.

She could never risk loving Linc, creating a family with him within the greater Ballantyne clan and then, like before, having it all ripped away. She wouldn't survive losing another family, losing the people she loved again. Linc and Ellie and Shaw could only be a lovely memory.

That was the way it had to be, the way it would be, so why was her stomach churning and bile creeping up her throat at the thought? Why did the notion of getting on a plane and leaving them behind make her feel like she was facing her executioner? *You're losing it, Harper, so get off your butt and do something! Call Reame, find out what progress he's made with finding Kari. Contact your producer and see if they have decided where they are sending you next.*

Get real. Stop fantasizing about something you can't have, and let these crazy notions about loving Linc, having it all, go. You have to move on.

Mentally and, sometime soon, physically.

But for now, step off the crazy train, dammit. She pinched the bridge of her nose and sighed. Maybe exercising wasn't a bad idea after all; maybe she could sweat out her stupidity.

Ten

Linc stood in front of the glass case holding Connor's alexandrite ring, a glass of whiskey in his hand. Around him, the rich and elite of Manhattan, and a few dozen other cities, drank French champagne and popped dainty canapés into mouths filled with perfect teeth.

Sage's edgy, interesting, modern collection was a roaring success, and the Ballantyne collection of rare precious gemstones was going to be talked about for a long time to come. Amy had volunteered to babysit Shaw and Ellie, and when he'd checked in with her ten minutes ago, both kids were asleep.

For the first time in, well, ages, he was having fun, and that was only because Tate was with him, sharing her pithy observations about his guests. She looked exquisite in a deep red lace dress. The high-waisted bodice was accented with a rose-printed lace, velvet strips and crystals. She'd found the dress in a vintage shop in SoHo, she'd told him, but Linc was more interested in the slight swell of her breasts peeking out from the neckline, her creamy shoulders and the smooth leg the thigh-high slit in the dress occasionally revealed.

She was beautiful, Linc thought, looking across the room to where Tate stood, talking to a tall, black-haired man who had his back to him. The man turned, and Linc saw his distinctive profile... Tyce Latimore, Sage's ex. Linc looked around the room to find his sister and saw her by the bar, talking to Reame. He'd once hoped that something would spark between Reame and Sage, but it never had; Reame treated Sage like a sister.

Linc turned his attention back to Tate and narrowed his eyes when Latimore placed his hand on Tate's back to guide her to the bar. His protective instincts revving in the red zone—there was vibe to Latimore that made Linc think that there was something unbridled and dangerous lurking beneath the smooth veneer—Linc pushed his way through the crowd to reach the bar. Sage, seeing Latimore's approach, slid off her seat and sauntered away, her ex's gaze following her, his expression benign but his eyes blazing. When he reached the bar, Linc pulled Tate to his side and gave Latimore a hands-off-or-I'll-beat-the-crap-out-of-you look.

Latimore just lifted a dark eyebrow and smiled sardonically before holding out his hand for Linc to shake.

Linc shook his hand but deliberately kept a frown on his face. "Are you messing with my sister, Latimore?"

"Since she's currently not talking to me, and hasn't for a couple of months, that's not a feasible assumption," Tyce replied, his voice deep and dark. Linc thought he saw sadness flash in his eyes but dismissed the thought; the Korean French American was far too much of a player to be fazed that his sister was ignoring him.

"My warning still stands. You hurt Sage again and the three of us will take you apart." Linc pushed the words out through gritted teeth.

Linc heard and ignored Tate's surprised gasp. Tyce held his stare but banged his whiskey glass on the counter of the bar, and when he spoke, his words were bitter. "Yeah, you Ballantynes are such freakin' paragons. Have you ever considered that she might have hurt me, that one of yours might have hurt one of mine? You don't have the monopoly on family and loyalty, Ballantyne."

Latimore released a muttered curse and held his hand up. "Forget I said that." He fixed a smile onto his face, but Linc noticed that it didn't reach his deep brown, almost-black eyes. "It's been lovely meeting you, Tate. I hope we do so again."

"Not damn likely," Linc muttered.

Latimore flashed him a disparaging smile before Tyce's attention was caught by movement at the door. Linc followed his gaze and saw his sister, in a midnight blue ball gown, taking a glass of champagne from a passing waiter's tray. As if she knew that Tyce was looking at her, she lifted her head, and their eyes clashed and held. Linc's eyes bounced from his sister to Latimore and back again, slightly uncomfortable at seeing the blazing attraction and undisguised lust on Sage's face.

Oh, God, she looked at Latimore like he did at Tate, like the thrill of riding the lightning bolt was worth ending up as a charred crisp.

"Holy smokes," Tate breathed, lifting her hand to fan her face. "That's some intense sexual attraction."

Linc signaled to the bartender for another glass of whiskey before frowning down at Tate. "Please do not mention sexual attraction and my sister in the same sentence," he growled.

"She's all grown-up." Tate pointed out the obvious, and his frown deepened.

"Not helping, honey." Linc nodded his thanks at the bartender and took a fortifying sip of his drink. Staring down into the liquid that was the same color as Tate's eyes, he shook his head. "God, that's going to end badly."

"Tyce and Sage?" Tate clarified.

"Yeah. I'd hoped they were over, but any fool can see that they aren't done with each other. And what did he mean by that your-family-hurting-mine comment?"

"A business deal that went south? A party invitation that wasn't sent? His grandmother had an affair with your grandfather?"

Linc rolled his eyes. "You're letting your imagination run away with you. No, Latimore doesn't come from family money. He's got to where he is by his own hard work."

"And you admire that."

"I do," Linc reluctantly admitted. "And I worry about the fact that Sage is so much wealthier than him."

Tate tipped her head to the side. "Does it bother you that you are so much wealthier than I am?" she asked him.

"No, that doesn't mean a damn thing," Linc said brusquely, wondering if he should feel insulted.

"Then why do you assume that it's a problem for him?" Tate asked. "The reality is that most men would be less wealthy than your sister. She could probably buy a small third-world country."

Linc smiled, acknowledging her point. "Only a small one, she wouldn't be greedy," he replied, only half joking.

"For what it's worth, I like him," Tate stated, crossing one leg over the other and revealing a very silky thigh. It took Linc thirty seconds to get his head out of the bedroom and to register Tate's words.

Jealousy, acid and unwelcome, flared. "You and the rest

of the female population of the city," he groused. "He's said to be one of the best-looking and most talented bachelors in Manhattan."

"He is a fabulous artist," Tate agreed. "His sculptures are amazing."

"That's not the talent I was referring to," Linc said, his voice desert dry.

Instead of blushing, Tate erupted into laughter. When she could speak, she looked at him with mirth-filled eyes. "Oh, lucky, lucky Sage."

"Dammit, Tate!" Linc muttered, scowling into his drink.

Seeing his ferocious expression, her mouth quirked with amusement, and she lifted her hand in a placating gesture. Funny, he wasn't placated.

"His, um, talents aside, Tyce is a very good-looking man. He has a blinding smile, and his mixed heritage has resulted in a very, very sexy face. His body isn't too bad, either."

Linc groaned. "God, shoot me now."

"But he has sad eyes, and behind the charm and the charisma, I sense a man who hasn't had it easy. He has demons nipping at his heels," Tate stated, her tone now serious.

Linc wanted to believe that Latimore had all the depth of a puddle, so he wasn't happy with her pronouncement. Then again, nothing about this conversation made him happy. Especially Tate's comments on how attractive she found his sister's ex. "And you can tell this, how?"

Tate sipped her champagne. "Call it woman's intuition."

God, he hated those airy explanations, those inexplicable feelings women got that allowed them to make major assumptions on minimal information. But the hell of it was that he couldn't discount her pronouncement. Still, where Tate saw sadness, he saw danger, and he was worried that Sage was part of whatever game Tyce was playing.

Because Tyce Latimore, he was convinced, was playing a very dangerous game with someone.

Reame's hand gripping his shoulder pulled Linc out of his reverie. He sent his friend a weary smile, and when Reame's eyes remained serious, Linc frowned. Oh, crap. Something had happened. Something he didn't want to hear.

"Can you leave?" Reame asked Linc. He gestured to Beck and Cady, who were cheek to cheek on the dance floor. "I know that we are celebrating Beck's engagement, but we need to talk."

Linc slapped his glass on the counter and nodded. Tate put a hand on Linc's arm to hold him in place. "Is this about Kari? If it is, then I have the right to know."

Linc caught the slight grimace that crossed Reame's face. Linc knew that he wanted to tell him the news in private, so that they could discuss how to tell Tate… Dammit, this news would rock her world.

"Why don't you join Jaeger and Piper, Tate? I'll be back in a minute," Linc suggested, keeping his voice ultracalm.

Her fingernails pushed into his hand like sharp little daggers. "Is it about Kari?" she demanded.

Reame nodded.

"Then I'm coming, too." Tate shot Linc a hard look when he started to protest. "My sister, Linc, my problem. I am paying Reame's bill, remember?"

Well, no, because he had no intention of letting her do that. But that was an argument for another day. Linc rubbed his jaw and, seeing the fiery determination in Tate's eyes, realized that this was a fight he wasn't going to win.

"I already called for your car," Reame replied. "It's waiting outside, and we'll talk on our way to the airport."

"We're flying?" Linc asked, placing his hand on Tate's lower back as he guided her out of the ballroom.

"Yeah, I called your pilot and told him to file a flight plan," Reame explained, leading the way.

"So where are we going, Reame?" Tate asked, trying to keep the question light, but Linc heard the panic in her voice. "To a jail?" Her voice broke. "A rehab center? A hippy commune?"

Linc helped Tate into her thigh-length black woolen coat. Reame shook his head, his face somber. He looked at Linc, who nodded, silently telling him to get it over with.

Reame placed his hands on Tate's shoulders. and released a heavy sigh. "No, Tate. You're flying to Texas to a hospice about an hour north of Austin. Your sister is there."

"At a hospice? Working there?" Tate asked, puzzled. "No, that can't be right. Kari doesn't do sick people. She wouldn't be working there."

Linc closed his eyes; he'd already made the connection that Tate hadn't. He linked his fingers with hers and squeezed and waited until she looked at him. "Honey, Reame is trying to tell you that she's in the hospice. As a patient."

They were somewhere over Pennsylvania when Tate changed from her ball gown into soft jeans and a thigh-length, moss green jersey that Reame had had Amy pack for her. She scrubbed the makeup from her face and pulled the pins out of her elaborate hairstyle and brushed out the curls, pulling the heavy mess into a tight braid.

Her mind buzzing with both fear and shock, Tate walked back into the main cabin and took a seat opposite Linc, who'd changed into beige chinos and a black sweater over a black-and-white-check shirt. Jo was now back at The Den and watching the kids; Tate trusted her implicitly, and it was a relief not to worry about them. She could focus on Kari and her situation.

As Tate settled into the butter-soft leather chair opposite him, Linc sat up and pushed a glass in her direction. Tate picked up the glass, took a sip and welcomed the burn of rich, expensive cognac. Feeling a little of the icy disbelief melting, she lifted her eyes from the glass to look at Linc.

"Tell me what you know. All of it."

Linc glanced at a folder on the seat next to him but didn't bother to pick it up. He'd read it, absorbed it and his ultrasharp brain wouldn't forget any of it. "Reame's man in Austin tracked down a friend of hers. They've been room-mates since Kari split up from Ellie's dad."

"Has she spoken to Kari lately?"

Linc shook his head. "No. Kari refused to allow any-one to visit her, to call for updates on her condition. She didn't want anyone to watch her die."

"We watched her mom die. It was horrible," Tate choked out. "She'd hate people to see her like that."

Tate crossed her legs. "Does she have cancer?"

Linc looked gutted. "Yeah. Stage-four brain cancer. She entered the hospice as soon as she came in from New York after seeing you."

A shudder passed through Tate. "Dear God, that was only a month ago. How did she manage to travel with Ellie, to fly to New York and back?"

"Her friend was with her, apparently. And she was a lot better a month ago. Apparently she has one of the fastest, most aggressive cancers on record, and she went down-hill fast."

Tate wrapped her arms around her body and rocked in her chair. Lifting a hand, she gestured for Linc to con-vey all the information he had. Linc remained silent for a beat before speaking. "From what Reame managed to find out from the friend, she discovered a lump behind her ear when she was pregnant, and she ignored it. When

Ellie was six months old, five or so months ago, she had the lump removed and they did a biopsy, and it was found to be malignant. That led to a battery of tests, and they discovered the brain tumor."

"Inoperable?"

"Yeah. They closed her up and told her that she had, at the maximum, four to six months...if she was lucky."

Tate felt her tears sliding down her face. "God, she must be so scared."

Linc leaned forward, placing his forearms on his thighs, and Tate noticed the grooves beside his mouth, his narrowed eyes and his tense shoulders. Yes, Kari was her sister, but she was also Shaw's mom. He'd loved her once. Linc was hurting, too.

She reached out and covered his bunched fists with her hands, sighing when his fingers linked with hers.

"Her main concern, apparently, was for Ellie's welfare, and she was determined to leave the little girl with you."

"Why didn't she just ask me to look after her like a normal person? Why all this cloak-and-dagger stuff? Why involve you? I don't understand her!" Tate cried.

"Kari never goes directly from A to B, Tate, she always makes a couple of detours. Why be simple when you can complicate the hell out of something?"

Linc made the observation in a voice saturated in frustration but devoid of criticism. Tate's head snapped up, and she watched as he pulled his hands away from hers to rub his face. He swore bitterly, his curses reverberating off the cabin walls.

"I've cursed her six ways to Sunday, Tate, but I swear I never wanted this to happen to her." Linc slammed his head back into the seat and closed his eyes, misery etched on his face. Of course he hadn't, no more than she had.

"Cancer doesn't care who you are, what you do or what

you've done," Tate said, standing up to move across to him. Draping an arm around his neck, she sank down on his lap and curled up against his chest, sighing when his arms went around her. She felt so warm here, so safe. But this was a haven she couldn't linger in, a port she couldn't harbor in for long.

A few months ago she would have imagined giving and receiving comfort from Kari's ex, sitting in his masculine, powerful embrace, thinking that this was her favorite place in the world. She wanted this wonderful, amazing man and his love in her life, but she couldn't ask for it and she certainly didn't deserve it. Love had never treated her kindly. Sure, Linc enjoyed her, he might even like her a little, but she wasn't the stay-at-home-mom, happy-to-be-his-wife woman he said he wanted.

She was never quite what anyone really needed, but at this moment she needed comfort and would settle for a little affection. She wanted to feel alive, to be grateful for what she had. But she did she have a right to take comfort from this man? He was Kari's first, and Tate suspected that a small part of him still loved her. She was the mother of his child; they had a connection she could never have with him. Tate felt the lump in her throat expand and felt the tingle of tears.

This wasn't fair, she raged. None of this was fair, and even less of what was happening made sense. Kari was facing the end of a life lived on her own terms, and, because of that, Tate had become a foster parent after years of being resolutely single. And she'd fallen in love with her sister's ex.

She was questioning everything about her life. Did she really want to return to her busy, lonely, nomadic existence? Did she truly want a life without Linc and Ellie and Shaw? Was she still a rolling stone, or was she turning into a bit of a boulder?

This was all so complicated, Tate thought miserably, pushing herself up from Linc's chest. And she had to start unraveling the mess. To do that she needed to start looking at the situation with clear eyes and a sensible attitude. Right now, she should be concentrating on Kari and her horrible situation. The sensible course of action was to distance herself from Linc, focus on Kari and Ellie and how she was going to navigate the next few weeks.

Tate tried to swing her legs off Linc's lap, but his hand gripped her thigh, keeping her in place. Tate lifted her head to look into his face and saw his need, blazing in his eyes.

"I need you, Tate. I need to feel warm and alive and like the world is not spinning out of control. For some reason, I find that feeling when I'm making love to you."

She heard the plea in his voice, felt the tension in his hand, saw it in his thin lips. She understood his need, she found peace in his arms, too, a solace that took her away from the here and now. And, God, they needed to leave the here and now, just for a little while.

Then Linc slid his hand up her cheek, tunneled his fingers into her hair, and his mouth was on hers, hot and demanding, a little desperate and a lot wild. His tongue pushed between her lips to mate with hers in long, hot, ravenous strokes that sent shivers and shocks over her skin. God, she needed him. She needed his heat and his virility, to feel the long play of his muscles under her hands, to touch his skin, to have him slide inside her, filling her, completing her.

Linc was the person she'd always want. It would be so easy to hand this situation over to him, to allow him to make the decisions for her, to relinquish control. So easy but that was a slippery slope, and soon she'd lose herself in him. She couldn't do that; she'd worked too hard to find her true authentic self. Being independent allowed her to keep people at arm's length. If she gave that up, she'd allow herself to be vulnerable, to risk her heart. She loved Linc, she did, but she couldn't give him the power to destroy her.

She could only control the now and here, and they had this time, these few hours before they had to deal with a desperately ill Kari. In no time at all she'd have to make some tough decisions, one of which would be to walk away from Linc and Shaw and the life with him she fantasized about. The life she couldn't have.

But for now, for the next four or so hours, she could love him. He was hers.

"Don't walk away from me, Tate. Not now, not yet," Linc said, his voiced gritty from emotion. She jerked her head up, and her eyes met his, filled with raw, palpable desire.

God, how well he knew her.

"I'm in a jet flying at thirty thousand feet," Tate joked but it fell flat. "I'm not going anywhere."

"You know what I mean," Linc growled. "I need all of you, all your hopes and fears. Give them to me, just for the next few hours. Give me you, *all* of you."

She wasn't strong enough to withstand his silent plea for something real, something life affirming, so she gave up the fight. Straddling his lap, she placed tiny butterfly kisses along his jaw, up and over his cheekbone, onto his temple. She rested her forehead against his and looked into his smoky eyes. "Is it wrong to want you, knowing that she is—"

Linc tucked a loose strand of hair behind her ear. "Us enjoying each other isn't going to change what she is going through. Do you want me, honey?"

Tate sighed, her breath sweet on his lips. "I do. So

much." She had to work to keep her words of love from passing her lips. He didn't need that from her; he just needed to lose himself in her. And she loved him enough to give him exactly what he needed.

Linc pushed his hips up so that his erection pushed into her. "Then let me make you mine." He closed his eyes as if he were facing a wave of pain. Or pleasure. "I need this, we need this. Here. Now."

"The pilots?" Tate asked, sending an anxious glance at the closed door.

"The do-not-disturb light is on. They'll leave us alone." Linc pulled up her jersey to stroke her sides, his fingers on her ribs just below her breasts. "You feel amazing."

Tate dropped her mouth on his, and their hot, frenzied kiss went on and on, two mouths desperate to mate. Tate pulled his sweater and shirt up his chest, desperate to get her hands on Linc's skin, and they broke their kiss for him to pull the garments over his head. Linc, impatient and demanding, helped her peel her sweater off and then held her away from him to look down at her sheer bra that did nothing to conceal her pointed nipples.

"You are so damn sexy," Linc muttered, bending his head to suck her through the lace. She held the back of his head and arched up into him, lost in his touch, in how incredibly feminine and powerful he made her feel. This was the ultimate aphrodisiac, she thought, having an incredibly sexy man want you with every fiber of his being.

This was what being alive felt like.

Without warning, Linc banded a strong arm around her back and lifted her up, surging to his feet as he did so. Letting her stand, his hands went to the band of her jeans, flipping open the button and pulling down the zipper.

"Take your bra off," he commanded and Tate did as he asked. When her torso was free of the lace, she dragged her breasts across his chest, enjoying the rough hair, the sinewy muscle underneath his skin.

"I want you." She panted, reaching down to palm his erection now throbbing beneath her touch. Linc groaned, pushed her panties and jeans down her hips and steadied her as she kicked off her ballet flats and stepped out of her jeans. Linc pulled her to him, making sure that her most sensitive parts were intimately connected with his fabric-covered erection.

"Get naked," Tate breathed after pulling her mouth off his to speak.

"Shh, baby, slow it down," Linc told her. "We have a couple of hours."

Tate shook her head, and, holding his head in her hands so that he had to look at her, she spoke. *"Now."*

Breaking their contact, Linc pulled off his socks and shoes, stepped out of his pants and groaned when her hand encircled his long, steel-hard length. He felt amazing, all harnessed power. Linc muttered something about a condom and pushed her hand away to slap his against a small cupboard above his head. Ducking his hand inside, he pulled out a strip of foil packets.

Tate grabbed the foil packet from him, tore it open and pulled out the latex sheath. Rolling it onto Linc—accompanied by his grateful groans—she pressed her lips into his chest, holding him with both hands. She didn't like how much she loved making love to him, how much she loved him.

She wished he could love her back, that he could heal her fears, convince her that he'd never hurt her, that he'd never leave her. That there was some way for them to be together.

Linc's hand stilled between her legs. "Tate, honey? You okay?"

Tate flashed him a smile. "I'm grand, why?"

"You tensed and you had a strange look on your face."

Yeah, that's my how-the-hell-am-I-going-to-survive-loving-you face. Tate forced a smile and moved against his hand. She linked her arms around his neck, and when he boosted her up his body, she buried her face in his neck. "Make love to me, Linc."

"That would be my absolute pleasure," he growled, pulling her down to the settee, where he stretched out on top of her, her legs opening to allow him inside. He surged inside her and he filled up every hollow, dark, shadowed part of her. He was her brownstone just off Park Avenue, big and bold and so damn permanent. He was the soil she could imagine planting her roots in, the home she never thought she needed. He was her soft place to fall. He was, Tate thought as he pulled her closer and closer to oblivion, her everything.

Eleven

In the administrator's office in the hospice just north of Austin, Linc managed the introductions and guided Tate to one of the visitors' chairs, watching Kari's doctor as she moved to sit behind her large, paper-strewn desk.

Linc took the chair next to Tate and flicked a glance at her worried face. Her mouth, the amazing mouth he'd kissed with ferocious abandon earlier, was pulled tight, and her body was taut with tension. *Dammit, Kari, sick or not, why couldn't you have just had a conversation like a normal person?*

Why did everything have to be a drama?

Linc listened with half an ear as Dr. Mitchell made small talk with Tate, asking about her childhood with Kari and inquiring about Ellie.

Drama, Kari excelled at it. And that was the difference between the sisters; Tate was a straight shooter, someone who looked at life the way it was and not how she wanted it to be. Was she perfect? No, but he didn't expect her to be. She carried more emotional baggage than she did real luggage. She was wary and insecure but she wasn't flighty, selfish or dramatic, and he...

He loved her.

Linc gripped the arms of his chair and stared down at the carpet below his feet. He'd never expected this, not with Tate, but, yeah, he *loved* her and it felt nothing like he'd expected it to. He'd thought that if he ever fell in love again the feeling would be accompanied by angels singing or African drums. That he'd feel swamped, drowning under the rush of emotion, but he felt none of that. It just felt right.

It felt as if his soul had found its warm spot to curl up in, like he'd found a safe place to shelter from the storm outside. He felt as if he had another source of strength to draw upon, an alternate source of wisdom that was now accessible to him.

This love he felt, this was deep and real and nothing like he'd ever experienced before. It was the phone calls they shared during the day, the silly text messages that got him through those endlessly long, tedious meetings. It was how he felt at the end of the day walking into his house and seeing her there, filling his home with her warmth, her laughter and her perfume. It was the fantastic, mind-blowing sex that always left him aching for more, and it was that indescribable feeling like she was in his corner, utterly and absolutely on his side. He'd started off not trusting her because she was a Harper, but now he trusted her because she was Tate, a fascinating and unique product of her Harper past.

Linc sucked in a deep breath as the realization rolled in that, while he might be in love, she might not be feeling the same. Tate had set objectives for her life, and love and a partnership—in whatever form that took—wasn't something she was looking for. So many people had disappointed her; the people who were supposed to love her best never had, and as a result, she had enormous trust issues. Tate wouldn't easily believe that he was in it for the long haul, that he was prepared to love her and Ellie, for the rest of his life.

He knew that she felt something for him—so he'd just have to take it slow, get her used to the idea that she was exactly where she was meant to be.

And they'd have to find a way to work around her need to be independent, her career. He wanted her to have it all; he didn't want her to sacrifice a damn thing for him. It was the twenty-first century; if he could be both a dad and businessman, then Tate could have her career and be a mother and a wife.

Linc rolled his head on his shoulders, trying to ease some of the tension in the cords of his neck. Dr. Mitchell looked at each of them, and then leaned back in her chair, her expression gentle and sad.

"Ms. Harper, I regret to tell you that your sister passed away early this morning. I am so very sorry."

Linc closed his eyes as sorrow seeped into him. Yeah, Kari drove him nuts but she had given him an amazing son. *Kari, rest easy.*

Linc clenched his hands around the arm of his chair before placing his arm around Tate's very stiff shoulders. He looked at her and tried to gauge her reaction. To Linc it looked like she'd shrunk in on herself; she looked smaller and frailer. But it was her expression that scared him or, more accurately, it was her lack of expression.

For the first time, he couldn't discern any emotion in her eyes. There was no sadness, no anger, no regret. Linc turned in his chair and forced his fingers through hers, and he grew concerned when she didn't respond. She'd retreated to a place where he couldn't reach her, Linc suddenly realized. This was the same place she'd said she retreated to during her childhood, when the pressure and pain of living with her mother and sister became too much. The same place she went to when her father disappointed her time and time again.

Tate was on her island and he couldn't get to her...

"I have tried to contact you, but your phone has been going straight to messages for the last six hours."

"I was at a function and didn't think to turn it back on," Tate told her tonelessly.

Dr. Mitchell cleared her throat, and Linc looked at her, his eyebrows raised. "Kari deteriorated quickly when she got here. It was almost as if she stopped fighting."

"I have to organize her funeral," Tate said, staring straight ahead.

"Kari left explicit instructions. She didn't want a funeral and her body is already on its way to a home to be cremated."

She made arrangements for her funeral but not for her kids? Linc shook his head. "Her ashes?" Tate asked in a monotone voice.

"She ordered the funeral home to dispose of them," Dr. Mitchell replied, staring down at the folder she'd opened on her desk. "She did, however, leave a will."

"A will? Kari?" Linc asked, unable to keep the skepticism from his voice.

Dr. Mitchell nodded. "It's part of the admission process. We insist that our patients sort out their affairs."

Linc frowned as a thought suddenly occurred to him. "How did she pay you? The Kari we know—*knew*—didn't have the cash to pay for a private facility."

"We do take pro bono cases. Kari was one of those."

Hearing that, Linc immediately decided that he'd leave

a check to cover Kari's expenses. She was, after all, the mother of his child.

Dr. Mitchell looked at Tate. "Kari wanted me to explain her wishes, but if you'd prefer to deal with a lawyer, then you can."

Tate's eyes had yet to leave the doctor's face. "No, you can tell me," she said, her voice even but still devoid of emotion.

"Before she died, Kari did make arrangements to have Ellie adopted. In fact, she worked with an adoption agency and preapproved a couple for Ellie to go to."

Ellie wasn't going anywhere! She was Tate's. And his. He couldn't lose his two girls.

"Kari wanted to give you the option of adopting Ellie, as well. Essentially, the paperwork at the adoption agency has been completed. It just needs either your signature or the Goldbergs' signatures, and Ellie has a new family."

"Did…" Tate cleared her throat. "Did Kari indicate where she'd prefer Ellie to go?"

Dr. Mitchell shook her head. "She said either of the options was fine. Essentially, she left the choice up to you."

"I see…" Tate softly replied and Linc released a sharp breath, desperate to know what was going through Tate's mind right now.

Oh, Tate, come back. Feel angry, feel sad. Please, don't shut down, and, God, don't shut me out.

"Everything you need to proceed is in the folder, Tate." Dr. Mitchell closed the folder and handed it to Tate, who took it with a rock-steady hand. "I am very sorry for your loss."

Linc placed his hand under Tate's elbow and felt her jerk her arm away. He frowned at her profile, set in stone, and felt her sliding away.

He silently cursed, hot, heavy words that gave him no

relief. He would fight as hard as he could, for her, for them, for the family they were in the process of building, but if she chose to run, there would be little he could do about it. Running away was, after all, what she always did when life became complicated or people demanded more than what she wanted to give.

It would be interesting to see how he coped with the tsunami of pain that was bound to follow her departure.

Hi Tate!
Just to let you know that we'd love to have you host our new, US-based travel show. It's a show developed for your unique delivery style and personality and we're excited to work closely with you on this project. Details and the contract to follow and let me know when we can meet.

Tate read the email again and tossed her phone onto the bed and shoved two hands into her messy hair. She'd been back in The Den for two days, and she felt as if she was operating on fresh air and emotion. Her sister, the person she'd both loved and hated, was dead.

Her daughter was now Tate's responsibility.

She was in love with Kari's ex.

Kari was dead…

And she had the offer of a new job…

Tate rested her forehead against the cool wall of her bedroom, too numb to think, still too stunned to cry. A part of her wanted to scream, to hurl curses at God and Fate, but mostly she just wanted to curl up into a ball and go to sleep.

Is this what an emotional meltdown felt like, Tate wondered, panic creeping up her throat. For the first time ever, she didn't know what to do, how to act. Should she run?

Should she stay? Should she talk to Linc or just pick up her niece and her stuff and leave?

Talk or run? Stay or go?

Her indecision terrified her.

"Hey, sweetheart."

Tate turned around and looked at Linc, leaning his big shoulder into the frame of the door. So solid, so protective, a guardian through and through. God, it would be so easy to throw herself on Linc's broad chest, feel his arms banding around her, silently assuring her that she was safe, that he'd protect her. Because that's what Linc did, the core of who he was. At eleven he'd scooped up the Ballantyne siblings and placed them under his wing, determined to shelter them through their grief. He was Connor's heir apparent, and he felt utterly responsible for the well-being of Ballantyne International. He was insanely protective of Shaw and still worried about his grown-up, very capable siblings.

Linc saw himself as a white knight, and she and Ellie roused his every protective instinct. What she saw in Linc's eyes was not love or affection; it was his need to watch over and care for those around him.

Tate placed her palm on the wall. As much as she wanted Linc, physically, she couldn't allow herself to lean on him. She needed to stand on her own two feet. Find some perspective, some clarity. Distancing herself would give her that.

It would allow her to make smart decisions, decisions that would stand the test of time. Kari and her mom were the queens of hasty, off-the-cuff choices, and most of them had blown up in their faces. She wouldn't do that; Ellie was too important, too precious to treat lightly.

Tate felt Linc's hand on the back of her neck and closed her eyes when he kissed her temple.

"How you doing, sweetheart?" he asked, and Tate's heart sighed. She fought the urge to turn her face into his neck, to wrap her arms around his waist and to rest there for a while. She was exhausted; emotionally and physically drained.

Tate forced her feet backwards, and Linc's hand dropped from her neck. "I'm..." Sad? Gutted? Emotionally whipped? "I'm okay."

Linc frowned at her. "Really? Because I'm feeling like someone used me as a floor rag."

He lifted a hand to her face and ran his thumb under her eyes, across her cheekbone. God, she felt as if being touched by him was what she was put on this earth to do. Tate jerked her head at the thought and stepped back again, shaking her head. *You're not doing this, Tate, you're not going down that road. Distance, dammit!* Creating distance was her best coping mechanism, the way she avoided disappointment and heartbreak. And bad decisions.

Distance had served her well in the past.

"I've had a job offer," Tate blurted, keeping her voice flat.

Linc's eyebrows rose and a muscle jumped in his cheek. His hand fell to his side. "Really? Where?"

"I don't know too much about it except that it's a US-based travel program, which will be a change."

"What about Ellie? How are you going to manage her and the job?"

Linc threw up his hands in frustration when she didn't respond. He correctly interpreted her silence. "Oh, come on, Tate! You can't seriously be thinking about giving her up. She belongs with you, any fool can see that—"

"How do I support her? She doesn't come with a trust fund, Linc! I have to clothe and feed her and educate her! How do I do that? If I give up my career for her, where do I find another job where I can be with her and support her?"

"Here, at The Den," Linc stated. It took a moment for the words to register, for the pennies to drop.

Tate frowned, not sure that she'd heard him correctly. "You're offering me the nanny job?"

"I trust you with Shaw. I like having you in my house, and I'd pay you well."

She loved Shaw and Ellie, but there were so many places she still wanted to see, to share with the world. She adored her job, and he was asking her to walk away from it? "Are you completely nuts?"

"Probably. But I'm also in love with you, and I'm trying to finding a way to make you stay," Linc said, in an annoyingly calm voice. "I thought I'd ease you into living with me...us."

Tate placed her fist into her sternum, utterly shell-shocked by his prosaic announcement. Linc just held her eyes, his hands in his pockets, waiting for her reaction.

Tate lifted her fist to her mouth, her eyes blurring with tears. She heard his words, but she couldn't trust them, she couldn't allow herself to take the risk of believing him.

He couldn't, shouldn't love her... She wasn't what he needed. He needed a woman who was completely and utterly focused on him and on their life at The Den; she'd always have one eye on the horizon, dreaming about another place she wanted to explore. Linc deserved a woman who gave him exactly what he needed and wanted, and while she loved him, she was terrified that he'd one day realize that he'd mistaken his need to protect her and Ellie with love.

Besides, she needed to leave, to test her theory that distance gave her perspective. Would what she felt for Linc be as strong away from him as it was with him? Somehow she thought not.

"We agreed to keep it simple, Linc. To not let it get emotional. You told me I'm not what you wanted! You want a domestic goddess, a stay-at-home mom, a compliant wife."

"I'm pretty sure I never mentioned the word *compliant*," Linc muttered. He rubbed the back of his neck, obviously frustrated.

"You told me that I deserve to be happy, and you, for some reason, make me happy." Linc pulled his hands from his pockets and reached for her, but Tate danced out of his grip, knowing that if he touched her, she'd never leave his arms again.

She had to—she had to run, she had to put the distance she needed between them.

"Make some ties, Tate, commit to me, to us. Stop protecting yourself from life and love," Linc said, his eyes sad but determined. "Be brave, Tate. Love me, embrace the life I'm offering you."

Tate wished she could, but it wasn't possible. Tate slowly shook her head. She couldn't risk hurting him, hurting herself. No, it was better if she left now, while both their hearts were still, sort of, intact.

When she had distance from him, when she wasn't confused by all the emotions swirling between them, she'd feel differently, she'd feel as she always had: that she was right in her belief that she was better off alone, that she didn't need love in her life.

Tate knew how to run away; she knew what she had to do.

She'd pack up and find a hotel, which is what she should have done weeks ago when she first acquired Ellie. She'd meet with the adoption agency and the Goldbergs and see if Kari was right, if being with them would be the right choice for Ellie. If they could give her a good life, no, a *wonderful* life, she'd hand over custody, hoping that the Goldbergs would allow her to have contact with Ellie going forward.

She would take the new job she'd been offered, and life would return to a new type of normal.

Tate closed her eyes against the wave of pain at the thought of not having Ellie or Linc or Shaw in her life, but she knew it would pass, that each day would get better. Keeping it simple, being on her own, was the way she had to live.

It had worked for ten years; it would work again.

She had to do this. She had to tell him.

Linc beat her to it. He lifted a hand, his eyes steel gray. "Don't bother saying anything, I can see the answer in your eyes. You're going to run, because that's what you Harper girls do."

"It's for the best, Linc."

"BS! Instead of staying, talking it out, working it out, you're running." Linc linked his hands behind his head, the cords in his neck tight with frustration. "You kept telling me you were different from Kari, Tate."

"I am."

Linc shook his head and flashed her a cold smile. "Are you? You took what I offered, and when it became a little uncomfortable, a little heated, you decide to walk, run, whatever the hell you Harpers call this."

He's trying to hurt you, wanting and needing to lash out, Tate told herself, but his words still whipped her with the ferocity of an Arctic storm.

"It's not like that, Linc." she said, silently begging him to believe her.

"Funny, it feels exactly the same." Linc strode over to the door. He placed his hand on the door frame and gripped it tight. "Can you be gone by the time Shaw comes home from pre-K? I don't want him upset any more than he needs to be."

She didn't want it to end like this. "Linc—"

Linc spun around, and his lightning-filled eyes pinned her to the spot. "All I've ever wanted, Tate, was someone to stay. No matter how hard it got, just to stand next to me. And, because I'm such a flippin' fool, I thought that person might be you."

Tate, her heart cracking, watched him walk through the doorway, heard the clatter of Linc's feet on the stairs and then, a minute later, the heavy, hard thud of the front door slamming closed.

Tate sobbed as she watched his hunched figure walk down the sidewalk away from the house, walking out of her life.

Just as she'd told him to.

Twelve

Two weeks later, Ellie, sitting on the carpet in the Goldbergs' comfortable lounge, held a small feather duster and waved it in front of an orange cat's nose. The cat swiped the duster with its white paw, causing Ellie to release a girly laugh.

This is what Ellie needed, Tate thought. Two parents, comfortably well-off, a nice home, a cat. Two people who absolutely adored her, who would sell their souls to raise this precious, precious human being. Giving them Ellie would be the right thing to do, the kind thing to do; it made sense in every corner of the universe.

Ellie chuckled again and lifted her eyes to meet Tate's, the perfect little person demanding she share the fun. Tate felt her heart roller-coaster around her chest, trying to resist the urge to scoop Ellie into her arms and chant "mine, mine, mine."

Sandra and George both had college degrees and good

jobs; they had extensive family and lots of nephews and nieces so Ellie would have lots of cousins to play with. They had a solid support group, and, best of all, they were completely open to Tate visiting Ellie, to allowing her to be part of her life going forward.

They were an excellent choice; she could see why Kari was so taken with them. Ellie's laugh washed over her, and Tate closed her eyes. Just put them out of their misery, give them the gift of Ellie and get on with your life, the life she'd spent the last two weeks planning. She was taking the job she'd been offered, had accepted the very hefty salary, and had demanded, and been given, a lot more creative control. This was her show, and she was going to put her stamp on it.

The show had to be stunningly successful; she was sacrificing everything she loved for it and her career. It had better be worth it.

Tate folded her hands over her stomach and stared at Ellie. She had just two weeks before she had to fly out to Aspen to shoot the first episode, and after that she'd pass custody of Ellie to the Goldbergs. She just had to get them to sign the adoption papers and arrange for them to have temporary custody until the adoption was court approved.

She was doing what was best for Ellie, but how could she walk away knowing that Ellie wouldn't be a daily part of her life? How could she miss the first time she walked, her first proper word, the toddler tantrums and her first day at school? She wanted to wipe away tears caused by snotty friends, childhood scrapes or stupid boys. She wanted to help choose her prom dress, go shopping with her, watch her marry, have kids of her own.

She wanted it all. She wanted Ellie. She wanted Shaw, as well. And Linc. She needed her family, as cobbled together as it was. She needed to be the mom, the wife, the lover… God, if she couldn't be any of those, then she'd settle for being the damn nanny.

She just wanted to be with them, around them. And even if Linc wasn't interested in her anymore—she'd noticed that that he hadn't called her once—she could still be Ellie's mom. Yes, it meant sacrificing her career as a travel presenter, but surely there was something else she could do to earn money? Maybe she could arrange culinary tours for travel agencies or become a travel agent or write for a foodie magazine. She could work at night, when Ellie slept; anything was possible if she tried.

But if she allowed this little girl to slip away because she was too damn scared to be her mommy, she'd regret it for the rest of her life. If she walked away from Linc, from Shaw because she was scared, because she put her career and her independence before the people who made her heart sing, she'd never forgive herself. She loved Linc, she loved the family they'd started to become.

She'd been so convinced that she'd needed distance, that she was better off alone, that she didn't need love in her life. She was so full of it…

If anything, she'd quickly realized that she'd been completely, comprehensively, *asininely* wrong. It turned out that she needed love and intimacy, she needed Linc to be the best version of herself. She was a shadow of the person she was with Linc, loving Linc. He made her stronger, wiser, simply better.

She'd messed up badly, and she'd hurt Linc, hurt what they had by running away, instead of planting her feet on the ground. She'd hit him hard by doing exactly what Kari did, leaving him because she didn't have the guts to stay.

She'd fulfilled his worst fears about her, and she couldn't be more ashamed of herself. She kept telling him that she was nothing like her sister, but when the chips were down, she was. For that, at the very least, she had to apologize. At the very best, and if Fate was a little kind, maybe they could talk, maybe she could find a way back into his arms. She'd swallow her pride, grovel and beg if she needed to. She just wanted to have contact with him, somehow, in some way.

Ellie waved the feather duster, her bright smile showing off one bottom tooth. "Ma…ma."

Tate placed her hand on her heart and nodded. Yes, she was her mama. Maybe not by blood but by love…

Tate bit her lip and turned to look at Sandra and George who were looking sad but not surprised. "I'm sorry, I can't. She's mine."

Sandra leaned forward and patted her knee. "We know. We've known it from the first moment you walked in the door."

Tate released a half sob, half laugh. "Then why did you let me come back?"

George shrugged. "We hoped that we were wrong."

"I'm so sorry," Tate said, standing up. "I didn't mean to lead you on, to play games with your expectations. I really didn't know for sure until a minute ago."

George nodded and stood up. Sandra bent down to pick up Ellie, gave her a quick cuddle and her eyes misted over with tears when Ellie leaned toward Tate, her body language telling them all where she wanted to be. Tate settled her on her hip and bent her knees to snag her bag from the settee.

"I hope you find a baby soon," Tate said, feeling embarrassed and more than a little guilty.

Sandra nodded. "Goodbye, Tate. Goodbye, Ellie."

At the door George shook her hand and didn't bother to walk her down the path to the road. Sucking in cold air, Tate pulled up the hood on Ellie's little snowsuit and kissed her cheek. "I love you, my darling El."

Ellie patted her cheek and buried her face in Tate's neck.

"So, what the hell do we do now, El? I'm open for suggestions." Tate tipped her head, pretending that Ellie had answered her. "Do you think that we should find Linc, that we should go to him and tell him that I was wrong, that we miss him and that we love him?"

Elli laughed and blew Tate a kiss. She'd take that as a yes. "Right, any ideas on how to do that?"

Ellie rested her head on Tate's collarbone and within minutes she was a dead weight in her arms, fast asleep on her chest. That, Tate decided, was her daughter's way of telling her that she'd created the mess they were in and that she'd have to fix it.

Well, she'd try.

Linc ran down the steps to the kitchen for the third time that night and wearily took the glass of whiskey Reame held out to him. Shaw was acting up tonight, just as he had been for every night since Tate left two weeks ago. It felt like forty damned years.

God, he was furious that she'd left him to deal with a confused little boy who thought he'd done something wrong to chase her away. He was incensed that she'd confirmed his worst fears about her, that, like Kari, she bailed when life got sticky.

He'd genuinely believed she was better than that. Then again, he hadn't exactly excelled at getting his point across that night. He'd hadn't taken the time to explain that he wanted her any way he could get her, that he didn't expect her to sacrifice a damn thing for him, that she could have her career, that she didn't need to change anything to become the woman he thought he might, one day, want. She was all he wanted, exactly as she was.

But she'd run and he found that hard to forget. Or forgive. She'd hit him exactly where it hurt the most.

"If you grip that glass any harder it's going to shatter," Reame told him in a mild voice.

Linc looked around his living room and saw that, in between him running upstairs to soothe an upset Shaw, his siblings had arrived. Yeah, not what he needed.

Tate was missing from his house and his life, and, despite his anger and disappointment, he still needed her. He needed her in his arms, kissing his son and her daughter good-night, making love to him when the kids were asleep. He missed Ellie, missed his happy little girl. Because she was his, as much as Shaw was. But most of all, he missed Tate with every fiber of his being.

He never felt the same sort of constant ache when Kari left; he'd been pissed and annoyed and sad on Shaw's behalf, but he hadn't felt like someone was using his heart as a hockey puck. Linc stared at his drink before lifting it to his mouth, grimacing at the awful taste of his favorite ten-year-old rare whiskey.

God, he felt like a shadow of himself.

Reame placed a hard hand on his back and guided him toward the sitting area. His pal pushed him down into the vacant seat next to Sage. Linc wanted to tell him to back the hell off, but he didn't have the energy. Since she left he'd had the minimum amount of sleep. At least he could blame his red-rimmed eyes on lack of sleep and not on the tears he refused to let anyone see.

His fault for falling in love with another Harper woman.

Reame sat on the arm of Beck's chair. "So, what are you

going to do about her?" he demanded, finally acknowledging the mammoth in the room.

Linc stared out of the window to the garden and noticed that it was snowing… God, he hoped they were warm. Of course they were, he mocked himself. This was the woman who looked after herself all over the world; she knew how to take care of herself. *She doesn't need you…*

"Nothing," Linc replied in an I'm-not-discussing-her tone of voice.

"Wimp" Beck mocked.

Linc glared at him, but Beck just grinned, amused. There had been a time when a watch-it look from him meant something, but no longer.

"There are so many unanswered questions," Sage mused, tucking her feet up under her, leaning her shoulder into Linc's.

"She left. That's the end of the story. No additional questions or explanations needed," Linc bit out.

"You can growl all you want, but we all know that you are desperate to know whether she gave Ellie up for adoption and whether she's signed a new contract."

"She's keeping Ellie."

Linc sat up and looked at Reame, narrowing his eyes at his oldest friend.

"She can't keep Ellie and do the show, so that means she'll be sacrificing her job. She loves her job," Linc stated. *Dammit, Tate! If you'd stayed, you could've had it all.*

"All I know is that she's keeping Ellie," Reame reiterated.

"And how do you know that?" Linc demanded.

Reame returned his hot look with one of his own. "Why do you want to know? You are the one who let her go."

"She left," Linc said, his teeth grinding together. "I told her I loved her, but she still left. Reame, dammit, tell me!"

Reame, the bastard, tossed him a smug smile. "I called her earlier today and asked her."

Jaeger laughed and Reame shrugged. "PI skills 101," he explained.

"So, bro," Beck asked, his ankle on his knee, "are you going to man up and go to her and try and sort out this mess?"

Linc kept his eyes on Reame, and Reame responded with a it's-time-to-get-your-ass-into-gear look. "She's not Kari, Linc," Reame stated.

Linc nodded. "I know."

She wasn't. Linc felt his head swim. The last of his resentment toward Kari faded away, and images of his time with Tate flashed on the big screen inside his head… Tate making cupcakes with Shaw, cuddling Ellie, her bright smile when she saw him for the first time at the end of the day. Tate naked, her expression blissful as he ran his hands over her fine skin, down her hip, between her thighs.

Tate, messy haired and bighearted. Tate in tears, crying over Kari. Tate…

Just Tate. His world didn't make sense without her in it. He needed her in his world.

Linc looked down when he felt Sage patting him down with a dishcloth, Beck standing over him and picking glass off his chest. Reame was holding his hand, and suddenly he realized that blood was dripping from his palm onto the leg of his jeans, some drops finding their way onto the laminated wooden floor under his feet. Linc looked at his hand again and noticed that he had a two-inch shard of glass sticking out of his hand and that he wasn't feeling a damn thing.

"I'm going to pull this out, and then I'll decide if we need to take you to the emergency room, bro," Reame told him.

"Does it hurt, Linc? Are you okay?"

Linc looked at Sage and managed a smile. "Not as much as my heart does."

"Can you fix it?" Sage asked him, picking up the bottom piece of his broken glass from the floor by his feet.

"My heart or my hand?" Linc nodded decisively. "Damn right I can fix both."

"Excellent news," Reame said, examining his hand. "The not-so-excellent news is that this is deep, and you need stitches."

"Crap." Linc looked at the kitchen towel that Beck was pressing into his hand. "I was going to leave you lot to babysit, and I was going to find Tate."

"Not tonight you're not," Reame told him. He gripped Linc's uninjured hand and hauled him to his feet. "You have a couple of painkillers and at least six stitches in your immediate future."

Linc looked from his very bloody hand to his oldest friend. Screw the blood and stitches. "Take me to her, Reame. I know that you know where she is."

Reame looked at his siblings, his eyebrows raised. "We need a translator. Do we know anyone who speaks fluid idiot?"

"Very funny," Linc retorted. He saw the commanding officer look on Reame's face and grimaced. "Is there any point in arguing?"

"You can, but it's not going to change the outcome," Reame, the bastard, cheerfully told him. "One, or all your sibs, will stay here to look after Shaw."

Linc watched as more blood fell from his hand to the floor. "Damn, now it hurts."

"Since you crushed a crystal glass in your hand, it damn well should," Jaeger told him. "Moron."

His hand was on fire, his heart was battered, and he

had to put up with crap from his siblings? On what planet was that fair? Linc sent Jaeger a screw-you look. "Remind me to kick your ass."

"You and whose army, sweetheart?"

Linc snatched up his cell and headed for the stairs. "Idiots," he muttered, taking the fresh kitchen towel from Reame and pushing it into his gushing, burning hand. "Idiots everywhere."

Jaeger's chuckle drifted to him. "And you are their king."

After running scenarios and practicing what she wanted to say, it still took Tate most of the evening to gather her courage to go to Linc. Finally, a little after eleven at night, Tate, using the key she had never bothered to return, let herself into The Den. Navigating the house by feel, she carried a sleeping Ellie up to the third floor and placed her in the crib she'd been sleeping in up until a couple of weeks before.

Slipping out of her coat, Tate grabbed the baby monitor off the bedside table and crept down the stairs to the second floor. She opened Shaw's door and walked over to his bed, dropping down to kiss his cheek. Taking a deep breath and wondering, not for the first time, whether she was completely nuts coming over to talk to Linc so late, she eased open the door to Linc's bedroom and frowned at his empty bed. So... Huh, avoiding explanations by slipping into bed with him wasn't an option.

So much for that fantasy.

After running back up to the third floor, Tate found Sage fast asleep in her bedroom.

If Sage was looking after Shaw, then Linc was out.

Out working? Or out drinking? Clubbing? God, *dating*?

Tate walked down the stairs and sat down on the settee next to the front door. What if Linc came home with a woman, what would she do? How would she cope? What if he'd changed his mind about her staying? What if he didn't want to talk?

She felt her insides ripping apart, and she was about to run up the stairs and collect Ellie when she heard low male voices and a key in the front door. Tate watched the door swing open, and then Reame and Linc walked in, shrugging out of their coats.

Linc's eyes widened when he saw her, and his eyes flashed with an emotion she didn't immediately recognize. Relief? Surprise? A combination of both?

Tate immediately noticed his bandaged hand and his bloody shirt and bounded forward. She touched his chest and looked into his pain-filled eyes. "God, are you okay?"

Linc's eyes just bounced from feature to feature as if he couldn't quite believe she was there. "You're here. Hi."

Tate touched his cheek and smiled. "Hi back." Worried, she looked at Reame. "Is he okay?"

Reame nodded. "Crushed a glass in his hand and he needed a whole bunch of stitches." Reame held out a pill bottle which he dropped into Tate's hand. "He did a good job of slicing his hand so he needs to take two of these in the morning. That's if you are going to be here in the morning."

Tate held his eyes as her fingers slipped into Linc's un-injured hand. "I plan on being here."

Reame cocked his head at her, his gaze probing. "You staying this time, Tate?"

Tate nodded. "If Linc wants me to."

Linc didn't speak. He just opened the front door and jerked his head, a clear gesture for Reame to leave. Reame took his time picking up his coat and pulling it on, his eyes filled with amusement.

"Coffee would be nice. It's cold out there," Reame teased and Tate frowned. She liked Reame, she did, but she needed to be alone with Linc.

Linc scowled at Reame and gestured for him to leave. "Out!"

"Such gratitude," Reame grumbled good-naturedly as he moved out into the night. Tate called a soft goodbye but wasn't sure if Reame heard her because Linc quickly slammed the door behind him.

Linc turned back to her and placed his hands on her biceps, and suddenly Tate was inhaling his cologne, looking into his smoldering eyes. She was home...

"Did you mean that?" he demanded. "About staying?"

Tate lifted her hands to rest them on his chest.

"Yes, I'll stay." Tate pulled her bottom lip between her teeth. "If you want me."

"I'll always want you, Tate."

She released her lip, and Linc swiped his thumb across the skin to ease the sting. He pulled her closer and slid his hand around the back of her neck, using his thumb to lift her face up. "We need to talk, but we'll get to that. But first, this."

His mouth covered hers, and Tate felt his cool lips on hers. His sigh hit her mouth, and she instinctively opened hers, and his tongue slipped inside, a hot, slow slide. She'd missed him, missed his clever mouth and his ever-changing eyes, his big body, both clothed and naked.

She'd felt adrift these past couple of weeks, more alone than she'd ever felt in her life. Her world had faded to grayscale, to wishy shades of gray. Life with Linc, with the kids, his and hers, infused her life with color. She felt alive with him; just sitting next to him made her feel like the best version of herself.

God, she loved him. She could stand here, on her tiptoes, and be kissed by him for the rest of her life. If that was all she could have of him, she'd take it.

Linc pulled away from her and rested his forehead on hers, his hand cradling her cheek. "That was about fifteen days, eight hours and ten minutes overdue."

"I have no idea what's happening here, but as long as you keep kissing me, I'm good."

Linc grinned, and his smile had her heart doing back-flips. "FYI, I plan on kissing you for a long, long time. In fact, that talk is going to be delayed for a while, because I plan to kiss you for the rest of the night."

Tate allowed Linc to lead her to the stairs, her hand firmly clasped by his uninjured one. "Just kiss me?" She mock pouted. "Nothing else?"

Linc stopped and turned around to look down at her, and Tate's heart hitched at the pure emotion she saw on his face. "Tate, I'd give you the world if I could, right now. Seeing you standing in my hallway is all my Christmases and birthdays rolled into one. The only time I've ever come so close to feeling as happy was when Connor showed me the adoption papers stating that I was officially a Ballan-tyne. There's nothing I wouldn't give you." Linc squeezed her hand. "Come upstairs with me."

Didn't he realize that she'd go anywhere, do anything for him, with him? Tate slowly nodded and ran up the stairs with him.

Thirteen

The smell of good coffee pulled Tate from a heavy sleep, and she woke up slowly, immediately looking for the source. As her eyes focused, Linc sat down on the side of the bed, Ellie on his knee, her beautiful face full of smiles. Having been the focus of Linc's exquisite attention for most of the night, Tate was full of smiles, as well.

Tate pushed herself up and leaned over to nuzzle Ellie's cheek. "Mornin', baby."

Linc raised an amused eyebrow when she leaned back. "And where's my 'morning, baby'?"

Tate overexaggerated her sigh and hooked her hand around his neck to pull him down for an open-mouth kiss. "Mornin' baby," she said, her voice husky with laughter.

Linc grinned. "Much better."

"Where's Shaw?" Tate asked, placing her hand over her mouth to hide her yawn.

"Still asleep." Linc pushed the cup of coffee into her

hand. "Drink this, have a shower and I'll wake Sage up and tell her that she's on kid duty for a little while. Last night was amazing, but we really need to talk."

Oh, God, he looked and sounded so solemn. Had he changed his mind? She couldn't bear it if the happiness, the hope she'd been feeling, was suddenly snatched out of her hands. Fear and insecurity, hot and hard, bubbled up her throat. "Yes, okay."

Tate pushed her hair back as Linc stood up. Tate took a moment to admire her sexy man dressed in a berry-colored sweater and dark pants. She couldn't wait… She couldn't stand the tension for one more minute, so she pushed a nervous hand into her hair and sent him a troubled look.

Tate spoke, and the butterflies in her stomach took flight. "Did you mean what you said, on the stairs?"

"Are you doubting me? This?"

Tate gave him a quick nod. She looked at the door and fought her instinct to run. "A little. I'm feeling hopeful and happy, and I'm scared it's all going to evaporate." Tate looked into her coffee cup and told herself that running was no longer an option. Yes, she was risking her heart and her future, but Linc was worth it. She had to talk, to lay it on the line; she had to trust him with all that she was. Her hopes and her fears. "I'm scared that you are confused about what you want, I'm worried that you might change your mind about me—" Tate gestured to Ellie "—about us."

It wasn't one person walking into his life and hoping to stay; it was two.

Linc sat down again, rested his chin on Ellie's head and sent her a steady look. "I've been up for hours, Tate. So far, I've contacted my lawyer to get the paperwork started on all the adoptions that need to happen to make us a proper family—me to adopt Ellie, you to adopt Ellie and Shaw.

I've contacted an agency to find an experienced nanny. I've also spoken to Jo, told her that you're back, have asked her to look after the kids for a couple of hours here and there so that you and I can have some alone time. I think we deserve that. I had to run to my office to get something out of my safe—does all that sound like I'm confused about you and what I want?"

Tate, unable to take in all the implications of his speech, just stared at him. Linc leaned down, Ellie in his arms, and brushed his lips against hers. "What about what you want, Tate?"

She swallowed, desperately looking for some moisture in her mouth. "I want it all, Linc. I want you and the kids and…"

"And what, honey?"

Tate tapped her finger against her coffee cup and forced herself to be honest. "I want my career. I love what I do, but if the choice was between you and the kids and my career, then I choose you. I can live without my career. I can't live without you and the kids." She wrinkled her nose. "But a part of me still wants to take this work opportunity even though I understand that might not be possible or feasible or realistic." She bit her bottom lip. "Or not what you want."

"Because you think that I want a stay-at-home mother for my wife, a wife who knows her place?"

Tate, not sure how to respond, just shrugged and stared down into her cup of rapidly cooling coffee. She felt Linc's finger pushing her chin up, and she gasped at the emotion blazing from his eyes. "I thought that was what I wanted, Tate, but I was so damn wrong. All I need is for you to be happy. If taking the job makes you happy, then do it. Take it. In fact, I insist that you do."

God, he made it sound so simple, but it wasn't. "Linc,

if I took the job, I'd be away from home a few days every week for a good six months. That's a lot of time away."

Linc looked stubborn. "Our relationship is not about sacrifices, sweetheart. It's about compromises and being organized. And I have enough money at my disposal that I can organize the hell out of any situation."

"Tell me what you are thinking," Tate begged, utterly amused by the idea that she could have her man and her kids and her career.

"I meant to tell you that I never intended for you to give up your career. If I can have mine, you can have yours. That's why I mentioned that I contacted an agency to find us a nanny. We'll find someone we all like, and some weeks the nanny and the kids will travel with you, some weeks I will. Maybe with the nanny, depending on my work load, maybe without. Some weeks, depending on your work load, the kids will stay here with me. It's all figure-outable."

It was, Tate thought, her heart expanding with excitement and delight. Together they could do it all. Tate curled her hand around the back of Linc's neck and pulled his head down so that she could brush her lips against his.

Before they went any further, she had to apologize, to ask for his forgiveness for making such a massive mistake by running when she should have planted her feet next to him and stayed. "Linc, I'm sorry I left. So sorry."

Linc tipped his head. "Do you plan on doing it again?" he asked, his voice heart-attack serious.

"No." Tate placed her hand on her heart and shook her head. He had to believe her, she couldn't bear it if he didn't. "God, no! I promise."

Linc's eyes filled with relief, and the corners of his mouth quirked upward. "Then we're good."

"Thank you." Tate breathed the words against his

mouth, desperately wanting to thank him for making all her dreams come true. "Thank you for being wonderful and thoughtful and sensitive to my needs. Thank you for giving me my career. Thank you for forgiving me for running away." Tate's eyes filled with tears.

"Thank you for loving Ellie. For loving me," she said, her voice choked with emotion.

Linc wiped away a tear with his thumb before dropping his forehead to rest it on hers. "I'm going to spend the rest of my life loving you, Tate. Because you, more than anyone else I know, are so worthy of being loved."

Linc pulled back and tapped her nose. "Take a shower and I'll see you downstairs. We'll start planning the rest of our lives over breakfast."

"Sounds good," Tate murmured. "Actually, no, that's the sound of all my dreams coming true."

She hadn't told Linc that she loved him yet.

The thought hit Tate as she walked down the stairs twenty minutes later. How could she have neglected such an important detail? She did love him, with every fiber of her being. She hoped he knew that, but in case he didn't, she'd tell him as soon as she saw him.

He'd given her so much, yet she still hadn't given him the words he needed the most. God, she sucked at being in love, but she would learn. She was as determined to make Linc as happy as he made her.

On an impulse Tate sat down on the bottom stair and looked around the hallway, her hand running over the polished step next to her thigh. She loved this house, she realized, and it wasn't because it was situated on one of the best streets in Manhattan or because it was worth a fortune. She loved it because all the people she loved lived here. Tate looked up at the portrait of Connor on the wall opposite her, taking in his patrician face and his merry blue Ballantyne eyes. She was sorry she'd never met Linc's father, but she thought she would've liked him. So many generations of Ballantynes had grown up in this house, and it sounded like Linc had plans for Shaw and Ellie to do the same.

Love, she felt, had seeped into the bones of this house, into the walls, into the foundations. Sometimes she felt that she could hear whispered laughter, hot spots of warmth, the suggestion of spiritual energy. She didn't think the place was haunted, but she did feel like the previous occupants had left a little of their happiness behind.

Jo had been right when she'd said that this house had the ability to heal. In this house, around the Ballantynes, she felt happier, centered, more focused. She felt like she was home.

Tate heard footsteps behind her and twisted her torso to look up the stairs. Linc stood at the top of the stairs staring at her with a strange look on his face.

"I thought you were downstairs."

"I took Ellie up to Sage and grabbed something from my room."

The odd look on his face remained as he looked at her.

"What's the matter?" Tate demanded. "Are the kids okay?"

Linc shook his head as if to clear it and half jogged down the stairs. "Shaw is still asleep, Ellie is cuddling with Sage."

Tate started to stand up, but Linc's hand on her shoulder kept her butt glued to the stair. "No, stay there," he said. "This spot is as good as any."

"To do what?"

"This." Linc sat down next her and immediately pulled

her to him and started to kiss her, his hand going to her breast. Tate laughed and pulled back.

"I'm fairly adventurous, Ballantyne, but your sister is upstairs and might need to use these stairs," Tate drily told him. "And your siblings all have a key to that front door, and they frequently use it, and at odd times, too."

Linc grinned, and then his face turned serious. "Does that bother you?"

"Does what bother me?"

"Does it bother you that The Den is Grand Central Station? I love this house, but if it doesn't suit you, if you want something more private, then we can move."

"I love your house, Linc. I don't want to live anywhere else."

Linc smiled. "I want this house to be ours, Tate, the kids will ours, that we do this together as equal partners. We *can* have it all. It'll be crazy trying to juggle two careers, the kids, but I'm convinced we can fuse it all together into one glorious mess."

"Yours, mine…ours." Tate pushed the words out between her lips, stunned once again by his generosity, love bubbling in her stomach. She placed her hand on his hard thigh and rested her forehead on his shoulder. "Yeah, I think we can do that. But The Den, this is where I want to live."

She heard Linc's relieved sigh and felt the kiss he pressed into her hair. Tate didn't want to move; she just wanted to sit here, listening to the house and inhaling Linc's sexy, citrusy cologne.

"I love you, Linc," she whispered, pushing herself over the last barrier between them.

"You, Shaw and Ellie and the kids… What we have together will always be the center of my world, the reason the earth spins for me," she added, her voice low and intense.

So much emotion swirled between them, but Tate finally embraced her passionate feelings instead of bolting from them. "I don't love often, Linc, but when I do, I love with everything I have. I'll always love you."

"I love you, too, sweetheart," Linc replied, his voice husky. "Come here."

Tate scooted onto his lap, straddling him, his thighs hard under hers. She held his face in her hands and looked into his mesmerizing eyes, happy to see laughter and contentment brimming in those stunning gray depths.

"Love you," she murmured, desperate to tell him again.

Linc jerked her toward him, and his mouth covered hers, demanding that she translate that emotion into her kiss. Tate was more than happy to oblige, and within minutes she was chest to chest with Linc, rubbing the juncture between her legs against his rock-hard erection. Her hands pushed under his sweater and shirt, needing his skin on hers, desperate to show him how much she loved him, desired him, how much her body had missed his.

The door behind them opened, and Tate heard an outburst of laughter as far too many Ballantynes crowded into the hallway. Tate pulled back and lifted her eyebrows at Linc.

Linc sent her a half amused, half sour look. "They thought I might need help talking you into staying."

"Guess we weren't needed after all," Jaeger stated.

Tate looked over her shoulder. Yep, the entire clan, Jaeger and Piper, Beck and Cady and Reame were standing in the hallway, watching them with open amusement.

"Have you guys heard about this new thing they've invented?" Beck asked, shedding his coat and throwing it on the pile that was building on the settee. "It's called a bedroom. And you have impressionable kids in the house."

"And Sage is here," Jaeger added.

Tate looked from one sibling's face to the next, and in the eyes of each, she saw that they were happy for Linc, that she was now part of this crazy, extended family. They liked her, they approved of her, and they might, in time, come to love her. Her eyes collided with Reame's, and he winked at her.

Tate turned back to Linc, and, staying on his lap, she decided to mess with his cocky siblings. "Linc, does the conversation we've just had mean that I am the de facto mistress of The Den?"

Linc, because he knew her so well, immediately picked up on the teasing in her voice, but he kept his face bland. "Yep. Pretty much." He pushed his hand into his pocket and pulled out Connor's ring, the color a deep, happy green. "Though if you agree to wear this ring, we'd make that, and a bunch of other things, legal."

Tate ignored Cady and Piper's squeals, keeping her eyes on Linc's beloved face. "Is that a proposal, Linc?" she asked, amused.

"Sure is." He smiled. "If you agree to marry me, to stay with me for the next sixty or so years, it comes with the added bonus of becoming mistress of The Den and bossing that lot around."

So happy, Tate thought. She didn't know she could feel this full, so blissful.

"Only sixty years? I think we can do better than that," she replied with a radiant smile.

"Is that a yes?" Linc asked with a catch in his voice.

"Yes, that's a yes! I love you, and I can't think of anything more I'd like to do than spend the rest of my life with you." Tate said, dropping a soft kiss on Linc's mouth. She lifted her head and grinned. "But bossing your siblings around holds a certain appeal."

"Go away," she told Linc's family—no, her family—

smiling as she tossed a look over her shoulder toward their audience. "I have plans for your brother."

Nobody was more surprised than her when all of them picked up their coats. Reame grabbed the door handle, and Tate watched, utterly astounded as they started walking out of The Den.

Tate immediately felt bad. She'd been joking, dammit! She started to call them back when Linc clapped his hand over her mouth, his face suffused with laughter. "Good job at getting rid of them, sweetheart."

"I was joking!" Tate wailed. "Make them come back!"

"Not a chance in hell," Linc muttered, standing up with her in his arms. "Because I have plans for my brand-new fiancée. Naked plans."

Tate sent another look at the door, biting her bottom lip. "But—they—"

Linc rolled his eyes, placed her on her feet and jogged to the front door. Yanking it open, he shouted to his family who were halfway to the sidewalk. "Come back for dinner! Bring food!"

Linc slammed the door behind him and slapped his hands on his hips, looking down at Tate with one sexy eyebrow raised. "Happy now?"

Tate ran the tip of her finger down the long ridge in his pants. "I will be."

"Damn right you will be," Linc growled. "I'll race you to the bedroom. You get a five-second start."

Tate started running up the steps, and as she hit the landing she nearly barreled into Shaw. He immediately launched himself at her legs. "Tate! You're back! I missed you! Spike missed you. Come say hi to Spike. I played the drums at school…"

"For God's sake," Linc muttered, shoving a frustrated hand into his hair.

Tate, her arm around Shaw's shoulder, laughed out loud when she saw Sage walking down the stairs from the third floor, carrying Ellie. When she met Tate on the landing, Sage immediately noticed Linc's ring on her finger and lifted it up to take a better look. "Oh, my God! Is that Connor's ring? Are you going to marry him?"

Tate grinned down at Linc at the bottom of the stairs, her eyes on his as Shaw tugged at her arm and Ellie moved from Sage's arms to hers. "I so am."

With an arm around Shaw's shoulders and holding her best girl, Tate laughed before saying, "Since everyone is awake, do you want to call the rest of the clan back, Linc?"

"Might as well," he grumbled, hands on his hips and looking frustrated. "Bloody madhouse. I think we should move out."

Tate laughed again and shook her head. "Not a chance. I love this house, our children and you."

Linc's eyes softened, and Tate noticed his Adam's apple bob in his throat. "I love you more."

He lifted his phone out of his pocket and texted his brothers and Reame. When he was done, his eyes moved from Tate and his kids, to his sister.

He smiled, looking relaxed and happy. "Happy to have another brother off your hands, Sage? And, I'd like it noted, that you didn't even have to pay Tate to get rid of me."

Sage nodded, but Tate noticed the tender emotion in her eyes. "I might reward her by redesigning Connor's ring. It's a little old-fashioned. As for taking you off my hands, I have to admit that you are fractionally less annoying than my other two brothers."

Linc winked at Tate before looking at Sage, his expression contemplative. "And that raises the question—how are we going to get *you* off *our* hands?"

Tate placed her hand on Sage's shoulder. "And that's

brotherspeak for him, us, hoping that you, too, will find love, Sage."

Sage groaned and covered her face with her hands. *"Ugh."*

Linc cocked his head. "So, what exactly is going on between you and Latimore, Sage?" he asked, gray eyes teasing.

Sage threw her hands up in the air and scowled. "I swear my guardian angel was drunk when she put that man in my path."

Tate kissed Ellie's head and squeezed Shaw's shoulder. Looking down at her man, she smiled, utterly in love. Frankly, if her guardian angel was responsible for all her happy, she was doing a hell of a job and deserved a raise.

* * * * *

If you liked this sassy, sexy story from Joss Wood, pick up her other Mills & Boon Desire novels!

TRAPPED WITH THE MAVERICK MILLIONAIRE
PREGNANT BY THE MAVERICK MILLIONAIRE
MARRIED TO THE MAVERICK MILLIONAIRE

***

And don't miss the next
BILLIONAIRES AND BABIES *story,*
A FAMILY FOR THE BILLIONAIRE

by Dani Wade.
Available September 2017!

"I don't need you to save me."

"That's not what this is." But even as he said it, he wasn't entirely sure that was the truth. He didn't think about it in terms of saving her. He thought about it in terms of *helping*. Of course, why he felt this compulsion to help Kate was another question that he didn't want to investigate too deeply right now.

"Then tell me what this is about. The truth, Seth."

The truth? Hell. The truth was he was worried about her. He couldn't stop fantasizing about her. He was glad that she hadn't married Roger. He knew how hard single mothers had it and he didn't want it to be that hard for her. It shouldn't be that hard for anyone, but especially not for her.

He didn't say any of that. Instead, he closed the distance between them and cupped her face in his hands. "This," he said, lowering his lips to hers, "is the truth."

* * *

Little Secrets: Claiming His Pregnant Bride
is part of the Little Secrets series:
Untamed passion, unexpected pregnancy…

LITTLE SECRETS: CLAIMING HIS PREGNANT BRIDE

BY
SARAH M. ANDERSON

HarperCollins
PUBLISHERS
Since 1817

First Published in Great Britain 2017
By Mills & Boon, an imprint of HarperCollins*Publishers*
1 London Bridge Street, London, SE1 9GF

© 2017 Sarah M. Anderson

ISBN: 978-0-263-92830-3

51-0817

Our policy is to use papers that are natural, renewable and recyclable products and made from wood grown in sustainable forests. The logging and manufacturing processes conform to the legal environmental regulations of the country of origin.

Printed and bound in Spain
by CPI, Barcelona

Sarah M. Anderson may live east of the Mississippi River, but her heart lies out west on the Great Plains. Sarah's book *A Man of Privilege* won an RT Reviewers' Choice Best Book Award in 2012. *The Nanny Plan* was a 2016 RITA® Award winner for Contemporary Romance: Short.

Sarah spends her days having conversations with imaginary cowboys and billionaires. Find out more about Sarah's heroes at www.sarahmanderson.com and sign up for the new-release newsletter at www.eepurl.com/nv39b.

To everyone who stood up for what they believed.
You continue to inspire me!

One

Of all the things Seth Bolton wanted to be doing today, attending the wedding of a guy he went to college with was pretty low on the list.

Besides, he hadn't even liked Roger Caputo. Seth had been forced to live with Roger for three hellish months in college when Seth's roommate had backed out and Seth had been desperate to cover the rent without asking his family for help. That Roger had been a senior and unable to get any roommate but a freshman should have been the first clue to how Seth's three months were going to go.

It wasn't that Roger was a bad guy—he was just a jerk. Entitled, spoiled, inconsiderate—every privileged white-guy stereotype rolled into one. That was Roger.

Seth couldn't imagine who was foolish enough to marry Roger, but clearly someone was. Seth had no idea if he should pity this woman or not.

He gunned the engine up the incline, following the road as it snaked through the Black Hills. The wedding was supposed to start at five thirty—Seth was running late. It was already five forty and he had at least fifteen miles to go.

For some reason, the wedding was being held at a resort deep in the Black Hills, forty minutes away from Rapid City.

Why did people have destination weddings? Well, he knew why. The late-summer sun was already lower in the sky, casting a shimmering glow over the hills. They weren't black right now, not with the sun turning them golden shades of orange and red and pink at the edges.

It was *pretty*—not that he was looking as he took the next curve even faster. Roger must've found one hell of a woman if she wanted to tie herself to him with all this beauty around her.

Or maybe the jerk had changed. It was possible. After all, Seth himself had once been the kind of impulsive, restless kid who'd stolen a car and punched a grown man in the face because the man had dared to break Seth's mother's heart. Sure, that man—Billy Bolton—had married his mother and adopted Seth, despite the punch. But still, that was the sort of thing Seth used to be capable of.

Maybe he was still a little impulsive, he thought as he flew down the road well over the speed limit. And yeah, he was definitely still restless. The last year living in Los Angeles had proved that. But he'd gotten good at controlling his more destructive tendencies.

So people could change. Maybe Roger had become a fine, upstanding citizen.

The road bent around an outcropping, and Seth

leaned into the curve, the Crazy Horse chopper rumbling between his legs. This was a brand-new model, in the final stages of testing, and he was putting it through its paces. The new engine had throwback styling combined with modern power and a wider wheelbase. The machine handled beautifully as he took another curve and leaned in hard. Seth felt a surge of pride—he'd helped design this one.

Damn, he'd missed these hills, the freedom to open up the throttle and ride it hard. LA traffic made actually riding a chopper a challenge. And palm trees had nothing on the Black Hills.

His father and his uncles, Ben and Bobby Bolton, owned and operated Crazy Horse Choppers, a custom chop shop in Rapid City, South Dakota. Crazy Horse had been founded by their father, Bruce Bolton, but the Bolton brothers had taken the company from a one-man shop in Bruce's garage in the early eighties to a company with sixty employees and a quarter of a billion in sales every year.

Seth had never had a father growing up, never expected that he would be a part of any family business. But when Billy adopted Seth ten years ago, the Bolton men had embraced him with open arms.

And now? Seth was a full partner in Crazy Horse Choppers.

He still couldn't get his head around the meeting yesterday. His dad and uncles had called him into the office and offered him an equal share in Crazy Horse. And Seth was no idiot. Of course he'd said yes.

At the age of twenty-five, he was suddenly a millionaire. A *multimillionaire*. Considering how he and his mom had sometimes been on welfare when he was a little kid, it was a hell of a shock.

But Seth knew it wasn't straight nepotism—he worked hard at making Crazy Horse Choppers a successful business. He'd just gotten back from living in Los Angeles for a year, managing the Crazy Horse showroom and convincing every A-to D-list celebrity that a Crazy Horse chopper was good for their image. And he'd excelled at the job, too. Getting Rich McClaren to ride up the red carpet at the Oscars on a Crazy Horse chopper—right before he won the award? Seth's idea. The free advertising from that had boosted sales by eight percent overnight.

The McClaren stunt was the kind of strategic thinking that Seth did now. He didn't just react—and react poorly. He planned. The best defense was a good offense.

Even now—he wasn't just going to a former friend's wedding. A quick internet search had revealed that Roger was a real estate agent now, part owner in his own agency. He was up-and-coming in the civic world of Rapid City. And after a year in LA, Seth was back in Rapid City. Maybe even permanently.

Seth was not going to this wedding to wish Roger and his new bride happiness, although he would. Seth was going to the wedding because he planned to be an up-and-comer himself. God knew that he had the money now.

The Bolton men might have given him a place at the table, but Seth was going to damn well keep it.

He screamed around a curve but saw something that made him ease off the throttle. There was a limo at a scenic overlook—but something wasn't right. Seth couldn't brake fast enough to stop without crashing, but he slowed enough to get a better look.

Something was definitely wrong. The limo was parked at a crazy angle, its bumper hanging in the roadway. Was there someone behind the wheel? He didn't see anyone enjoying the view.

He was late—but he couldn't in good conscience ride on. Seth pulled a U-turn on the road and headed back to the overlook. Did his phone even have service out here? Because if this wasn't some crazy wedding photographer stunt and the driver was having an emergency…

The limo was still running when Seth pulled up alongside it. His heart leaped in his throat when he realized that the front wheel on the passenger side wasn't exactly on solid ground. The driver had stopped just before the wheel went off the edge of the overlook completely. Hitting the gas would mean certain death.

He hopped off the bike and hurried to the driver's side. He hadn't been wrong—there *was* someone behind the wheel. A woman. Wearing a wedding dress and a…tiara?

Definitely not the limo driver.

She wasn't crying, but her eyes were wide as she stared at nothing in particular. Her color was terrible, a bluish shade of gray, and she had what appeared to be a death grip on the steering wheel. Basically, she looked like someone had shot her dog. Or ruined her wedding.

For all of that, she was quite possibly the most beautiful woman he'd ever seen.

How many brides were wandering around this part of South Dakota? Was this Roger's bride? If so, what was she doing *here*? Where was Roger?

He knocked on the glass of the driver's-side door.

"Ma'am?" he said in what he hoped was a comforting voice. "Could you roll down the window?"

She didn't move.

"Excuse me? Ma'am?" This time, he tried the handle. Miracle of miracles, the door was not locked. When he opened it, she startled and swung her head around to look at him. As she did so, the limo shuddered. "Where did you come from?"

"Hi," Seth said in a soothing voice, hanging on to the door as if that could keep the car from plummeting off the side of the hill. "I'm going to turn this off, okay?"

Her eyes blinked at different speeds. "What?"

Seth leaned into the limo, keeping an eye on her in case she started to freak out. The limo was actually in Park, thank God. She must have taken her foot off the brake when he startled her. "I'm Seth," he told her, pulling the key from the ignition. "What's your name?"

Seth didn't expect her to burst out laughing as if he had told a joke. Clearly, this was a woman whose actions could not be predicted. Then, as quickly as she'd started laughing, the sound died in the back of her throat and she made a strangled-sounding sob. "I'm not sure."

Bad sign. He had to get her out of the limo. "Can you come talk to me? There's a bench over there with a great view of the sunset." He tried to make it sound like he was just here for the vista.

"You not going to tell me to get married, are you?"

Seth shook his head. "You're here for reasons. All of those reasons—I bet they're good ones."

She blinked at him again, her brow furrowed. He could see that she was coming back to herself now. "Are you here for a reason, too?"

He gave her a reassuring smile. "Everything happens for a reason."

This time, when she started laughing, he was ready for it. He chuckled along with her as if they were at a comedy club in downtown LA as opposed to on the edge of a scenic overlook in the Black Hills. He held out a hand to her and bowed at the waist. "Seth Bolton, at your disposal."

For the longest second, she just stared at him, as if he were a *Tyrannosaurus rex* that had emerged from the undergrowth and was roaring at her. "I'm not imagining you, right? Because you're kind of perfect and I made a mess of everything."

"I'm very real—the last time I checked, anyway," he joked, which got a small, quick smile out of her. He kept his hand out, the picture of a chivalrous gentleman. *Take it*, he thought. He would feel so much better if she were on solid ground next to him.

She placed her hand in his and it took everything he had not to close his fingers around hers and yank her out of the driver's seat—and into his arms. Instead, he tightened his grip on her ever so slightly and waited as she swung her feet out and stood. Her layers of dress settled around her—silk and satin and chiffon and all of those fabrics that his aunt Stella made dresses out of for her fashion line.

He didn't think this was one of Stella's dresses. Stella designed classic gowns that looked deceptively simple. This gown?

There wasn't anything simple about it. The bride looked a little bit like an overdone cupcake, with sparkles and sprinkles. The skirt was huge, with tiers and layers of ruffles and lace. How had she even fit behind the wheel in that monstrosity?

Her golden-brown hair was swept up into some elaborate confection that matched the dress, but at some point it had tilted off its bearings and now listed dangerously to the left. Pearls dripped off her ears and around her neck, but her ring finger was bare.

What did she look like when she wasn't dressed up like a bride? All he could see of her was her face and her bare shoulders. And her cleavage, which was kind of amazing—not that he was looking. His body tightened with awareness even as he tried to focus on her eyes. It didn't help, staring down into her face. Everything tugged him toward her with an instinctive pull that wasn't something he'd planned on, much less could control.

His first instinct had been right—she was gorgeous, he realized as she lifted her gaze to his. A sweetheart face, wide-set eyes that were the deepest shade of green he'd ever seen. The kind of eyes a man could get lost in, if he weren't careful.

Seth was careful. *Always.*

He knew exactly what happened when a man lost his head around a woman. So it was final—no losing himself in her eyes. Or any other of her body parts. She might be a goddess, but she was obviously having a very bad day and he wasn't about to do a single damn thing that would make it worse.

So he locked down this intense awareness of her.

She wasn't for him. All he could—and should—do was offer her a helping hand.

"Hi." He launched another smile, one that had broken a few hearts, in her direction. "I'm Seth," he repeated because he honestly wasn't sure if she'd processed it the first time.

"Kate," she replied in a shaky voice. She hadn't pulled her hand away from his yet. Seth took an experimental step back—away from the limo—and was pleased when she followed. "I…I'm not sure what my last name is right now. I don't think I got married. I'm pretty sure I left before that part."

In his time, Seth had seen people involved in accidents still walking and talking and functioning almost normally because they were in a complete state of shock. Big dudes thrown from choppers and yet walking around and cracking jokes with one of their arms hanging out of the socket. Later, when the adrenaline had worn off, they'd felt the pain. But not at first.

Was this what this was? Had she been hurt? He looked her over as surreptitiously as he could, but he didn't see any injuries—so this was just a mental shock, then.

"Kate," he said, his voice warm and friendly. "That's a pretty name. What would you like your last name to be?

"Burroughs," she said firmly. "I don't want to be Kate Caputo. I can't be."

Seth let out a careful breath. That answered that question.

He had found Roger's runaway bride.

Two

Kate felt like she was moving in a dream. Everything was blurry at the edges—but getting sharper. How much time had she lost? A couple of hours? A couple of days? The last thing she remembered was…

She had been sitting in the little room set aside for the bride to get ready, staring at the mirror and fighting back the rising tide of nausea. Because she was pregnant and she was supposed to be marrying Roger and—and—

"Easy," a strong, confident male voice said.

She looked down to see that her hand was being held by a man who was *not* Roger and they were *not* at the lodge she had especially selected for the beautiful sunset. She looked around, startling again. None of this looked familiar. Especially not him. She'd remember him. "I don't…"

The man's arm went around her waist and even

though she didn't know who he was or what was going on, she leaned into his touch. It felt right—comforting. *Safe.* Whoever he was, he was safe. Maybe it was all going to be okay. She could have cried with relief.

"I've got you," he said, sounding so very calm when there was nothing to be calm about. "It's all right."

She laughed at that. "No, it's not."

"It's not as bad as you think, I promise. Roger will get over this, and so will you."

She wasn't sure she believed that, but his arm tightened around her waist. Kate couldn't have said if she leaned on him or if he picked her up or how, exactly, she got to the bench. All she could focus on was this man—with dark hair and dark eyes and tanned skin, wearing a motorcycle jacket over what looked like a pair of suit trousers. He sat her down on the bench and then took a seat next to her. "You're cold," he said, picking up her hand and rubbing it between his.

"Am I?" Yes, now that she thought about it, she could feel a chill in the air. The way he spoke to her called to mind someone trying to capture a bird with a broken wing.

Then something he'd said sank in. "You...you know Roger?"

The man—Seth? Had he said that was his name? Seth nodded. "I lived with him in college." He stood and peeled off his leather jacket and even though Kate was having a terrible day, she was struck by how nicely this strange, sympathetic man filled out a button-up shirt. He even had on a tie—but somehow, it didn't look stuffy. It looked dangerous, almost. "Frankly, I think you're doing the right thing," he went on as he settled his jacket around her shoulders. "Assuming he hasn't seen the light and become a better human, that is."

"No, I don't think he has," she said slowly. His jacket was warm and soft, and she immediately felt a hundred times better. She had been cold for far too long. It was good to realize there could still be warmth in the world.

Then she realized what she'd said. "I didn't mean that," she quickly corrected, feeling the heat rise in her face. She blinked. Seth was staring at her with a level of focus that she wasn't used to. Roger certainly didn't listen to her like this.

But even thinking that made her feel terrible. She was supposed to be marrying Roger and she wasn't. She didn't have to add insult to injury by—well, by insulting him. "I mean, he's not a bad guy. He's a great catch." On paper.

On paper, Roger was handsome and educated, a successful small-business man. On paper he was perfect.

She couldn't marry a piece of paper.

She was supposed to be marrying a flesh-and-blood man who didn't love her. She was fairly certain about that.

"Even if he somehow magically turned into a great catch—which I doubt," Seth said, fishing something out of his pants pockets and sitting next to her, "that doesn't mean he's a great catch for you."

Her breath caught in her throat as he closed the distance between them. As he lifted her chin and stared into her eyes, Kate knew she should pull away. She couldn't let this stranger kiss her. That wasn't who she was.

She was Kate Burroughs. Only child to Joe and Kathleen Burroughs. A real estate agent who worked for her parents at Burroughs Realty—which was now Burroughs and Caputo Realty.

She didn't make waves. She did the right thing, always. She got good grades and sold houses. She didn't get unexpectedly pregnant. She most definitely didn't leave her groom at the altar, and under no circumstances could she be attracted to a man who wasn't her fiancé.

At least, that was who she'd been yesterday. It seemed pretty obvious that she wasn't that same woman today.

He had such nice eyes. A deep brown, soft and kind and yet still with an air of danger to him. He was dangerous to her, that much was clear, because he was going to kiss her and she was going let him and that was something the woman she'd been yesterday never would have allowed, much less entertained.

"It's going to be okay," he said softly. Then he touched her cheeks. With a handkerchief.

Kate hadn't realized she was crying until Seth dabbed at her cheeks.

When he was done, Seth pressed the handkerchief into her hand and leaned back. She wouldn't have thought it possible, but she got even more embarrassed. *Really, Kate? Really?* She wasn't even close to holding it together and she wanted to kiss this complete stranger?

She'd lost her mind. It was the only rational explanation.

She was relieved when Seth turned his gaze back out to the landscape. The sun was getting lower and the world was crimson and red. "Bolting on a wedding," he said slowly, "may not be cheap and it may not be easy. You may feel…"

"Like an idiot," she said bitterly.

"Confused," Seth corrected. "You're trying to talk

yourself into going back, but your instincts made you leave. And it's a good idea to listen to your instincts."

"That's easy for you to say. Your parents didn't shell out thousands of dollars on a fairy-tale wedding and invite hundreds of guests, all of whom are probably wondering where the hell you are and what's wrong with you."

He made a huffing noise, as if she'd said something idiotic instead of stating the facts of the matter. "Correct me if I'm wrong, but your parents aren't marrying Roger. None of the guests are, either. You can put on a good show for them because of the sunk cost of the reception, but at the end of the day you're the one who has to go home with him. For the rest of your life." She shuddered involuntarily. Seth put his arm around her shoulders and, weak as she was, she leaned into his chest. He went on, "If he hasn't changed, then you don't want to be stuck with him."

She sniffed. She knew she was crying again, but she was powerless to stop. Seth was warm and he smelled good and it was okay if she cried. "I don't. I really don't."

"Leaving him at the altar is cheaper and easier than getting a divorce," he said with finality. "Better to feel foolish now than to wake up tomorrow knowing you've made a huge mistake. Besides, if you realize you should have married him, you can still do that. If he really loves you, he'll understand."

That was what she needed to hear, because that was the truth that she felt in her heart. She was making a horrible mess for Roger and her parents, and she didn't want to humiliate him or their families and friends.

But at the end of the day, she was the one who had to

live with him. With herself. And she *knew* she wouldn't be able to make the marriage last the rest of her life. How far would she and Roger get before she couldn't take it anymore? A year? Three? The divorce—because there would be one. Seth was right—would be ugly. Especially because of the baby.

She lost track of time, quietly crying into Seth's shoulder and his handkerchief as the sun got lower in the sky. Purple joined the reds and oranges. It was truly a beautiful late-summer day. Perfect for a wedding.

And where was she? Marrying her Prince Charming? Celebrating? No.

She was sitting on a bench with a man who had been Roger's roommate. A man who understood that Roger was better on paper than he was in real life.

A man who didn't think she was insane for running away from her own wedding.

"I'm pregnant," she announced because she hadn't been able to tell anyone yet and that single fact—those two little words—had completely altered the trajectory of her life.

Seth stiffened and then said, "Oh?" in a far too casual voice.

"Roger is the father," she went on in a rush of words. "I'm not the kind of person who would cheat on my fiancé." Ironically, though, she was the kind of person who'd abandon her fiancé. What did that say about her? "It's his child and I should probably go back and marry him because we're going to have a baby. Together."

Seth didn't say anything, nor did he spring to his feet to lead her back to the limo. Back to her doom.

Wait—how did the limo get here? Had she stolen it?

And was it stealing if she'd rented it for the whole evening?

"Easy," Seth said again in that soothing voice of his. She could feel it in her chest, warm and comforting. "You might not believe this, but people have babies without being married all the time. It doesn't mean you've doomed your kid from the beginning."

"How can you say that?" And how was he reading her mind?

His arm tightened around her shoulders. "Because I've lived it, Kate. I won't let anything happen to you—I promise. Now," he went on even as she gasped at that honest promise—something she'd never heard cross Roger's lips, "do you remember where the limo came from?"

"Um…" She sat up and dabbed at her eyes again. The waterproof mascara was doing its best, but it was no match for this day and his handkerchief was paying the price. She tried to focus on the limo. "Stein, maybe?" It felt right—Stein Limo. That was a thing, she was pretty sure.

"Ron Stein? He's a great guy."

She stared at him in confusion. "You know the limo guy?" She didn't even know Seth's last name, but he knew Roger and now the limo guy. Was there anyone Seth didn't know?

"He rides," Seth said, as if that explained everything. "I'll see if I can make a call and let him know where his limo is. But I need you to stay right here, okay?"

"I don't know where you think I'd go. I'm not walking home." She wiggled her toes and realized she wasn't wearing her shoes. Where the hell were they?

But even the thought of going home made her wince.

She had a home—with Roger. They'd bought it last year, after finally setting a date for the wedding. It'd been a big sign of their commitment to each other.

No, that wasn't right. She didn't have a home with Roger. She owned part of a house. She shared a property with him. They split the bills right down the middle. They'd maintained separate bank accounts, even.

She'd lived with Roger, but it'd never felt like home.

"Promise me, Kate." His eyes were intense and serious. "You're not going anywhere without me."

"I promise." It wasn't like she'd sworn to love, honor or obey—but there was something to that promise that resonated in her mind.

Why could she make such a promise to this man she didn't know but couldn't to the one she did?

He gave her a satisfied nod of his head, leaned over and slid his hand inside his jacket, right over her left breast. She stiffened and he paused. "Just getting my phone," he said, purposefully not touching her. "Don't move." He stood and walked off to the side, far enough away that she couldn't hear what he was saying. But he turned back to her and gave her a little smile that set off butterflies in her stomach.

She ignored them and settled back on the bench, trying to get a handle on everything that happened.

It was a lot. But she'd had a good cry and Seth's jacket was warm and she felt better. Her mind was clearer and she could look past the next five minutes without having a panic attack.

She hoped.

She tried to rationally go over the facts. She was pregnant. She wasn't marrying Roger. She couldn't go back to the house she shared with him and she didn't think she could go to work on Monday. Her parents had sold half of Burroughs Realty to Roger in anticipation of the wedding. He owned it now.

She'd worked for Burroughs Realty her whole life, starting when they had her making copies and greeting clients as a little kid.

But they hadn't seen fit to give or even sell her part of the agency. Instead, they'd used it almost like a dowry, rewarding Roger for taking her off their hands.

Why hadn't she realized that before? She was a good real estate agent. She sold her market well. She was more than capable of being a full partner in the family business and running the office.

But it was Roger Caputo who was being rewarded with his name on the front door. Because why? Because he was marrying her?

She was their daughter. Wasn't she good enough on her own?

Oh, what would her parents say about all this? Especially once they found out she was pregnant? Her mother would try to be supportive—Kate hoped. The prospect of a grandbaby would be exciting, once the humiliation of a broken wedding passed.

But her father? Joe Burroughs was a dyed-in-the-wool workaholic who demanded perfection—or at the very least, that everything be done his way, and in his mind, those two things were the same.

She had to face the facts—her father might disown her for this, and if he did, he might forbid Mom from seeing Kate. Hadn't he already chosen Roger over her?

Just as she began to panic at the thought, Seth looked up at her again and smiled. It was a very nice smile, seemingly real and not the kind of expression one directed at a crazy person. He hadn't treated her like she was nuts at all, actually—even though the situation certainly did seem to warrant a little concern.

Instead of telling her she was insane to walk away from Roger, he'd agreed that tying herself to him was a bad idea. Anyone could have said the words, but Seth wasn't just saying them because she was having a really bad day. He was saying them because he actually *knew* Roger. Maybe not well, but he'd lived with Roger. He understood what that was like in a way that her friends and even her parents might not. Seth was speaking from a place of wisdom, and that counted for a lot.

It didn't make any sense that she felt safer with a strange man who rode a motorcycle she did with the man she'd been with for four years, but there it was. Seth didn't know her at all, but he was more concerned with her well-being than anyone else. After all, how long had she been here? At least half an hour, maybe much longer. And had anyone come looking for her? Roger? Her parents? Any of the wedding guests?

No. Seth had stumbled upon her, noticed something was wrong, and he was actively making sure she was okay. He'd given her his leather jacket and dried her tears.

He glanced at her again, another smile on his lips— which set off another round of butterflies in her stomach. Now that her mind had cleared, it was hard to miss the fact that her Good Samaritan was also intensely handsome.

No, no—she was not going to be the kind of woman who defined herself by her attractions to men. It was blatantly obvious that she couldn't run from Roger's arms straight into a stranger's. She was pregnant, for God's sake. Romance should be the last thing on her mind.

She needed a place to stay tonight. Maybe tomorrow. She needed a job that didn't involve Roger or her father. She needed…

A plan. She couldn't sit here at a scenic overlook forever.

Had she managed to bring anything important with her—her wallet, money, credit cards, her license—*anything* that could help her out tonight? She rather doubted it—she didn't even know where her shoes were.

Seth ended his call and began to walk back toward her, and Kate realized something.

She needed him.

Three

"Come on," Seth said, pulling her to her feet. She was not a tiny thing—she was only a few inches shorter than he was—but there was still something delicate about her. "I'm going to take you to a hotel." Her eyes widened in surprise but she didn't lean away from him. Not that that mattered. "And I'm going to leave you there," he added with a smile.

"Oh. Of course," she said, her cheeks blushing a soft pink. "Thank you. I don't think I can go back to the house I shared with Roger." She cleared her throat. "Are we taking the limo?"

"No. I talked to Ron—he's going to send someone out to pick it up. They did have cops looking for it but he's reported it not stolen. He's not going to press charges."

She blinked at him. "Is that because of you?"

The short answer was *yes*. Ron had been furious that

Kate had driven off with his limo—apparently it was his most expensive ride. He'd already fired the driver for dereliction of duties.

Ron's temper burned hot, but it always fizzled out quickly. Ron had been buddies with Billy Bolton for years and Seth had seen him in action plenty of times. He had to blow his top, and then he could be reasoned with.

Seth had waited until Ron finished blustering and then had convinced the man not to fire his driver—who had reasonably thought he'd had another hour before anyone would care about the whereabouts of the limo—and to inform the police that no theft had been committed.

But that's not what he told her. Instead, Seth said, "Ron's a great guy. He understood." Kate notched an eyebrow at him—clearly she wasn't buying that line.

But that was his story and he was sticking to it. Kate had already had a terrible day. The prospect of being arrested and booked for grand theft auto would only make everything a thousand times worse and he didn't want that, especially now that she'd calmed down.

He hadn't lied when he'd told her he'd keep her safe. This pull he felt to protect her—from the consequences of taking a limo, from Roger, from her thoughtless parents, from the harsh realities of life as a single mother—it wasn't something that made sense on a rational level. He didn't know her. He had no claim to her.

But by God, he wasn't going to cast her to the winds of fate and call it a day.

"Okay," she finally said, exhaling heavily. Which did some very interesting things to her chest. "Then what do we do next?"

"We ride." The color drained out of her cheeks. "Have you ever been on a motorcycle before?"

She shook her head, her tilting hair bobbing dangerously near her left ear. He reached up and tucked it back in place as best he could. He managed to do so without letting his fingers linger, so there was that.

"I've been riding for years," he assured her. "All you have to do is hold on. Can you do that?"

"I…" She looked down at her dress. "Um…"

She had a point. He eyed the confection suspiciously. The skirt was a full ball-gown style, layered with ruffles and lace. It spread out from Kate's waist in a circle that was easily five feet in diameter.

Ron had made it clear—Seth wasn't driving the limo. But Kate in that dress on the back of the chopper was a recipe for disaster. He could just imagine the wind getting underneath her skirts and blowing that dress up like a balloon.

"Is there any way to reduce the volume?" He tried to think back to what his aunt Stella had taught him about women's fashion. "An underskirt of some kind that we can remove?

Her face got redder. "I have on a structured petticoat. It's separate from the dress."

"Can you get it off?"

Kate's hands went to her waist. "I'm…I'm wearing a corset. I can't bend at the waist very well. And the skirt is tied on behind." She sounded unsure about the whole thing.

Seth mentally snorted to himself. Because if there was one thing a groom enjoyed on his wedding night, it was fighting through complicated layers of women's clothing. Petticoats and corsets—what was this, the 1800s? "How did you get into it?"

"I had help. My bridesmaids…"

Seth realized that if he wanted to get her on the bike anytime soon, he was going to have to play lady's maid. Which was not, he mentally reminded himself, the same as undressing her. At no point was he getting her naked.

No. Definitely not undressing a beautiful woman he wanted to pull into his arms and hold tight. Just… removing a few unnecessary layers of clothing. So that she could safely sit on his bike. That was all.

Trying to keep his mind focused on the task at hand, he eyed the bodice of her dress. "Do you need to take the corset off?" he asked reluctantly, because that seemed less like removing layers and more like just stripping her completely bare.

She shook her head quickly. "I was able to drive in it, apparently. If we can get the petticoat off, it should be fine."

Of all the things Seth thought he'd be doing today, falling to his knees in front of a runaway bride and lifting the hem of her skirt over the voluminous petticoat was not something that had made the top ten. Or even the top one hundred. But that's what he was doing. He lifted the satin of her dress, rising as he moved the fabric up.

There should have been nothing sensual about this, lifting her skirts. She was still completely dressed. The petticoat stood between him and her body. God only knew how many layers were built into it, because she was still shaped like an inverted top. So this should have been nothing.

But there was something erotic about it.

Focus, Bolton, he scolded himself. This was just an action born of necessity. He had to get her someplace safe, where people she knew could step up and take over. Taking care of a pregnant runaway bride was not in his skill set, and besides, it wasn't like he was attracted to her anyway.

Sure, she was beautiful—more so now that she'd calmed down. And yes, he was curious about what she looked like without the overdone hair, makeup and dress. And fine, he did feel a protective pull toward her. But that didn't add up to attraction any more than helping her adjust her outfit to ride on the bike was undressing her.

And that was final.

After a few snags—the petticoat was *huge*—he succeeded in getting the skirt up to her waist. He handed the bunched-up fabric to her and eyed the next layer. He could just see the bottom edge of her corset—white satin trimmed in baby blue. It appeared the waistband of the petticoat was underneath the corset.

This just kept getting better, because if he had to undo the corset, he'd have to remove the dress completely. He hoped it wouldn't come to that. If he were going to properly undress this woman, it sure as hell wouldn't be at a roadside pull-off.

He could see her chest rising and falling quickly. Did she feel the tension, too? Or was there something else?

He managed to pull his gaze away from her chest and found himself lost in her eyes. Her pupils were wide and dark and damn if she didn't look like a woman who was being undressed by a lover.

He put his hands on her waist, just below the bunched

fabric of her skirt. Her waist felt right under his hands, warm and soft—and a little hard, thanks to the corset.

Who was he to talk about instincts? Yeah, she shouldn't get married when her instincts told her to run. But his were telling him to pull her against his chest and tuck her into his arms and not let go. And fighting that instinct only got harder when she lifted her gaze to his because she took his breath away.

"Turn around," he told her because he needed not to get lost in her eyes.

He needed to keep a cool head here—among other body parts. She was not for him. Only a complete asshole would take advantage of a woman in this situation. Seth was many things, but he didn't think he was an asshole, complete or otherwise.

She turned in his arms, and Seth forced himself to step back and assess the situation. Luckily, the corset didn't ride as low in the back as it did in the front. He could see where the petticoat was tied—in a knot.

Of course it was knotted.

He was tempted to just cut the damn thing off her body, but then a shiver raced over her skin. Brandishing a blade wasn't the best way to keep her calm, so Seth gritted his teeth and got on with it. It felt like it took forever, but after only a minute or so, the knot finally gave. "Now what?" he asked as the waistband sagged down around her hips.

She didn't answer for a moment. "I had to step into it and they pulled it up because…" She swallowed. "Because it's so structured, it won't fall on its own. So I guess you'll have to push it down and I'll step out of it." Her voice shook.

Just for the ride, Seth repeated as he grabbed the

waistband of the petticoat and worked it over her hips. *Structured* must mean *able to stand upright on its own*, because the damned fabric had no give in it at all. What kind of fresh hell was this, anyway?

The petticoat slipped over her skin, and he had to bite back his groan. He barely knew this woman and he wasn't even sure he liked her. But as he revealed the frilly lace of the white thong and the bare cheeks of her bottom, *liking* had nothing to do with it. His mouth went dry and his hands started to shake.

His instincts—they were pushing him past protective and into raw lust. He was strong, but how strong did one man have to be? Because he wasn't sure he could handle the way that thong left her bottom completely exposed.

Then it only got worse as he wrestled the petticoat down and revealed inch by creamy inch of her legs and bare skin. Why couldn't she be wearing those support-ive bike shorts that some women wore instead of this scrap of lace? Why couldn't she be wearing a simpler outfit? Why couldn't she be someone who didn't inspire this reaction in him?

It only got worse when he hit the top of her thigh-high stockings and the blue garter on her right leg. Of course it matched the blue trim on her corset.

Roger, Seth concluded, was an idiot to let this woman go. Because Seth was pretty sure that he was going to have fantasies about this moment for the rest of his natural life.

He struggled not to touch her skin—but his hands shook even harder with the effort of it. Although he had to fight all that "structure" for every damned inch, he managed to get the petticoat pushed down to the ground, which meant that he was at eye level with her bottom. And it was perhaps one of the nicer bottoms he had ever seen. Firm and rounded and begging to be touched.

Except it wasn't. This was not a seduction. This was an action born of necessity. He would not touch her. She'd already had a bad day, and being groped by a biker wouldn't make anything better.

"Now what?" His voice cracked with the strain of trying to sound normal. "Do you just step out?" That was when he realized she didn't have on shoes. They were standing on gravel. Had she been missing her shoes the entire time?

"I...I don't want to lose my balance," she said in a strangled-sounding voice. Before Seth could process what she meant by that, she turned. Which was good due to the fact that he was no longer staring at her ass.

But now he was staring at her front. The thin lace of her virginal white thong covered the vee of her sex and everything about Seth came to a screeching halt. His blood, his breath—nothing worked. He couldn't even blink as he stared at her body.

It only got worse when she placed one hand on his shoulder for balance. Seth squeezed his eyes shut because there was no point in looking if he couldn't have her, and he *couldn't* have her. Offering anything beyond assistance would be a mistake. She'd run away from a wedding today. She was pregnant with another man's baby. None of her was for him.

Even though his eyes were closed, the scent of her body surrounded him, torturing him. It wasn't the scent of arousal, but there was no missing the sweet notes of flowers—maybe lilacs, and a hint of vanilla that had been buried underneath the layers. Her smell reached out and stroked him, making him shake with need.

She stepped out of the petticoat and—thankfully—let go of the skirt. It fell, covering her legs and hiding that lacy thong and those white thigh-highs and that garter belt from his eyes. Seth gave himself another few moments to make sure he had himself under control.

Then she let out a little cry and stumbled. He moved without thinking, catching her before she fell. His arms folded around her body and finally, he was able to pull him to her.

But despite his awareness of her body—and the fact that her arms went around his neck so that he could feel her breasts pressing against his chest—he didn't miss the way she shivered or how her breathing was ragged.

"Easy," he said, coming to his feet with her in his arms.

"I stepped on a rock," she said, her voice wavering. She sounded like she was on the verge of tears again, and that hurt him in a way he hadn't expected.

He wanted to make sure she didn't hurt. He'd wanted that from the very beginning. But now, it felt more personal.

He didn't understand this strange drive to take care of her. He could've called her a ride. Surely someone could've come to get her. Rapid City had taxis, and for a price they could've made it out this far.

But he hadn't. He hadn't done anything except hold her close and make sure she was okay.

He didn't want to think too much about why.

He carried her over to his bike and sat her on the back. He gave thanks that his father had built this prototype with the passenger seat behind the driver's seat.

Part of Billy Bolton's rigorous testing was to make sure that he took Seth's mom, Jenny, out for rides with him. Billy claimed that sometimes, the additional weight of a passenger would reveal design flaws that needed to be tweaked. Because Seth didn't want to consider any other options about what happened when his parents went out riding, he accepted that explanation at face value.

"I'll put the petticoat in the car and then we'll go, okay?" he said. "But you're going to have to straddle the bike. See if you can figure that out with your skirts." He waved a hand over her dress and hoped like hell he wouldn't have to take the whole thing off to get her corset removed.

But even as he thought that, his brain decided it would be a really great idea. He would kill to see Kate Burroughs in nothing but a corset and some stockings and a garter. Splayed out on the bed, a package that Seth was almost done unwrapping.

He slammed the brakes on that line of thought. *Nope.* She had too many bags to carry, and he was a single twenty-five-year-old man. He had no interest in tangling with someone whose personal life was as messy as Kate Burroughs's was. No matter how good she looked, no matter how sweet she smelled, no matter how much she'd clung to his neck.

No matter how right she'd felt in his arms.

She nodded and he went back to get the petticoat. It was all dirty with rocks and bits of grass stuck in it. He shoved it into the back of the limo and glanced around, hoping against hope that there would be a purse with a wallet, but nothing. There was some champagne that was probably warm, though. But he didn't think that'd help anything right now.

He locked the limo and left the keys on the ground on the inside of the front driver's-side wheel, where Stein had told him to leave them. True dark was settling now and it was going to be a long, cold ride back to Rapid City. It wouldn't be so bad if he had his jacket, but he couldn't let her freeze to death behind him.

The other logistical problem was that he only had one helmet. He had no idea if it would fit over her hair.

He went back to the bike and picked up the helmet. "Let's see if this works," he said. At the very least, she had managed to straddle the bike. The skirt had hiked up over her calves, and her legs were going to be cold by the time they got out of the hills, but there was no way he could risk having her fall off if she was riding side-saddle. Maybe if she pressed herself against him, his body could take the worst of the wind. He'd be a Popsicle by the time they made town, but he'd take it for her.

But even that noble sentiment was almost completely overridden by the image of her arms around his waist, her chest pressed to his back, her legs tucked behind his. Of that lacy little thong and the corset.

Of a wedding night that ended differently.

He pulled at the collar of his shirt. Yeah, maybe he wouldn't freeze.

She looked up at him, her eyes wide. "I can't thank you enough, Seth," she said, her voice soft. "I'm having a really bad day, but you're making it better."

If she were anyone else, he'd cup her cheek and stroke her skin with his thumb. He'd tilt her head back and brush his lips over hers. He'd offer comfort in a completely different way.

But she wasn't anyone else. She was Roger's pregnant runaway bride. So instead of kissing her, he settled the helmet over her hair. It didn't work. He pulled it off. "Let me see what I can do here." She tilted her head so he could get at the elaborate updo—it probably had some sort of name, but he didn't have any idea about women's hair. He could see the pins and clips—sparkly stuff in her hair. And hairspray. Lots of hairspray. He began pulling them out and shoving them into his pants pocket. What would her hair feel like without all this crap in it? Soft and silky—the kind of hair he could bury his hands in.

He really had to get a grip. The whole mass of hair sagged and then fell. It looked awkward and painful, but he was sure he could fit the helmet on now. "There."

She looked back at him as he settled the helmet on her head and strapped it under her chin. She looked worried. "This will be fun," he promised. Cold, but fun. "Just hold on to me, okay?"

She nodded. Seth took his seat and fired up the engine. It rumbled beneath him. He loved this part of riding. Bringing the machine to life and knowing that a journey was ahead of him.

After a moment's hesitation, Kate's arms came around his waist. His brain chose that exact moment to wonder—when was the last time he'd had a woman on the back of a motorcycle?

Of course he'd ridden with women before. That was one of the reasons to ride a bike—women loved a bad boy, and Seth was more than happy to help them act out their fantasies. Motorcycles were good seduction and he was a red-blooded American man. He wasn't above doing a little seducing.

But there was something different about this—about Kate. This wasn't a seduction, leaving aside the fact that he knew what her thong looked like. This was something else, and he couldn't put a name to it.

Then he felt more than heard her sigh against the back of his neck as the helmet banged his shoulder. He winced but didn't flinch as she settled her cheek against his back, her arms tightening around him even more. Her body relaxed into his. Which was good. Great. Wonderful. The tighter she held on, the safer this ride would be.

Except his body was anything but relaxed. He was rock hard and she'd know it if her grip slipped south in any way.

He needed to get her to a hotel and then he needed to get on his way. He had a future as a partner of Crazy Horse Choppers. He had plans for the business. He had motorcycles to sell.

None of those things involved a pregnant runaway bride.

He rolled away from the scenic overlook and hit the road back to Rapid City.

Kate Burroughs wasn't in his plans. After today, he wasn't going to see her or her stockings ever again.

That was final.

Four

"Good morning, Katie," Harold Zanger said, strolling into Zanger Realty with a smile on his face and a bow tie around his neck. "It's a zinger of a day at Zanger, isn't it?"

As cheesy as the line was—and it had been cheesy every single day for the last month and a half—Kate still smiled. She smiled every day now. "It is indeed, Harold," she said.

Harold Zanger was one of her father's oldest friends. They'd been playing poker together for a good forty years—longer than Kate had been alive. Harold was almost an uncle to her.

Kate had not gone back to Burroughs and Caputo Realty. She just couldn't—especially when her parents had made it clear that splitting Roger off from the business was going to be quite complicated, which was one way to say that her father wasn't going to do it because he was beyond furious with her.

So it had been Kate to decide that, rather than grovel before her father and Roger, she'd start over. She was the one who put distance between them.

It had hurt more than she wanted it to, to be honest. Although she'd known it wasn't likely, she'd wanted her parents to put her first. She'd wanted them to take her side and tell her it'd all work out. She'd wanted her mom to get excited about the pregnancy.

She'd wanted the impossible. Oh, Mom was excited—to the extent that she'd underlined the word *excited* three times in the congratulations card she'd sent. Other than that, there'd been no discussion of pregnancies, no trips down memory lane, no planning for the baby's room.

There hadn't been anything, really, since Kate had walked out of their house and driven back to the hotel where she'd been staying since Seth had dropped her off and paid for three nights.

And the hell of it was, it wasn't like they had put Roger first. No, Joe and Kathleen Burroughs had done what they always did—they'd put their business first. Burroughs Realty—Burroughs and Caputo Realty now—had always been the most important thing. Her father hadn't disowned her outright, but it was clear that, for the time being, there was no point in pursuing a family relationship. Joe Burroughs was a workaholic and Kathleen refused to go against her husband's wishes.

No, the business came first, and Roger was now part owner of the business, which meant that Roger came first. So Kate had left because she hadn't wanted to make things difficult for her mother.

Harold Zanger, gregarious and happy, had offered her a job. Kate strongly suspected it had put a strain on his friendship with Joe Burroughs, but Harold insisted everything was fine. Of course, he was an eternal optimist, so perhaps everything was. Harold had given her a desk and a blazer and some business cards and told her to "get out there and sell some houses, sweetheart."

If anyone else had called Kate *sweetheart*, she would've walked, but Harold had been calling her sweetheart since she was old enough to crawl—probably even before that.

So here she was. Ready to get out there and sell some houses for Zanger Realty.

"Today's the day," Harold said, snapping the suspenders underneath his Zanger Realty blazer, which was a delightful shade of goldenrod. "Something big is going to happen today, Katie my girl. I can feel it."

There was comfort in familiarity and Harold said this to her every morning. She hadn't believed it at first—she still didn't really believe it—but Harold's optimism was infectious.

"Today's the day," she agreed.

"Your big sale," Harold all but crowed, "is going to walk through that door. I just know it."

"I'm sure it will," she said with an indulgent smile. Really, it was sweet that Harold believed what he said, because that was just the kind of man he was and had always been. If opposites attract, then that held true for friendships, too. Joe Burroughs had been a pessimist, convinced that tomorrow the bottom would fall out and the world would end and so he'd better sell a house today so that his family would have something to live on. Disaster was always lurking right around the corner for Joe Burroughs, so he had to miss his daughter's concerts and plays because there was work to be done.

Harold was the opposite. Today was a good day. Tomorrow would be even better. It would all work out in Harold's world, and Kate would be lying to herself if she said she didn't need that in her life right now.

Because she was three months pregnant. She'd sold exactly two houses—but they hadn't been big sales. She'd earned enough on commission to rent a two-bedroom apartment and buy some secondhand furniture. But she had to sell a lot of houses in the next six months if she wanted to be able to take time off when she had her baby.

Roger would pay child support. Just because he didn't love her and she didn't love him didn't mean that he would leave her out to dry. Roger wasn't a bad guy, really.

But when they had sat down face-to-face and confronted the aftermath of their relationship and the baby that would always tie them together, it had been clear—he'd been relieved that she'd walked away. And he hadn't even tried to hide it. He'd gone on their honeymoon trip to Hawaii without her and he hadn't missed her at all.

Even more than that, Roger had been relieved when her father had not asked him to give up his stake in the real estate business. Which really had Kate wondering—had he been marrying her because of her or for the business?

She knew the answer—the business—but she couldn't think about that.

If she ever had another wedding, she would be damned sure she was marrying someone who wanted her. Not her family's business. Not her name.

Her. Kate Burroughs. Future single mom and semi-professional hot mess.

Aside from child support, Roger made something else clear—they were done. He wasn't going to be an active part of raising his child. It was painful, it really was. But at the same time, it was also a relief. She wouldn't have to worry about navigating around Roger at the same school plays and concerts that her own father had skipped. She wouldn't have to negotiate who would get the baby for Christmas and birthdays. It would be simpler without Roger.

It would be harder—she was under no illusions that being the single mother of a newborn wouldn't be the hardest thing she'd ever done. But she only had to negotiate with herself.

She was on her own. For the first time in her life, she didn't have to answer to anyone. Not her father, not Roger, not her mother. There was something freeing about that. Terrifying, but freeing.

Harold went back to his office and Kate turned to her listings. She had been a real estate agent for years, so it wasn't like she was learning on the job. She knew what to do. She had grown up at Burroughs Realty, copying things for her parents and then going with them when they looked at houses. She'd learned how to stage a house when she was in high school. Her parents had paid her for her help, although not a lot.

She could sell a home in her sleep. But she needed buyers and sellers. She needed someone to walk through that door and instead of asking for Harold, to ask for

Kate. That was what she'd had at Burroughs Realty. She had been a Burroughs, and any Burroughs would do for some people. The name was the important thing.

As her thoughts often did when she was faced with the weight of her future, she imagined that one person in particular walking through the door—a tall, dark, mysterious biker. A man who looked dangerous and yet treated her as if she were worth protecting.

Seth Bolton.

She had not seen him since he had taken her to a local hotel and shaken her hand in the lobby. He hadn't even suggested that he come up to the room and make sure she got settled. He was too good a guy for that.

That had to be why she couldn't stop thinking about him. It had felt like…like there was unfinished business between them. Which was ridiculous. They didn't have any business together to begin with. She'd had the worst day of her life and he'd taken pity on her. That was all there was—a Good Samaritan doing a kind deed for a woman having a really terrible day. Because there was no way a man like that was single or available. And even if he were—why would he be interested in her? She had not made the best of first impressions.

Looking back at what had happened over six weeks ago, she could see with a little objective distance that she had been in a state of complete and total shock. Discovering she was pregnant had left her stunned. Deciding she couldn't marry Roger had been a realization that sent her reeling. Each shock mounted upon the next. She still didn't remember stealing the limo, but at least she hadn't been arrested. Whatever Seth had done or said to the limo owner had worked. The cops hadn't gotten involved, and she was beyond grateful for that. He had helped her see that her reasons for running were valid, made sure she was okay and let her cry it out.

But gratitude wasn't the only reason she kept thinking about him. There'd been the way he'd untied her petticoat and slid it down her legs. And the way she'd wrapped her arms around his waist and leaned into him on the long, cold ride back to Rapid City. Hell, even just the way his jacket had smelled—leather and something lighter, maybe sandalwood. He'd smelled good.

She was not fantasizing about the man. Oh, sure, he drifted through her dreams every so often, but that didn't mean she was fantasizing about him, specifically.

It was the fact that he had taken care of her. And she had needed to be taken care of. That was all.

She didn't need to be coddled anymore. She'd gotten back on her feet. Her parents and Roger had handled the entire disaster with a surprising amount of good humor—for them, anyway. But that didn't change the fact that, moving forward, she needed to sell a house. A lot of houses. Heck, even one big sale would get her through the winter.

While she was wishing for the impossible, she might as well ask for a pony. Sadly, Santa had never delivered on that one, either.

As she mused, she worked on assembling a potential list of houses. A family from out of town had called and said that the husband might be relocating to Rapid City. Nothing was definite yet, but there was a good chance that they'd move and if so, Kate was going to be the one to sell them a house. Harold had gifted her with this opportunity, rather than keep it for himself.

The Murray family had given her their standard list of requirements—three bedrooms, two baths, a fenced backyard, a two-car garage. She was putting together a list of potential homes and praying that Mr. Murray decided to take a job in Rapid City when the door jingled.

On reflex, Kate said, "It's a zinger of a day at Zanger. Can I help you?"

Then she looked up at the same moment a hearty chuckle reached her ears. There was something familiar about that chuckle, warm and comforting.

She froze. There was something familiar about the man standing in the entryway. Tall, dark. Black hair, dark eyes—that motorcycle jacket settled over his shoulders like a second skin.

And that smile. She didn't remember everything from her wedding day. But that smile? She'd been dreaming about that smile for a month. She was helpless to *stop* dreaming about it.

It was entirely possible, she decided as she stared at him, that she was still asleep because her fantasy had just walked into her office and into her life, hotter than ever. This was the man who'd talked her off the ledge. Who'd supported her when she'd admitted that marrying Roger would've been the biggest mistake of her life.

Who'd practically stripped her bare at a roadside overlook.

"Kate," he said, his voice stroking over her name in a way that made her toes curl. "I was hoping I'd find you."

Okay, that did it. She was definitely dreaming. "Seth? What are you doing here?"

If she were dreaming, the answer would be *I have come to sweep you off your feet, my darling. Let me take you away from all of this and solve all your problems.*

"I looked you up."

She blinked. "You did? Why?"

"I wanted to see how you were doing." He took another step into the office. "How are you doing?"

Her breath caught in her throat. As odd as it seemed, not many people asked that question. The fallout from leaving Roger at the altar had shown her who her true friends were—and the number was few and far between. Really, her mother was the only one who asked that question and was actually interested in the answer.

Except for Seth Bolton, a stranger who had seen her at her lowest moment. Instead of running, he'd stood by her side. He'd taken care of her. He'd made everything better.

Was it any wonder she'd been dreaming of him nearly every night?

This wasn't possible. She could not be watching Seth walk into her office, that sexy smile on his face, asking about how she was. It simply wasn't possible.

"I...I'm fine," she told him. "I mean, I'm all right."

"Good." His smile deepened and she was stunned to realize that he had dimples. What a difference. That made him hot and sweet and more than everything she dreamed of. "I meant to check in on you earlier, but I had some business to deal with first."

She lifted her eyebrows at that. Was he serious? She was nothing to him, other than a strange afternoon that had probably become an amusing anecdote. *Did I ever tell you about the time I found a runaway bride in the middle of the Black Hills?*

She would expect that if he remembered her at all, he'd remember the crazy woman who stole a limo and refused to marry the father of her child. Nobody should've found her desirable. Memorable, maybe. Definitely not someone worth worrying about.

"Well, as you can see, everything's okay." That was a gross generalization. She was exhausted and hormonal and worried sick about how she was going to make everything work out.

But she wasn't the same lost woman he'd found by the side of the road, either. She held her head high and faced every challenge she met with open eyes. She had a job and a purpose. She didn't need to be coddled anymore.

Not even by someone as attractive as Seth Bolton. Was it possible that he was even more gorgeous now? He took another step closer and she swore she could feel the tension between them hum, like he'd plucked the string of a violin.

The jacket was the same, but he had on a gray T-shirt with some sort of logo on it and a pair of well-worn jeans that were black. They hung low on his hips and she realized she was staring at the vee of his waist as if she'd never noticed that part of a man before.

She jerked her gaze back up, her cheeks hot. His lips quirked into a smile that did things to her. Things she hadn't felt in over a month.

No, she scolded herself. It was one thing to fantasize about a great guy she'd never have to face again. It was a completely different affair to lust after a flesh-and-blood man standing in a real estate office.

Why was he standing in a real estate office? She cleared her throat and tried to relocate her lost sense of professionalism. "Was there something I could help you with?" Or had he just come here to make sure she hadn't completely fallen apart? She hoped not. She didn't want him to think of her as this pitiful creature who couldn't function.

That string of tension that had been humming between them tightened as his eyes darkened. His gaze swept over her face, her body. Was he checking her out? Or just checking for signs of her pregnancy? It was still pretty early. Her clothes still mostly fit, although she'd already gone up a cup size in bras.

"Actually, there is," he said. "As crazy as it sounds, I'm settling down."

Oh. That sounded like…like he was setting up house with a girlfriend. Or a wife. Well. So much for that fantasy. She was not about to poach anyone's man. At least now he'd stay safely in her dreams and she wouldn't make a fool of herself over him.

She stood from the desk, straightening her tacky Zanger jacket. "I can handle all your needs. Your *real estate* needs," she added, her face burning.

Well. So much for not making a fool of herself over him.

For a second, she wished she were someone different—someone more together and charming and…

Well, someone who wasn't pregnant and coming out of a long-term relationship.

He didn't laugh. Or even snort. Instead, something in his eyes changed—deepened—and warmth spread through her body. She recognized that warmth—*desire*. It was like running into an old friend from high school she hadn't seen in a few years. She hadn't realized how much she'd missed it—until here it was.

When was the last time she had felt desire? At one point she was sure she had enjoyed sleeping with Roger, but she couldn't remember when it stopped being fun and started being routine. It hadn't been bad. It just hadn't been good.

Kind of like Roger himself.

Seth was still smiling. It would be great if she could get her act together today. Within the hour, even though that was probably too much to ask.

Still, she had to give it a try. "What sort of properties are you looking for? Because a home is very different from a condo." There. That was a viable thing to say that didn't make her sound like an idiot.

And if she wasn't making any sense, she was blaming that on the pregnancy, which went right back to Roger. So if she was flabbergasted before Seth for the second time in a few short weeks, it would be entirely Roger's fault.

She motioned for Seth to sit because standing was getting more awkward by the second. Seth took the chair in front of her desk and crossed one of his legs, bringing his heavy leather boots into view. Up closer, Kate could see that the T-shirt was for Crazy Horse Choppers, which fit with the leather jacket and the motorcycle.

In other words, he looked like a badass biker dude.

Except for those dangerous dimples. Because it took everything hard about him and made it something else. Something that had her pulse pounding in her veins, heating her from the inside out. "Tell me what you're looking for."

He held her gaze for a beat too long before he spoke. "Well, I've been back in Rapid City for about a month and a half."

Wait—did that mean he'd been living somewhere else until...until when? Had he come back for the wedding that wasn't? "Where were you before?"

"I'm not sure if you recognize my name or not but my family owns Crazy Horse Choppers."

"Um…no? I'm sorry," she quickly added. "I mean, of course I've heard of Crazy Horse Choppers."

They were one of Rapid City's most famous local businesses, started twenty or thirty years ago by a local boy made good and now run by his three sons, whose names hadn't ever really registered for Kate. She thought there'd been a reality show featuring the three unruly biker brothers a number of years ago. Kate had been in high school when it'd been on the air—and it hadn't been interesting to her then.

Clearly, she'd underestimated the power of a bad boy in a leather jacket.

She shook her head, trying to push that thought away. She was definitely going to blame that line of thinking on the pregnancy hormones. "I just didn't make the connection between you and the company," she explained. "I'm not up-to-date on motorcycles. I'd never even been on one until…"

Until he'd stripped her petticoat off her and set her on the back of his bike and she'd wrapped her arms around his waist and held on to him.

She wouldn't have thought it possible, but her face got even hotter.

"I lived in LA for a year while managing the Crazy Horse showroom we operate there," Seth said, ignoring her red face. "My father and my uncles recently made me partner in the company, so I'm thinking I need to set up a permanent base."

She eyed him. She had no idea how old Seth was, but he seemed young to be a partner in such a successful company. Was that just because it was the family business and he was family? Or was he really good at what he did?

Of course it was because he was good at what he did. He'd talked her down from the ledge, hadn't he? The man could probably sell motorcycles to anyone.

"'Permanent base'? That's not how most people describe buying a house." In fact, it sounded more like he was setting up a strategic military outpost or something.

He shrugged. "My uncle Bobby has wild expansion plans. He expects me to travel and represent the brand. But the company is based here, so I need to maintain a residence. I anticipate that I'll only be in Rapid City maybe half the year. The other thing—"

"The other thing?" A house would be a great sale. As partner to a successful and growing business, he'd want something that spoke of his power and, one assumed, wealth. Or at the very least, a condo with all the bells and whistles.

"I'm in the planning phase for a new project for Crazy Horse," he went on, ignoring her interruption. "We're going to need an industrial space for a museum."

Her mouth fell open. A house was terrific. A house *and* an industrial space?

She'd be able to live off that commission for months. She could take time off to be with her baby without having to worry about money.

Seth Bolton was her guardian angel. It was really that simple.

He was staring at her expectantly. "Kate? You okay?"

"What? Oh. Yes. Yes! I'm just…a museum?"

That grin made it plenty clear that she wasn't fooling him. "My granddad and my dad have been building choppers for thirty years. My dad's kept one of everything he's ever built, including a lot of prototypes that never saw production. He's got close to four hundred motorcycles stored in the original Crazy Horse factory. I think we can build the brand loyalty if we take those bikes out of storage and put them on display. Harley-Davidson did something similar and they've had a great response."

"Wow…" she said, which was lame and stupid but really, how was she supposed to react here? Seth Bolton was hot, kind, supportive…hot—and now also an amazing salesman and a whip-smart business owner?

Her fantasies weren't this good. They just weren't. If he also loved babies and puppies and was single, then she'd know for certain that she was having the best dream of her life.

Nothing about this made the least bit of sense. Not only was the man of her dreams—literally—sitting in front of her, suddenly in the market for a great deal of real estate, the commissions of which could carry her through the next several months, but he was part of Rapid City's most famous local family.

Underneath the desk, she pinched her leg. But nothing changed. Seth was still sitting in front of her, dimples in full force, ready to discuss all his real estate needs while also giving her those searing looks.

She was in trouble. The very best kind of trouble.

Five

One thing was clear, Seth realized as he sat across from Kate while she called up listings to give him an idea of what was on the market.

He should have checked on her sooner.

He remembered a hot woman. Okay, that had been more her body than her face because she'd had a very bad day and had looked like hell. But it was hard to forget skimming that petticoat down her legs, revealing her gorgeous ass in that little scrap of fabric—not to mention the stockings and garter.

He shifted in his seat. The woman sitting across from him in a tacky yellow blazer with Zanger embroidered on the chest wasn't *hot*.

Kate Burroughs was beautiful.

Without the false eyelashes and lopsided hair—and without the lost look in her eyes—Kate was simply stunning. Even more so because today, while it was clear that she was shocked to see him, she wasn't in a state of shock. And what a difference that made.

He might be imagining things, but she even seemed happy to see him. Surprised, sure. Excited about the business he was throwing her way, yes. But Seth saw the way she looked at him—especially the way her whole face had softened when he'd asked how she was doing.

He should've come sooner. But he'd had to represent Crazy Horse Choppers at two trade shows and Julie's soccer season had started, and although it wasn't good for his image as a tough biker, Seth was the kind of guy who went to his baby sister's games and cheered her on from the sidelines. Then there'd been a pow-wow on the reservation and career day at the school where his mom taught and moving out of his folks' house into the hotel and putting his stuff in storage and…life happened.

But he hadn't forgotten Kate Burroughs. That wasn't possible, not after their memorable introduction. But it wasn't until he'd come to the belated realization that at the age of twenty-five, he couldn't continue to live in a hotel that he had decided to seek her out.

It'd taken a lot of digging. She had apparently been the Burroughs in Burroughs and Caputo Realty for some years. Seth wasn't entirely sure what the deal was, since she was now at Zanger Realty and Roger was still at Burroughs and Caputo Realty. The whole situation was messy and Seth was not interested in messy.

Which did not explain why he was currently sitting across from the messiest woman he'd ever met.

That wasn't fair, though. She'd been a mess the day of her failed wedding, yeah. But the woman before him now? If he hadn't known she was pregnant, he never would've guessed. She looked amazing. Her golden-brown hair was free of the shellacked mass of curls that had overwhelmed her delicate features. Her hair was away from her face, but the rest of it fell in gentle waves down her back. Her eyes were the same star-tlingly bright green he remembered and today, they were clear and hopeful instead of lost and afraid. With-out the heavy layer of makeup, he felt like he was see-ing her for the first time.

Seth had seen a lot of attractive women in his time. Los Angeles was overflowing with them. But that was hotness for public display and public consumption.

Kate was more of a quiet beauty. There was just something about her.

Which was the only possible explanation as to why he was here. He couldn't stop thinking about that something and it went way beyond thongs and gar-ter belts.

"So if you'll be traveling a lot, a condo would prob-ably be the best property for you. The exterior main-tenance is…" Seth scowled at her. Anyone else would have been terrified. But Kate merely lifted her eyebrows and…smiled? "No?"

"Don't condos—by definition—have other people living in close proximity?"

She tilted her head to one side, studying him. "Yes. It's not a stand-alone building. You would have neigh-bors with whom you'd share walls."

He shook his head. "No. LA was full of people who talked all the time because they were afraid if they didn't, no one would notice how important they were. I couldn't stand it." Among other things. He'd hoped that getting the hell out of South Dakota would be the answer for this restlessness.

It hadn't been. Traveling the world and selling motorcycles was probably the cure for what ailed him.

Yet here he was, buying a damned house while planning on barely living in it. He went on, "I want peace and quiet. No neighbors."

"You're talking to me," she pointed out, pinning him to his chair with her gaze.

"You're different," he said and the funny thing was, it wasn't a line he was feeding her. He meant it. He couldn't have said why, but she was. "So I need a house."

"With enough land to protect you from nosy neighbors. What else do you need? I'm assuming a garage is important—or room to build your own?"

He had to hand it to her as she grilled him on the number of bathrooms and bedrooms he required or if he wanted a finished basement or would he consider building from scratch—the woman knew what she was doing. He'd had some vague notion of a house that he now realized didn't look all that different from his parents' home.

But his parents' home was built for a family. And Billy's bikes, but it'd been sprawling enough to house the fourteen-year-old boy Seth had been when Billy had married Jenny Wawausuck and adopted Seth and big enough to hold them all when Julie had been born the next year.

It'd been a family home. And that was not what Seth wanted, as he had no plans to start a family anytime soon. Not even by accident. He was careful.

So he wasn't settling down. Not even a possibility. Billy Bolton—hell, all the Bolton men—might be dyed-in-the-wool family men, but Seth was a Bolton in name only.

Still, he needed a place to keep his stuff and the freedom to come and go—and have guests over—without his parents keeping tabs on him.

He looked at the photos of the four or five houses she'd pulled up, but nothing jumped out at him. "I need to walk through them," he said.

"Absolutely," she agreed. "Pictures can tell us a lot, but they can't give you a real sense of how the house will work for you. I'll need to schedule tours, if that's all right. Only a few of these houses are empty. Unless you are looking to buy today?"

Seth snorted. "This isn't a snap decision. I want to make sure I find the right place. Even if I don't live there full-time, I still want it to be home." He didn't know if that was possible or not, but at the very least, he wanted something he could be proud of.

Besides, owning and caring for his own home would just further prove to his father and his uncles that they'd made the right decision in making Seth a partner in Crazy Horse Choppers, and he couldn't let the Bolton men down. Not after everything they'd done for him.

His parents hadn't been huge fans of Seth relocating to a hotel and, aside from room service, neither was Seth. But as much as he loved his family, he hadn't been able to move back in with them after a year in LA. So if he had to pay for a hotel, then he paid for the hotel. He had the money to spare.

Kate nodded eagerly. "And if none of these houses are right, there are always more houses coming on the market. Sometimes we get notice before properties are officially listed—as long as you've got the time, the right house for you is out there."

She made it sound like it was only a matter of patience. Seth was not always the most patient of people. His dad said it was because he was still young and stupid—although Seth didn't feel particularly young or particularly stupid.

Seth was afraid it was something else. Billy was a good father—but it wasn't his blood that ran through Seth's veins. What if this restlessness wasn't just youth?

What if it was something he'd inherited from his birth father, the sperm donor?

Seth pushed that question away. He didn't like to compare himself to the man who'd abandoned Jenny Wawausuck when she'd been pregnant, never to show his face again. Seth was a Bolton now. The past didn't matter. Only the future.

A future where he owned a sizable chunk of a family business as well as his own home. "That's fine. Saturday? We can make a day of it. Unless you have other plans?"

Because he had no idea. It was a fair assumption that, since she was no longer at the office where Roger worked and—he glanced down at her hand—she wasn't wearing any ring, she wasn't actively involved with anyone. Kate didn't strike him as the kind who rebounded indiscriminately.

But that didn't mean she might not have something to do on a Saturday.

Kate smiled and damn if Seth wasn't dazzled by it. "Saturday would be perfect. Now tell me about this museum you're planning. Does it need to be close to the production facility? Do you want to build to suit or adapt a preexisting space? Do you have a handle on how much square footage you're looking at?"

Seth took a deep breath. The museum was his idea—he'd toured the Harley-Davidson museum in Milwaukee a while back and had been damned impressed. He didn't want to replicate that facility, because the Crazy Horse collection was vastly different from the Harley collection.

Seth still remembered the first time Billy had taken him to see all the choppers that he'd built. Seth had been like a kid in a candy store. The original choppers were impressive, but what had blown his teenaged mind had been the wild prototypes Billy had created over the years.

That was what he wanted to capture—that feeling of shock and awe that only a Crazy Horse chopper could inspire. And he wanted to capitalize on that experience. The motorcycle business had its ups and downs and having a secondary stream of income—or even tertiary stream—to help even out the lows was a good business decision. After several interesting discussions—and only one fistfight—the Boltons had agreed to spot him the capital. He just needed a property.

Besides, it wasn't like he was making it up as he went along. He had a master's in business administration. He hadn't needed a college degree to build choppers—he'd been doing that by Billy's side since he'd been thirteen.

But running a business was not the same thing as welding a frame. And the Bolton men had been good to Seth for last ten years of his life. His father and his uncles were demonstrating a great deal of faith in Seth. He couldn't screw this up and run the family legacy into the ground. His adopted last name meant he had to make sure the family business stayed relevant and important.

"We're still in the idea phase," he finally said. Which really meant it was all still in his head. "At least sixty thousand square feet. I'm envisioning the museum, a gift store, a café—maybe an area where we can have special exhibits. And possibly a showroom. We're still selling bikes out of the factory, but I don't think that's sustainable. If it's closer to the original factory, that'd be ideal, but it doesn't have to be. I hope that makes sense," he added.

Her eyes lit up. He couldn't tell if she was excited by the vision or the commission it would generate. Which was fine. He didn't need her to be excited about his big plans. Once he'd realized she was in real estate, the whole reason he'd come looking for her at work was to give her the commission. It'd been important to him.

He honestly wasn't sure why—she wasn't his responsibility. But he needed several properties, and he wasn't on a first-name basis with any other real estate agents. So why shouldn't he help out a soon-to-be single mom? God knew that Seth's mom could've used a hand up before Billy came into their lives.

He was paying forward the good fortune Billy Bolton had brought into Seth's life. It was that simple.

But it didn't feel simple when Kate leaned forward, her gaze locked on his. It felt messy and complicated and…right.

"It makes perfect sense," she told him. "But I'm going to need to do some research as to what's available. Do you have a budget in mind?"

Seth shifted nervously. The budget was, predictably, the part Ben and Billy objected to the most. "I'd like to get a list of potential properties and the associated costs first so we can budget for design and building after that." Billy was not in the mood to spend millions and millions of dollars on this. The only reason he'd agreed to the museum in the end was because Seth had promised that he'd take care of everything and Billy could just keep right on building bikes.

Kate nodded and took a few notes. "This will be a process," she warned him. "We could have a house under contract in a matter of weeks. The commercial property is much more involved—months of looking at properties, negotiating with sellers and dealing with architects."

Months of riding around with Kate, spending time with her when neither of them were under extreme duress. Months of getting to know her. Months of seeing that particular smile.

"Are you trying to talk me out of this?" God knew Billy had. He hated anything that distracted from building bikes.

And yeah, it was true that they didn't have a company without the bikes. But no one could compete in today's market without having a plan for the future.

So this was Seth's plan. He'd buy a house so he could be on hand to manage the museum project and the Bolton brothers. He'd prove that he had what it took to help the company and the family prosper.

That he had what it took to be a Bolton.

Kate's cheeks flushed as she dropped her gaze to the desktop. "No," she said quickly. "I just want you to go into this with realistic expectations." She looked up at him through her lashes. "It means we'll have to work together. A lot," she emphasized, as if the idea of spending more time with her was a deal breaker instead of one of the main reasons he was here in the first place.

Seth fought the urge to reach across her desk and cup her cheek in his hand. "Kate," he said in all seriousness, "why do you think I looked you up?"

Six

Kate was always polished and professional when she showed houses. Nobody wanted a real estate agent who was slovenly. That was just a fact. She was careful with her hair and makeup and put forth her best appearance.

But for this afternoon with Seth? She had gone above and beyond her normal preparations. She hadn't just carefully applied mascara—she'd primed and preened, showered and shaved until she was as glamorous as she could possibly be on her budget. If she'd had the cash, she would have gotten her hair blown out. As it was, she'd used hot rollers to tease her hair into a delicate half twist that she'd seen on Pinterest. It'd taken her a good half hour, which was a solid twenty-five minutes longer than she normally spent on her hair.

She was also thankful her best pair of trousers had buttoned. True, that button was straining as she drove her car toward the first house on the schedule for the day. If she were alone in the car, she'd undo the button and let her stomach relax.

But she wasn't alone. Seth Bolton was in her passenger seat, filling the space with his raw masculinity and leather jacket, tapping his fingers on his jeans. They were a dark-wash denim today, not nearly as scuffed as the black ones he'd worn the last time she'd seen him. And instead of a distressed T-shirt, he had on a gray flannel shirt. She'd never thought of gray flannel as a particularly attractive fabric before, but on him?

Yup. Keeping her button fastened and her baby bump sucked in.

Every day it seemed her clothing shrank just that much more. And for a woman who'd maintained a steady weight since she'd lost the freshman fifteen during her sophomore year, to suddenly be faced with a wardrobe that might not fit today and most definitely wouldn't fit tomorrow was more than a little daunting. Not to mention that she had to buy replacement clothes on a supertight budget.

She could tell by the way Seth fidgeted that he wasn't used to being a passenger but despite that, he hadn't changed the radio station or adjusted the mirrors or any of the other things Roger had always done every time she'd had to drive him home after he'd had too much to drink.

After all, Seth had arrived at Zanger Realty this morning on a motorcycle that didn't look familiar. Not that she remembered much about her wedding day fiasco, but she was certain that the bike hadn't been candy-apple red.

She'd never been into bikers before, but looking at

that beautiful machine this morning as Seth straddled it, his hair tousled from the wind, those dimples in full force...

She shivered and pushed those thoughts aside. She really needed Seth to buy a house. Even if his big ideas about the museum of motorcycles fell through, as long as he bought a nice house with a big piece of land attached, it'd be enough. But if there was something more...

She was being absolutely ridiculous as she turned onto the street of the first house. "We've got thirteen houses today," she warned him.

"Is that a lot? It seems like a lot," he said in a thoughtful voice before he turned that winning smile on her.

It was a good thing she was sitting because that smile was dangerous to her balance. "I've done more in a day. I don't anticipate you'll love them all."

"You mean, we might have to do this again sometime?"

Was she imagining things or did he sound happy about that prospect? "If you don't find something you like, we might."

"That would be too bad, wouldn't it?"

He was just a Good Samaritan, she reminded herself. A hot, kind, wealthy Good Samaritan. He'd probably been a Boy Scout or something and this house-hunting expedition was the adult equivalent of helping an old lady across the street.

He'd comforted her on the day of her not-wedding. He'd made sure that she was safe and secure in a hotel that night. He hadn't taken advantage of her confusion or vulnerability.

Seth Bolton was a hell of a good guy. Maybe the best she'd ever known.

"Saturdays are usually free for me—after about eleven," he added. "We could have a standing date."

Oh, Lord—how was she supposed to react to that? "We might have to do that," she said, keeping her voice carefully professional. "Even if you love a house today, there are still the commercial properties to deal with."

A standing date didn't mean anything. Hell, it wasn't even a date. For all she knew, he always looked at women with that intensity. He probably wasn't flirting on purpose and besides—why would he flirt with *her*? She was pregnant and had not demonstrated the best of judgment. He might not hold abandoning Roger against her, but he'd be well within his rights to blame her for settling on Roger in the first place. Frankly, who could blame him?

So there wasn't anything here. He was using her as his real estate agent out of the kindness of his heart. It was a generous thing to do, but that was it.

She absolutely should not be thinking about Seth and dating in the same breath. No dating. He was a client. That was final.

How many times would she have to repeat that before she believed it?

"This property," she said as she pulled up in front of the split-level ranch in the Rapid Valley neighborhood because she was a professional and would not ask if his Saturdays were free because he was single, by God, "has a three-car garage." It was the only redeeming feature of the property, but she wasn't going to say that out loud. It was an ugly house. The shrubs were overgrown, the paint was peeling—absolutely no curb appeal, and she could tell from the pictures that the inside was in no better shape.

If it were up to her, it would be a complete teardown. But it wasn't. All she could do was sell the positives of any home. She almost hadn't put this house on the list, but sometimes seeing a house a client definitely didn't want helped clarify what they did, and since Seth had been vague about what he wanted—beyond no neighbors—she had to work from the process of elimination.

"So there would be plenty of room for a workshop and multiple motorcycles. Or a car, assuming you have one?"

"I own a car." He chuckled. "And a truck. Don't forget that I grew up in Rapid City. We have this thing called winter—maybe you've heard of it?"

She shot him a look. "I'm familiar with the concept."

Oh, there were those dimples again. She really needed to stop making him smile. "I also have three personal motorcycles, but I've been known to test out prototypes. It'd be great to have space for all of them."

In the week and a half since Seth Bolton had walked into Zanger Realty, Kate's dreams had gotten a lot more vivid. It wasn't like she hadn't dreamed of him before—she had.

Maybe it was the pregnancy hormones—that was her answer to every strange new change in her mind and body. Because her dreams now weren't just nonsensical images all jumbled together. Her dreams of Seth stripping her down—again—and this time instead of shaking her hand and riding off into the night, he laid her out on a bed and spent the evening feasting on her body.

She always woke up unsatisfied, with an edge of longing that no dream could fully erase.

Seth looked at the property. "It's kind of ugly."

"But there's a lot of potential," she pointed out. He slanted a side-eye look at her and she realized that she had said that with a little too much fake enthusiasm. "Okay, it's a little ugly. But there are things you can do to make it less hideous."

"You're really selling it," he said drily. "I guess we should look inside?"

"Never judge a book by its cover," she agreed.

He snorted. "The Boltons are a family of bikers. They look like mercenary criminals but underneath, they're all great big teddy bears." He paused, hand on the handle. "Don't tell my dad I called him a teddy bear."

She laughed as they got out of the car. "It's all confidential," she reminded him.

The split-level ranch did not improve in appearance outside the car. "It better have one hell of a kitchen," Seth commented, kicking at the unmowed grass.

Kate winced. Well, now she knew that a good kitchen was important. "Don't see what it is. See what it can be."

Seth scowled at her. "The other twelve aren't this ugly, are they?"

"No. I don't normally tell people this, but we're going in order from what I think you're least likely to buy. But," she added before he could suggest skipping half the list, "I've been wrong before. People can be surprising in what they want, and I don't know you well enough yet to be able to say definitively what you'll like and what you won't."

Seth's gaze snapped to hers and there it was again, that tension between them that hummed like a string, and Kate's brain took that moment to remind her this was the man who'd stripped her skirts off her and gotten a full view of her wedding thong.

He took a step closer. "I imagine," he said, his voice low, "that if we make this a standing date, you'll figure out what I'm looking for real quick."

She could feel the heat in her cheeks, but she couldn't look away, couldn't put any distance between them. "I imagine I will," she murmured.

His eyes darkened, and he looked dangerous in the very best sort of way.

Against her will, her body pitched toward his. His lips parted—he had nice lips, full and warm and...

"Kate." His voice stroked over her name like a lover's kiss as he took another step closer.

"Seth," she replied. It came out high and breathy.

Good God, what the hell was she doing? She couldn't—really, she *couldn't*. She was pregnant and coming off a failed long-term relationship and he was a client and...and...well, there were just a lot of really good reasons why she couldn't act on any of her fantasies right now.

She pulled away before she did something idiotic, like throw herself at him. "We..." She cleared her throat and tried again in her real estate agent voice. "We should go inside."

Some of the heat in his gaze cooled. "We should," he agreed. But he didn't sound happy about it.

And he didn't get any happier as they toured the house. The place was just as hideous on the inside as it was on the outside. The kitchen still had original appliances, the carpet was probably early 1980s—a cream color that had dimmed to a dull gray with grime. The wallpaper was peeling in the bathroom, and the tub was the stuff of horrors.

Kate cleared her throat. "As you can see, there is room to grow."

Seth snorted again. "But what? Is that mold, do you think? You shouldn't be breathing this air." He ushered her out of the bathroom, his hand on the small of her back. When they were in the hallway, he didn't remove it.

"You have to look into the future. Do you want room for a girlfriend or a wife?" She swallowed. "A family?"

His hand dropped away from her waist. "I don't have any plans for family anytime soon and I'm not seeing anyone," he told her. He stopped in the middle of peeking into the linen closet. "How are things going? With the pregnancy, I mean."

Kate blushed from the tips of her ears to her toes. "Good." Aside from her parents and Roger and Harold, few people knew she was pregnant. It had been hard enough to explain to everyone why the wedding was off without the added complication of an unplanned pregnancy. She had wanted to keep it quiet for long as long as possible.

Which meant she wasn't very good at talking about it yet.

Seth peeked into the third bedroom and winced in horror at the walls. "Is Roger going to step up?"

"In his way," she admitted. "He's been willing to provide child support."

Seth heard what she didn't say. "But nothing else?"

The concern in his eyes did things to her that had nothing to do with his dimples or her inability to stop blushing. He cared, damn his hide. He cared about her and her pregnancy, and she had the urge to tell him about all the strange things happening to her because he was the only person who'd asked. "No. We should look at the basement."

They went downstairs. The heart-of-pine paneling had seen better days, just like everything else in this house. "So he's not going to be a father to his child. Typical."

Kate was surprised by the bitterness in Seth's voice. "That's an accurate assessment of the situation," she said. When he gave her a hard look, she added, "Which is for the best, honestly."

"If you say so." He surveyed the rest of the basement room, his hands on his hips. "I think we're done here. We can cross this off the list."

"Done." They headed outside. "No more split-level ranches?"

"Good Lord, no," he said, getting back into the car. "I like the idea of having room to grow, though. There's always the possibility of houseguests, at the very least. Julie might come over."

She nodded and tried not to imagine what sort of houseguest this Julie would be. Young, pretty and not pregnant, most likely. Kate shook her head trying to get images out of her mind and focused on her job—the job she desperately needed.

She wished she could show him her favorite house— the one in the Colonial Pines neighborhood that had been on the market for almost a year. If she'd been able to afford it, she would have snapped that home up in a heartbeat. But even with combining her and Roger's incomes, the house on Bitter Root was out of reach— it was over twice the price of homes like this one and she didn't want to push Seth into more house than he wanted.

So she put that house out of her mind and focused on her job. "We have other options. One down, twelve more to go."

Seth groaned.

Seven

"I take it from the expression on your face that this one's a no, too?"

Seth was all for wood-burning stoves, but not ones that left scorch marks up a wall and dark shadows on the ceiling. "How is it possible that the house hasn't burned down?" Even as he said, his foot hit a particularly creaky board and he hoped like hell he wasn't about to fall through.

Kate sighed and put a hand to her lower back. "These are the houses at this price range," she began, closing her eyes and stretching.

"Then we go up." He had the money.

Even though Seth and his mom had lived comfortably—more than comfortably—for ten years with Billy Bolton, old habits died mighty hard. Seth had been looking at the cheaper end of homes simply because there was a part of his brain convinced that was all he should spend on a house.

That part of his brain was wrong. He could afford homes that cost four times the ones they'd spent the day staring at.

He was a partner in a wildly successful business. He had to start thinking like one. And living like one, too. Which would be good for Kate, too. A more expensive house for him would be a bigger commission for her.

He watched Kate sway as she massaged her lower back. They had walked through thirteen houses—only three of which were even remotely habitable. And she was pregnant. He had kept her on her feet all afternoon and clearly, she was tiring.

God, he was a cad. He wished he could make this easier on her. But he wasn't going to buy a mediocre house just so she wasn't on her feet as much.

Not that she looked pregnant. Instead, she looked *lush* and it took most of his willpower to keep from touching her. Her hair shone and her figure—she was a perfect hourglass. A voluptuous, decadent hourglass figure that he wanted to appreciate properly.

But he didn't. He was a gentleman, by God. But then she made a moaning noise and what was left of his will-power went up in smoke.

He stepped in close and pushed her hands aside. This was a bad idea, and yet he settled his hands on her hips, rubbing his thumbs in circles along the small of her back, and damned if she didn't feel right under his touch.

"Would you buy any of these houses?" he asked, try-ing to focus on relieving her tension instead of the way her body filled his hands.

For a long second, she didn't respond. She held her back straight, and her arms awkwardly hung at her sides. But then he must've found the right spot because all of a sudden, she sighed heavily and leaned back into his touch. "I would not," she admitted. "But my housing needs are different than yours. If I were to buy a home, it'd need to be a family home."

"Where are you living now? Not with Roger, right?" When Seth had found her at the scenic overlook, she had made it very clear that she couldn't go back to the place she'd shared with Roger. Seth knew that she had been at the hotel for a week—because the room had been charged to his credit card. But where she'd gone after she'd checked out, he didn't know.

"No, not with Roger." She sighed again, leaning back into him some more. "We… You shouldn't…"

"Hush," he said, closer to her ear than he should've been. She was right—he shouldn't be touching her like this and certainly not in a crappy house he wasn't going to buy. Funny how that wasn't stopping him. "Was this the last house?"

She nodded, not pulling away as he worked at her tired muscles.

"I'm taking you to dinner. No argument," he said quickly when she jolted. "We'll discuss real estate things. But I'm hungry and you need to get off your feet."

He could feel the tension in her body and there was a moment when he knew she was going to say no. And really, why had he asked? He was tired, too. He'd been sociable and chatty all afternoon and he should've been absolutely done with other people.

Instead, he was kneading her tired muscles and hoping she'd say yes. To dinner, that was. Nothing else.

But she wasn't going to. He let go of her hips as she stepped away from him. When she turned, her eyes were in shadows. "Dinner?"

It wasn't a no. He wanted to take her to an expensive place, with haute cuisine and complicated wine lists. He wanted to show her he was more than a biker, more mature than any other twenty-five-year-old. God knew he had the money now to wine and dine her. Hell, he could buy a restaurant for her if she wanted.

Suddenly, he realized he didn't want to take her to a fancy place. Yeah, he wanted to impress her—but for some reason, it also felt important that he show her who he really was.

And who he really was, was a biker. A multimillionaire business owner, yeah—but choppers were his life. "Sure. There's a great burger place not too far from here, but it's whatever you want."

She tucked her lower lip under her teeth and worried at it. The effort it took not to stare was surprising. "I should buy you dinner," she announced. "You paid for the hotel."

No way was that happening. "The hotel was a wedding gift. A not-wedding gift," he corrected with a smile when she opened her mouth to argue. "Dinner's on me. What are you in the mood for?"

He hadn't heard a no yet—but he still hadn't gotten a yes, either. "I'm sure you have someone you'd rather have dinner with."

Well, wasn't *that* an interesting statement? Was it possible that Kate Burroughs was jealous? It was, of course. But—jealous of who?

Then she answered the question for him. "This Julie—she's probably waiting on you?"

Seth knew it was not a good idea to laugh at an expectant mother. He fought it as hard as he could, but he lost ground little by little. His lips twitched up and then they broke open into a wild grin and the next thing he knew, he was chuckling.

Kate looked indignant. "What's so funny?" she demanded, crossing her arms in front of her chest.

The sight of that had Seth standing straighter at attention. "Julie's my little sister. She just turned ten. She's a year younger than Clara, and almost the same age as Eliza. We're all cousins." At this point, he couldn't explain his family tree without a whiteboard and color-coded markers. The all-purpose designation of "cousins" would have to do. "They are a tough pack of middle-school girls. You should see them play soccer sometime—they're brutal."

He didn't know what she had expected him to say, but it was pretty clear that wasn't it. Kate's mouth opened and then shut, her brow furrowed, then her mouth opened and shut again.

Seth smirked and took her by the elbow, leading her out of the house that might well burn down tomorrow. Gallantly, he opened the driver's-side door and bowed her into her seat. "You have two minutes to decide if you want burgers or not. I'm hungry."

It took less than two seconds before Kate said, "I would kill for some french fries," in a tone of voice that made it sound like french fry cravings were a crime. "Does this place have ice cream?" she asked hopefully.

"Malts *and* milkshakes."

She sighed, a noise that shot straight through him. "Burgers it is."

In short order, they were sitting in Seth's favorite booth at Mike's All Night Diner. Kate looked around nervously because Mike's was not quite a bar, but it was popular with a certain clientele. In fact, her car had been the only car in a parking lot full of bikes. But this was a family restaurant. People came here to eat. If they wanted to get drunk and brawl, there were bars for that.

"You come here often?" she asked as a guy in motorcycle leathers walked past them.

Seth shrugged. "Often enough. Don't forget, I own part of a motorcycle company. This was normal when I was growing up."

In fact, now that he had her here, he wasn't sure that this was a good idea. The odds of him being recognized by one of his dad's buddies were pretty decent and this could be an intimidating crowd. Kate stuck out worse than a thumb, sore or not, and word would probably get back to his dad.

Damn.

She really didn't belong in a place like this. He should've taken her to a classy place, with linen tablecloths and snooty waiters and artistically displayed food on oddly shaped plates.

Then again, he'd been so busy since he'd officially returned to Rapid City that he hadn't had time to catch up with the old gang. It just wasn't a priority—not right now, anyway.

Not that he would ever admit it out loud and certainly not in a joint like this, but Seth had missed his sister and even his parents. However, the phrase "you can't go home again" turned out not just to be a tired cliché but an absolute truth. Seth loved his family, but he didn't fit in their household anymore.

Still, he hadn't seen a single home today that made him want to give up his suite of rooms at the Mason Hotel. There, at least, he could come and go as he pleased, the bed was always freshly made and if he ate out too much, well, it wasn't that different from how he'd lived in LA.

The waitress took their orders—Kate went with a chocolate shake and Seth ordered an extra side of fries. Once they were alone again, he waited.

She didn't make him wait long. "Can I ask you a question?"

God only knew where this would go. "Of course."

"How old are you?"

Seth notched an eyebrow at her. "Does it matter?"

He had the feeling she was older than he was—not much older, but she might be anywhere from twenty-five to her early thirties. And really, was that such a big leap from twenty-five? No. It wasn't. It wasn't like he was thinking improper thoughts about a grandmother, for crying out loud.

He cleared his throat and shifted in his seat. It wasn't like he was thinking improper thoughts about her at all. She was his real estate agent. The only thing that mattered between them was that she helped him find the right properties.

Yeah, right.

"No, no," she defended weakly. "It's just that you seem a little…old to have a sister who's only ten."

He couldn't stop the smirk if he wanted to. "Technically, she's my half sister. My mom married into the Bolton family when I was fourteen."

He could see her doing the math in her head. It really wasn't complicated—except, of course it was. And he still didn't have a whiteboard to help explain the ways the Bolton half of his family overlapped with the Lakota half.

"Oh. I just assumed…"

"That I'm really a Bolton? I am—Dad adopted me. But I'm also a full-blooded member of the Pine Ridge Lakota tribe." He hoped that was enough of an answer for her, because he didn't want to get into his birth father, the sperm donor. Not at Mike's, not ever.

She dropped her gaze to the table, and he saw that she was nervously twisting the straw wrapper around her fingers. Seth had a moment of panic—his heritage wasn't going to be an issue, was it? He'd grown up on the reservation with his tribe, where he'd been loved and protected and then, when Billy had adopted him, the Bolton name—and reputation of his dad—had shielded him from the worst of the bullying off the reservation.

But that didn't mean he didn't know racism existed, in both subtle and overt ways. Once he'd left the rez, he'd seen how kids at his new high school had talked about other Native kids. He heard stories from his friends on the rez. And his dad had made damn sure he knew how to defend himself.

Part of that defense mechanism was not announcing his heritage until he was sure of his reception. And sometimes, that meant he never found the right time to tell a paramour before the relationship drifted away.

Within his family, his ethnicity wasn't just accepted, it was normal. *Welcomed.* His dad and his uncles came to powwows and helped out at the school on the rez and had married into the tribe. They hired Seth's uncles and cousins and friends from the rez to work in the factory. It all overlapped and blended together. Just like it had in Seth.

They'd never demanded that to be a Bolton, he had to give up being a Wawausuck. His legal name was Seth James Wawausuck Bolton. He was safe to be both, and that freedom was not something he took lightly.

It shouldn't matter what Kate believed, really it shouldn't. Because there was nothing more than a professional business relationship between them.

Except...

Except for the way she'd leaned into his touch as he'd rubbed circles on the small of her back. And the way she'd looked when he'd stripped the petticoat off her. And the way her entire face had lit up when he'd walked into her office—and that was before he'd told her why he was there.

Okay, it mattered, what she thought. It mattered a lot.

Kate opened her mouth just as the waitress arrived with their food and said, "Anything else?" as she unloaded enough french fries to feed an army.

Seth eyed the plates of food. Mike didn't mess around with his burgers, and the malt was huge. There was easily enough food for five on the table, but Kate was staring at it with something that looked like devotion. "I think we're good," he said.

The waitress left and Seth turned his attention back to Kate. She was staring at him openly. "Is it a problem?" He wasn't talking about the food.

"Of course not," she said easily. But she looked worried. "It's just..."

She picked up a fry and slid it slowly between her lips as she nibbled at the tip.

Who knew that eating french fries could be so erotic?

"You obviously have a really complex family history," she finally said.

Seth snorted. "That doesn't begin to cover it." Which was not an observation that let him relax. Crap, why had he brought it up at all? Oh, right—because Kate had thought Julie was a girlfriend and it had been important to make sure Kate knew that wasn't true.

He sighed and picked up his burger. Deep thoughts about identity and fathers could wait. "Eat, Kate. I know you're starving." And one fry at a time wasn't going to make much of a dent in this meal.

They made good headway into the food. Kate ate delicately—but she ate, thank God. Finally, she said, "I'm glad you came for me at Zanger, Seth."

"Are you?" Because there were several different ways he could interpret that statement. She might be happy about the commission, the chance to say thank you for the hotel room or...

"I'd been wondering about you," she replied, not quite meeting his gaze.

He let that statement settle around the table as he scooted the extra fries toward her. She'd cleared her plate. "In a good way?"

She nodded. "I..." She took an especially deep breath. "Most people wouldn't have done what you did for me."

Which part? Depositing her safely at a hotel? Or stripping off her petticoat? "I think you underestimate people."

That got a rueful chuckle out of her. "No, I don't. I

almost married Roger. And you haven't even met my father. People like you are rare, Seth." She looked at him through thick eyelashes. "You're special. You just don't realize it."

That sure as hell seemed to answer at least one question. A question that set his blood to pounding in his veins.

His hands itched to settle around her waist again. She wanted special? Hell, he could show her special. Slow and tender and hot and very, very *special*.

He put the brakes on those thoughts—something he was doing a lot around her. She was not technically available. She was expecting and they were working together and he didn't have any interest in being a rebound.

Well, not a lot of interest, anyway. But when she looked at him like that he had to admit that yeah, maybe he was a little interested.

"You know what I think?" he said, snagging a few more fries.

"Split-level ranches are the work of the devil?"

He snorted and damn near choked on a fry. "That, too. But seriously—I think you don't realize how special *you* are."

Her cheeks shot past a delicate blush and straight on over into red. "I'm not special. I'm a mess. You know that."

He considered that statement. "The situation is messy, maybe. But," he went on as she gave him an arch look, "that doesn't make you a mess. You believe leaving Roger at the altar makes you an utter failure, and when I look at you, all I see is one of the strongest, bravest women I've ever met."

She gasped, a hand covering her chest, right over her heart. "Seth…"

"No, I'm serious." He wasn't going to let her undermine her worth. "You walked away from a crap marriage and gave up your family business, right?"

She nodded, her eyes getting suspiciously bright.

"You know why? Because you're going to have a baby and you'd do anything—*anything*—to give that child the very best life possible. To walk away from everything you know, even though you know it's going to be hard—because it's the right thing to do? You amaze me, Kate. You simply amaze me."

Aw, hell. Sincere compliments were a bad idea, because now she was crying. Quiet tears slipped down her cheeks, and he couldn't stand that.

He leaned over the table and cupped her face in his hand, swiping at her tears.

"I'm sorry," he said softly. "I didn't mean to make you cry."

"Don't you dare take that back." She sniffed, grabbing a napkin and dabbing at her eyes. "That's the nicest thing anyone's ever said to me."

Wasn't that a shame? Her former fiancé, her father—had anyone ever noticed who Kate really was?

He sat back as she took a bunch of deep breaths and got herself under control. "Sorry—hormones," she said, giving him a watery smile.

"Don't apologize. It was rude of me to ambush you with compliments."

That got him a slightly less watery smile. "It was, wasn't it?"

A strange silence settled over the table and then a movement behind Kate caught Seth's eye. Oh, hell—it was Jack Roy, one of Billy Bolton's oldest friends. Seth gave a friendly nod of his head to Jack, hoping the man would just keep moving without stopping.

No such luck. "Seth! Finally out and about?" Jack stood over the table, grinning down at Kate. "And who do we have here? Hello, beautiful."

Later? Seth was going to stab the man. Repeatedly. Jack Roy was a born flirt and had the kind of face a lot of women went for. And now he was smiling down at Kate and she was blinking up at the man, stunned by the force of his smile.

"Jack," Seth said, hearing the tension in his voice but seemingly unable to sound any more relaxed, "this is Kate Burroughs, my real estate agent. Kate," he went on, mentally willing Jack to get the hint and leave, "this is Jack Roy, head painter at Crazy Horse."

"And a whole lot more," Jack murmured in a seductive voice that Seth had heard him use on every female he'd ever met.

Kate's cheeks colored again as she dropped her gaze to the table. Crap, this was terrible. Not only was Jack interrupting just as things had gotten interesting, now the man would probably call Dad up and ask if Billy knew Seth had been having dinner with a pretty real estate agent. How much had Jack caught? Had he seen Seth cup Kate's cheek? Or wipe away Kate's tears?

Damn it all. Seth pivoted and launched a careful kick in the direction of Jack's shins. The man flinched but, to his credit, didn't even let out a stream of obscenities.

Instead, he turned that smile up to full power. "You make sure this one treats you right," he said, a hint of steel behind his seductive voice as he nodded at Seth.

Kate's eyes widened in surprise. "Oh, no—we're just working together."

The quick defense pricked at Seth's pride, even if it was exactly what she should have said because it was the truth. "I'm buying a house," he added.

By God, if Jack made some sort of crack about how Seth was all grown up and a big boy now, the man's handsome nose would never look the same.

Jack's mouth opened and then he closed it. "Well, then," he said, notching a knowing eyebrow at Seth. Hopefully Kate couldn't see it. "I'll let you two get back to *business*." He reached down and appropriated one of Kate's hands, bowing over it. "Ms. Burroughs, it has been a true pleasure." Then the bastard kissed her knuckles.

A rumbling noise startled everyone at the table. It was only when both Kate and Jack turned to look at Seth that he realized the noise—a growl—was coming from him.

Jack's mouth curved into a knowing grin and Seth realized he'd walked right into Jack's trap. The jerk had intentionally provoked Seth with that kiss.

"Jack," Seth managed to get out without strangling the man.

"Seth—be good," Jack said with another wink before he finally, finally left.

Seth scowled at the man's back as he walked away. When he glanced back over at Kate, she was staring at him with what looked uncomfortably like confusion on her face.

Well, this evening was shot to hell. And he wasn't even sure what he'd wanted before Jack had interrupted.

This wasn't a date—Kate had said so herself. This was business.

This wasn't personal.

"Come on," Seth said, leaving a fifty on the table. "I think we're done here."

Eight

The ride back to the real estate office was tense. Or maybe that was just how Kate felt—because there was no missing the tension. Her dinner sat heavy in her stomach, and her head was a muddled mess. Her back hurt, her feet weren't any better and she was so tired she could barely see straight.

She just wanted to go home and go to bed and, inexplicably, she wanted to do so curled in Seth's arms. She wanted that *so* badly.

What kind of hormonal torture was this? There was no good reason why she should be craving Seth's arms around her, his chest pressed against her back. As fantasies went, it was downright boring.

Except if she went to sleep in his arms, then she'd wake up there and then...

No, *no*. She was not following that train of thought to its logical conclusion. Not a bit.

It wasn't that she'd been scared when that friend of his had shown up. The guy was obviously a smooth talker who considered himself God's gift to women—not that he'd done anything for her. Because he hadn't. She'd been able to empirically realize he was an attractive man but compared to Seth, he was like a cardboard cutout next to a real man.

Then there'd been that kiss on her hand. If Kate didn't know any better, she would've thought that kiss had been to intentionally provoke Seth. There hadn't been a single bit of heat to Jack's lips—but when Seth had growled?

That noise had shot right through Kate, primal and raw. God, it'd sounded so *good*. Almost like he'd wanted her and was more than willing to fight for her.

But to what end? She and Seth were not together and no one present was a caveman. In her experience, no one fought over her. Hell, Roger hadn't even bothered to be upset when she'd jilted him.

This was only the third time they'd ever met face-to-face. The first time, she had been a hysterical runaway bride. The second time, she'd been too stunned to put together two coherent sentences. And today...

Today, he'd told her he wanted to buy a much more expensive house—which came with a much bigger commission. He'd rubbed her back and bought her dinner.

She was not the kind of girl to rebound with the first hot guy she saw. Or the second. Or any guy. Kate Burroughs did not do anything so impulsive or crazy or...fun.

Right. That was final. No fun. She was not interested in Seth.

It didn't matter that he just kept right on drifting

through countless dreams, ones that always started with him riding up on his chopper before moving to him undressing her to hot, passionate lovemaking to...

Holding her while she slept. Making sure she felt safe.

Stupid hormones. She didn't want to do anything that would jeopardize their business relationship because she needed this business relationship more than she needed an attractive, wealthy man to rub her back.

They pulled up in front of the real estate office. Kate turned off the car but neither of them made a move to get out. Instead, they sat in silence and Kate had no idea if it was awkward or not.

"So," she finally began, unable to take the tension for another moment. "We looked at all the houses that were under two hundred and fifty thousand dollars. Do you want go up to three hundred thousand?" That was what most people did. They could handle increases of twenty-five to fifty thousand dollars at a time. And as much as she needed this commission, she didn't want to make this all about her.

But Seth wasn't most people. "I can't imagine there's a huge jump from what we saw today with a couple thousand dollars. Let's look in the three-fifty to five-hundred range."

She took a slow breath. The house on Bitter Root was four seventy-five. Would he like her favorite house or not? "Half a million is a lot of money, Seth. There's no need to buy more house than you'll use." Certainly not because of her. She didn't want to bankrupt the man just because he had a soft spot for...

Well, not for her. For pregnant women, maybe. But not for her.

He turned, facing her fully. There was something in his eyes—the same sort of almost possessive look he'd had when he growled earlier.

Heat flashed through her body as he stared at her. He'd looked earlier like he was willing to fight his friend over her. He looked very much the same now.

"We can't do this," she heard herself say before she completely lost her mind.

He lifted his eyebrows, and she immediately felt stupid. "Do what?" he asked, almost—but not quite—pulling off innocence.

"I'm not looking for a relationship." Well. So much for not making this awkward.

"Fair enough." He turned even more, resting one elbow on the dashboard and another against the back of the seat. "What are you looking for?"

Oh, hell. That was a question she most definitely hadn't seen coming. "I'm sorry?"

"You have to admit, Kate—there's something between us. I went to your office because I need to buy a house and an industrial property—but those weren't the only reasons." He leaned toward her—not close enough to touch her, but his gaze drifted over her and he inhaled deeply. "I couldn't stop thinking about you. I know that how we met wasn't exactly normal—"

Kate rolled her eyes. That was being generous.

"Look, I'm not in the market for a relationship, either," he went on, politely ignoring her unladylike response. "I don't plan on sticking around all the time. Settling down isn't in my blood."

Wasn't that what he'd basically said before? He was buying a house he only planned to live in for maybe six months out of the year? No, Seth Bolton wasn't the kind of guy who started playing house on a whim.

But still, hearing it baldly stated like that was physically painful, like someone was jabbing her hand with a pin. "What are you saying?"

"I need a house and you need a commission. That's all there has to be. But if you want something more…" His gaze darkened, and Kate swore it got ten degrees warmer in the car.

"More?" Her voice came out the barest of whispers.

She shouldn't be asking. She should, instead, get out of this car and thank him for his business and promise him that she would have a fresh slate of houses in a new price range that were sure to meet his needs by Saturday at 11:00 a.m. Their standing date.

"I think we want the same thing." His voice was low and serious, and another flash of heat ran through her body. Ironically, she shivered. How was he doing this to her? She was not sexy—not after being on her feet all day and mowing through that many fries. She was not desirable—her pants barely buttoned.

Yet here Seth sat, looking at her as if she were the ice cream and he couldn't wait to start licking. Her body felt warm and liquid, like she could melt right into him. "You're not looking for long-term. You don't want to be hurt again and you've got a baby on the way to think about. But it might do you good…" His voice trailed off as his gaze caressed her face.

"*What* might do me good?" She was powerless to do anything but ask that question, because it appeared that all common sense had abandoned her in the face of one hot, protective biker dude.

He didn't answer her for the longest second and

Kate thought she just might die on the spot. "Rebounds can be fun. Something short and sweet, no strings attached—something to help you get past those years lost to Roger. I think you deserve a little fun, Kate."

God, it sounded so good. So right. Because really—one conversation with Seth that didn't even involve touching, much less kissing, and she was already more turned on than she could remember being in years. Seth would be amazing. Simply amazing. Maybe the best she'd ever had, in her limited experience. And who knew what would happen after the baby came. She would be struggling to get through the long nights alone. Romance would be the last thing on her mind.

What if Seth were her last shot at romance—or even just good sex—for a long time? Years, even?

Was she willing to let go of that part of herself?

She wasn't, and she almost, almost said *yes* right then and there. Her mouth opened and the word was right on the tip of her tongue. *Yes*.

But she couldn't get it out because she wasn't the kind of person to willingly enter a sexual relationship just for the fun of it. Casual sex had never been casual. Not for her.

Still… "And you're fun?"

That smile—oh, she was not going to be strong enough. "I can take care of you, Kate. Even for a little while." His eyes darkened. "Just something to consider."

And the thing was, he seemed sincere about it. He wasn't boxing her in. He was focused on her, yes—but not intimidatingly so. "You're serious, are you?"

Please, let him be serious.

He nodded, the tip of his tongue touching his top lip. Jesus, she'd never seen anything so seductive. "You don't have to decide anything now. My offer's on the table. But promise me you'll think about it?"

She hated to ask this next question—but it was important she make a counteroffer. "And if I pass?" Because she needed the commissions he would bring in. She didn't want this to be some quid pro quo situation.

"Then you pass." He shrugged, as if rejecting his advances were no big deal. "Unlike some people, I know where the line is and I know not to cross it. I can keep business and pleasure separate."

Oh, that hurt. Because with Roger, they hadn't been separate. With Roger, she wasn't sure how much pleasure had been involved at all. The longer she was away from him—and her father—the more she was certain that Roger had only been with her because she came with the company.

Had there been any evidence to the contrary? No. There'd been no late-night calls, drunken or otherwise, professing that he really loved her and wanted her back. No daytime calls, either. No flowers. No big romantic gestures, like standing under her bedroom window and blasting their song until she realized she'd made a mistake.

Nothing. They didn't even have a song. When she'd asked what he wanted to play for their first dance, he'd shrugged.

And to think, she'd almost married *nothing*.

That did not mean that she wanted to jump into bed with Seth. It did mean, however, that the fact that he was making sense should be a source of concern.

So what if something short and sweet and fun sounded perfect? So what if it was Seth, who had made her feel safe from the very first moment she'd laid eyes on him? So what if the one man who seemingly gave a damn about her was the one offering to show her a good time—with no strings attached?

She had a baby on the way. There would always be strings attached.

"I can't," she said softly, unable to look at him when she said it. Because even if he was offering to make at least one of her fantasies come true, that wasn't her. Kate Burroughs wasn't that girl. She did what was expected of her and smiled and nodded and went along to get along. She did not have casual sex with a hot biker dude simply because it'd be fun and safe and so, *so* satisfying. That wasn't who she was.

Was it?

The silence in the car grew heavy and she didn't want to think about what would come next. Oh, she knew Seth wouldn't hurt her. Funny, how she trusted him with that. She simply didn't want the awkwardness. They'd laughed and joked and had an otherwise really lovely day together and she didn't want to ruin that.

"Then we won't. No harm, no foul." He didn't even sound upset by her refusal.

She peeked at him through her lashes. She didn't know what she'd been expecting, but that look bordering on concern wasn't it. Shouldn't he be mad? Insulted? Frustrated, at the very least?

Not concerned. Not for her. "And you're okay with it?"

He gave her a look as if she'd asked if he didn't like to kick puppies in his free time. "Why wouldn't I be? Besides…" he went on, leaning ever so slightly toward her. The tension between them tightened and she felt her own body move in his direction. "It's a woman's prerogative to change her mind."

And with that parting shot, he was gone before she could blink, out of the car and around to the driver's side and opening her door and—again—holding out a hand to her like he'd be honored if she joined him. "Otherwise," he said when she put her hand in his, his strong fingers closing around her own, "I'll see you at eleven next Saturday. We'll take more breaks and I'll buy you dinner again—no arguments, Kate," he scolded, cutting her off before she could protest. "I'm not going to run you into the ground."

And maybe it was the hormones or the exhaustion or the way he'd growled at his friend—or maybe it was the offer of something fun and easy—but whatever the reason, Kate didn't let go of his hand when she had her feet underneath her, nor did she step away from him.

She'd never known anyone like Seth Bolton, and she might not be able to make sense of what was going on in his head—because, again, he was attracted to *her*? But she was flattered and touched and interested all the same.

She shouldn't be, but she was.

Instead of putting distance between them, she held his hand and maybe even pulled on it a little, drawing him in closer. Not close enough to kiss, but close enough that she could feel the heat radiating off his chest, warming her on the chilly fall night.

"I'll…" She shouldn't say this but damn it, what the hell. "I'll think about it."

Seth's fingers tightened around hers and he favored her with a smile so dazzling she almost had to sit down again. "Do that," he said, his voice a caress on the wind.

And just when she thought he was going to lean in and kiss her, he instead took a step back. "Until next week, Kate."

He waited until she'd gotten the office door unlocked before firing up his motorcycle and riding off into the dim light.

Oh, sweet merciful heavens—she really was going to think about this. About Seth and all those dream fantasies that had kept her company for the last several weeks. About how she might not get another chance for a lover for years because once the baby came, she'd devote herself to her child.

Would she really let this golden opportunity pass her by? And if she did, would she spend the rest of her life kicking herself for letting Seth Bolton slip through her fingers?

Was she out of her mind?

Nine

So that was a *no*, then.

Seth took one look at Kate and sighed. She was wearing a black pantsuit with a white blouse that was buttoned up almost to her chin. Her glorious hair had been scraped back into a severe ponytail and there wasn't a smile to be seen anywhere despite the fact that it was another lovely late-October Saturday. She looked more like she was on her way to a funeral than a house tour.

And if that didn't make her position clear enough, there was no missing the way Kate's pretty mouth twisted into a scowl when Seth walked into Zanger Realty at ten fifty-eight in the morning.

Definitely a *no*.

He shouldn't be disappointed. This had been the most likely outcome, after all. There was no getting around the reality of the situation, and that reality was that Kate was expecting and she didn't want to get involved with anyone.

He should be relieved. Her personal life was a mess and only an idiot would put himself in the middle of that. Her rejection was going to save him a lot of trouble and not a little heartache.

And yet—relief was not the feeling that had his stomach plummeting. No, he was not disappointed. And if he were, it was about the fact that he was going to be missing out on some great casual sex. After all, he didn't have to worry about getting her pregnant, right?

But that didn't explain the weight of sadness that settled around his shoulders. He and Kate could've been great together, but now? They'd never know.

Still, he was a gentleman and a man of his word. He was not going to make this awkward, nor was he going to try to change her mind. He would not badger, nag or wheedle. He had no interest in being with a woman he had to wear down. He'd seen those kinds of guys in action in college and "pathetic desperation" didn't make anyone attractive. Good sex became great when everyone involved was equally enthusiastic about it.

So he straightened his shoulders and put on a friendly grin, even if it took effort to do so. "Good morning, Kate. What will we be looking at today?" Because the answer obviously wasn't each other.

Her scowl deepened as she stared at something on her desk. She looked positively insulted by his presence, which didn't make any sense. She hadn't even been insulted when he propositioned her. Shocked, maybe. Curious? Definitely. But not insulted. What the hell was going on?

"I have nine houses in your new price range on the schedule. We should get going."

The *no* couldn't have been louder if she'd shouted it. What a shame. "Nine sounds good," he said, striving his hardest for friendly. "Thirteen was too much last weekend." She still wasn't meeting his gaze, so he charged ahead. "I made dinner reservations at the Main Course for six thirty, but if you don't think we'll be done before then, I can change the time." She hadn't been comfortable at the diner—or at least, she'd been okay until Jack showed up.

Tonight would be different. They'd have a quiet dinner, just the two of them and a bunch of house listings. No interfering family friends, no distractions.

Although, given the body language she was putting off, maybe they could use a few distractions. Because even closed down, she still called to him on a fundamental level that had nothing to do with reason or logic.

He'd made his offer last week because he'd convinced himself that he could show her a good time, no strings attached. But today? When the answer was no?

He should be able to let it go. He'd asked, she'd said no, end of discussion.

But looking at her now, he wasn't sure his offer had been only about her. Because he still wanted her. Desperately.

She hadn't answered yet. "Kate? We're still on for dinner, right?" He expected any number of polite excuses—she'd had a long night, she had other plans, she would be too tired. She had an actual funeral, thereby justifying the outfit. Something.

So when she looked at him through her lashes and said, "That sounds nice," in a tone that stroked over his ears like a lover's kiss, he didn't know what to make of it. And when she shot him a nervous smile before dropping her gaze again, he had even less of an idea.

Because that wasn't a *no*. It sure as hell wasn't a *yes*, either.

What if he was looking at a *maybe*?

Five hours later, he had absolutely no idea what to make of Kate Burroughs. Through eight other houses, she'd kept her distance, never getting within two feet of him. Not like he was going to grab her, but still. She was definitely not close enough to touch. No accidentally brushing hands as they stood in a narrow hallway—of which there were several. No putting his hand on her lower back to guide her out of a room. No gentlemanly offers of his hand or his arm for her to lean against as they walked over uneven paver stones.

However, every single time he'd glanced at her, he'd caught her watching him. She always looked away quickly, as if she were going to pretend she hadn't been staring, but he could feel her gaze upon him. She'd also thawed—slowly at first, but she'd gotten notice-ably warmer to him as the day had progressed. She'd left her scowl behind at the first house—a markedly more habitable dwelling than nearly anything they'd looked at the previous week. By the third house, her lips had gone from a tight line to a gentle smile and by the fifth house, she was laughing at his jokes again. By the sev-enth house, her eyes softened and she let her gaze lin-ger upon him when he'd glance at her, like she didn't want to look away.

She was still absolutely captivating.

He had to play this cool. As much as he desperately

wanted to pull her into his arms and show her exactly how good they could be together, he didn't dare. She had to come to him, and besides—her decision was separate from their business dealings.

So he was doing his best not to think about anything other than real estate. It was a battle he wasn't necessarily winning, but he was trying.

"This isn't bad," he said, standing in the middle of a gleaming kitchen with a professional six-burner stove, a fridge with cabinet facings on the door and an island with a marble countertop. The whole thing was done in whites and grays with splashes of red and bright blue for accents. This was the last house of the day and they were on schedule, with a whole thirty-five minutes before their dinner reservations.

Kate snorted. "Four hundred and seventy-five thousand dollars and it's not *bad*?"

"Compared to what we looked at last week, it's amazing," he conceded.

He stood at the island, trying to get a sense for how the room flowed. And the fact that he was thinking about the flow of rooms was odd. He'd never considered work triangles and flow before. He and his mom had lived in a cramped two-room place before Billy Bolton had come into their lives, and then they'd moved into Billy's house and it'd been great simply because it was a real house with a room—and a bathroom—all his own.

The kid he'd been would take the first decent option he got. But he was a man of means now. He could afford to be picky.

He looked up at Kate, who was staring at the kitchen with open longing. Picky, indeed. "What do you think?"

"It's not going to be my house, Seth," she said in a quiet voice.

Something in her tone pulled at him. She sounded almost sad about that and he remembered what she'd said last week—she'd arranged for him to look at the least likely house first. This was the last house of the day, which meant she thought this was the best house they'd looked at yet.

"But you have a professional opinion, Kate. What do you think?" When she didn't answer right away, he added, "I'd appreciate it if you're honest."

About this kitchen, about the houses they looked at, about whether or not dinner was going to be painfully awkward.

About him. He wanted her to be honest about what she wanted from him. Just the commission or something else?

When she still didn't answer, Seth wished he could take it back. He never should've offered her a sexual relationship last week. He should've left it at flirting and making her smile, at making sure she was landing on her feet.

But then Jack had shown up and watching him hit on Kate had been more than Seth could take. She was *his*, not Jack's and not Roger's.

Except she wasn't. She wasn't a possession he could do with what he pleased. She was a complicated woman who had her own life to live.

"I'm just asking, Kate. Your opinion is important to me. Just tell me what you think. I've never done this before."

"You've never bought a house before?"

"That, either."

Her lips twisted to the side in a scowl that he now recognized as confusion. "You've never propositioned a pregnant older woman before?"

Finally, they were at the heart of the matter. "Oddly enough, no. There's a first for everything, isn't there?" He gave her a warm smile, hoping that would help.

He wasn't sure it did. "But you've offered to have no-strings relationships with other women?"

He tried to process the line of thinking behind that question. How long had she been with Roger? Kate didn't strike Seth as the kind of woman who'd had a lot of casual relationships. "I went to college."

The scowl was back. But at least this time he'd earned it. He braced for her cutting rejoinder, but instead she squared her shoulders and said, "This is an amazing house," in what he thought of as her real estate agent voice. "The master suite has that Jacuzzi bathtub and the office on the first floor has an amazing view. It sits on two acres so you don't have any neighbors within immediate line of sight and although it only has a two-car garage, there's more than enough room to expand or even build a separate workshop. The property is fenced so if you're ever going to have a dog or children, there would be a huge backyard for them to play in."

"It is a great house on paper," he agreed. "But I can read. I want to know what you think of the house, Kate."

"It was originally on the market nine months ago for five ninety-nine," she went on, ignoring him. "But was overvalued and the market has been a little soft at this price range. The owners are probably desperate to sell, so we might be able to get them down to four-fifty."

He might never figure this woman out, but he was

going to have a hell of a good time trying. "Kate." She swung around to look at him. "Do *you* like it?"

She blinked at him in confusion and he had to wonder, had anyone ever asked her what she liked before?

Then she exhaled heavily, looking defeated. He didn't like that look on her. "Roger and I..." she started, her voice trailing off. Then she tried again. "We'd already purchased a house when this came on the market and besides, it was out of our price range. But I've been through it several times now and..."

Her hand stroked over the marble countertop affectionately as she walked to the sink, making his gut tighten. He wanted her to touch him like that, to hear that longing in her voice when she talked to him.

Great. Now he was jealous of a house. Bad enough he was jealous of Jack, but at least that was another guy. The house was just a house.

She leaned against the sink and stared out the window into that big fenced backyard and damned if she didn't look like she belonged here. She loved this house and for some insane reason, he wanted to give it to her.

"The house just makes *sense*," she went on, a note of defeat in her voice that he didn't miss. "The way the rooms are arranged, the way everything works together—it's one of the best houses I've ever been in. Nothing to compromise on, nothing I'd want to change. I've always been able to see myself living here. It'd be a wonderful place to raise a family."

He understood what she was saying. She hadn't been able to afford it even when she'd had Roger's income to kick in and now? Even if the price could be negotiated down more, it'd still be beyond her. Instead, she was going to have to watch someone else buy her dream home.

Unless... "Question." She turned, her eyebrows raised. "We haven't started on the industrial properties for the museum. What happens if I buy a piece of property for, say, four million dollars? Will your commission be enough to buy this house?"

The color drained out of her face, which was not the reaction he'd been hoping to get. "Seth," she said softly, sounding even sadder—which had not been his goal. "You can't just snap your fingers and solve all of my problems. I got myself into my own mess and I am going to get myself out of it, too." She swallowed, her eyes huge. "I don't need you to save me."

"That's not what this is." But even as he said it, he wasn't entirely sure that was the truth. He didn't think about it in terms of saving her. He thought about it in terms of *helping*. Of course, why he felt this compulsion to help her was another question he didn't want to investigate too deeply right now.

"Then tell me what this is about. The truth, Seth."

The truth? Hell. The truth was he was worried about her. He couldn't stop fantasizing about her. He was glad she hadn't married Roger. He knew how hard single mothers had it and he didn't want it to be that hard for her. It shouldn't be that hard for anyone, but especially not for her.

He didn't say any of that. Instead, he closed the distance between them and cupped her face in his hands. "This," he said, lowering his lips to hers, "is the truth."

Then he kissed her.

Ten

Oh, God—Seth was kissing her. And somehow, it *was* the truth.

Because the truth was, she wanted him to kiss her and more than that, she wanted to kiss him back.

How had she thought that she could talk herself out of this need? God knew she'd tried. For a whole week, she'd diligently reasoned that it didn't make sense to fall into bed with Seth Bolton. It was a bad idea and the list of reasons why was long. Safer to keep their relationship strictly platonic.

In fact, she had gotten up this morning determined not to let things get to this point. But now that they were here—now that he was brushing his lips over hers, soft and gentle and asking for permission…

She sighed into his mouth and wrapped her arms around his waist. However many reasons there were not to do this, none of them trumped the simple fact that she *wanted* Seth. She wanted to hold on to this last chance to be Kate Burroughs before her identity was redefined by motherhood. She wanted her baby, but she didn't want to lose herself, either.

So she kissed him back. She opened her mouth for him and slid her tongue along the seam of his lips and thrilled at the groan of desire that rumbled out of his chest. She pressed her body to his and let the warmth of his solid muscles sink into her skin.

She stopped trying to fight this desire. She stopped trying to fight herself.

Seth was the one who broke the kiss. He pulled back and rested his forehead against hers, his chest rising and falling rapidly. "I shouldn't have kissed you," he said, his words coming out in a rush. "But I can't regret it."

This was it, her last chance to stop this madness before it consumed her.

Too damned bad she wanted to be consumed. "Yes, you should've."

He gave her a quizzical look. "Was I reading you wrong? I thought you weren't interested."

She had tried so hard not to be. "Seth, this is a bad idea." His face fell. "But that doesn't mean I'm not interested. I don't *want* to be interested in you. My life is complicated enough. But I can't help wanting you."

Dimly, she was aware that they were locked in an embrace inside a stranger's home. True, the home had been unoccupied for months. But ethically, she was pushing her luck. "We need to leave."

He nodded and stepped back, but he didn't let go of her. Instead, his arm slid down around her waist and he held her tight to his side. "Where do you want to go? Dinner or…"

She would need to eat—eventually. But she needed him more. "Or?"

He guided her toward the door. "What about your place?"

She hesitated. It was such a small apartment. She knew she shouldn't be embarrassed for him to see it—it was clean and neat. But after spending the day in some of the nicer homes in Rapid City, her apartment would look pathetic in comparison.

Besides, she didn't want Seth in her apartment because then she would have all these memories of him there. Every time she walked into her bedroom, she would remember him stretched out on her bed, the sheet around his hips and his chest bare. Every time she tried to fall asleep, his presence would keep her awake.

She needed to keep a little distance between the rest of her life and what was going to happen in the next few weeks. Because she couldn't imagine that this would last more than a few weeks.

Just long enough for her to taste true passion. Just enough memories to keep her going through what would be a few years of long days and sleepless nights. That's all she was doing with Seth—making memories.

"Your place?"

"I'm currently living in a hotel. But," he added, opening the door for her, "it has room service. If you're sure?"

Was she sure this was a good idea? No. She was pretty sure it wasn't.

But was she sure that Seth would take great care with her? That he would deliver on exactly what he had promised—something fun and satisfying, something to erase the lingering bad memories of Roger from her mind? Something *good*?

She leaned up on her tiptoes and brushed a kiss across his lips—a promise of more to come. "I'm sure. Are you?"

That smile—confident and cocky, sensual and heated—*that* was exactly what she was looking for. "You have no idea."

Twenty minutes later, Seth said, "We can order room service later," as he guided her into the room and kicked the door shut behind him.

Then she was sinking into his arms and wondering why, exactly, she'd fought against this so hard. It didn't mean anything. She was attracted to Seth and he was attracted to her, and she simply hadn't had enough fun in her life for so long that she almost couldn't remember what it felt like to enjoy herself.

Well, to hell with that. Because she was going to enjoy this time here, with this man. "Okay?" Seth asked again as his hands settled around her waist. They hadn't even gotten to the bed—he was still leaned against the door. But he wasn't going to let her go.

"Okay," she agreed, sliding her hands underneath his jacket and flattening her palms against his chest. It had been unseasonably warm today and he had on another Crazy Horse T-shirt. His body was hard and hot under her touch, and touch him she did.

He let her. He stayed still while she explored the planes of his chest. He didn't yank her clothing off, didn't try to skip the foreplay and get straight to the sex. He let her take her time and that felt important.

She didn't know how long they had together, but she didn't want to rush it.

"You never did tell me how old you are," she murmured as she pushed the jacket from his shoulders. He let go of her waist long enough for the leather to hit the floor and then she was studying his arms. She hadn't seen them before—the muscles that strained at the sleeves of his shirt, a tattoo visible on his right biceps. "Good Lord, Seth. Look at you."

"Twenty-five. And I'd rather look at you. Except… without these clothes." He peeled her black suit jacket off her shoulders. "Black and white are all wrong on you. You need bright, vibrant color, Kate. You're gorgeous in color."

She felt her cheeks get warm. "It was the only thing that fit," she admitted—and that was only because the pants had elastic in the back. Otherwise, she would've been showing houses in yoga pants.

"Ah. And here I thought you were sending me a message—hands off."

She could feel that her whole face had turned red and it only got worse as he reached for the buttons on her slacks. It wasn't like he hadn't undressed her before—he had. He had lifted her skirt and peeled off a petticoat and been within inches of her most personal areas. But it was different now. Her body was changing faster every single day. "I'm different. Since the last time we did this."

His mouth curved into a dangerous half grin. "We've done this before? I'm sure I would remember."

"You know what I mean," she said, whacking him on the side of the arm. "You have undressed me before. At least partially."

"Trust me, babe—I have not forgotten. I never will." He worked the zipper down and then slid his hands underneath the fabric, along her skin. "And this time, I'm not going to settle on 'partially.'"

She didn't have on a thong today, nor did she have on stockings and a garter. The best she could do was a pair of bikini-cut panties—white—with a little pink bow on the front and her new, very serviceable white bra. The underthings were innocent, almost—the most innocent thing about this particular situation, anyway.

She could feel the palm of his hand moving over the fabric of her panties and then lower, over her hips. The slacks gave way as he stroked down her skin. He followed the pants, falling to his knees before her as she revealed her skin and this time, she couldn't drop a skirt to hide.

This time, she didn't want to.

They felt like they were starting from the same spot—but it was different, too. She hadn't known anything about Seth the first time she'd balanced a hand on his shoulder so she could step free of extraneous fabric. She hadn't known if he was rich or poor, old or young. All she had known then was that she was safe with him.

She still was. "Tell me what you want," Seth said when she had stepped free of the slacks. He grabbed them and threw them out of the way, then began to slide her trouser socks off. "I want to give you what you need."

Her eyes fluttered shut and she tried to put words to what that was.

She wanted to be selfish. She didn't want to swallow down her disappointment in bed to protect anyone's feelings. She didn't want to accept mediocre sex because Roger was incapable of putting forth the effort to get better. She didn't want to settle because it kept the peace.

She needed to know what Kate Burroughs wanted. She needed to know that person was valuable and desirable and worth the risk.

She needed Seth to fight for her.

She needed to fight for herself.

"Anything," Seth said as her other sock and shoe were also tossed aside. He sat back on his heels and ran his hands up and down her bare legs, warming her skin. "Be honest, Kate."

"I don't want to regret this," she said, because that was the most honest thing she could think of. "I don't want to regret you."

"You won't. And I won't, either," he assured her. He leaned forward and pressed his lips against her thigh. "I had the most erotic dreams after the last time," he whispered against her skin as he kissed his way up her leg.

"I'm different now. Everything's changed." She felt huge and she knew she was only going to get bigger. Rationally, she knew it was because of the baby, but it was still hard to know that an ugly black suit was the only thing she could wear for her standing date with Seth Bolton.

She didn't feel ugly now, not as Seth moved to the other thigh and began to kiss and nip at her skin. She watched in fascination.

"You were gorgeous two months ago, but now?" Seth leaned back and began to undo the buttons on her shirt. He had amazingly long arms, powerful muscles. Everything about him was powerful and he was here with her. How did this make any sense?

"But now?" he said in such a sincere voice that even though it didn't make any sense, she had no choice but to believe him. He got the buttons undone, and she shrugged out of the shirt, letting it fall. "My God, Kate—*look* at you."

She was going to protest that there was nothing to look at—at least not anything good—but he sat forward and pressed a kiss right below her belly button. And then one below that. And then one even lower. What started out as a sweet, tender gesture rapidly became something else entirely.

"Seth," she said, her knees beginning to shake as his mouth moved over the thin cotton of her panties, coming ever closer to her sex.

"Tell me what you need, Kate," he said, bringing his hands up to cup her bottom—and bring her closer to his mouth. "Do you need this?"

He skimmed his teeth over her panties, pulling the fabric aside. She was so shaky that she had no choice but to bury her fingers in his thick black hair and hold on. He looked up at her and squeezed her bottom, a knowing smile tugging at the corner of his lips. "Come on, Kate—you have to tell me."

"Yes," she whispered. He was slow and methodical—and focused entirely on her. He wasn't keeping an eye on the clock or an ear on the game. He wasn't wishing he were anywhere else. She had his undivided attention and that, more than anything else, was what she needed right now.

That and his mouth on her. "More." It came out half an order and half a plea.

His grin sharpened. "Good girl. I want to hear what you like." Then he buried his face against her sex.

"Ohh..." That. Definitely *that*.

Somehow, he pivoted her so instead of her standing, she was leaning against a wall. He scooted her legs a little farther apart and pressed himself between them. He still gripped her bottom with one hand, but with the other, he reached around the front and pulled her innocent-looking white panties to the side. Not off—just to the side. "How about this? Do you need this?" he asked, pausing just long enough that she knew if she said no, he'd stop.

She didn't want him to stop. "I do," she said, her voice little more than an exhale.

He kissed the top of her thigh, teasing her. "Are you sure?"

For some reason, the question irritated her. She was tired of people not listening to her, tired of them assuming they knew best. She wanted Seth to make her feel gorgeous and sexy, she wanted the release of a good orgasm—but more than that, she wanted him to listen. She wanted to be heard.

She tugged on his hair—hard—pulling him back to where she needed him. "I said yes," she hissed, watching as his eyes fluttered shut and he inhaled her scent deeply. "And I meant it. I won't beg, Seth. You're going to give me what I want and that's final."

He moaned. He was on his knees in front of her, his face buried against her sex, and he *moaned*. It was a noise of pure want and it shot straight through her. And then he kissed her, right where she needed his mouth. His lips moved over that nub of skin and nerves and then it was her moaning as she held him to her. His tongue flicked out and traced a pattern on her skin, one that she would feel for the rest of her life.

He was marking her, and she was his to be marked.

As his mouth worked her body, the rest of the world fell away. She stopped worrying about her rounded tummy or her woeful closet. Commissions and tours and kitchens—they all fell away. Even the fantasy that had been Seth—him stripping her at the scenic overlook and instead of putting her on a motorcycle, doing this exact same thing—it fell away because that hadn't been real. It'd been a bedtime story she'd told herself, a lie to convince herself that she was still Kate Burroughs and that was good enough.

This? This was not a lie. She was Kate Burroughs and Seth wasn't some mysterious, handsome stranger, he was a man—a warm, solid, flesh-and-blood man—who wanted her. More than that, he was putting her first. Hell, she hadn't even gotten his shirt off. She wanted to see his body, to touch it and taste it.

She wanted him all for herself. Not for anyone else, not for a commission. She wanted Seth Bolton because he was a man she liked, a man who cared about what happened to her. A handsome, confident man.

A man who was very good with his mouth. There was something naughty about this. They hadn't made it to a bed—no one was naked. But there was something freeing about it, too.

"God, Kate—you taste so good," he murmured against her sensitized flesh, his words vibrating right through her. "Better than I imagined."

Well, they were being honest. "I dreamed of you doing this, too," she told him. The hand that was still on her bottom slipped underneath her panties so he could grip her harder. It wasn't enough. She heard herself say, "I need more, Seth."

The request shocked her. Had she ever said that be-fore? If she had, she was pretty sure it hadn't gotten the desired result. When had she learned that, even in bed, she had to be quiet and go along to get along? Whose bright idea was that?

"Mmm, something more." He leaned back. The next thing Kate knew, her panties had been pulled down and Seth was back between her legs. This time, in addition to his mouth, his fingers began to work her. He stroked up and down and found that sensitive nub again, teas-ing it with his teeth as he slipped a finger inside her.

The relief was so intense that she could've cried. He thrust that finger into her in time with the movements of his tongue and his lips, and it was everything she'd ever wanted and never gotten.

Then, just when she was sure she couldn't take another moment, he added a second finger and she was lost.

Eleven

Kate's grip on his hair bordered on painful, but Seth wasn't about to do anything to stop the incoming wave of her orgasm. He could take a little pain for her.

She was so beautiful when she came. Her color was high and her eyes were glazed over with lust. And her body? Damn, her body. There was something so lush and gorgeous about her that even though he was inside her, he couldn't get enough. He had never been this hard for a woman, never this desperate.

"Seth—Seth!" she gasped as her body convulsed around him. He leaned in, putting just a little more pressure against the spot that drove her wild. The noise she made—he wanted to capture it in a kiss and hold it deep inside him, but he didn't dare let her go.

Her back arched off the wall and then the crisis passed and she slumped, her legs giving out. He managed to catch her before she toppled them both over. "I've got you, babe," he whispered against her breast as he studied her.

For a long few minutes, they stayed in this awkward pose, him on his knees, her half draped over him. She was breathing hard, and he wasn't much better off.

He needed to move. It was torture to sit on his heels in these boots, torture to keep these jeans buttoned. He needed to lay her out on the bed and show her *that* had just been a preview of what was to come.

But when he shifted to stand and sweep her into his arms, he realized there were tears running down her cheeks. "Kate?"

She blinked at him. "Seth…" she murmured, sounding almost as confused as she looked.

"Oh, God—I'm sorry," he said, scrambling to his feet and pulling her into his arms. He crushed her in a hug and then realized perhaps *crushing* was not the best option right now, so he shifted to make sure he was merely holding her firmly. "I'm sorry," he repeated.

"What? No—no, you don't understand." She sniffed and pulled away, scrubbing at her cheeks with the back of her hand. "That was amazing, Seth. I don't think… I'm sorry. I'm not upset. It's the hormones. I've never— This isn't— I…" She trailed off, looking, if possible, even more confused.

Oh, thank God. He hadn't hurt her, hadn't crossed the line—hadn't misread the situation. "So you're okay?"

She smiled—a watery smile, but a smile all the same. "Honestly, I'm not sure if I've ever been better. It was amazing. You," she said, poking him in the chest, "are amazing. And wearing far too many clothes."

"I can fix that." He grabbed the hem of his T-shirt, but she batted his hands away.

"I want to do it."

"Never let it be said that I don't give a woman what she wants." He let his hands fall to his sides as she began to tug at his T-shirt. She was in no hurry, her movements languid and relaxed. Her tears had dried and all that was left was that knowing smile, satisfied and ready for more. He'd put that smile on her face and by God, he'd leave another in its place.

She pulled his shirt over his head and let it fall to the side. "Good heavens, Seth—you're stunning."

She skimmed her hands over his chest, brushing his nipples and taking the measure of his waist. He fought to keep the groan from escaping. "I aim to please."

She paused at the button of his jeans and shot him a look. "What about you? What do you want?"

The word *everything* popped up in his head before he could think. But he didn't say that, not out loud. This was short-term, fun. No strings attached. He could have everything, for a limited time only.

For some reason, the thought made him sadder than he expected. He didn't expect it to upset him at all, frankly. He expected to get lucky and have a good time and call it a day. He didn't *want* anything more.

Kate began working at his button fly, drawing his attention back to her. She was simply the most beautiful woman he'd ever seen. He wanted to burn that ugly black suit and deliver Kate to his aunt Stella, the fashion designer. He wanted to wrap her in vibrant blues and golds and greens. He wanted to see Kate in all of her glory, instead of her beauty hidden.

He pulled the ponytail holder out of her hair and sank

his fingers into her locks. "Beautiful," he said as he arranged her silky hair around her shoulders.

She shoved his pants down and he kicked out of his boots. That left him in nothing but his boxer briefs—which were barely keeping his erection contained.

Kate straightened, a shy smile on her face. He knew she was no innocent, but there was still something unsure about her. Which she only reinforced when she asked, "Now what?"

He didn't particularly want to think about Roger Caputo right now, but again he had to wonder what the hell had been wrong with that man. Kate was a gorgeous, passionate woman and Roger had just let her go. Was he that damned blind that he couldn't see what was right in front of him?

If Kate were his, Seth would do everything in his power not just to keep her, but to keep her safe and whole and so blissfully happy that she never had to worry about anything.

Too damned bad she wasn't his.

"Bed," he said, having trouble thinking straight. He was personally familiar with the concept of lust—but this? This was different. More intense. He was *desperate* for her, and he had never been desperate before. Hard up, maybe. But not like this.

She ducked her head and turned toward the king-size bed. But Seth reached out and turned her back toward him. "Wait for me, babe," he murmured, drawing her in close so that he could feel her breasts pressed against his bare chest. He fisted his hand in her hair. Tilting her face to his, he brought his mouth down upon hers.

He kissed her with everything he had. She made a squeak of surprise but then she melted into him. She tasted so good—he couldn't get enough of her. And when her arms came around his waist and she slid her hands down to cup his ass, he got even harder.

He wanted to take his time with her—he *was* taking his time with her—but the intensity of his desire was blinding. He began to walk her back toward the bed, never taking his mouth from hers.

She came alive against him. He could almost see the moment when she forgot to be self-conscious and nervous. He could definitely taste the sweetness of that moment. He captured her little noises and need with his lips. He let go of her hair long enough to unfasten her bra and cast it aside, and then he had to look.

"Sweet Jesus, Kate," he groaned, cupping her breasts in his hands. They were full and heavy, her nipples a deep russet red. "Perfect," he said, brushing his thumbs back and forth over her tips and watching them tighten.

She gasped her arousal. "They're not usually that— oh, Seth," she moaned as he lowered his head to one and replaced his thumb with his tongue. "They got bigger. More—oh! More sensitive." Her hands found his hair and, just like she had held him to her sex before, she held him to her breast now.

The words were slow to penetrate the fog of desire in Seth's mind, but penetrate they did. More sensitive— that meant he needed to be gentle. It meant that if he played his cards right, he might be able to drive her to orgasm just by playing with her nipples alone.

The back of her legs hit the bed and she sat abruptly. Seth came off her breast with an audible *pop*. She blinked up at him, apparently surprised as to how she'd landed where she was. "Seth," she whispered. She stroked her hands down his chest, and his stom-

ach—then she hooked her fingers into the waistband
of his briefs and pulled.

They had all night. That was what Seth kept telling
himself when his cock sprang free. He held his hands at
his side, giving her the space to explore without making
any demands. Because they had all night and he had
nowhere he had to be tomorrow morning and by God,
he was going to make this memorable for her.

"Wow," she said, tracing the tip of her finger along
the side of his erection, making him quiver. "I had no
idea." Seth was powerless to keep the growl inside.

Maybe he wouldn't despise Roger. True, the man
had apparently never done anything good for Kate, but
on the other hand, it was going to be easy—and enjoy-
able—to blow Kate's preconceived notions of sex and
intimacy out of the water.

She wrapped her hand around his shaft and stroked
once, twice—all while staring at him intently. "Is it
okay if I do this?" she asked, stroking him again.

"God, yes." Why wouldn't it be?

"I just…" But she didn't finish the thought. Instead,
she stroked him slowly, driving him past the point of
thinking. And that was before she leaned forward and
pressed her lips to his tip.

And suddenly it was too much. Before she could
take him into her mouth, Seth grabbed her by the hair
and pulled her away. "I can't— Kate," he said, not even
able to get a coherent thought out. He leaned down and
crushed his mouth over hers, desperate to be inside her.
But at the very last second, his lone remaining functional brain cell kicked into gear—the condom. It wasn't
like he could get her more pregnant—but safe sex was

good sex. He forced himself to pull away from her and went to grab his jacket, fishing the condoms out.

When he turned back to the bed, Kate was leaning on her elbows, watching him intently. There was something so right about her, about them being here together. *Everything*, he thought, staring at her. She was everything.

He prowled across the hotel room, kneeling on the bed next to her. He was supposed to be saying things to her, he was pretty sure—sweet nothings about how gorgeous she was, how excited he was—how great he was going to be for her.

He had nothing. Not a damned thing. And when she reached out and gripped his erection again, the need to be buried inside her was overwhelming.

He rolled on the condom and fit himself between her legs. "Yeah?" he asked, dragging his erection against the folds of her flesh.

Her hips arched into him as her eyes fluttered. "Yes, please," she whispered, wrapping her arms around his neck and bringing him close so she could sear him with her lips.

"So polite." He was going to push her past that. He wanted her demanding and bossy, confident in her desires and in his ability to fulfill them.

He shifted and found her opening and then, as carefully as he could, he began to thrust. Her body was tight around his and the sensations—damn, the sensations. He'd always liked sex. Careful sex, of course. He wasn't going to get anyone pregnant and leave them high and dry. He was *not* that guy. But sex itself had always been fun.

This? Burying his body inside Kate's went far past fun, he realized as they fell into a rhythm. Being with

Kate wasn't a fun Saturday night. It was suddenly as vital to him as breathing.

She rose to meet him as he plunged into her again and again and he completely surrendered to her. Her hands gripped his shoulders, his arms. "Oh, God— Seth," she cried, her body tightening around his.

"Yeah, babe—yeah," he ground out, straining to keep his orgasm in check long enough. He wouldn't dare leave her unsatisfied. It simply wasn't polite.

She thrashed her head against the pillow and dug her fingernails into his back as her body gripped his with such strength that he couldn't hold anything back. He gave himself over to her and held on as she came.

He collapsed on top of her, both of them breathing hard for a few moments as his head cleared. This time, when he leaned back to withdraw, he was ready for the tears—because they were there again. She looked at him and smiled and then laughed and said, "It's good crying, I promise."

He was willing to take her at her word that this was a hormonal thing. "You never cried before?" he asked, getting rid of the condom and draping himself around her.

"No," she said, sounding tired and sated and happy. "Or laughed. But then, I don't ever remember having orgasms like that, either."

Roger was an idiot. A clueless idiot. "I am ever at your command, my lady."

She laughed again. "I think you were right."

He propped himself up on his elbow and began to trace her collarbone with his lips. "About what?"

She cupped her palm around his cheek and lifted

his face so he had to look at her. Her eyes sparkled. "I think you're going to be very good for me."

His chest puffed up with pride and he nipped at the space where her shoulder met her neck. "It was only the beginning, Kate. I can be even better for you than that in just a few minutes." He lowered his mouth to her breast again, but just then her stomach rumbled. He bit back his smile and leaned away, putting his hand on her stomach. If he didn't know she was pregnant, he wouldn't be able to tell. Soon, maybe. "Maybe we should have dinner first? I picked this hotel for the room service."

He would do anything for that smile of hers. Everything. "I'd like that."

Seth called in their orders while she got cleaned up in the bathroom. When she came back out wearing her boring white shirt again, he growled.

"I am not going to be naked when room service shows up, thank you very much. Besides," she went on as he stared at her legs, "you can always take it off again later."

"Woman," he groaned, falling back on the bed as if she'd shot him. "Come wait with me."

They curled up under the covers and turned on a game, although they didn't watch it. Seth was too busy touching her skin, massaging her shoulders, stroking her hair, to pay any attention to sports. By the time dinner showed up, he was more than half hard for her all over again.

And the whole time, he kept thinking that it was a damn shame that he had no plans to stay in Rapid City on a permanent basis. Though even if he were staying, he wouldn't want to keep this thing between them going. Kate didn't need a long-term relationship that was nothing more than casual sex. She needed a man who could settle down and stay in one place, someone who could be a good dad and shoulder his half of the load—if not more. She needed someone who would be there every night and every morning and that, sadly, was not Seth. He simply didn't have it in him.

He'd always been restless. Although his mom had never said so one way or the other, Seth attributed his wanderlust to his birth father. The man had disappeared before Seth had been born, never to be seen on the reservation again. Seth had no idea if his father was kind or hard, laughing or serious. All he had ever known about the man was that he left his girlfriend and his unborn child behind without a second look.

That was why Seth's new position at Crazy Horse Choppers fit him so well. He'd already spent a year in Los Angeles, hobnobbing with the rich, famous and the wished-they-were-famous. His uncle Bobby was always looking for the next big thing. Billy just wanted to build motorcycles. Ben kept an eye on the bottom line—but Bobby? Bobby wanted to take over the world, and he was more than willing to use Seth as a means to that end.

Seth was going to get this museum project started because he believed it would be both a great way to extend the Crazy Horse Choppers brand name and also expand their revenue streams. But beyond that, it would showcase the occasional mad genius that was the Boltons. And after that?

After that, Seth was looking toward the future. American-style motorcycles were beginning to take off in popularity in Asia. His uncles and his father—they were family men. All Boltons were. They loved their wives and were actively involved in their children's lives. It would be hard to ask them—even Bobby—to pack up and head to Shanghai for six months or so to open up the Asian market.

But Seth? He was unattached. No wife, no children. Just a restless wanderlust and an up-to-date passport.

That night, after he had pulled Kate on top of him and teased her breasts until she cried out with a shattering orgasm, he lay in the dark, listening to her breathe and feeling her warm body pressed against his. He decided he wouldn't tell her about the possibility of Asia. Not yet, anyway. It was still several months away, and he had to get the museum project going first.

Which meant he had several more months of nights like this.

Twelve

Just like it had every Saturday for the last three weeks, Kate's heart sped up when Seth Bolton walked into Zanger Realty. Today was no exception.

Rain had dampened his hair and a few stray drops clung to his eyelashes, and he was impossibly more handsome now than he'd ever been. When his gaze locked on hers from across the office, she could see how much he'd been waiting for this moment, too.

Because she had been waiting for *him*.

"Ms. Burroughs," he said, his voice going right through her.

"Good morning, Mr. Bolton." It was a little game they played, pretending to be professional when there might be someone else around, even though Harold Zanger rarely came into the office on Saturdays. She stood. "We have a busy day ahead of us—two industrial properties I think will work for you. And after that, are you ready to buy a house?"

He was buying the home on Bitter Root. Her house—although it wasn't hers. Soon, it would be his.

She'd always known she'd be sad when that house sold. But oddly, she was happy that if anyone else had to buy it, it was Seth. He'd take good care of it.

His eyes darkened as his gaze swept over her body. Because he was buying a house today, she had splurged on some new clothes that fit—she'd get her commission before the bills came due. The broomstick skirt with an elastic waist and the tunic top with a deep vee at the neck weren't outright maternity clothes, but she had read that it was a wise financial investment to buy regular clothing one size larger than she had been wearing because she would probably need them after she had the baby.

And although she knew this wasn't a committed relationship, she wanted to look her best for Seth. She couldn't do anything about her rapidly changing body—although Seth seemed to appreciate her new curves far more than she did—but by God she could at least put on flattering clothes. And lingerie. The new lacy black bra—yet another size up—and the matching panties made her feel like she could still be sexy.

Especially when Seth looked at her like that.

"I'm certainly looking forward to celebrating my new home," he said, his voice low. "You look *amazing* today, Kate."

She felt his words—and his desire—in her chest. Everywhere. A shiver went through her—the kind of shiver that promised better things to come. "I've always found home ownership to be *inspiring*." She couldn't wait until the ink was dry on the legal documents and the key to his new house was in his hands. Normally, she would buy clients a gift basket to welcome them to their new home—a candle, a few knickknacks that seemed to match the personalities of the buyers.

Today? She wanted to welcome him to his new home in ways that had nothing to do with candles.

His grin deepened and he took another step into the office, leaving wet footprints on the carpet behind him. "Incredibly inspiring," he agreed. "But assuming the rain moves off, we'll need to make a small side trip."

"Oh?"

His grin tightened and suddenly he looked nervous. "My sister's regular game got delayed because of the storm, but it's supposed to clear off soon. I promised I'd try to stop by. If they win today, they're in the championship."

"This is Julie, right?" They'd talked some about their families, but only enough to scratch the surface. What could she say about her parents? Her mother was a doormat and her father was a steamroller?

His family life seemed vastly more complicated. The man outright dismissed the notion of living in one place for more than six months at a time and yet he was the most devoted big brother she'd ever met. For a man who wasn't the least interested in setting down roots, he was perfectly happy to spend a crazy amount of money on a luxury home.

After a month of spending time with Seth, she was no closer to understanding him, really.

"Yeah. She and my cousins make up half the starting line. We won't have to stay for the whole game, but I do want to put in an appearance."

She was not looking for anything more permanent. She *wasn't*. She was appreciating this time with Seth as the gift it was. But still, his offer to include her in a family thing warmed her.

Wait a minute. "Will your parents be there?"

He dropped his gaze. "Yeah. The whole family will be."

Oh, dear. Of course, once she had figured out she would be spending time with Seth, she had looked up the reality show the Boltons had done a number of years ago—even catching glimpses of the teenage Seth working with his father.

Seth had been a cute boy on the verge of manhood then—but the Boltons? Billy was like an angry grizzly bear, Ben Bolton glowered sullenly anytime a camera was shoved in his face, and Bobby? Well, the last Bolton brother wasn't dangerous-looking like his brothers—but he was smooth and sharp and good on camera. And their father? He was the epitome of every tough old biker ever.

And Seth wanted her to meet these people?

"We don't have to," he said into the silence. "They can be overwhelming—trust me, I know."

It was tempting to say that they wouldn't have time for a side trip. Or to say she wasn't dressed for standing in a wet field. Or that she wasn't feeling up to it. All of those would be perfectly fine excuses to save her from meeting the Boltons en masse. Because meeting the whole family—that felt huge. Far too big for a casual relationship like the one she and Seth had.

But family was forever. Or, for a long time—until they disowned you, anyway. And she'd feel terrible if she caused any sort of trouble for him with his extended family just because she might be a little intimidated by a group of bikers. He was willing to go above and beyond for his family, and she couldn't fault him for that. If anything, she admired him all the more.

So despite her misgivings, she put on a smile and said, "We can do that. But we better get going if we want to have time."

When Seth opened her car door for her, she was past panic and straight over into stark terror. "You're not introducing me as your girlfriend," she told him, staring at his hand. "That's not what this is, right?"

He didn't answer for a long moment, and she suddenly didn't know how he'd answer that question.

Worse, she didn't know how she wanted him to answer that question.

"Right," he finally said, slow and serious. "You're my real estate agent."

Oh, this was a mistake. An epic, huge, grandiose mistake.

But she was going to make it anyway.

After he helped her from the car, they began the long trek to the playing field. Apparently showing up late meant that they got the worst parking spot. Although she'd worn boots to walk around the potential museum sites, she still had to hold her skirt by the hem to keep it from getting wet in the tall grass.

Which was fine because if she was holding her skirt, then she wasn't accidentally holding Seth's hand.

When they reached the playing field, Kate looked around. "Is that them?"

Most of the parents on the sidelines were regular-looking people sitting on folding chairs with coolers.

But at the end of the field, there was a group of big, burly men around a cluster of pickup trucks with the tailgates down. The trucks were massive and even at this distance, she could tell they were top-of-the-line.

And the Boltons were *loud*. Kate could hear them bellowing words of encouragement to the players on the field.

"That's them. Don't be intimidated. They're a lot nicer than they look. All bark, no bite—that sort of thing."

She shot him a look.

They paused at midfield, and Seth turned her toward the game. "We're rooting for the green team, the Mustangs. The forward? That's Julie. The right guard's Eliza and the left is Clara—my cousins. They're unbeatable." He said it with obvious pride when any other man his age might have been embarrassed or at least put out to have to give up part of his Saturday on a regular basis to watch little girls kick a ball around. But not him. He really did love his family.

The thought made Kate unexpectedly sad. She hadn't played soccer when she was young—but she'd had dance recitals and choir concerts, and had even acted in a few plays in high school. Her mom had come— but not her dad.

As they watched, Eliza passed the ball to Clara, who faked out a player on the other team and then kicked the ball to Julie, who bounced it off her chest and then kicked it in just past the goalie. The green team erupted into cheers—as did the parents on the sidelines. Especially the group of Boltons at the end of the field. Seth let out a tremendous whoop and the girls on the field pivoted as one and waved at him before their coach bellowed something and they all trotted off down the field.

"They seem pretty good," Kate said as they began to make their way toward his family—and her doom.

No, no—not her doom. Just a really awkward meeting with her not-boyfriend's parents. No need to panic.

"The Mustangs came in second in the championship last year. I think they're going to win it this year. Julie's unstoppable and Eliza is a monster on the field."

Kate kept an eye on the game. Julie and Eliza looked a great deal like each other but Clara? Kate had a feeling that if they all stood still next to each other, she'd be able to see the resemblance, but Clara was much lighter in coloring than the other two.

And then it was too late to turn back because the biggest of the three men stood up from the tailgate and bellowed, "Seth! About damn time. Where the hell have you been?"

Kate recognized him. It was Billy Bolton, the biggest and meanest-looking of the brothers. He was older than he'd been in the reality show, his grizzled beard shot with silver—but he was still a force to be reckoned with.

Then Billy's gaze landed on Kate and she froze like a deer in the headlights.

One of the women—petite and brown and who looked a great deal like Seth—put her hand on Billy's knee. "Language, honey."

A kid about eight or so looked up from the book he was reading. "Seth is here? Yeah!" He hopped up and gave Seth a high five and immediately began telling him about some complicated…card game? Kate couldn't tell.

A little girl, maybe five, squirmed out of Ben Bolton's arms and came charging up to Seth, who caught her easily. "Set!" she crowed. "Spin me!"

Kate's heart clenched at the sight of Seth making a

little girl squeal with joy while simultaneously carrying on a very important conversation with a kid. Of course he was great with kids. He was perfect, apparently.

And she was…not.

The woman who'd shushed Billy Bolton stood and made her way over to Kate and instantly, every hair on the back of Kate's neck stood up in warning. "Ignore my husband. Hi, I'm Jenny Bolton. And you are?"

"Kate." Kate swallowed, trying to remember who she was supposed to be right now. But that wasn't easy because every single pair of eyes at this tailgate party were now staring at her. Two other women, both about the same age as Jenny Bolton, closed ranks, standing behind Jenny. "Kate Burroughs," she finally remembered when the one woman with long, dark brown hair raised an eyebrow at her. "Of Zanger Realty. I'm Mr. Bolton's real estate agent."

Someone snorted, but Kate kept her focus on the women. Because it suddenly occurred to her—why had she been worried about the Bolton brothers?

She should have been worried about the Bolton *women*. Including but not limited to the three younger ones running up and down the field.

But maybe not the littlest one. Seth paused in spinning what Kate assumed was another cousin just long enough for the girl to grin at Kate and say, "Your skirt is pretty. Does it twirl?"

"I'm not sure," Kate answered honestly. "Twirling makes me dizzy." And God knew her sense of balance wasn't what it had once been.

"But that's the best part!" The girl giggled and then she and Seth were off again, making big, dizzying circles.

"Real estate?" Jenny's eyes narrowed as she took in

everything about Kate. The woman looked too much like Seth not to be his mother. The woman to Jenny's right was taller, more statuesque, perhaps a little lighter in coloring, but she bore a strong resemblance to Jenny. The woman to Jenny's left, however, had vivid blue eyes and an almost icy demeanor. To a woman, however, they were wearing stunning tops underneath their coats. Kate looked longingly at Jenny Bolton's soft peach sweater. She had a feeling that no matter how much her commission was, she wouldn't be able to afford a sweater like that. The same went for the diamonds in Jenny's ears and around her neck. And that had nothing on what the woman with blue eyes was wearing.

Kate refused to be intimidated by the unified wall of womanhood that was currently looking her up and down. Crap—could these experienced wives and mothers tell she was pregnant? Or were they just judging her by regular feminine standards?

"We were looking at an industrial property not far from here and had time to check in on the game before we signed papers on Mr. Bolton's house this afternoon." All of which was 100 percent the truth and had nothing to do with how good Seth was in bed.

After a moment's hesitation that spoke louder than any niceties could, Jenny said, "I see," in a tone that made it clear that she did—far too well.

Kate swallowed. This was not going well. Feeling desperate, she turned her attention to the rest of the group. "No need to get up," she said when it was obvious no one would, anyway. She gave a little wave. "It's a pleasure to meet you all. I enjoyed your show." Bobby Bolton, still as handsome as ever, grinned—but his brothers both groaned. Kate pressed on. "And

I'm excited to help your company move forward into its next venture." There. That was a perfectly professional thing to say.

No one reacted. "Kate's done an amazing job finding the right properties," Seth announced into the awkward silence.

She could feel her face heating up. Somehow, turning tomato red didn't seem to be the reasonable reaction here.

Then it only got worse because in the middle of that quiet lull, her stomach growled so loudly that it briefly drowned out the sounds of the game. "My apologies," Kate said hastily, wondering if a woman could actually die of embarrassment at a soccer game. "We haven't had time to grab lunch. We should go…"

But the words had no more gotten out of her mouth than the Bolton women descended upon her. "We have food," the paler one said in a surprising British accent. "I'm Stella—Bobby's wife. Clara's mother."

"Besides," the other added, "Connie won't turn loose of Seth for a good twenty minutes and Davey has to talk to someone about Pokémon—all the better if it isn't me. I'm Josey—Ben's wife. The rest of this brood is mine."

"You should sit," Jenny said, moving forward to put a hand on Kate's arm and leading her to a folding chair. "We have chicken or burgers."

And just like that, Kate wasn't on the outside anymore.

She had no idea if that was a good thing or not.

Thirteen

Dimly, Seth was aware that there was still a soccer match going on. But that wasn't the game he was playing right now.

"She's pretty," Bruce Bolton, Seth's grandpa, said. He turned his flinty eyes back to Seth. "What's she doing here with the likes of *you*?"

Seth tried to laugh that off. Over the years, he had learned to hold his own against the Bolton men. But that usually worked best when they'd chosen sides. The Boltons united was a fearsome sight to behold.

Like right now. The three brothers and their father were all staring at Seth, expecting a reasonable answer. It was at that moment that Seth realized he might have overplayed his hand. Time for some damage control. "Like I said, she's my real estate agent. I'm closing on my house this afternoon." They stared at him like he had lost his ever-loving mind.

"I wouldn't waste my time with a lovely lady like that on real estate," Bruce grumbled. Then he winked at Seth.

"The second site we looked at this morning seems like a good fit for the museum," Seth went on, desperate to keep the conversation away from how pretty Kate was. "It's halfway between the highway and the factory. It costs a little more up front, but the site's already been cleared."

If Seth had had any hope at all that talking shop would distract the Bolton men from the pretty real estate agent currently being coddled by the Bolton women, that hope died on the vine. "You be careful with her," his uncle Ben said.

"I am. I mean," Seth quickly corrected, "it's not like that. We're just working together."

His dad's glare hardened, and Bobby rolled his eyes in disbelief. Even Bruce looked like he wasn't going to buy that line. Seth wasn't a little kid anymore, but he began to sweat it. What if he couldn't convince them there was nothing unbecoming between him and Kate?

The Boltons were family men, and if they thought Seth was leading Kate along under false pretenses, Seth didn't want to even think what they might do. He wouldn't put a shotgun and a preacher past them, though.

But the moment the thought drifted through his brain, something weird happened. Instead of shuddering in horror at the thought, he could see Kate walking toward him, her belly rounded under a simple white dress—not that cupcake confection she'd been wearing the day he'd met her. A smile on her face as she came toward him…

He shook the thought from his head and glanced back over to where his mom and his aunts had surrounded Kate. Jenny had taken a seat next to Kate and appeared to be asking her a series of rapid-fire questions—about what, Seth was afraid to ask. Josey was piling a plate with food and Stella stood back a little ways, watching it all unfold. Kate glanced up and caught his eye. Her cheeks blushed a soft pink before she looked away.

"Yeah," Bobby said, chuckling. "*Just* working together. What did you say her name was?"

"Kate Burroughs."

"And she sells real estate?"

Seth nodded, feeling like he was sixteen and getting busted for staying out past curfew—again.

Bobby's grin turned sharp. "Wasn't there a wedding…?"

Of course Seth should've known that Bobby had his finger on the pulse of Rapid City gossip. "Yeah. I told you guys about that—I found the bride by the side of the road? That's her." He hadn't necessarily wanted to share that particular tidbit of information, but it was better to get out in front of this sort of thing.

Of course, being in front of anything with this crowd only guaranteed that he'd be run over. "You don't say," Ben said. *"Business."*

Honestly, Seth wasn't sure what this thing with Kate was anymore. It was, in fact, business. But it was also something casual and fun, a rebound to help Kate get back on her feet. And yet…

"Nothing but," he lied.

Not a single one of his male relatives bought that lie. Maybe because Seth didn't buy it himself.

Thankfully, something happened on the playing field

and for a moment, everyone's attention focused on the game. The Mustangs were up by three now, with fifteen minutes left in the game. The championship match seemed within their grasp.

He glanced at Kate again. Connie was practically in Kate's lap now, completely enamored of this fancy new person who wore pretty skirts. Kate leaned over, putting her at eye level with Connie. She had a big smile on her face and she clapped when Connie spun for her.

Something in his chest tightened. Kate was going to be an amazing mother. But he knew how hard it was to be a single parent. He didn't want that for her, damn it all. But aside from throwing two commissions her way, he didn't know how to help.

Kate caught his eye and gave Seth a tight smile. Then, as if by mutual agreement, they both looked away.

When Seth turned his attention back to his family, he found himself squarely in the crosshairs of his father. Billy threw an arm around Seth's shoulders and hauled him off to the side. "You're telling me," Billy began with no other introduction, "that you hired the runaway bride to be your real estate agent on purpose?"

Seth had had his disagreements with his adoptive father over the years. Billy was a hard man who did things his way. He wasn't afraid of a fight, either.

But for all that, he was a remarkably fair man. From the very beginning, he had treated Seth as if he were an equal. Seth wouldn't be half the man he was today if it weren't for his father. And he hated disappointing his father.

But he could tell that Billy was disappointed in him.

"She jilted her fiancé and he kept the house they had together. Her family didn't back her up and she had to quit their real estate office. I'm just helping her out. She needs the commissions."

All of which was true. Or at least, it had been a month ago. Now?

Billy gave him a hard look, one that had Seth standing up straighter. "Women are not to be trifled with, son."

"I am not trifling with her," he defended quickly. He'd made no promises to Kate beyond the next month or so. He was not leading her on with talks of love and marriage. There was no discussion of forever or happily-ever-after. No allusions to a future that existed past the new year. Ergo, it was not trifling.

"We're sending you to Shanghai," his father said in the kind of voice that Seth had seen make grown men damn near wet their pants with terror. "In the new year. Bobby thinks it could be six, eight months there, with a possibility of Mumbai afterward."

So it'd been decided? Good. Great. He loved it when a plan came together. So why was he filled with a crushing sort of disappointment? "And I'll be ready."

"Does she know that?"

"Of course she does. She knows my job is everything."

His father gave him a long look. "And yet you brought her to your sister's soccer game."

It was not a question. "I don't know how many times I have to say this," Seth ground out, pulling away from his father's embrace. "I'm not leading her on. We have a business relationship. We understand each other perfectly, damn it. And we were in the neighborhood."

Billy was not buying any of this. "If you get her pregnant," he said, as if he were Kate's father instead of Seth's, "your mother and I will expect you to do the right thing."

"I am not going to get her pregnant," Seth retorted. It was impossible to get her pregnant again. "Even if there was something going on between us—which there is not—I would never casually risk her health and well-being and you, of all men, should know that." For a moment, his dad looked almost chastised. Seth forced his shoulders to relax. "Now. Are you done threatening me so we can watch Julie play?"

He expected his father to glower or maybe even yell. So when Billy Bolton cracked a rare smile, Seth was completely caught off guard. "Make sure you're doing the right thing, son," he said, giving Seth a slap on the back that was hard enough to send Seth stumbling. Billy stepped around Seth and went to watch his daughter outplay the other team.

Seth glowered at his father's back. *Of course* he was doing the right thing. He was helping out a single soon-to-be mother. He was ensuring that she would have enough money to live on for the next year, if she wanted to. And he was helping her get over Roger. By the time Seth left for Shanghai, Kate would be financially secure and ready to move on with her life. Without him.

How was that not the right damn thing?

The garage doors shut behind them, sealing her and Seth off from the rest of the world. The afternoon had passed in a blur of legal documents and signatures, but the end result was now official—the home on Bitter Root was Seth's.

She wasn't going to be sad about that. She was just

going to be happy for him, and happy that he was willing to share this home with her, even for a little while.

He opened her car door and held out his hand, just like he always did. "I must say," he said, as she slipped her palm against his and let him help her from the car, "this has been one of the stranger days of my life."

"Buying a home is often very strange," she agreed. But that's not what made today strange for her.

The whole day had been a glimpse into a life she desperately wanted but would never get to have. This house was perfect for her and the family she was going to raise—but she couldn't afford it, not in this life or the next.

Just like Seth's family—aunts and uncles, grandparents and siblings, all coming together for something as mundane as a child's soccer game because they cared. They put family first.

Of course she knew that there were kind, loving, supportive families in the world. And hers was certainly not the worst, by far. But seeing the way that Seth's family had lined up to protect him from an outsider—her? And then there'd been that moment where, apparently by some unspoken agreement, she hadn't been on the outside looking in. She'd been made welcome and fed and, okay, so maybe his mom's questions about Seth's new house had really been thinly veiled questions about Seth and Kate's relationship. But there was no mistaking the fact that Seth's family would do anything for him—for any member of the Bolton family.

She wanted that unconditional love and support for her child. She wanted that for herself, but she was used to doing without.

Holding her hand, Seth unlocked the garage door. He

pulled her inside and then let go long enough to find a light switch. While he did so, she pushed aside her melancholy feelings. There was no point in moping over what she couldn't have. She needed to focus on what she did have—a gorgeous, caring, wealthy man who, for reasons she still didn't fully understand, was more than happy to give her almost everything she wanted.

"Welcome home, Mr. Bolton," she said when he found the light switch. He really was too handsome, she thought when he turned back to her. She tried to strike a sultry pose.

Seth's eyes darkened dangerously. "It's good to be home, Ms. Burroughs." He prowled toward her, the energy that made him so good in bed vibrating off him. "I feel like celebrating. How about you?" He paused, waiting for her answer.

"Yes." Because this was as good as it got. She could make love to Seth in his home and hold on to these happy memories through the long, lonely nights ahead.

He flattened her against the door with his body, hard and hot against hers. But even when he covered her mouth with his, taking and demanding—there was still a gentleness to him.

"Now, Seth," she whispered against his neck, grabbing the belt of his jeans. She didn't want to wait. She didn't want gentle. She just wanted this memory.

"Babe," he growled, and then he picked her up. She squeaked in alarm—she wasn't getting any lighter these days—but Seth cradled her to his chest as if it were the easiest thing in the world. Just like she had from the very beginning, she felt safe in his arms. She knew he wouldn't drop her.

"I apologize for the lack of furniture," he said as he carried her toward the kitchen.

"Don't," she said, throwing her arms around his neck and kissing his jaw. Tucking every contour of his face, every muscle in his neck, away into her memory. "Don't apologize for any of it."

He sat her on the island counter and kissed her again, harder this time. She managed to get his buckle undone and then he was shoving her flowing skirt up, pulling her panties down. "I need you so much, Kate."

"Yes," she hissed, shoving his pants out of the way. When was the last time anyone had needed her? Roger certainly hadn't. He'd barely even wanted her. Her parents had relied on her because she was cheap labor.

But who needed her because she was Kate?

No one. Just Seth.

They normally took their time with foreplay, but she didn't have the patience for it today and neither did he. He set himself against her and then, with one delicious thrust, buried himself deep inside. Moaning with pleasure, she fell back on her elbows as he grabbed her hips and slammed into her again and again.

She loved being with Seth, but this rawness, this need—this was what had been missing. She had thought he'd been holding himself back out of deference to her being pregnant. But today?

Today, he was like a man possessed. Seth pounded into her again and again, his fingertips gripping her hips with brute strength. Kate sprawled on top of the island, surrendering to him completely. Already, she could feel the orgasm spiraling up and up. Pulling her along until her back was arching and she was grabbing at his forearms, desperate for anything to hold on to. When her climax broke, it broke hard, wrenching a guttural cry from her lips. She didn't hold back, either.

She was Kate Burroughs and he needed her.

Seth flung back his head and made a sound that triggered another, smaller shock wave that left Kate completely boneless with satisfaction. He thrust one final time, the cords in his neck strained with the effort.

Then he fell forward, panting hard. She tangled her fingers in his hair and held him to her breast. They hadn't even gotten undressed on the way. It had been the most intense sex of her life, and she was glad it had been with him.

Seth withdrew and pulled her up, crushing her against his chest. Kate could feel the tears running down her face, but this time, it wasn't because the intensity of the orgasm had been overwhelming. She didn't even think it was the hormones, although they weren't helping.

This was supposed to be short-term. Fun. Seth had helped her secure her future. He made her feel desirable and beautiful even though her body was changing constantly. He'd introduced her to his family. And after all of that, he still made passionate love to her.

How was she supposed to let him go?

Fourteen

He could not wait for his bed to show up. An air mattress with two sleeping bags on it wasn't cutting it. Going back to the hotel would have been the smart thing to do. But he hadn't been able to wait to have Kate in this house with him and she was game, so an air mattress it was.

He wanted her in ways that didn't make a whole lot of sense. Which had to be why he was awake at some ungodly hour of the morning, trying to make sense of it all.

Thankfully, Kate was still asleep. She lay curled against his side, her burgeoning belly nestled on his hip, her leg thrown over his. Her breathing was deep and regular, and every so often, she'd twitch a little in her dreams. He hoped they were good dreams.

He gently stroked her hair and tried to think. In the midst of everything that had happened yesterday, Seth had almost overlooked one of the things his dad had said when he'd been telling Seth to man up.

They were sending him to Shanghai in a matter of months, then maybe to India. Which was great. Seth loved to travel. He liked to see the sights and try new foods and…

It wasn't like he had misled Kate. Part of their conversation about him buying a home had revolved around the fact that he was not going to live in it year-round. But he hadn't told her exactly what that entailed.

It was one thing to live in LA for a year. Sure, it took a little while to get from LA to Rapid City and back, but it was doable. Seth had made it home for birthdays and anniversaries and holidays with a few more frequent flyer miles under his belt and a growing distaste for airport coffee.

But Shanghai? Mumbai? Bangkok, maybe? Those weren't quick trips home.

It would be best for everyone, he reasoned, if the break was clean. He did not want to string Kate along. There was probably a great man out there who would appreciate everything she had to offer. Seth wouldn't stand in the way of that by giving her false hope that whenever he made it home, they could pick up where they left off.

Yes, a clean break was best. It just made sense.

Kate stirred against him. "Seth?" Her voice was heavy with sleep. "What's wrong?"

"Nothing," he told her, tightening his grip around her shoulders. "I'm just not used to the air mattress. Go back to sleep."

For a moment, he thought she was going to do just that. After all, he had run her all over God's green earth yesterday—industrial sites, soccer fields, soul-sucking house closings—not to mention several rounds of explosive sex. Plus, she was pregnant and he hadn't missed the yawns she'd hid behind her hands during the signings.

But then she put her palm on his chest and leaned up on her elbow. The room was too dark to see her face, but he knew she was staring down at him. "What aren't you telling me?"

I love you.

The words almost tumbled right off his tongue without his permission. He just managed to get his mouth closed around them before they complicated everything. Because if there was one way to make sure the break wasn't clean, it was those three little words.

"Seth?"

"I'm going to Shanghai," he told her, suddenly glad that they were having this conversation in the dark. He didn't want to see the hurt in her eyes. "My dad confirmed it yesterday at the soccer game."

The silence was heavy. "When?"

"After the holidays." He ran his hand up and down her back, willing her to lie back down. He didn't want to have this conversation about him leaving now. He didn't want to have it ever.

The realization was stunning. He loved her. When the hell had that happened?

"How long will you be gone?" Just because he couldn't see her face didn't mean he couldn't hear the sorrow in her voice. And that cut him deep.

"I'm not sure. At least six months. Probably a year."

"Oh."

Suddenly, he was talking. He couldn't let that one

single syllable be the end of this. He couldn't let this be the end.

"I knew this was a possibility, I just thought we might have a few more months. The Boltons are all family men," he explained. "Dad won't leave the shop, anyway. Bobby would go, but he doesn't like to be away from his wife and daughter very long and Stella doesn't like to take Clara out of school. Ben's a homebody and Josey wouldn't leave her school for that long," he explained, desperately trying to make her understand.

"So it has to be you?"

"It's a family business. They made me part of their family." When she didn't reply right away, he added, "I owe them, Kate. You don't know what it was like before they came into my life. Mom and I—we got by okay, but sometimes we were on welfare and in the winter, it got cold. She went to bed hungry so I'd have enough to eat, you know? She tried to hide it from me, always saying she'd eat after I went to bed, but I knew the truth. And I hated that she had to. I *hated* it."

His voice caught in his throat and it took a few moments before he could speak again. Kate didn't rush into the silence, though. She waited.

"I never wanted to see my mom suffer like that. And then, when Billy and Mom got together, that all went away like magic. Suddenly, we had plenty of food and I had my own room and clothes that fit—and I had a dad. I'd never had a dad before." He could still feel the sense of awe he'd felt in court, when the adoption had been finalized. The entire Bolton clan and almost half the reservation had shown up. "I had a *family*."

She sat up, although she didn't take her hand away from his chest. He clutched it, holding her palm over his heart. "I would never ask you to give up your family," she said solemnly. "Not for me."

He rested his hand on her stomach. She had hardly started to show, although now that he had been sleeping with her for a month, he could see the small changes in her body. He was going to give that up, too. He was going to leave before she got to the end of her pregnancy. He wasn't going to be there to see the baby born. He wouldn't see how her body changed with motherhood.

No, he knew that she would never ask. Because that wasn't who she was and that wasn't their deal.

"Kate," he said hoarsely, and then stopped because he couldn't be sure what he was going to say next.

She moved then, straddling him. The faintest glimmer of starlight came in through the bare windows—just enough that he could make out the generous swells of her breasts. His body responded immediately because he couldn't get enough of her.

He might never get enough of her.

She took him into her body and set a slow, steady pace that heated his blood all the same. Nothing stood between them now. "I will miss you," she whispered as he cupped her breasts and teased her nipples. She sank her hands into his hair and pulled him up. "God, how I will miss you."

She shuddered down on him, and he quit trying to fight it. He was lost to her.

What could he offer her? A nice house? Financial stability? Great sex, definitely.

But he couldn't offer her himself. He couldn't be there when she needed him. So instead of telling her that he loved her, that she was everything, he forced himself to say, "I will, too, babe," because it was the truth—just not the one he wanted it to be.

"So this is it, then?" Seth asked as he looked over Bobby Bolton's expansion plans for Shanghai.

"This is it," Bobby said, lounging in the chair in front of Seth's desk. "Setting up the showroom in Shanghai, training the staff, making sure everything goes smoothly for the Asia launch. In a perfect world, it'll take you six months."

"The world ain't perfect," Seth said, the sour feeling settling in his stomach. He didn't speak Chinese. He wasn't fluent in the local power structures. He needed to figure out his target market and the best way to reach them.

Even assuming he found the right bilingual staff who understood motorcycles, Seth was looking at a year in China.

He had jumped at the chance to go to LA for a year. He loved his family, but there was no getting around the fact that the Boltons could be overwhelming. And even then, Bobby had made a habit of stopping in every few months, unannounced, to see how things were going.

China was the ultimate fresh start. Seth should've been thrilled by this prospect.

"You know," Bobby said in a kind of voice that Seth had long since recognized as manipulative, "we could send someone else. I've made a few contacts..."

"What? No—I'm going. I'm a partner in this company. This is my job." He was a Bolton. He worked for the family business. He wasn't about to shirk his duties because he'd accidentally fallen in love with Kate.

The sour feeling in his stomach got more awful.

"The museum project is barely off the ground," Bobby went on, as if Seth hadn't spoken. "We still need to select the architect, finalize the design, and then there's the actual building to oversee."

"You're going to handle that." Of all the brothers, Bobby was the one who traveled the most—and that wasn't just because his wife was British. But the man practically turned into a homebody from September to May while Clara was in school.

Bobby stared at him flatly. Seth heard himself continue, "This was the deal, man. I promised to do this and I'm not going to go back on my promises to you guys. We're family." Bobby didn't respond, and an odd sort of dread churned around with the sourness. "Aren't we?"

"Have you ever spoken with your dad?" Bobby asked unexpectedly.

What the hell kind of question was that? "I talked to him this morning when I came into work. Why?"

"No, I mean your birth father. Have you ever talked to him?"

It shouldn't have hit Seth like a sledgehammer to the chest—but it did. "No. I don't even know who he was. All I know is that he left. Mom was pregnant and he left her alone."

He did not like the way Bobby was looking at him. The man was perhaps the most intelligent of the three brothers, but he hid it behind a veneer of playboy charm. There was no getting around the fact that Bobby played a long game. "She's pregnant, isn't she?"

The hits just kept on coming. "I'm not the father."

There was no need to ask who had figured it out. Kate had come to Julie's championship game—the Mustangs had easily won. And if no one had asked her if she was expecting, that was because her body made that question irrelevant. She was soft and round and glowing. Any idiot could see that she was with child—and his family was not full of idiots.

However, no one had asked. Kate's impending joy had been the elephant in the room that they had all avoided talking about at the game and ever since. Even Billy had skirted the subject, instead favoring Seth with hard looks that said more than words ever would.

Now Seth was going to leave Kate behind. Because his first priority was his family. Because that was what Boltons did. Family was first. Family was everything.

And Kate was…

He was going to be sick.

"I made a promise to you guys and to the company," Seth said slowly. "I haven't made any promises to anyone else." Which was true.

So why did saying it feel like a betrayal?

Because Kate was spending almost every night in Seth's bed and every morning in his arms. Because they ate dinner together and talked about their days.

Because he had asked her if she wanted him to go with her to her doctor's appointment where she found out she was having a girl. He'd discussed names with her. Because he had a diamond solitaire pendant with matching earrings already wrapped in silver-and-red paper with her name on it—his parting gift to her before he left.

Because, like an idiot, he had completely fallen in love with her. Deeply, irrevocably in love.

It didn't help that Bobby was still staring at him. Usually, you couldn't shut the man up. But today, he was acting more like Billy than ever. "Who else does she have? I did some digging, you know. Her ex-fiancé stayed with her parents' firm. An old friend had to give her a job. And then a certain knight in shining armor rode in and threw some big commissions her way. But if you leave, who else will she have?"

It was not uncommon for the Bolton brothers to come to blows. Bobby and Billy were like oil and water, and although Ben did his best to keep them from pummeling each other, Seth had seen a few noses get busted in his time.

Aside from that one incident before his parents had gotten married, Seth had never been a part of a family brawl. Mostly because he wasn't nearly as big as his dad and his uncles, but also it didn't seem right to take on the men who'd made a place for him.

But right now? Right now, he wanted to break Bobby's jaw. And maybe a few other bones, just for good measure. "If you're going to say something, just say it."

Bobby cracked that smooth grin of his. Seth wanted to push it in with his fist. "Wouldn't be surprised in the least if your aunts didn't descend upon that poor woman. Your mom, especially, wouldn't like the idea of Kate being all alone when she has that baby."

No, of course Mom wouldn't. Even though Seth was twenty-five years old now. Even though Mom had been married to Billy for almost eleven years, Jenny Bolton still ran an after-school support group for pregnant teenagers because she didn't want anyone to feel as alone as she had when she'd been pregnant with Seth.

"Are you done yet?" Seth ground out. "Because I don't know what you want me to do here, Bobby. You show up with a plan that will have me in Shanghai for almost a year and then simultaneously make me feel like crap for doing my job? Go to hell. And get out of my office." It felt damn good to be able to say that.

Bobby stood, in no hurry to go anywhere. He straightened his cuffs and popped his neck from side to side. "I'm not the one making you feel bad, kid." He headed for the door, but paused with his hand on the knob. "And we *are* family, Seth. Family is the most important thing we have." The words settled in the room like silt at the bottom of standing water.

Seth understood what Bobby was saying. His uncle had just been playing devil's advocate—but they still expected him to put the family first and do his best to open up the Asian market. "I understand."

He was definitely going to be sick.

Bobby gave him a measured look. "Do you?" And with that parting shot, he was gone.

Fifteen

"Katie, my girl," Harold Zanger said, striding out of his office and snapping his suspenders. "How are you getting on this fine day?"

Kate patted her ever-growing stomach. "Fine," she said with a smile as Harold beamed. She left out the part where she had to pee every seven minutes and her back hurt. According to the doctor, things were going perfectly. She only had another three months to go.

"Is that Mr. Bolton of yours going to be coming around?" Harold asked the question in a too-casual manner.

But Kate didn't miss the *yours* in that question. "I don't think it's physically possible for him to buy any more real estate," she said, dodging the question.

Seth was not hers. In fact, with Christmas weeks away, he was less hers every single day.

They hadn't talked about it, but she knew he was

leaving soon. And she knew it was selfish, but she didn't want him to go. The last three months with him had been the best three months of her life.

Harold gave her a kindly look. "He's done all right by you, hasn't he?"

Kate looked away. "He has. But then," she said, forcing a smile to her lips, "so have you."

Harold patted her on the shoulder. "You're a sweet girl, Katie. You deserve better." Tears stung in her eyes as Harold gave her shoulder a squeeze and then turned away, politely pretending she wasn't about to cry. "I'm off to show some houses today," he announced loudly, giving his suspenders another snap just for good measure. "You'll hold down the fort?"

"Of course," she said, smiling through it all.

Seth had done right by her. Thanks to the purchase of the house—which still had next to no furniture in it—and the industrial property, she was able to plan to take six months off with her little girl, whom she'd decided to name Madeleine.

More than that, he had given her back her sexuality. Kate hadn't even realized what she'd been missing until Seth had come into her life. But now? She wouldn't settle for anything less. He had built her up instead of wearing her down, and never again would she go along just to get along.

Seth was leaving and she was going to let him go. It would be selfish to hold him here, but God, she was going to miss the hell out of him.

She was lost in these thoughts and others—what should she get him for Christmas?—when the chimes over the door jingled. "It's a zinger of a day at Zanger, how may I..." She looked up to see a familiar figure standing in the doorway. Her stomach curdled because she recognized that man—and it wasn't Seth.

"Roger?" What the hell was he doing here?

He looked like hell. Oh, he still looked good. His hair was combed, his face cleanly shaven, his suit nicely pressed. But as he stepped into the office, Kate could see the shadows under his bloodshot eyes. He looked like he hadn't slept in a week, maybe longer. "Kate," he said, and then stopped when she stood up. His eyes widened. "God, you look so…"

She didn't know if it was anger or adrenaline—she hadn't seen him in months. Not since he'd agreed to pay child support but promised that he'd never have anything to do with her daughter. "Pregnant?" she finished before he could say something crass. "Yes. I'm pregnant. I told you that, remember?"

He didn't even have the decency to look ashamed at coming within a hairbreadth of insulting her. "Yeah, I know. I just didn't…" He waved a hand in her general direction.

She blinked at him. "If you're implying that I was lying about being pregnant—"

"No, no. I believe you. You just look…"

How had she ever thought she could love this man? It'd been a crappy lie that she had forced herself to buy into because, for some reason she still didn't understand, her dad liked this man. Maybe it was because Roger and her father were too much alike. And Kate did exactly what her mother had done—shut up and went along with what her father wanted.

Well, no more. Seth had spent months telling her how gorgeous she was, how beautiful she looked—even as she got huge. She was carrying Roger's daughter and all he could think about was that she'd gotten fat.

He could go to hell.

"Did you have a reason for being here or did you just feel like insulting the mother of your unborn child?"

Roger recoiled.

"And I swear to God, Roger, if you ask if I'm sure it's your child, I will not be held responsible for my actions."

"Jeez, Kate—calm down. I didn't come here to pick a fight."

When, in the history of womankind, had telling a woman to "calm down" ever worked? Because it sure as hell didn't now. "Then why are you here?"

He scrubbed at the back of his neck. "Listen, I've been thinking—that kid's not even born yet. You're not going to need any child support for what, another year or so?"

Good Lord, just when she thought it couldn't get any worse, it did. "What are you talking about?"

"I heard you had a few big sales," he went on, completely missing the horrified shock in her voice. "To Bolton, of all people. I would've thought he'd come to me if he needed something—we're friends."

Liar, Kate thought. She'd been spending nearly every waking moment with Seth for the last several months and not once had Roger made an effort to talk to either of them.

She didn't say that, though. Instead, she focused on what Roger was really saying. "Yes, I sold some property. I happen to be a real estate agent. What's it to you?"

"You don't have to get all upset," he said, his eyes

darting around the office. "I'm just saying, it would probably be best if we delayed the child support payments for a little while. That's all."

"Best for who?" Roger tried to smile, but it was more of a grimace. "Roger, what the hell is going on? I'm pregnant and you rolled in here to insult my appearance and try to get out of your financial obligations to a child you helped create?"

"Hey, I didn't ask you to get pregnant."

"News flash, I didn't ask to get pregnant. It was an accident, but if you're going to act like I did this all by myself, I'm going to have to explain some basic biology to you. What do you want?"

The silence was awkward, but she debated whether or not she needed backup. How fast could Seth get here?

"See," Roger began, and she heard the whine in his voice that made it clear that he hadn't gotten his way with something, "there were some investments that didn't pan out and business has been slow and…"

"And you're suddenly broke?" she supplied.

"*Broke* is a strong word. But there have been some cash flow difficulties."

She mentally translated those passive statements. Why hadn't she ever noticed that when Roger screwed up he never owned his mistakes? "You lost all your money, didn't you? What's the matter, my dad cut you off?"

That grimace again. Roger looked like a cornered animal trying to bluff its way out of a dangerous situation. "Look, are you going to help me out or not?"

The nerve of this man. And to think, she might've been stuck with him. "You want me to help you out by releasing you from your financial obligations to your own child for an indeterminate amount of time because you made some unwise investment choices and you don't have me to bail you out—am I getting all of this right?"

Finally, he looked ashamed of himself. As well he should. "I wouldn't put it quite like that. We could get married, you know."

She almost gagged. "No," she said with as much force as she could. "I don't have to take your crap, Roger. I don't love you. You never loved me. And if you try to bail on child support, I will sue you back to the Stone Age."

"Come on, Kate—"

"No," she repeated again. "You kept the house. You kept the wedding gifts. You went on the honeymoon without me. What do I get? Child support. I had to rely on a family friend to give me a job. You gave me nothing, Roger. You are legally obligated to provide for your child. And I will hold you to it. There's nothing else I want from you."

He jerked as if she had slapped him. "When did you get so bitchy?"

Oh, that just did it. "Get out. I'm not your doormat anymore."

"But—"

"*Now,*" she repeated, putting as much menace as she could into her voice.

The jerk had the nerve to just stand there and stare, his mouth open in shock.

She was reaching for her phone when the door behind him jingled and suddenly, there was Seth Bolton, stepping around Roger and putting himself in between that jerk and Kate. "Roger," he said, his voice cool. He looked back at Kate. "Everything okay here?"

"Yes," Kate said before Roger could attempt to turn on the charm—not that Seth would fall for it. "Roger was just leaving, after renewing his commitment to paying child support." She left the *or else* hanging invisibly in the air.

Roger was an idiot, but not such a great idiot that he was going to argue with her in front of an audience. "We can talk later," he said in a conciliatory tone.

"No," she said, standing up as straight as her belly would allow. "We can't."

"Let me see you out," Seth said, almost—but not quite—sounding friendly. He crowded Roger toward the door and opened it, waiting.

Roger's shoulders slumped in defeat. He looked back at Kate and said, "You look great, you know."

There was a time when Kate would have clung to that halfhearted compliment as proof that Roger did care for her, that she was doing the right thing staying with him. Now?

Too little, too late. She did not return the compliment.

Roger opened his mouth as if he were going to say something else, but Seth cleared his throat. It was the most menacing sound Kate had heard come out of him yet.

Then the men were outside and Kate half wanted Seth to take a swing at Roger and half just wanted the idiot to go away.

She was going to have to take Roger to court—that much was obvious. Lawyers were going to be expensive, but she wasn't going to let him weasel his way out of this.

She sank down in her desk chair and dropped her head into her hands. He hadn't even asked if she was going to have a boy or girl. Why was she surprised? She wasn't, really. Of course Roger was going to disappoint her. He really didn't care. Not about the baby, not about her.

The door jingled again and there was Seth, shutting it firmly behind him. "He's gone," he said, looking at her with open concern. "Are you all right?"

Kate's throat was thick with emotion—damned hormones. "I stood up to him," she said around the lump in her throat. "He doesn't want to pay child support and I told him I'd sue him if I had to. God, what a hassle."

Seth grinned at that. He glanced back at Harold's dark office and then came around her desk, pulling her up into his arms. "You were amazing," he agreed. Rubbing her back in just the right place. "I wish I could've seen the whole thing."

She was crying—but she was also laughing. "Oh, you would've hit him. I would've liked to have seen that." Seth leaned back and stroked her tears away. She loved that her random bouts of hormones didn't freak him out. "I can't believe I almost married him."

He cradled her face. "I'm so glad you didn't."

Kate almost lost herself in the tenderness of the moment. No—she couldn't fall for Seth all over again. "Did he say anything to you outside?"

Seth snorted. "He seemed hurt that I hadn't used him for my real estate agent."

"Lord."

Seth hugged her tighter, and she sank into his

warmth. He was always here when she needed him, lending her his strength. Without him, she might have buckled and agreed to marry Roger. She might have let Roger out of his financial obligations.

She would've been miserable. But she wasn't. Upset, yes. Pregnant, definitely. But she'd refused to roll over to make someone else happy. Seth had shown her she could fight for what she wanted and for that, she would love him forever.

He stepped all the way around her and began to knead his thumbs into her lower back. God, it felt so good. "What are you doing here?"

"I needed to see you," he said, sending a thrill through her. Then, after a long pause while he worked on a particularly sore spot, he added, "We finalized the plan for the Shanghai showroom."

All of her good feelings disappeared in a heartbeat. Because this was it—the end. "Oh?" she got out in a strangled-sounding voice.

"Yeah." Kate couldn't tell if it was a consolation or not that he sounded almost as depressed as she felt. "Best-case scenario is Shanghai for six months, but it'll probably be closer to ten, maybe even twelve."

She shut her eyes, although that didn't change things. "That's great," she lied, because his job was important to him. His family was important to him, and she could not allow him to damage those relationships for her.

"Yeah," he said again, sounding positively morose about it. "It's going to be really exciting. I'll leave on the second."

They were down to days at this point. Sixteen days. And then he would be gone from her life and she would still be here, arguing with Roger and trying to do the best she could with what she had.

Suddenly, she couldn't bear it. She turned, throwing her arms around his neck. "I wish I could go with you."

His hands cradled her belly. "I couldn't ask it of you. I wish I could stay."

She shook her head against his shoulder. "I couldn't ask it of you, either."

He pulled a small box out of his pocket. "I got this for you."

She stared at the Christmas wrapping. She didn't want to open it—didn't want to accept the fact that the best thing that had ever happened to her was winding down to its natural conclusion. "Thank you. I haven't had time to get you a present yet."

"I don't..." He pulled her back into his arms and held her for a long moment. Then, almost by unspoken agreement, they both pulled back. Lingering would do no one any good. "Promise me," he said, taking her hands and staring down into her eyes. "Promise me you'll take care of yourself and Madeleine. Promise me you won't..." He swallowed, his eyes suspiciously bright. "Don't wait for me, Kate. There's a great guy out there who is going to be really lucky to have you and I don't want you to pass him up."

"You're being ridiculous," she said, hiccupping. She was almost seven months pregnant. The number of men who would look at her and see anything but baggage could probably be counted on one hand.

In fact, there might only be one of them. Standing right in front of her.

"If you need anything," he went on, ridiculous or

not, "you call my parents. My mom's an expert about single moms with new babies. Okay?"

"Seth—"

"Promise me, Kate," he insisted, squeezing her hands.

All good things came to an end. And that was what this was. The end. "I promise."

She'd never realized how much that sounded like goodbye.

Sixteen

An odd sort of tension settled in and made itself comfortable between Seth and his family. Sure, they all opened presents together Christmas morning. But even Julie, who professed to still believing in Santa Claus, was giving him looks that he didn't want to think about. She was too much like their father sometimes, and he was in no mood to be judged by a ten-year-old.

His mom would look at him and sigh and damned if it didn't sound like disappointment. And his dad? The temperature dropped a solid ten degrees anytime he walked into the room.

No one spoke about it. No one asked about Kate. They barely talked about Shanghai. Just tension.

Just Seth slowly going insane. He hadn't seen her since that day in her office—the day he'd given her the necklace. She hadn't opened it. He almost called her

Christmas afternoon but he told himself he'd wanted a clean break and that it was for the best.

That didn't explain why he called Kate on New Year's Eve and asked her to come spend it with him. She must have been doing okay, because she refused and in a way, he was glad. He was flying out first thing on the second to LA and from there, to mainland China. If she came over for one last night, he honestly had no idea how he was going to leave.

He was miserable and pissy and worried sick about her being alone for Madeleine's birth. Even though he knew that if the shit hit the fan his family would step up and make sure Kate was taken care of, he still worried. What if Roger came back? What if she had to sue him for child support? What if there was a problem with Madeleine? Hell, what if there wasn't? He remembered how hard it'd been for everyone the first few months after Julie had been born. And Julie had had Mom, Dad and Seth to take care of her. How would Kate handle the sleepless nights and diapers and feedings by herself?

He did his best not to worry as he packed up his stuff. His dad took him to the airport. It was still pitch-black at five in the morning, but at least it was clear. Flying out of South Dakota in the middle of winter was always dicey.

True to form, they didn't talk. Billy just glowered, and Seth? He tried to focus on the future. He'd never been one to settle down. Wandering all over God's green earth was who he was. He knew it. Kate knew it. His family knew it.

At least, he thought they did. They got to the airport and Billy silently helped unload Seth's bags and Seth couldn't remember ever having been more miserable than he was right now because this felt wrong. Everything about it was wrong.

Panicking hard, Seth stood before the only man he'd ever called father. "I'm not Madeleine's father," he said, wishing he could take the words back even before he was done saying them.

It was not Dad's business—it was none of anyone's business. But he knew, deep down inside, that Billy Bolton was disappointed in him.

Billy jammed his hands on his hips and stared up at the midnight-black sky. "No, I didn't figure you were."

"I have to put the family first."

Once, long ago, Seth had punched this man in the face for daring to break up with his mom. It was the only time he'd ever struck Billy, and the man hadn't yelled or hit back. Instead, he'd looked at Seth with disappointment in his eyes—the same disappointment in his eyes right now. "Neither of them is family, but you already know that baby's name."

Seth's throat closed up. "You guys made me a Bolton. That wasn't something I took lightly. I'm not going to let you or the business down."

Seth hadn't realized he was staring at the sidewalk until Billy's massive hands settled on Seth's shoulders. "Son," he said, and it just about broke Seth's heart to hear that word spoken with so much sadness, "God knows I tried to do right by you and your mom. And God knows if it weren't for motorcycles, I'd either be dead or in jail."

"I know," Seth said, wishing for numbness because he couldn't take this. The business kept his father going and he couldn't turn his back on that.

Billy's grip on him tightened. "Look at me, Seth." Seth raised his head, swallowing back tears. "The business is important, but we could lose it tomorrow and it wouldn't change anything about you and me and our family. We will always be family because we chose you, and more important, you chose us." He gave Seth a little shake. "You don't have to prove a damned thing to me. You never did."

Then he pulled Seth into a mammoth bear hug before quickly shoving him away. "Write your mother," he called out as he got back into his truck and drove off.

Seth stood there for a moment in the freezing air, shaking.

He hadn't chosen the Boltons—his mom had. His aunt had—they'd both married brothers. He'd been part of the deal, but not as a voting member. He'd just…

He'd spent the last ten years of his life living and breathing motorcycles and the motorcycle business because when he welded a frame Billy approved of or pitched an idea Bobby got behind, it made Seth feel like he was part of something. Crazy Horse Choppers had given him a place. A purpose.

That was what mattered.

Wasn't it?

Not that anyone was buying real estate right now— no one really wanted to move on the second day of the year in the middle of winter—but Kate went to work anyway. She couldn't handle staying alone in her crappy apartment all day, staring at the lovely Christmas card her mother had sent.

She wore the stunning diamond pendant necklace and matching earrings Seth had bought for her. She wasn't an expert in diamonds, but she'd listened when the jewelry salespeople had talked cut and clarity and all that and she was wearing probably close to four carats of diamonds. It wasn't a stretch to say that she was wearing close to fifty thousand dollars' worth of jewelry—a fortune.

He'd spent that on her. It was a hell of a farewell gift and, if worse came to worst, it would take care of her and Madeleine for a long time.

But she couldn't bear the thought of selling Seth's gifts. She'd sold her engagement ring because she hadn't wanted to hang on to another reminder of Roger—and she'd needed the cash. But Seth's pendant?

She wore it on a long chain so it nestled next to her heart. It was the only way she could keep him close.

That, and being here at work. There were so many memories of Seth here. Hearing the door jingle and looking up to see Seth standing there, that grin on his face. She didn't want to entirely leave those memories right now, either. It was easier to pull those memories around her like a blanket at the office. She was even gladder that she'd never had him over to her apartment. It would've been too much.

She glanced at the clock—again—and slid the diamond along the chain. Seth should've landed in LA by now. He was probably holed up in a bar, waiting for his flight to China. Was he thinking of her? Was he wishing that she'd taken him up on his offer to ring in the New Year—just one more night together? She'd known she needed to say no to him, but now she wished she'd said yes. Because it already sucked, letting him go. What would one more night have hurt?

The baby fluttered in her stomach, and Kate put her

hand to where Madeleine was kicking. This was what she had to focus on now—impending motherhood. For all intents and purposes, she was all Madeleine had.

No, it wasn't exactly true. Seth had made her swear that if she needed any help, she'd contact his family. Part of Kate knew that wasn't a good idea because, while she genuinely liked his parents and his sister, that would presume a relationship that otherwise no longer existed.

On the other hand, it was clear from her mother's Christmas card that there wouldn't be a close relationship with her parents. And Kate was just coming to grips with the fact that she had a long, cold, dark three months of being extremely pregnant ahead of her.

It wouldn't be so bad if Madeleine were already here. The baby was going to take every little bit of energy Kate had—and probably some she didn't have. She wouldn't be able to dwell on Seth's absence once Madeleine arrived.

Kate tried diligently to focus on listings. The family she'd spoken to a few months ago was being relocated to Rapid City and anticipated moving by March. And since Kate had recently been in a vast majority of the homes currently on the market, she could with great confidence eliminate most of them.

That was what she was supposed to be thinking about. But even in that, her thoughts turned back to Seth. He'd purchased the house that she had long wanted—but refused to furnish it without her input. The house could be such a showplace, but right now, it was little more than an exaggerated bachelor pad, stacked with boxes that had been in storage. She hoped Seth would hire a good interior decorator when he came home and make something out of that house.

She was making another cup of tea in the small kitchen tucked behind Harold's office when the door jingled. "It's a zinger of a day here at Zanger," she called over her shoulder, pouring the hot water over the tea bag. Who knew? Someone had actually come looking for a house. It was a good thing she was here. "I'll be right with you."

She walked out into the main part of the office and then pulled up short so quickly that water splashed all over the place.

She was hallucinating, because it wasn't possible that Seth was here.

Then he smiled and she realized that no, she couldn't be imagining this. Seth Bolton himself stood in the doorway of the office.

He'd come for her.

He couldn't have come for her.

"Seth? What are you doing here?"

His smile faltered a little. "I've been thinking," he said, taking a hesitant step into the office.

"But... You are supposed to be on a plane? Or in LA by now. You're not supposed to be here."

"I couldn't leave," he said, his voice hoarse. "I couldn't leave you."

The room started to swim and the next thing she knew, she was in Seth's arms and he was lowering her down into her chair. "Breathe, babe," he said, kneeling in front of her and holding her hands.

"You're not supposed to give up your job with the company for me," she said, her voice cracking. "I would never ask you to put me before your family."

"You're not asking," he said, stroking his thumbs over the back of her hands. "Kate, I screwed up. I want to make it right and then, if you still want to be done, I'll go."

He'd come back for her. She didn't want him to leave again. She wasn't sure she was strong enough for that.

"We had an agreement," she said weakly. "Fun. No strings. You're not going to stay in Rapid City. That was the deal."

"I want to renegotiate the deal. I'm looking for something fun. Some strings attached. Slightly more permanently based in Rapid City. At least until Madeleine is old enough to travel."

At that moment, the baby chose to shift, sending flutters all over Kate's belly. Seth cupped her stomach and leaned down to kiss it through her clothes.

"You can't mean this," she said, giving up the fight against the tears. What was it about this man that always had her at her weakest?

He looked up at her, so handsome and perfect and *here*. "I never knew my father. He ran out on my mom before I was even born and I thought…I thought I was restless. That I needed to see the world—and that was because of him. But I don't think I'm restless. I just think I hadn't found a reason to stay in one place."

"Don't say that," she begged. "Don't break my heart, Seth. I can't take it."

"I couldn't take it, either—so I won't."

"I won't let you do this. I will not let you give up the family business for me. I'm not…"

His gaze sharpened. "You *are* worth it, Kate. And you know what? I'm a Bolton and if there's one thing I know about Boltons, it's that family is everything. Kate, you are *my* everything. What kind of man would I be if I didn't fight for you?"

She threw her arms around his neck and buried her face against his cheek. "No one has ever fought for me before," she wept. "I just don't want you to regret it."

"Have a little faith in me," he said, his voice shaking. "And have faith in yourself. Do you love me?"

"Of course I do," she sobbed. "How could I not?"

"Then marry me, Kate. And not in some big lavish ceremony with a crazy dress that has petticoats and corsets and ruffles and strings. We can get married at the courthouse, for all I care. It's not the wedding that counts—it's you. You're my everything, Kate, you and Madeleine. Let me be your family. It doesn't mean I won't do stupid things like nearly flying halfway across the world when I belong right here. That means I will fight for you, for us. Every day of my life, so help me God."

"But your job…"

He leaned back and gave her a cocky look. "I'm a partner in the firm. It's not like they can fire me. And besides, it'll work out. It might be a little messy, but I'll fight for what I want. I don't have to prove myself to them. I just have to prove myself to you." He swallowed. "If you'll have me?"

"Yes," she said, pulling him into a kiss. "God, yes, Seth. I couldn't even think with you being gone."

The baby shifted again, harder this time—demanding attention, no doubt. Kate gasped as Seth rubbed her belly. "I couldn't miss this. She will always be my daughter, from the very first moment."

This was everything she'd ever wanted. She wasn't perfect, not by a long shot—but Seth understood who she was and loved her anyway. She cupped his cheek with her hand. "Seth?"

"Yeah?" He turned his head and pressed a kiss against her palm.

"You were right."

His eyes darkened as she ran her hands through his hair. "Oh? About what?"

"You're good for me," she replied, leaning forward to brush her lips against his. "Very, very good for me."

He grinned against her mouth. "Babe," he all but growled, pulling her into his embrace, "I'm just getting started."

Epilogue

"You don't think she'll run, do you?"

Seth shot Bobby a dirty look as the judge cleared his throat. "Shall we begin?"

Jack Roy began to strum his guitar as Julie walked into the judge's chambers, strewing rose petals before her. Davey walked next to his cousin, intensely focused on the rings he was carrying. Clara, Eliza and Connie giggled while their mothers shushed them.

Billy smacked Bobby on the arm and Ben made a noise of warning deep in his throat. Seth ignored them all because just then, Kate walked through the double doors, holding a sleeping Madeleine in her arms instead of a bouquet.

Seth's heart clenched at the sight of his family. Not that he hadn't seen them this morning—he'd gotten up with Madeleine at two so Kate could sleep.

But his aunt Stella had worked her magic, designing a simple cream wedding gown that clung to Kate's ample chest and flowed softly away from the waist. Compared to the monstrosity that Kate had almost gotten married in the first time, Seth was thrilled to realize this dress wouldn't require three lady's maids to remove.

Madeleine wore a similar outfit, although her fabric had been dyed with the faintest pink. Seth couldn't see his daughter's feet because the dress flowed well past Madeleine's legs.

"Beautiful," Billy whispered, sounding almost wheezy about it.

"Mine," Seth replied.

"I'm proud of you, son," Billy went on, his voice low enough that no one else could hear him. "I knew you'd do the right thing."

The last six months had been a whirlwind of change. Kate had moved into their home and Seth had given her free rein to decorate it as she saw fit. Madeleine had come two weeks early, healthy and beautiful. Seth had been with Kate for the entire twenty-two hours of labor.

He'd personally hired a man he'd worked with in LA who, it turned out, spoke semi-fluent Mandarin to spearhead the Shanghai showroom.

And Seth? He'd stayed in Rapid City, overseeing the museum expansion.

Expanding his family.

Today, not only would Kate become his wife, but Madeleine would legally be his daughter. He and Kate had debated getting hitched immediately—Seth's preference—but Kate had decided she wanted to wait until Madeleine could be a part of the ceremony.

Seth caught the eye of his future in-laws. Kate's dad was scowling, but he'd put on a boutonniere and he was here, so that was something. Kate's mom was dabbing at her eyes. Seth hoped that for Kate's sake, they could have a cordial relationship, if not a close one.

Then Seth turned his attention back to his bride.

The judge, it turned out, was an old riding buddy of Billy's. He'd been happy to combine a wedding and an adoption.

Kate made her way up to Seth and handed Madeleine off to Jenny. Then, before their families, God and the state of South Dakota, he married his bride and adopted his daughter.

He was a Bolton and this was his family. By God, he would do anything for them. They were the right thing. They always would be.

* * * * *

If you liked this story of pregnancy and passion,
pick up
PRIDE AND PREGNANCY
by Sarah M. Anderson!

And if you enjoyed Seth's story,
don't miss the other novels in
THE BOLTON BROTHERS *series:*

STRADDLING THE LINE
BRINGING HOME THE BACHELOR
EXPECTING A BOLTON BABY

All available now from Mills & Boon Desire!

***

Don't miss the next LITTLE SECRETS *story*
THE BABY MERGER
by Yvonne Lindsay
Available September 2017!

MILLS & BOON®

Desire™

PASSIONATE AND DRAMATIC LOVE STORIES

Join Britain's BIGGEST Romance Book Club

- **EXCLUSIVE offers every month**
- **FREE delivery direct to your door**
- **NEVER MISS a title**
- **EARN Bonus Book points**

Call Customer Services
0844 844 1358*

or visit
millsandboon.co.uk/subscriptions

MILLS & BOON®